FORGIVE ME FATHER,
FOR I HAVE SINNED

"Is there," Clement repeated, "something you wish to confess?" He tried not to sound harsh.

"Yes. But it wasn't my fault, you understand. I merely do that which must be done . . ."

The voice was filled with a razor-blade kind of pain. Clement felt slightly dizzy. He was conscious all at once of the stale air within the confessional, the perspiration that trickled under his cassock, the dryness of his chapped lips.

". . . Usually I'm fine. I mean, for years I might be fine. No one would ever know, ever suspect. And they mustn't, you understand? You must never tell. I only kill the bad ones."

HOMETOWN HEROES

SUSANNA HOFMANN McSHEA

AVON BOOKS  NEW YORK

This is a work of fiction. The events described are imaginary, and the characters are fictitious and not intended to represent specific living persons.

AVON BOOKS
A division of
The Hearst Corporation
1350 Avenue of the Americas
New York, New York 10019

Copyright © 1990 by Susanna Hofmann McShea
Published by arrangement with St. Martin's Press, Inc.
Library of Congress Catalog Card Number: 90-37235
ISBN: 0-380-71675-5

First Avon Books Printing: August 1992

AVON TRADEMARK REG. U.S. PAT. OFF. AND IN OTHER COUNTRIES, MARCA REGISTRADA, HECHO EN U.S.A.

Printed in the U.S.A.

RA   10 9 8 7 6 5 4 3 2 1

For Bill McShea, whose intelligence, sensitivity, and humor sustained me in this and in so much else.

HOMETOWN HEROES

PROLOGUE

It was the most beautiful car she had ever seen. Wine red with sweeping black fenders. Under moonlight bright as day it shimmered, not a nick on it. So shiny it looked wet.

"This car sure don't look three years old," she said. She leaned back into the leather seat. She tried not to be nervous, unaccustomed as she was to such lavish surroundings. "Jeepers, it even smells new."

He didn't say anything. Instead he reached over and flipped on the radio. It was a factory-installed radio, not the kind people usually stuck into their cars as an afterthought. He fiddled with the dial, looking for a station.

"What with the war an' all, I bet this was one of the last cars they built."

"Maybe," he said absentmindedly. It was nothing to him. Nothing. Not the car, not his fancy tuxedo and wing-tip shoes, not even the red carnation he wore in his lapel. The radio crackled with static, then broke forth with the sweetest, purest sound.

"Don't sit under the apple tree with anyone else but me . . ."

"I'll be glad when the war's over," she said. "My daddy says it's gonna be over soon, too. Well, thank God, that's what I say." She looked sideways at him, but still he didn't respond. This boy was that word they had in vocabulary class the other day. Taciturn, that's what he was. It was hard to figure what he was thinking. Most senior boys didn't want the war to end. They wanted to see some action. If she'd had to lay money on it (which she didn't have), she'd bet this boy didn't care if the war ended tomorrow. She wondered if that made him a coward. Maybe it made him smart.

He had nice breath. It smelled of peppermint. "Listen," she said, cozying up to him, "it was real nice you askin' me out tonight."

"Uh-huh."

"Prom night an' everything. I mean, I can tell you how bad I felt sittin' at home, everyone else goin'."

He seemed to grip the wheel tighter. She'd expected him to put his arm around her, but he didn't. He just gripped. Maybe he was worried about shifting. Maybe he wanted to treat her nice. With respect. He was a gentleman, that was for sure. Not like the others. He had class.

"My mother, she's sick," she babbled on, "an' I hadda stay with her till my daddy got home. He works at the hat factory over in Danbury. Oh, I told you that before. I forgot."

She was sure she was boring him. She started to sweat. She crossed her legs under the long frilly skirt, her best one. She plucked at an imaginary shred of lint on the arm of her sweater, a sweater that looked almost like cashmere but wasn't. Even her best outfit didn't go with his tuxedo.

"Listen," she said, giving up, "do you mind if I smoke?"

"No."

Well, at least it was something. A word. At least he wasn't deaf and dumb. She fished through her purse and found a pack of Marlboros. They were a new brand. Lucky Strike had gone from green to white. Green had gone to war, they said. Just like all the good men. Only boys and cowards and 4-Fs were left. She looked sideways again at this boy and felt a prickle of anger. Who did he think he was, anyway? He was spoiled, that's what. He wasn't making her feel comfortable, either.

"I know you had another date for the prom," she said airily. At first she'd been grateful, grateful that he'd take her out, even this late. Even after the prom was over. After his first date. But now she was mad. He probably thought he could use her. Probably thought she was cheap.

"Take me home," she said.

"What?"

He stared at her in disbelief. Headlights came toward them, and she thought they would crash. Still, she didn't flinch. She stared straight ahead. She held her breath. The car passed, and they were alone again on the deserted stretch of highway.

"Take me home," she said again, more loudly this time. "This just isn't working. We're not like they say meant for each other, so I'd 'preciate it if you'd take me home."

"Sure."

He said it like he didn't care. The hell with him, she thought. I don't care neither.

They drove in silence for some moments. Then he jerked the wheel, turning off the highway and onto a hidden dirt road. The rutted surface was overgrown. Weeds scratched the underside of the pristine Cadillac. Branches whipped against the shiny fenders.

"Hey," she said, getting alarmed now. "I said I wanna go home."

"Shut up," he said.

"Turn this car around," she demanded, trying to swallow her fear. The fear was a hard lump, a turtle in her throat. No one knew where she was. Not her father. Not her mother. She'd gone out the window, an old trick she'd done lots of times before. He could rape her, and no one would know. He could kill her. She shoved the thought from her mind and reached for the door handle.

She almost made it. Almost. She grabbed at the door handle, but her palms were slick and sweaty. She pulled at it, she fumbled. He had locked the door—she'd forgotten that.

"Not so fast," he said evenly, ramming the massive car to a stop. She could hear crickets through the open window. She could smell mud and decay. They were near the swamp, that much she knew. He grabbed her wrists. Brushing off her struggles, he rammed an elbow into her left breast, knocking the wind out of her.

"Please," she gasped. "I didn't mean it. We don't have to go back. I'll do anything. Really."

He hit her again, this time in the face. Crazily, she thought of her lipstick, her mascara. Makeup so carefully applied. She felt sick and dizzy. He slammed the flat of his hand into her face broadside, crushing her nose. She felt her throat fill up. Her sweater was bloody. She couldn't breathe. She would be sick. Then everything went black.

She never felt him pull her from the car, and she never felt him kill her, either. Betty Murphy, who wore the imitation cashmere sweater and the frilly skirt and the silk stockings saved for special occasions. Betty Murphy, who on an evening in June 1944 never went back through the open window into the safety of her own bedroom. Betty Murphy—no, she never went home at all.

1989 . . .

She heard him before she saw him. An old man with white Brillo hair, bent, stooped, tramping through the woods. Her woods. He wore shapeless khaki pants hitched low around his hips and a green plaid shirt. Brown and green and weather-beaten, he blended in with the trees. And he was careening straight toward her, staring fixedly at some invisible spot in front of his mud-crusted boots. He was crippled or he had lost something, she couldn't tell which.

"Stop!" Mildred Bennett cried just in the nick of time, the barest hair of a second before his head would have slammed her stomach.

"Huh?" The head snapped up. He looked at her with watery

blue eyes. Then he turned his eyes again to the ground and spit—yes he spit—practically on her brand-new white Keds. "Goddamn sons of bitches," he muttered.

"I beg your pardon," said Mildred. She bit off each syllable. She drew herself up to full height. She touched a strand of perfectly styled silver hair. She looked at him with ice blue eyes. Who did he think he was anyway? Ruining her morning walk. Defiling the air with his foul language.

"Horses' asses," he snapped, not bothering to look her in the eye. "They tramped around here like it was some kind of garden party. Clodhoppers!"

"Who did?" Mildred's curiosity got the best of her. She found her eyes scanning the thicket around them. Wet leaves. Broken twigs. Thorns. Spiderwebs. A far cry from New York City.

"The police, that's who." He said it as if she were stupid, as if she should know. She didn't like his tone.

"I'm afraid I must ask you to leave," she said stiffly. Hers was an imperious tone, a tone handed down from generation to generation. A tone few people argued with.

"The hell I will!" he snapped.

"I'll call the police."

"I *am* the police!" he shot back. Then he seemed to deflate. "At least I *was* the police. Once. I retired a while back."

Mildred eyed him closely. He had retired a fair while back, it looked like. He was seventy if he was a day. But there was something familiar about him.

"Chief Haggarty?" she ventured.

"Right," he said. "Forrest T. Haggarty."

"Goodness," she gasped.

"Thought I was dead, didn't you?" He grinned, exposing a big gold molar on the right side and a black gap on the left.

"Well, no," she stammered. "I . . ."

"Course you did." He waved a claw hand. It was arthritic, knotted like a pretzel. It could never pull a trigger. "It don't

6

bother me none. Lotsa folks think I'm dead. Well, I'm not, see?" He put his face smack up to hers, the tip of his beak nose almost touching her ski-jump one. For a minute she thought he might kiss her on the lips. She would die, she surely would. Then he winked.

"I'm alive and kicking," he said, "and I've got a job to do, so if you'll excuse me, girlie . . ."

Girlie? she thought. Girlie. I am fifty-eight years old, and he calls me girlie. He must be daft. Senile.

"I really must ask what you're doing here," Mildred pressed. She followed after him, branches and brambles whipping her face, raking through her swept-back hair. He seemed not to notice. He let fly a twig that stung her cheek.

"Oh yeah?" he called over his shoulder. "An' who're you ta be asking?"

"Mildred Bennett," she gasped with as much dignity as she could muster. For an old man he was difficult to keep up with.

"Priscilla Schroeder's girl?"

"Yes."

"That a fact?" He stopped and waited for her. His face showed new respect. "I knew your mother."

"She died."

"I know." If he'd had a hat he would have removed it, Mildred could tell. "I'm real sorry."

"Oh, it's quite all right." She was about to say, My mother was old, her time had come. But she looked at Forrest Haggarty, who was also old, and she reconsidered. "I'm just here to get the house in order. Find a real estate agent. Get it in shape so someone will buy it."

"It's a mighty big house," said Forrest. "They don't build 'em like that anymore."

"I know."

"You gotta have servants to run a place like that."

"I know."

"People don't have that kind of money. Nowadays."

"Some do."

"Most don't."

"I'm never going to sell it, is that what you're trying to tell me, Chief Haggarty?" He straightened up when she called him Chief. "I should just let them bulldoze the place down and put up one of those tacky overpriced developments of imitation colonials, right? Well, I won't do it. No sir! I'm not desperate for money. I can hold on, and I will."

"Right on, Millie!" Forrest Haggarty slammed a twisted fist into a semiopen hand and did a little jig. She should have been mad that he called her Millie, it was so presumptuous. Should have. But she laughed out loud.

"You know," he said smiling, "you're real pretty when you laugh. Just like your mother."

From the way he said it, she thought maybe he'd known her mother very well. Intimately even. God forbid. She pushed this thought away.

"So what's this business about the police?" she asked.

"You really wanna know?"

"Yes. I really want to know."

"Last night," he whispered, leaning forward, "right here . . ."

"Yes?"

"A woman was murdered."

"My God."

"Agnes Peabody. Age fifty-seven." He surveyed the woods around them. "Yup. An' from the looks of things, Agnes put up a good fight, too."

"Oh my."

"Oh my, indeed. You see that"—Forrest Haggarty pointed —"that kinda flattened area, leaves all mashed down, almost like a bed?"

"Yes."

"That's where they found the body. Agnes. An' over

there"—he pointed into what looked to Mildred like a solid wall of greenery—"well, there's a path broke through there. A new path. A desperate path. Branches all broken. Bits of fabric an' hair in the prickers. Yep, it looks to me like Agnes made a run for it. From the road. She gave it a shot, Agnes did. Couldn't run good, though. She had on high heels."

"Oh dear." Mildred pictured poor desperate Agnes Peabody crashing through the woods. Running. Falling. Dying.

"Uh-huh. One of 'er heels come off. They found it stuck in a stone wall. My guess is that she tripped there"—he pointed again—"and crawled to there . . . where he killed her. Where he molested her, too."

"He, who?" said Mildred.

"Dunno," said Forrest darkly.

"How did he . . ." Mildred let the question hang.

"The murder weapon was a rock," said Forrest matter-of-factly. "They took the rock away, along with Agnes. Won't be much help, though. You can't lift prints off granite."

"This is awful," said Mildred. "Perfectly ghastly."

"Funny thing," mused Forrest almost to himself. "Funny thing."

"I see nothing funny," said Mildred, shuddering inside.

"Her clothes, I mean."

"Her clothes?"

"Yep. She was all dressed up. Pretty dress. High heels. Hose."

"So?"

"So that was very unlike Agnes. Agnes never dressed up. Maybe for church an' that, but not otherwise. She was a widow. She was plain. Simple. Quiet. Lived over at Ballard Green."

"The senior citizens' complex?"

"Yep. They bent the rules so's Agnes could get in. Clarence didn't leave her much. So Agnes lived there with the old folks but she wasn't one to take charity. She worked around the park.

9

Gardening. Put in rose bushes, Lordy, you should see 'em. She was always in sneakers and muddy dungarees, hair a tangle. Naw, Agnes never dressed up."

"Maybe she had a date."

Haggarty looked at Mildred like she was crazy. "A date? Haw, that's a good one! Agnes Peabody? Christ on a crutch! Har, har, har!"

Mildred looked away, disgusted. There was no talking to this man. She would terminate this conversation right now.

"You didn't hear anything, did you?" Haggarty's eyes brightened at this possibility.

"No. My house is some distance away. And I had a little wine last night, only a split, but it put me out like a light. I do remember Winston waking, though."

"Winston? He yer husband?"

"No!" she said too loudly. "He's my bulldog."

"Humph," grunted Haggarty. "Too bad."

"Chief Haggarty," said Mildred coolly, "if you don't mind my saying so, you don't seem to think this is too bad at all. You seem to be enjoying this—yes, I really think you are."

"Enjoying?" He looked at her sharply, as though stung by her words. Then he shrugged his shoulders, dropping the pretense. "Look, I'm sorry about Agnes. I'm sorry as can be. But I've been waiting for this son of a bitch to slip up for more than forty years, and by Christ, it looks like he's done it this time. Naw, girlie, what you're seeing ain't enjoyment. It's hope."

"Don't call me girlie," she fumed. "And hope for what? I don't understand."

"Come on," he said, putting an arm on her shoulder. "Let's set awhile."

He led her through the woods to a clearing by the road. There was a battered pickup truck with red rust leaching through pitted white paint. It had big balloon tires and floodlights mounted on the cab. Haggarty flipped down the tailgate, and before Mildred could protest he lifted her up onto it. She saw him wince as he did so, but he seemed to ignore the pain and hopped up to sit next to her.

"Maybe you don't know it," he said, "but women have been disappearing in this area for a good long while. Years."

"Years," Mildred repeated. Maybe this man was crazy. Police work had addled his brain. "I see," she said carefully.

"You don't believe me."

"I didn't say that."

"You didn't have to. I may be old, but I'm not blind. I can see it on your face plain as day." Mildred looked away. "You're thinking I'm crazy just like they all do. Ha! Well I've got something the rest of them don't have."

She didn't ask what it was. You've got bats, she thought, that's what you've got.

"I've got memory." He tapped his head.

"I see."

"So listen up . . ."

Why not, thought Mildred. I've nothing else to do.

"Nineteen forty-four. Betty Murphy."

Her head snapped toward him. She felt a shiver. "I remember Betty Murphy. She was in my high school—in my class, too. Lived in a trailer park over by the dump."

"Yep. Not exactly your circle."

It was true. Betty Murphy wore tight sweaters and lots of makeup. All the boys dated her. For experience, it was said. She dated older men and army men on leave, too. When she disappeared in her senior year, no one was surprised. They all assumed she was pregnant.

"She ran off with a sailor or something," said Mildred.

"She disappeared," said Forrest. "Without a trace. Look, she didn't just run off. Her mother was an invalid, and Betty was devoted to her. She'd never have left without so much as a note. 'Sides, Betty was gonna be the first in the family to graduate high school. Think she'd run off three weeks away from graduation? Never."

"I don't see what that's got to do with—"

"I remember it well," Haggarty went on, oblivious to Mildred. "It was my first year as chief. I was only thirty-two. It didn't smell right to me then, and it's never smelled right to me since."

"That's only one person," said Mildred, "and a long time ago at that."

"Sure," he said. "I thought so too. Hoped so." He shook his head. "There's more."

Mildred steeled herself and waited. He would tell her things, horrible things. He would ruin the woods, ruin the house, ruin this place.

"Nineteen fifty: Marilyn Collins. Nineteen sixty-three: Emmy-lou Taylor. Nineteen seventy: Muriel Guthrie."

"Stop," she whispered.

"Nineteen eighty-one," he said more loudly, "Harmony Johnson."

"Please!" She wanted to press her hands to her ears.

"Nineteen eighty-nine," he shouted, "Agnes Peabody!"

"Why are you telling me this?"

"Because someone's gotta listen. All these women disappear, and people say I'm crazy!"

"Maybe they had reasons. Sometimes people leave. They want to disappear. I myself—"

"That's what they all said." Haggarty was ranting now. "The newspaper, the selectmen, my own men on the force. They said I was off my rocker! My own men!"

"Maybe—"

"Maybe nothing! Betty Murphy was gonna graduate, an' Marilyn Collins, she was just outta college. She was engaged, for Chrissake! Emmylou Taylor had two children. Sure she had trouble with her husband, and sure she was unhappy. She might of took off, but not forever. She wouldn'ta forgot Christmas! And Muriel Guthrie . . . oh, poor Muriel. Such a mouse of a woman, you never saw such a meek little thing. She loved this town. She *picked* it even, for her home, I mean. She wouldn'ta left. They'da had to drag her away. Then there was Harmony Johnson..." Forrest looked at Mildred with eyes that turned suddenly sad. "Well, I can't even talk about her. And now Agnes Peabody. It's just too much, I tell you. Too damn much."

Mildred was afraid he might break down and cry right there, he was in such a state.

"There, there," she said.

He shook his head, winding down but still aggravated. "No one even cares. Shit a fucking brick."

"Chief Haggarty!"

"Huh? Oh, pardon me. I forget myself sometimes." He seemed lost in thought for some moments, then shook himself. "Well, this is the break I've been waiting for. Because Agnes Peabody, see, she didn't disappear. She clawed her way into the woods and something scared him off. Your Winston maybe. Who knows."

As if on cue, an aged bulldog lumbered out from the bushes, wheezing loudly through twisted nasal passages, face dripping with drool.

"That," said Haggarty, "is the ugliest dog I've ever seen."

"He's a champion," Mildred shot back. A champion past his prime, she thought to herself. Just like you.

Forrest Haggarty eyed the dog with distaste. "Some champion."

"These things may not connect," she said gently. "All those others and Agnes, I mean."

"Oh, they connect all right. You bet your ass." He stopped short. "Whoops. Sorry."

"Oh never mind," sighed Mildred. "I'm getting used to it. Well," she said, trying to be polite, "I wish you the best of luck with your investigation. Now I've got to get back..."

She moved to jump down, but before she could Haggarty hopped off the truck and lifted her to the ground. Actually he lifted, then dropped her. His eyes widened in pain, and he let her go. Then he doubled over, his arms clasped tightly around his knees. Mildred stared helplessly. She guessed he was trying not to scream.

"Chief Haggarty," she blurted. She touched his shoulder. "What's the matter? Let me get help."

"It's my back," he gasped. "It's happened before."

"Can you straighten up?"

" 'Fraid not."

"Oh dear." This was horrible, a horrible predicament indeed. "I must get help." She turned to leave, but wavered. How could she leave him by the side of the road? Like that.

"Don't go," he pleaded through clenched teeth. "Just hoist me in the truck. Pay no mind if I scream."

"Into the truck?" She stared at him in disbelief.

"We'll call for help—"

"It's so high . . . those tires . . ."

"Try," he urged. "Please."

Mildred Bennett was stronger than she looked, and Forrest Haggarty was a lightweight bundle of sticks under his khaki and green plaid. She managed to lift his locked-up body without changing the bent position. She eased him on his side like a rigid doll onto the ribbed metal bed of the pickup.

"Don't you worry," she reassured him. "We'll call your family right away."

"No!" he shouted. "God, no. Not them. We'll call Trevor Bradford."

"Dr. Bradford?" He'd been the family doctor when Mildred was a child. "Surely he's retired."

"Yeah," Haggarty gasped. "He's retired, but he's a damn good doctor. And he's my friend."

"Okay," she said. "You just hold on tight."

"She's a stick shift. Ever driven one?"

"A long time ago." She tried to sound confident but wasn't sure she could cope with a stick shift—or anything else for that matter.

14

"Just put her in first and take it real slow. Oooooohhhhh."

"Okay. Okay."

"And don't go over any potholes."

"There are no potholes on my property, Chief Haggarty."

"Just go! Ooooohhhh. Ahhhhhhhhh."

Mildred didn't waste words. She climbed into the pickup, shoving aside papers that had spilled from a broken cardboard carton on the passenger side. She grabbed hold of the big wheel and put her sneakered foot to the clutch. Then she grabbed the stick and put it into where she hoped first would be. She took it low and slow and maneuvered the pickup to her house.

This was supposed to be my vacation, she muttered under her breath. Some vacation.

2   When she climbed out of the truck and ran back to see Forrest Haggarty, Mildred was afraid to move him. His body was clenched tight as a fist, his face bleached white with pain.

"Don't move," she said. "I'll call Dr. Bradford."

"Shit, Millie, where would I go?" He said it through clenched teeth. He tried to smile and failed.

Mildred returned moments later.

"He's on his way," she said. "Just hold on."

"Hold on," Forrest repeated numbly. "Hold on."

She unhitched the tailgate and climbed up next to him. She moved to pat his shoulder but stopped herself and took his hand instead.

"Talk to me, Millie."

"I beg your pardon?"

"Talk to me, for Chrissake. Talk!" His eyes darted wildly. "Anything, okay? Say anything." He squeezed her hand and she thought she heard the bones crack.

"Ow!" she cried. "Yes. Of course. Talk." Mildred wasn't

good at speaking extemporaneously. She had never mastered the fine art of idle chitchat. But sometimes when she gave blood at the blood bank, sometimes then, she'd babble on like a magpie. Because you couldn't think of two things, couldn't chatter and think about blood, too. Her bones crunched again, and words spewed from her mouth.

"My mother died."

"You told me that."

"Yes. Uh, she died. So I decided to come here to sell the house. And for a"—he squeezed—"*vacation!*" she screamed.

"Alone?"

"Yes." She exhaled. It was like sitting with someone in labor. Waiting for the next contraction.

"Family?" Haggarty asked.

"Family? Ah, yes, I had a family."

"Had?"

"I mean *have*. Of course. I have a family."

"Tell me about 'em." The man was relentless. *"Tell!"* he yelled, squeezing yet again.

"My son died when he was twenty-two." She said it all at once, slapping Forrest in the face with the words. Astounding herself at the same time. Eight years ago she had put it to rest. She had come to terms with her grief and she had carried on. "Only twenty-two," she repeated almost to herself. "Too young, of course, far too young. You never expect to bury your own child."

"I'm sorry, Millie. I shouldn't of asked."

She seemed not to hear him. "His name was Sam. You would have liked him, Forrest. Everybody liked him."

"You don't have to talk about—"

"He was my first, and I suppose I was overprotective. Connor used to tell me I was." She stopped, remembering, and her face transformed from sad to glad. "I remember he had one of those kazoos when he was a child, Sam did. He'd play it all the time, hum into the thing. 'Yankee Doodle.' 'The Old Gray Mare.' 'Three Blind Mice'..."

"'See how they run, see how they run. They all ran after the farmer's wife...'"

"'She cut off their tails with a carving knife!'"

"Right!"

"Yes, he played all those songs. Then I saw he was biting down on the kazoo, biting down to the tin or whatever metal it was. Sam was a very intense boy. I was sure he was ingesting that red paint. So I took the kazoo away."

Forrest didn't say anything.

"I'd give anything to hear that kazoo now." She seemed to shake herself, seemed to wake up. "Well, that's nonsense, of course. Utter nonsense."

"So what happened to 'im?" Forrest couldn't help himself. He wanted to know.

"Oh... he had just graduated from college. Princeton. With honors. He had a new sportscar. A TR-6. Yellow, I think it was." Mildred knew what color it was, knew exactly what color it was. She would never forget that color. Canary yellow. "It was our graduation present to him and, ah... well, he just went off the road one night. It was one of those twisty New Jersey country roads just like here."

"I'm sorry," he said again, feeling helpless, not knowing what else to say, not knowing that just in the listening he was helping a lot.

"They said it was suicide. Can you imagine? The very idea. It was an accident, of course."

"Was there alcohol in his blood?" asked Forrest. "The autopsy would have shown—"

"No," she said quickly. "No alcohol. No drugs. But—"

"Were there skid marks?"

"No! What's wrong with you? You sound just like them!"

"I'm a policeman, Millie. I'm only asking—"

"Well, don't. You hear? Just don't. It was an accident."

"Okay, okay. An accident."

"And I have a daughter. Grown. She and I are not close. She's fond of her father, but not of me. I have trouble sometimes, Chief Haggarty. I must say. Trouble sometimes"—she drew a breath—"expressing affection."

Mildred could not believe she was telling this. This was private family business—worse than private family business—this was nobody's business, and she discussed it with nobody. Not even family.

"Molly, my daughter, lives in New York, too. I see her sometimes. It's difficult. She lives with this . . . this . . . how shall I say it? Creature. He's got fleas in his beard. Probably loaded with social diseases."

There, thought Mildred. I've said it all. I'm an unfit mother who couldn't protect her own child. And I'm a snob, too. But she hadn't said it all, not yet.

"Husband!" cried Forrest.

"Who?"

"Your husband. Where's he?"

"I prefer not to discuss—"

"*Where!*" he cried.

"He's ah . . . he's . . ." She searched for a way to dodge this question. She looked at Forrest Haggarty. His eyes were bloodshot, his lower lip raw from being bitten. Maybe she could tell him. "He's gone!" she blurted truthfully.

"Gone where?"

"I don't know. He left. Me. Last week." Another secret, another private humiliation. Throughout the years Connor Bennett had gone through a series of relationships with other women. These relationships—or dalliances, as Mildred preferred to think of them—had pained her greatly. Each time Mildred did what she had been taught to do: she ignored the situation. She waited for it to pass as it always did. She put on a happy face, a mask face, and went about her daily routine with false cheer that hid her very real internal anguish. Sometimes she feared that if someone were to accidentally bump against her, she would break right apart. Once she did lose hold. She almost became publicly hysterical in the Food Emporium when Carl the butcher happened to ask—as he always did—"And how are you today, Mrs. Bennett? Will it be the veal or the lamb?" She had fled that time. Escaped. Barely. She had fled to the street where she put her head against the cold metal of a fire alarm box. She almost broke the glass with her forehead and pulled the lever. Almost.

Connor's most recent relationship didn't follow the pattern, however. It didn't pass like the others. The initial clues had been the same, of course, and infuriatingly obvious: the slightly sappy grin at unexpected moments, the whistle while he shaved, the new spring in his step, the cloying scent of Aramis, dovetailed as always with later hours at the office and, finally, the flurry of overnight business trips before winding down to sullen sulks. Only this last time it didn't work that way. The grin persisted. Worse, it evolved. It evolved from sappy to smug Cheshire Cat to determined. And one day not so very long ago Connor informed Mildred that he was leaving. Just like that.

"He ran away with his secretary. Someone half his age. And mine. Isn't that trite? You'd think he could have shown more imagination. He was a successful man, you understand. A respected man. President of the firm."

Connor Bennett's station on the corporate slag heap meant absolutely nothing to Forrest Haggarty, who would have shrugged if he'd been able to.

"No one knows where he is. Not the office. Not his friends. Certainly not me. Isn't that funny?"

"No," said Forrest, who thought a man, any man, had certain primary responsibilities, one of them being to look after his wife. "It's not funny at all."

She wiped at her face with her free hand. When Connor left, she had stretched out fully clothed on the living room floor.

She had turned her face into the kick pleat of the sofa. She could still remember the rough cold feel of the brocade fabric against her cheek. I can go crazy, she thought. I can go mad right here and now. It would be very easy. She was amazed that she actually had such a choice, but she knew as surely as she was breathing that she did. Yes, it would be so very easy. Molly would find her. Or Elana, the cleaning lady. Even dull Elana would find it hard to vacuum without noticing a catatonic mummy sprawled on the carpet. Of course they would try to coax her to speak, to move, but she wouldn't. And they would call whoever people called at times like this. Let their fingers do the walking. Look under L in the yellow pages. For Loony Bin. They would send her to a nice place with tall pines and white wicker lawn furniture and soft-spoken people who would tell her when to get up, what to wear, and what to eat. Yes. She could go mad, she really could.

Then she considered a second choice. Alternative B. She could go to the kitchen and grind up one hundred Bayer aspirin with a spoon. She could mix the pulverized granules into a dish of softened vanilla ice cream. And she could eat that ice cream. She knew this snack would kill her. Amazingly enough, she had heard a physician explain that such a recipe would achieve such a result. He told it to a circle of listeners at a cocktail party. She had been both fascinated and repulsed at the same time. The man, if memory served, was a psychiatrist. He was saying how he never feared prescribing Valium to depressed patients because you couldn't kill yourself with Valium. But aspirin and ice cream, now there was a combination. And these simple ingredients were in everyone's kitchen and bathroom. Mildred was chilled. The man was the Julia Child of suicide. As she lay there on her living room floor, it made her angry just remembering.

So she turned to Alternative C. Connecticut. She could flee to Raven's Wing. It, too, was a place of refuge. With that thought wrapped around her like a life preserver, she got up from the floor. She went to the bedroom. And she packed her bags. She packed them very full. Because she might not come back. Ever.

"There, there," she said. "I'm fine. Really."

"In a pig's eye."

"I do believe I hear Dr. Bradford coming." Thank God, she thought. How things had gone this far was beyond belief. She was used to privacy. She was used to self-control. Now she would pack Chief Forrest Haggarty into an ambulance and get back to normal, whatever normal was.

Trevor Bradford rolled up the long driveway in a big black Lincoln. He stopped smoothly on the gravel, climbed out of the cavernous interior, nodded at Mildred Bennett, and went straight to Forrest Haggarty.

Trevor was much different than Mildred remembered. The shoulders inside the tweed jacket were slightly stooped. His handsome face was deeply lined—from worry, more than smiles, it looked like—and she noticed a nick on his chin where he'd cut himself shaving. If Mildred had guessed that this nick was the result of Trevor's stubborn insistence on using a straight razor, combined with a slight tremor in his hand, she would have been right. But despite the added years, despite the slumped shoulders and the tremor, Trevor Bradford had a bearing about him. He was tall—six feet two when he stood to full height, and he always did. His silver hair was neatly parted on the side and combed to the right. His corduroy pants were freshly creased. And a gold Cross pen nested in his jacket pocket, ready to write a prescription should the need arise. Unfortunately the need arose less and less lately. Oh, he still made rounds of sorts. He looked in on old friends in Ballard Green with some regularity, visiting them as a friend, not a doctor. He never failed to ask, "How's that hayfever, Cora?" or "The pacemaker working okay, Al?" And more often than not when he left there would be a prescription note on the table by the front door. He didn't take money for this and would, in fact, have been put out had anyone tried to press a five or a ten into his hand. The occasional visits, the talking with friends, made him feel useful. And that was more than the rest of the world did.

"Well, Forrest, you really went and did it this time."

"Don't start," groaned Haggarty. "Don't start on me now. It hurts awful bad, Trevor. Awful bad."

"Just hold on. I'll get my bag." He nodded to Mildred to follow him.

"Everyone's telling me to hold on!" Forrest shouted.

"Will he be all right?" she whispered when they got to the car.

"It's not his back I'm worried about. It's his heart."

"Oh dear."

"Oh yes. The pain is putting a terrible strain on his heart. We'll fix that in a jiffy, though." Trevor flipped open his bag and broke a syringe out of a glassine wrapper. "What did he lift anyway? A sack of cement?"

"Not exactly," Mildred sniffed. She wished she'd lost a few pounds. "Shouldn't we call his family? Shouldn't we call an ambulance?"

"We'll talk about that in a bit," said Trevor, turning on his heel.

Mildred raced after the distinguished country doctor. "What do you mean, we'll talk about it? What's to talk about?"

"Hush!" he said. He shot her a look that shut her up. He rolled up Forrest's sleeve, dabbed on alcohol, and administered the injection. "You'll feel better soon," he said softly.

"Help me get him inside, will you?" Trevor looked to Mildred, who stared back in disbelief.

"Inside? In my house?"

"If you would." It was not a question.

"I most certainly will not. Surely he has family," she sputtered. "Surely there are medical facilities. You must take him away this instant."

"Take him away," repeated Trevor icily.

"I didn't mean it like that. I just meant—"

"I know what you meant," he said shortly. "Now, Mildred Bennett, you listen to me. I remember you very well, and you always were the contrary one."

Mildred stood there slack-jawed. She couldn't believe this. Then, somewhere, she heard her mother say, *You'll catch flies,* and she clamped her mouth shut.

"He's *got* a family, understand. A family that wants to put him in a home. Put him away."

"Oh."

"They're looking for an excuse. Any excuse. Tried to have his driver's license revoked. He had to take the test again, but he passed it, see? His eyes are good, and so's his mind. But his mind won't be worth squat if they put him in Craigmore."

"It's a very nice place," Mildred interrupted. "An expensive place. We were considering it for my mother."

"And she had the good sense to die before you could stick her there." He saw her wince but went on. "The mind atrophies there. I've seen it before. Forrest deserves better."

"So what do you expect me to do?" She was afraid of the answer.

"He needs to be flat on his back awhile. Complete bedrest." He saw her expression and held up his hand like a traffic cop. "A couple of weeks at most. It's a slipped disk. He's had it before. He'll be fit as a fiddle in ten days. Two weeks tops."

"Two weeks!"

"Listen," said Trevor quickly, "it won't be so bad."

"Not so bad!" How will I manage, she thought wildly. How will I cope? Bedpans. Bathing. Feeding. It's like having a baby. Worse than having a baby.

He seemed to read her mind. "I'll get you help. I'll call the DNA."

"What's that?" she asked miserably. "Some kind of genetic organization? Like the DAR?"

"No. The District Nursing Association. They send home nurses." Trevor seemed to turn something over in his mind. "But that would never do. They'd find out."

"Who'd find out?" Her eyes narrowed to slits.

"His family. They'd ship him up to Craigmore before you could bat an eye. No, the DNA is out." His eyes opened wide. "I know! I'll call Irene Purdy!"

"Who's she?" Mildred started to panic. Everyone would be moving into her house. Peace and serenity and time for licking of wounds would be out of the question.

"She's a country woman. Lives up on the mountain. Used to do midwifing and nursing before the state made her stop. Said she was practicing without a license."

"Great," said Mildred. "Just wonderful."

"But she was very good, very good indeed."

"I really don't think I can become involved, Dr. Bradford."

"Trevor."

"Trevor. His family could find out. I'd be sued. Charged with kidnapping."

"No you wouldn't, either. He's here of his own free will. I'm his friend. I'll just tell them he took off and went fishing. He does that all the time."

"Oh, I don't know . . ."

"Just keep him for two weeks. Hide him." He saw her waver. "Keep him safe. Please."

"Oh!" She stamped her foot. "You!"

"You'll do it?"

"I guess."

"Good. Now help me move him. Easy, Millie! Easy does it."

"Two weeks," she said evenly. "Two weeks and that's it." They carried Forrest up the front steps, and Trevor acted as if he never even heard her.

They laid Forrest gently on a bed upstairs. It was the hardest bed in the house, in a room with an adjoining bath and bedroom, so Irene Purdy could hear him during the night. Mildred thought he was asleep, but his eyes were half open.

"Say!" he cried, jerking awake. "What's that there? I'm not dyin', am I?"

Trevor's eyes followed from the tip of Forrest's outstretched finger. He saw a confectionery jar on the windowsill, the kind you fill with penny candy. Only it was filled with shimmering multicolored rocks, sort of like quartz, in soft soothing shades of cranberry, emerald, and amber.

"Rocks," pronounced Trevor.

"They are not," corrected Mildred. "They're salt glass. Mermaid's tears."

"Huh?" said Forrest, not taking his eyes from the fragments of stained glass.

"Salt glass because they taste like salt in your mouth," explained Mildred. "We thought they were magical when I was a child. Not merely beach glass or sea glass, but mermaid's tears, shed for lost sailors. My cousins and I used to hunt for them on the beach. They were a gift from the sea. Plain broken bottles, ground smooth, transformed, by the waves. They sparkle in the sand. We'd find money and shells and other things, too. It's amazing what you'll find on a salt glass expedition. But we always liked the salt glass best."

"They're real pretty," said Forrest dreamily. "You say they're from broken bottles?"

"Most likely."

"Naw, nothing so simple as that. Nothing so plain. Maybe from stained glass windows of sunken yachts. Or taillights from Jimmy Hoffa's car. Or a sultan's turban, yeah, from places like that. Exotic places."

"Maybe," said Mildred. But Forrest didn't hear her. He was blissfully asleep.

3 "Pssst!"

"Huh?"

"Hey, Forrest."

"Who's there?" Forrest Haggarty twisted on the pillows, his head going this way and that, but he didn't open his eyes.

"It's me, Forrest. Dontcha know it's me? Whatcha doin' there, all laid up? And you talk like a Yankee. I don't like it, Forrest. Tell me you're okay."

He should have been scared, but he wasn't. He recognized the voice and it was the most natural thing in the world that she would be talking to him. Here and now. Like this. While Mildred was gone God knows where. While he was a prisoner, wrapped and bound in a cocoon of smooth sheets and nubby handmade coverlet.

"That you, Patty Louise?"

"Course it's me, Forrest."

"Why you coming to visit me now? After all these years? Don't you dare tell me I'm dying, you who always were the big know-it-all. If you've come to tell me that, I'm not opening my eyes. Not looking at you, Patty Louise." He turned his face to the wall.

In truth, he *was* dying, but only of curiosity. Damned if he didn't want to see Patty Louise in the worst way.

"Are you quite through?"

"I suppose," he said to the wall.

"Well, open those beady eyes. You're not dying, okay? You're too mean to die, Forrest Haggarty."

He opened them then, not slow but quick, afraid she would vanish. Afraid she would dematerialize before he got to see. After all, she'd done it once before. Sixty-three years before.

"Jesus, Patty Louise, it is you. Jesus Night." He feared he might cry.

"Don't cuss, Forrest. I'll tell Daddy."

He hugged her to him then, feeling her spindly ten-year-old bones and her breastless chest. He hugged her so tight he had to stop himself, afraid he might crush the very breath out of her. His tears washed into her fine brown hair. He took her gently by the shoulders and held her at arm's length so he could take a real good look.

"You didn't grow none, Patty Louise. You're just the same."

"How else would I be?" But she looked at him with eyes that said, Boy oh boy, big brother, have you ever changed. Have you ever.

"That's a real nice dress," he said, changing the subject. "I remember that dress." He ran his finger along hand-stitched smocking that spanned her chest. He touched, barely skimmed, the lace on her starched Peter Pan collar. "Grandma made you that dress."

"It was my prettiest one. My favorite."

"It was the one you were wearing—"

"I know, Forrest." She cut him short, not wanting to talk about that. She moved to the foot of the bed.

"Don't go!"

"I'm not going anywhere, Forrest. See? I'll set right here." She sat cross-legged Indian-style, her sense of modesty forever undeveloped. He noticed that her patent leather shoes were still brand new, still no scuffs even on the soles.

"Did it hurt?" he blurted.

"Forrest."

"I can't help it, Patty Louise. Tell me that much at least. All these years, I never stopped wondering."

"It wasn't your fault, Forrest. I told you that then."

"It was me who went to the old barn looking for lumber.'"

"And me who followed you."

"I wasn't s'posed to go. I should have taken you back."

"It's okay, Forrest."

"I never should have pushed you, Patty Louise—"

"I was a brat, Forrest."

"If it hadn't been for that nail. A little bitty nail. Oh, Patty Louise, a thousand times I wished I'd stepped on it 'stead of you."

"Hush!" She pressed her hands to her ears and squinched her eyes closed, blotting him out. When she was sure it was safe, sure he was quiet, she opened her eyes and let the hands drop to her knees. She looked at him hard, seeming to turn a thought over in her mind.

"Okay," she said. "Okay. I'll tell you that one thing." She drew a breath. "It didn't hurt none, Forrest. Honest. The fever hurt and the dreams were terrible. But after, no, it didn't hurt at all."

"They have medicine now," he said. "For tetanus."

"I know." She said it like she wanted him to think she knew it all. A woman of the world at ten years old. "But it didn't hurt none. It felt, well, like swimming. Yeah. Like at the swimming hole when you dive down too deep into the chilly water and you need air so bad and you can see that patch of blue sky overhead and you know that's where the air is . . ."

"Yes?"

"And you swim and swim but you just can't make it. And you get so tired. Until finally you breathe anyway because what choice do you have?" She saw his look. "But it's okay, Forrest, 'cause you can breathe anywhere. Honest."

"You always were a good swimmer, Patty Louise." He said it accusingly. "You could hold your breath longer than anybody, even me."

"I knew you wouldn't understand," she said.

"So tell me about the others," he demanded. He sat bolt upright, not noticing that the pain in his back was gone. "Tell me about the family. Mama and Daddy especially."

"Oh no." She stuck out her chin in that defiant way he remembered so well. "I said one question. You asked it, you got it. Tell me about you."

He wondered how come she knew about tetanus shots but not about him.

"There's nothing to tell," he said. Nothing I'm especially proud of, but he didn't say that.

"Then I may as well go." She shrugged her shoulders with feigned indifference. She flipped a ribboned braid over her shoulder. She knew Forreset like a book.

"Okay," he said. "Okay."

"Start after the nail. After I—"

"Right."

He told her everything he could think of. He told her about aerated Wonder Bread and automatic washers, about pop-top cans and pantyhose, about color TV and interstate highways. He told her about cigarettes causing cancer and light beer with fewer calories, about automatic teller machines and Pac Man, about Post-it Notes and disposable diapers. He didn't tell her about Adolf Hitler, the atom bomb, or birth control pills. He didn't tell her about AIDS either. Because, after all, she was a ten-year-old stuck in 1923 and enough was enough.

Then, finally, after setting the scene, he told her about himself. He told her how their father lost all his money in the crash of 1929. How the man who had owned half of Chattanooga, Tennessee, and most of Lookout Mountain ended up without a plumb nickel. How the town repossessed the real estate for back taxes. He told how he—Forrest—started running moonshine at the age of sixteen, working for Boomer Sykes, a toothless, mean-spirited mountain man who operated a still deep in the woods. He even told how in moments of despair he drank that white lightning (also called skull crack), making himself half crazy and half blind. And how in a moment of such half blindness, when the world shimmered like salt glass, how he knocked up Boomer's fifteen-year-old daughter, Crystal Ann, who had smallpox scars and buck teeth and a two-digit IQ.

"You hit her?" said Patty Louise, not understanding "knocked up."

"Uh, something like that."

He told how he ran away then. Away from Boomer. Away from Crystal Ann. Away from Lookout Mountain and from his mother and father, who had always done for him, always protected him, but just couldn't anymore. Who now lived in a decaying farmhouse that leaned precariously to one side, that had water damage in the parlor and shingles that pop-pop-popped off the roof in double-time tempo.

"So where'd you go?" she asked.

"New York."

"New York City?" She said it as if it were Gomorrah.

"Right."

For nearly a decade he was a bum. To be fair, it didn't start out that way. At first Forrest tried to find work. Any work. And for a time he did find a raggedy string of menial jobs. Ice man. Street cleaner. He pried frozen coal from boxcars with a pick and shovel one frigid February. But soon even those two-bit-an-hour jobs disappeared, and he joined the breadline along with so many others, hat in hand. Broken. Dirty. Angry, too.

He slept in Grand Central Station or in a flophouse on East Fourteenth Street or curled up in some Godforsaken stairwell that smelled of urine and butts. He was luckier than most. He didn't have a family to worry about. He only had himself.

"Then the war came, and I straightened out," and Forrest. "It's awful to say, but the war was the best thing that happened to me. It saved my life."

He signed up right away. He'd been pretty good with a rifle on the mountain and was sure they'd put him in the infantry. He was wrong, though. They put him in the MPs.

"The Military Police. Me! Suddenly I had a career, though I can't rightly say I liked it much in the beginning. First they sent me to a POW camp in Texas, marching back and forth with my rifle. Guarding a bunch of bewildered Krauts. The heat was god-awful, the dust even worse. It was red, I remember that, and would work itself into your eyes and ears, into every pore of your skin. At the end of the day I looked like an adobe brick. I hated it there. So I put in for a transfer."

"Where'd they send you?"

"Rio Linda, California. A Nisei internment camp." Forrest's face flushed at the memory. "They were Americans, Patty Louise. I couldn't believe it. They weren't the enemy. They were fine people. Refined people. So polite and dignified, all the while other Americans were taking everything they owned hand over fist. Just like they did to Mama and Daddy. Only this time there wasn't no mystery about it. It was out in the open, legal and proper. I lost my faith in government then."

Forrest spent most of the remainder of the war teaching Nisei children how to play baseball, how to make slingshots, and how to play mumblety-peg. He helped them dig a swimming hole, a mud hole really, but that simple diversion carried the camp through an entire summer. He sipped bitter tea with parents and grandparents, carried extra blankets and canned goods into the camp on his back under cover of darkness, and found a source for sake in nearby Sacramento. From then on he made a regular sake run every Friday night. For all this he took no money. Save your money for a fresh start after this is all over, he told them. And he prayed it would be over, for even though he'd lost his faith in government, Forrest Haggarty never really lost his faith in God.

Sometimes he would dream grand dreams. Dreams of leading an insurrection or, at the very least, an escape. But he knew it was hopeless. On the outside every Nisei face was a mark, a sign, a walking WANTED poster.

"Then I got pneumonia," said Forrest. "Real bad, it was. I almost died. The army sent me to a hospital out there, then shipped me home. The war wasn't over yet, but it was for me."

"When you got home, Mama and Daddy were dead."

"Right. No one told me. I found their graves in the family

plot. I left wildflowers. Daisies. Queen Anne's lace. Black-eyed Susans. I bunched 'em up and tied 'em with a red rubber band. Then right before I walked away I set down a thistle flower, too. It cut my hand, but I didn't care. I set it on the grave, watered with my own blood. It was all I could do."

They were quiet for some moments. He could hear the ticking of a clock somewhere down the hall. A green-jeweled fly buzzed against the windowpane.

"One of my army buddies from Connecticut told me his hometown was looking for a chief of police. Connecticut, I says, that sounds like the end of the earth. Plus I was too inexperienced for the job. Barely out of my twenties. But then I figured Connecticut couldn't be much worse than New York or Amarillo or Rio Linda. And I saw how the pneumonia made me look older. So I gave it a shot. Hitched a ride up to Raven's Wing. They never had a full-time policeman before, never mind a chief. And danged if I didn't get the job."

Forrest remembered the proud feeling he'd had, a feeling that lasted until he sat on a stool in the Cannonball Pub and realized that all the other potential police chiefs were off fighting the war. The bar, like the town, was full of old men. Still, the job was his. He took it, grabbed hold, and never let go.

He told Patty Louise about Queenie and the children and the grandchildren, too.

"You see your grandkids, Forrest? Do they have you over for Sunday dinner and such?"

"I'm awful tired, Patty Louise." He closed his eyes, intending to rest only a minute. "Awful tired."

He didn't feel like talking anymore. There was lots more he could have told her. Lots more about his family and his years as chief. Lots more about Betty Murphy and the others too. He could have told Patty Louise how he remembered her all these years. How he saw her in the faces of these disappearing ladies. But right now he didn't feel like it. Maybe later he would.

4 "These pills," said Trevor as he was leaving. "Give him two when he wakes up, and two every four hours thereafter. Tell Irene. She'll know what to do."

"Yes."

"And call me tomorrow, no matter what."

"I will."

He turned to leave. "And, ah, thank you, Mildred. I really do thank you."

"Oh, it's nothing," she said automatically.

"Most folks wouldn't bother."

"Well, maybe they should bother," she said. "Maybe they should. It's not really a bother anyway." She looked at his hand on the door. Suddenly she didn't want him to leave. "Do you really think his mind's sharp?"

"He was talking to you about all those women, wasn't he?"

"Yes."

"His mind wanders sometimes," said Trevor grudgingly. "When we get old, we tend to live in the past. You'll find out someday ..."

Mildred was flattered. She thought she was old now. Too old for Connor anyway. Too old for Molly. Too old to get a job.

"... and retirement didn't agree with him. He missed the action." Trevor ran a hand over his silver hair. He seemed to choose his words carefully. "There's another thing too. None of us likes to fail. Take me, for instance. I keep remembering people I treated who died. The ones I lost. I remember them more and more. See their faces even. So maybe Forrest remembers those women who disappeared. It's sort of the same thing."

"I see."

"But if you want my honest opinion ..."

33

"Yes?"

Trevor looked at her as though he were about to betray a friend. "Well, I don't think anything really happened to those women. They had reasons to leave. All of them. They didn't disappear, they just left. It happens. One every ten years or so? Sure it happens. Kids disappear, too. You see them on milk cartons staring out of the refrigerator. Teenagers run away. And men, too, of course. They skip out on child support or alimony. No, there was nothing shady about these cases, just Forrest yearning for a little excitement. A little adventure. God knows," he sighed, "we could all use a little adventure."

"But what about that woman last night?"

"Oh, Agnes? That's another kettle of fish entirely. It's a pity. About Agnes, of course, but about Forrest as well. Sent him right off the deep end again. That's why I don't want his family to get hold of him just now."

"I see."

"I believe you do." Trevor Bradford smiled and took her hands in his. "You're a good woman, Mildred Bennett. Your mother would have been proud."

"Oh, go on," she laughed. "Get, before I do something stupid like inviting you to lunch. I'm a terrible cook."

"I've got a cast-iron stomach. Try me."

So she fed him cold quiche and Amstel Light beer. He didn't complain. It was the nicest meal he'd had in a long time.

"Maybe you'd like to come back," she said on the porch. "For dinner or something. And to look in on Forrest, too, of course." She added the last hastily.

Trevor looked slightly uncomfortable. He seemed to turn a thought over in his mind. "I've got a wife," he said quietly.

"Oh," she said quickly. "Of course."

"She's pretty sick."

"I'm sorry." She wasn't sorry, though. She was stung. He'd eaten her lunch under false pretenses.

34

"But, ah . . ." Trevor looked downright pained now. "I don't know how to say this . . ."

Just don't, she thought. Don't say anything at all.

". . . but I sure could use a friend."

"A friend?" Mildred stared at him dumbfounded.

"Company. Someone who's not sick. Not in pain. What I'm saying is I'd like to come to dinner. Or just to talk." The words came out bit by bit. "Retirement," he said almost to himself. "I guess it doesn't agree with me either."

"Well," Mildred said carefully, "I suppose you should look in on Forrest from time to time."

"Yes."

"And that Irene Whatshername . . ."

"Purdy."

"Yes. She'll need supervision."

"Of course," said Trevor quickly.

"Well, Dr. Bradford . . . Trevor . . . Stop by if you wish. To look in on Forrest. Or to chat." She waved her hand. "Whatever."

"I'll do that."

As she closed the door, she wondered if she had done the right thing. The proper thing. Oh what the heck, she decided. Maybe she could use a friend too.

5 At five-thirty the phone rang.
"Hello," said Mildred.

"Afternoon," said a woman's voice on the other end of the line. "Irene Purdy here."

"Thank goodness," said Mildred. "I've been waiting for you. Actually, I expected you an hour ago. He's liable to wake up any time now."

"I called to say I'll be there in the mornin'. 'Bout eleven, near as I can figure."

35

"Eleven?" Mildred gripped the phone tightly and tried to keep her voice steady. "That will never do. No, it won't do at all."

" 'Fraid it'll have to. There's a pool o' gasoline all over my garage floor. Leastwise I think it's gasoline. Looks like the tank rusted plumb through. I'm not about to flick my Bic in there. Ha, ha!"

Mildred stared at the wallpaper in the sitting room. Roses cascading in twining vines from ceiling to floor. Roses intertwined. Suddenly they looked like bars.

"It'll do that, you know. She's an old car. Volkswagen Beetle. I've had 'er since seventy-two. Running on the original engine. Course I change the oil regular, change it myself. Car'll last forever, long as you change the oil. Course the floor's rusted through. On the passenger side, mind you. I just put down one of those Rubbermaid drain mats. Don't have no passengers nohow. But now the tank's rusted through. I think that Vinnie Scarlatti over at the Texaco's been giving me bad gas. He'll pay for a new gas tank, you can bet on that."

"I'll pick you up!" blurted Mildred. "Just tell me where you are. I'll come get you."

"You'd never find me. I live on West Mountain . . ."

"I am somewhat familiar with this locale," Mildred lied.

". . . way in the woods. I got a log cabin. Built it myelf, log by log. Even the fireplace. Fieldstone. Chipped and shaped and lugged those rocks myself. Big suckers, too."

"I'll find you," insisted Mildred. She would find a way somehow, propelled by sheer force of will.

"Naw," said Irene. " 'Sides, you don't got a four-wheel drive. Betcha you don't got a four-wheel drive. I don't need it but you would."

"I have a Jaguar," said Mildred primly.

"A pansy car," hooted Irene. "Never make it up the hill."

"Then you can walk down." Mildred was getting annoyed now. This woman was so stubborn. She tried to filter shrillness from her voice. She didn't want to scare Irene away altogether.

"Three miles?" laughed Irene. "You kiddin'? With my bum knee? I got that knee from cleaning too many floors. I don't do floors, don't do housework at all. Hope Trevor told you that. I take care of the sick. Or the broken. That's it."

"I have a cleaning lady," said Mildred. (Don't back out on me now, Irene! Don't!)

" 'Sides," said Irene, not pausing for breath, "you can't come get me. You gotta stay with *him*."

"I don't gotta—I don't *have to*—do anything," snapped Mildred.

"Well, someone's gotta stay with him. For tonight at least. Like you said, he'll be waking up soon. He'll be disorientated. He'll try to run off, hurt himself real bad. Naw, you gotta stay with him. Give him a shota bourbon, he likes Jack Daniel's. A shot or two won't hurt him none. Then give him his dinner. You got any o' those chicken pot pies? Swanson's?"

Mildred felt like screaming. There was no way to get a word in edgewise. "Never mind," she said. "Never mind. I give up."

"Don't give up, honeybunch. Like I said, I'll be there in the mornin'."

"Don't call me honeybunch," said Mildred. But she said it to a dial tone. Irene had already hung up.

She decided to look in on Forrest. She tiptoed up the stairs and to the doorway. She didn't want to wake him. She peeked around the door at his prone form. He looked sound asleep. Ever so gingerly, she walked into the room on the balls of her feet. She eased up to the head of the bed. She bent down over the serene sleeping face. He looked so calm, peaceful, free of pain.

"What the hell are you looking at?" Forrest bellowed.

"Ahhhhhh!" she cried. She flew back several steps.

"You could scare a man to death that way. Lucky for you I didn't have my gun."

"Yes," said Mildred, clutching her chest with one hand. "Lucky."

"Where am I?" He tried to sit up, winced, and fell back into the pillows. "Where's Patty Louise?"

"You're upstairs. In my house. There's no Patty Louise here."

"Christ," said Forrest, sinking deeper. "Now I remember. I gotta get out of here."

"No, indeed," said Mildred.

"Huh?"

"You've got to stay here for ten days."

"The hell I will!"

"That's what Dr. Bradford says."

"What does Trevor Bradford know?" Forrest struggled to sit up. "Just you watch me."

"Lie still!" She ran to him then. She held him down, placing one hand on each shoulder.

"Lemme go!" He tried to twist away from her but couldn't. He was tired and he was hurting. "You don't understand. Please."

And then, all at once, he started to cry. Not loud. Not with heaving sobs. But with quiet tears that welled up in the corners of his eyes and spilled out the sides. He swung his head back and forth.

"There, there," she said helplessly. She felt a wave of pity for the man under her hands. "Now, now. It won't be so bad. Only ten days. You'll be fine. Trevor said so."

"Screw Trevor!" he said miserably. "I don't have ten days, don't you see? After three days, the trail gets cold. The odds jump enormously."

"What odds?"

"The odds of catching Agnes Peabody's killer, those odds."

"Oh."

"You forgot already. Ahhhh," he sighed, "the hell with it." He seemed to give up then.

"I suppose," he said, "I should become one o' them old people who make houses outta Popsicle sticks. I saw a lady in

People magazine who made an en-tire Cape Cod house outta Popsicle sticks. Lived in it, too."

"Oh."

"Or maybe I should be like the old fart they wrote about who collects twine. He's got the world's biggest ball o' twine now. Seven feet in diameter."

"Oh." It was all she could say.

"Ain't that nice. Get myself a hobby. Sticks or twine or some such shit."

Then he clamped his mouth shut and closed his eyes.

"Go away," he whispered.

She removed her hands and started to leave. "I'm sure the police have things well in hand," she said quietly.

He said nothing. Mildred felt like she could read his thoughts. The police are assholes, that's what he was thinking.

"I could move your police radio in from the car," she offered. "You could listen in at least."

He ignored her. He looked like a dead man. Mildred remembered an old saying from somewhere: *Happiness is something to do, someone to love, and something to hope for.* Forrest Haggarty had none of these things.

"Maybe I could help," she said carefully.

He seemed to stop breathing. Seemed to listen.

"I mean, I'm not very busy. I could do some legwork for you. Research or something. Your brain and my energy." She tried to laugh. "You could tell me what to do. How to begin." Her words drifted off weakly. "Oh," she said, "I suppose it's too farfetched."

"No," he said to the wall.

"What?"

"It's not farfetched, not farfetched at all."

"I don't know anything about police work . . ."

"I'll teach you. Go get my papers!" Forrest came to life. He fixed his blue eyes on her and looked like a man possessed.

"What papers?"

"The carton in the truck. My research. My notes. Go get it, girl."

Something inside Mildred Bennett took a flying leap. It was like the time she was seven and jumped off the diving board for the first time. It was a sense of excitement, a sense of adventure.

"Right," she cried, almost saluting. And she raced out the door.

6 In Raven's Wing, Connecticut, there are four churches on Main Street. The Congregational, the Episcopal, the Methodist, and the Presbyterian. The Catholic church stands alone —off on a side street—about a half mile from the center of town. Perhaps this is because Catholics were latecomers compared to their Protestant brethren. Perhaps all the prime Main Street property was occupied by the early 1800s. But perhaps also the location says something about preference or even prejudice.

After all, Catholics are different from you and me, folks would say. With their mumbo-jumbo Latin masses, grim-faced sexless women in voluminous black robes, and clickety-clacking rosary beads. They're clannish, they are. They don't eat meat on Friday. They send their children to separate schools. They fixate on the death of Christ rather than on the resurrection. *Mea culpa*, isn't that what they say? My fault. They're gruesome, that's what. Let them be by themselves.

He came to Saint Mary's Roman Catholic Church on Catoonah Street because it was remote in both location and style from the Protestant church of his youth. It was highly unlikely that any of his friends would see him here. And the atmosphere, to him, was soothing, though he didn't know why.

He sat ramrod straight in a pew toward the back, the very

same pew he had selected so many times before. The wood was slick under his moist palms. He took several deep breaths and tried to relax, concentrating on the flickering candles up front, which cast a mellow glow through the cavernous interior. He felt quite tiny, despicable really, under the vaulted ceiling. He looked from the candles to the statues, seeking some measure of comfort in their stony faces.

His eyes rested first on a statue to the right of the altar— some saint, he supposed—a man dressed like a friar with a rope around his waist and a sad smile on his alabaster face. He lingered longingly on this figure, caressing with his eyes the folds of the robe, the nape of the neck, the outstretched fingertips. Then his gaze shifted to the altar itself. It was carved from what seemed to be a single block of purest white marble. Multiple spires topped with gilt crosses rose from the sturdy yet intricately carved rectangular base. He sought out a compartment in the very center, a chamber covered in burgundy velvet with gold piping. Maybe Catholics thought God was in there, rolled up like a fetus in his tiny chamber. He liked the ritual of Catholics, liked their pomp and ceremony, too, but thought they themselves were childish and naive, clinging desperately to an impossible concept of afterlife.

Still, the very idea of retribution, of fire, of hell was intriguing to him. The concept of eternal damnation. Of punishment. He believed in punishment. He smiled to himself and wondered if he would ever be punished for the things he did. He doubted it.

Abruptly he frowned. His eyes traveled reluctantly from the purity of the altar to a life-size statue on the left. It was set within the confines of a concave niche within the stucco wall. He eyed it warily. Her pale blue robe and cloyingly sweet smile didn't fool him. Neither did the masquerade halo that hovered over her head, suspended by an all too obvious black metal wire. By rights she should have died instead of her son. She had brought forth a bastard, if the truth be told, then sent him defenseless into the world. Defenseless, into a world he thought could be changed. Then slaughtered on two slats of wood, a crown of bloody thorns pressed into his head. He had seen such thorns once. Two inches long they were, sharp and brittle as iron shards, on a bush in his mother's garden.

That garden had been beautiful, as so few things are today, a place of tightly manicured shrubs, red velvet roses, white pebbled pathways, and an ice-cold fish pond where a boy could chill his toes on a hot summer day. It was all gone now, of course, overgrown, full of poison ivy and briars. Gone, too, was the barefoot boy. And his mother? Gone. Dead.

Not that I care, you understand. I'm far beyond that.

He tried to push these thoughts from his mind. With increasing agitation, he looked at the brightly colored stained glass windows that loomed on both sides. Around and around they swirled. Turquoise blues and emerald greens and crimson reds. In and out, faces blending into splintered shards of glass, white robes flying, mouths twisting, eyes filled to overbrimming with scalding penitential tears.

Stop!

He rammed his head against the pew in front of him, rammed it with such force that it made a hollow clunking sound. Abruptly he snapped his head back upright and surveyed the rows of pews before him. No one even bothered to look his way. There were just a few old ladies in black, ladies enthralled with their own private chants and supplications. Please, dear Lord, cure my husband of cancer. Please make my arthritis not so bad. Please let my son-in-law find a job, they have a baby on the way. Oh please. Please please please! The word roared like thunder inside his skull—please—and he knew what was coming. Please. Leave me alone. God in heaven, leave me alone.

Again he hid his face, this time dumping it into his hands as though he were praying. It was a ruse, of course. A joke. He never prayed anymore. Maybe he had once—when had it been?

In his younger days, his littler days, before he discovered that he was not so helpless after all.

He dug blunted fingernails into his closed eyes and took refuge in the swirling colors and patterns that blossomed as he pressed.

Had he been rational, he would have admitted that this indeed was a prayer of sorts. His own prayer. His only prayer. A prayer that seldom worked. Because when the swirling started and the colors bled one into the other, he lost himself. Later he would make lame excuses for these lapses of memory . . . getting older . . . working too hard . . . maybe I had a few too many drinks. But it was disconcerting nonetheless.

He had responsibilities, after all. People counted on him. Believed in him too. Idiots, of course, but a following just the same. Sometimes he marveled at their blindness. He was a jigsaw puzzle held together with Crazy Glue and he knew this better than anybody. When he looked at himself in the morning mirror the sides of his face didn't match. And yes, this contradiction, the contradiction of his very being, gave him an almost erotic thrill.

But now he was in torment. Desperately, he twisted his head around and stared at an ornate wooden closet to the rear of the church. The confessional. Once, on one of his sojourns into this very church, he had peeked inside. Just a quick look when no one was around. It was dark and musty in there. It reminded him of the sticky chambers of porno parlors he had frequented not so long before. It smelled of dust and stale air and guilt. He held back the curtain, allowing the coffinlike chamber to flood with murky light. As he looked into that room, that place of the soul, he had taken inventory. A Spartan wooden seat. A bench padded in cheap red vinyl. A grilled screen that afforded no real privacy whatsoever. A priest would sit behind this screen, able to look up suddenly should the spirit move him. And this thought had filled him with dread. He had shrunk back and fled into summer sunshine outside. But even as he ran, even as he hurried down well-worn stone steps and out to the street—even then he had felt a chilly finger behind him reach out and brush the back of his neck ever so gently. You'll be back, it told him. You'll want to come back. You'll want to tell someone.

Confession. The word popped into his head. Why not? Priests are sworn to a vow of secrecy, after all. And he so wanted to share his secret with someone. To get a reaction. Admiration even. The thought was seductive.

I could, you know. I could tell.

With agonizing stealth, he moved his head a millimeter at a time. He turned ever so slowly and gazed at the draped chamber next to the door that hid the priest. They were in there now, the priest and the sinner. He could hear muffled murmurs. Only one priest on duty, ample resource to hear a few old ladies recite a litany of pathetically venial sins.

My sin will knock you on your ass.

The vulgar phrase jumped into his mind so suddenly, he almost laughed out loud. He clamped one hand over his mouth and bit into the meat of his palm hard enough to draw blood. With the other hand he reached up reflexively to pull down the brim of his hat even farther. He did not know that wearing this hat, no matter how stylish, made him conspicuous in a Catholic church. It made him look insolent, too, which he was.

You won't go in there, a voice said. *You don't have the guts.*

His body went rigid. He hated it when the voice started. Only crazy people hear voices.

Stop.

Never did have any backbone. Spineless, sniveling, pathetic little bastard.

Shut up!

He bolted to his feet. His upper lip was a blistered mass of perspiration bubbles. He clenched his hands at his sides, balling them into tight fists, lest the tremors within him escape. Blindly he sidestepped out of the pew.

Think you can get away? Think so?

He seemed to move through muddy water, each step taking an eternity. He thought only of escape. But then—at the last possible moment—he blundered right in front of a short, stout woman of indeterminate age who was about to enter the vacant confessional. She was dressed in black and displayed a prominent hairy mole on her protruding chin.

"Please," he croaked.

"Huh?"

"May I go first?" He thought he would die. He could not be saying this. He fully expected lightning to strike. "I have an appointment."

"You got an appointment for confession?" She looked at him as if he were crazy, and he wanted to kill her.

"No," he whispered, frantic now. The loudness of her question had attracted several startled glances. "Afterward. I have an appointment afterward."

She nodded grimly, chastened by reproachful stares from her friends from the Rosary Society. "What can you expect?" she muttered over her shoulder as he disappeared behind the curtain. "People today, nothing's sacred."

7   Clement Flynn shifted uncomfortably on his side of the confessional. He pulled at his Roman collar, which as usual was biting into the flesh of his neck. A device of torture, that's what it was, worthy of the Inquisition. A constricting noose that made him pay penance every time he had to swallow.

Clement sighed, bent his head, and touched index finger and thumb to the bridge of his nose. It was a pose recommended when he was a seminarian so many years ago—a pose designed to protect the privacy of the confessor while giving the impression that the priest was deep in thought.

Actually Clement was deep in boredom. He hated confession. No one bothered with it anymore, no one interesting anyway. Now they did it hidden behind the anonymity of a group—in public—and they called it reconciliation. The only ones who stuck to the tradition of private confession were people about to be dead, so they had no choice, and people who might as well be dead. People who clung to the old ways, most of them older women. Some were short and squat, some were tall and gaunt, but they all had one thing in common: monotonous sins. They whispered furtively of gossip, of envy, of an occasional white lie. Bless me, Father, for I have sinned.

Sin? Ha! These women didn't know from sin.

Though he knew it was wrong, Clement sometimes found himself yearning for the old days when real people confessed real sins. Like adultery. Now there was a sin you could hang your hat on. A sin of passion, a sin of pleasure, a sin of unspeakable guilt. Not some half-assed mealy-mouthed transgression like wishing a neighbor's fur coat was your own.

Once Clement had confided to a colleague, another priest from the diocese, about this yearning for the excitement of bigger, more meaningful sins. Then, to make matters worse, Clement tossed out a few gruesome possibilities. The confidant had looked at him oddly, and Clement knew he had gone straight to the bishop with word that Father Clement Flynn was losing his marbles.

Now the bishop kept Clement on a short leash. No more weekends off to New York, where he could lose himself and do a little sinning of his own. No more participation in pro-life demonstrations. No more buying vintage wines on credit at Hyde's Liquors. No more violent videos on the VCR. The bishop thought he was a crumbling cracker, plain and simple; he as much as said so. Clement hated the bishop.

Clement chastised himself for having these uncharitable thoughts. Tonight he would say an extra act of contrition. He sighed again and braced himself for the next person as he felt a form appear behind the screen.

"Uh, you a priest?"

Right away Clement knew something was up. For one thing, the person opposite him was a man, not a woman. That, in itself, was slightly unusual. For another, the man was obviously in strange territory. If he were familiar with the rites and rituals of Catholicism, he would have known that a priest and only a priest would be sitting where Clement was sitting.

"Yes, my son."

Clement also didn't know that this precise choice of words at this very moment was highly potent. He had pushed a sensitive button.

"Oh, God . . ." said the man, burying his head in his hands.

Clement fought the urge to look up, to offer a comforting look or even a touch through the grate, for such a gesture was absolutely forbidden. Instead he steeled himself and prayed for strength.

"Father," began the man in a whisper, "I seem to have wants."

"I see." Clement didn't see at all, but he was hanging in here.

"Needs."

"Yes," said Clement carefully. "Is there something you wish to confess?"

"I'm not Catholic," said the man. "It's just that I thought, I hoped . . ."

"That you are not Catholic does not matter," said Clement gently. "We are all God's children in his eyes."

"You called me son," whispered the man.

"Yes," said Clement. He didn't trust himself to say more. This man was obviously distraught. There was no script, no pose, for this confession.

"I would like to believe it." The man drew breath. "I've been so lonely."

The voice was filled with a razor-blade kind of pain.

Clement felt slightly dizzy. He was conscious all at once of the stale air within the confessional, the perspiration that trickled under his cassock, the dryness of his chapped lips.

"Is there," Clement repeated, "something you wish to confess?" He tried not to sound harsh.

"Yes. But it wasn't my fault, you understand. I merely do that which must be done . . ."

Clement rode along on a torrent of words as though on a roller coaster. They poured from the desperate man in a confused jumble, higgledy-piggledy, with no apparent rhyme or reason. Clement shut his eyes tight and tried to recall his one psychology class. When he was a seminarian there was so little emphasis on such things.

". . . usually I'm fine. I mean, for years I might be fine. No one would ever know, ever suspect. And they mustn't, you understand? You must never tell."

Clement couldn't be sure, but he had the distinct feeling that the man's fingers were now twined around the metal wires of the grate. Imploring. Or threatening.

"I won't tell," said Clement quickly, frightened now in spite of his best efforts to remain calm. "I'm sworn to a vow of secrecy, surely you know that."

"Yes." The man seemed to relax. "Anyway, I'm fine. Really. A rock. Only sometimes there is a voice. Bad memories, you know?"

"My son," said Clement tentatively, not realizing he was reinforcing the bond with his words, "it might be that a priest is not the best avenue right now." He had never sent a penitent away. Could he, would he, do it now? "Perhaps a doctor—"

"No doctors! I went to doctors, for years I went. They would do nothing. The voice, the teary eyes, the smell—God, the nauseating scent of perfume. Well, of course I'd do anything to stop it. Anything, you understand?"

Oh shit. That's what Clement Flynn thought right at that

very moment—Clement Flynn who never used vulgarity unless he was very angry or very frightened, and right now he was the latter.

"I'm here to tell you about it. To share these deeds."

"Deeds," repeated Clement dully, wishing for the life of him that the man wouldn't be so generous with this business of sharing. Wishing he would stop. Get up. Leave. Right now.

"I only kill the bad ones."

"You, ah, kill?" said Clement with false calm.

"Yes." The voice was matter-of-fact.

"Who," asked Clement woodenly, "did you kill?"

"Women," said the man simply.

Plural, thought Clement. Christ.

"How many?" he breathed.

"I'm not sure," said the man. "Twelve. Maybe twenty. Not all of them here. Some of them, but not all. That would be too risky . . ."

"I see," said Clement, wanting to scream. He fumbled inside his cassock for the rope of rosary beads and the crucifix. When he had been a child in parochial school so many years ago, the sister told him what to do should the Devil appear before him. He found the cross and clutched it.

"Hitchhikers," the man recited dreamily. "Whores, sluts. Women who parade themselves in front of men. You know. You must see them, too. Women like that don't matter."

Clement was reeling. Christ on the crucifix in his hand drew blood, he clutched it so tightly. He had to ask the next question, had to force himself. Because without the right answer this confession was meaningless.

"And you're sorry?" he said, leading the man to redemption.

"I beg your pardon?"

"You've come to ask for forgiveness?"

"I don't understand, Father."

"In order to make a good confession, in order to receive absolution, you must be sorry. And you must fully intend not to commit the sin again." He sounded like a catechism and inwardly cursed himself for it.

"I told you they deserved it."

The man's voice took on a new edge now. He sounded petulant.

"I told you I wanted to share this."

He said it as if he thought he should get a prize.

"God does not want you to share this"—Clement groped for the word—"this . . abomination!" The word thundered out. Clement could not stop himself. He ignored the biting pain in his hand and clutched the cross tighter yet. "God," he went on, "wants you to repudiate your actions. Renounce your sin. Beg for forgiveness."

"Beg?" repeated the man in disbelief.

But Clement plunged on, years of training coming to bear. "If indeed you have done the things you say, then you must be sorry. Do you understand? You *must*. There can be no equivocation here. For the sake of your own immortal soul you must be sorry and you must firmly resolve to amend your life. To"—he searched for the word—"to . . . stop. These things you speak of. You must stop."

Suddenly it sounded feeble to Clement's ears. To his horror the man started to laugh.

"If you cannot stop," Clement forced himself to continue, "if you cannot stop by yourself—and I'm afraid you can't—then you must get help."

"Help?" The man sneered the word.

"If you wish, I will accompany you to a doctor. Or to the police."

"God damn you," came a curdled whisper through the grate.

Father Clement Flynn knew the metal grate was strong, but in spite of this knowledge, he braced himself for an assault. And when the man hurled himself up from his knees, when the man strode angrily from the cramped confessional, only then did Father Clement Flynn say the words the sister had taught him long ago. Because in his heart Clement Flynn believed there had been three souls, not two, in his confessional. "In the name of the Father," he whispered, "and of the Son and of the Holy Ghost, begone Satan."

8 Mildred bunched up spilled papers in the front seat of the pickup, scooped up stray sheets that had fallen to the floor, and stuffed everything back in the broken carton. Then she held the bulging sides together with her arms and carried the heavy box upstairs.

"I'm afraid they're a little mixed up," she said breathlessly as she set the carton by the bed. The sides again burst open and papers spilled to form a carpet of yellow and white litter all over the braided rug, where Winston sniffed them with interest.

"No matter," said Haggarty with enthusiasm. "This stuff's just for background. You'll read it tonight, of course."

He said it like it was nothing. Reading hundreds of sheets of scribbled notes and old news clippings. Sure, she thought. Sure I will. But she said, "Of course."

"Agnes is most important. The freshest case. We'll concentrate on her tomorrow."

"Yes," she agreed. But the thought frightened her. Reading scribbles and clippings was one thing. Investigating a murder was another. She felt like Butterfly McQueen and almost said, "I don't know nuthin' 'bout investigatin' murder, Chief Haggarty." But she kept her mouth shut. She dropped to her hands and knees and started sifting through the mound of papers that surrounded her.

At sundown she put on the lights. The two of them sipped iceless bourbon and ate a dinner of cold roast beef sandwiches.

"Damn, that's good," said Forrest, smacking his lips after a sip. "That sure ain't Jim Beam."

51

"It's a custom blend. Made for my father. I was afraid it would have spoiled by now."

"It sure ain't spoiled. Lordy."

"There's a whole case in the basement. You can have it."

"Jesus," he said, almost falling out of bed. "You sure? You might be needing it. For a beau or something."

There aren't any beaus and I won't be needing it. But she didn't say that. "I'm sure," she said.

"Lordy." Forrest sank into the pillows and looked for all the world like he'd gone to heaven.

Soon he dozed off. He slept in fits and starts, waking unpredictably and eyeing her on the sly, as though doubting her commitment to this task. He needn't have bothered, though. By seven o' clock, Mildred was hooked.

First she scanned each scrap of paper and sorted it into one of five piles. To help her keep track, she put a place card next to each pile. Betty Murphy/1944. Marilyn Collins/1950. Emmylou Taylor/1963. Muriel Guthrie/1970. Harmony Johnson/1981. And a sixth place card, next to an empty space without any papers. Agnes Peabody/1989.

By two A.M. she had sorted through everything. One leg had fallen asleep. She struggled up and stumbled around the room to walk off the numbness. Then she walked down the hall, down the center stairway and to the kitchen, where she made herself a mug of instant coffee. She drank it down, set the mug in the sink, and splashed cold water on her face. She was exhausted. She pulled up a stool and sat, resting her head against the cool enamel of the sink, and closed her eyes.

Her mind was reeling with names and pictures, pictures of women she could almost see, almost touch . . .

June of 1950 should have been the best of times for Marilyn Collins. She had just graduated from Vassar with a degree in art history. In two short weeks she would be

*marrying Alexander Simpson, a match that pleased Marilyn's
parents, Gunther and Louise Collins. It was a match that
pleased Marilyn as well, because Marilyn loved Lex, at least
she loved him as much as she'd ever loved anyone. For a
combined graduation and wedding present, Gunther and
Louise were giving the couple a summer-long tour of Europe,
starting off with a week in Paris, where Marilyn had spent
her junior year.*

*Yes, the future looked bright for Marilyn Collins, and
June of 1950 should have been the best of times. But it
wasn't. Because Marilyn was pregnant with another man's
child.*

*On this muggy afternoon, Marilyn stood on hot patio
tiles and shifted from foot to foot. She glanced down at her
manicured toenails and noticed that the polish was chipped.
Then she looked up and into the face of a man who was not
Lex Simpson. Another sort of man. A man who would not
have been accepted so readily by her family. A man who
would raise eyebrows in town and set tongues wagging. A
man she was stubbornly attracted to nonetheless.*

*He looked back at her as though he were angry, as
though he hated her even. But she ignored the look.*

"What do you mean, you're pregnant?" he said hotly.

*"Just what I said." She teetered between the urge to
scream and the equally compelling urge to laugh out loud.
Pregnant was pregnant. What could be simpler than that?
She had always thought he was a smart person. Now he was
acting dense.*

*"It must have happened on spring break," she went on,
trying to mollify him, trying to recoup the old affection, too.
"I mean, I wasn't really sure. I've been late before—"*

"But you're sure now?"

*"Yes. I went to a doctor." She saw his expression. "Don't
worry, not a doctor here. One up in Poughkeepsie. I used
another name."*

He gripped the skimmer tightly and seemed to concentrate on cleaning the unrippled surface of the shimmering turquoise pool. He walked away from her and around the entire perimeter of the pool, skimming all the while. She saw him scoop up a dead frog, bleached white as milky ice, and deftly flick it over the hedge. The way he moved, he might have been playing lacrosse. Practiced. Precisioned. Passionless. It was the same way he made love too. She shivered and shoved that thought away.

It was a shock to him, of course it was. Her parents would be upset and Lex would be upset and things would be messy for a while. She supposed people might even call it a scandal. But everything needn't be ruined permanently. Plans would change, yes. But people would forget in time. Life would go on. It would just be different, that's all, and not really so terribly different at that. True, she would be a mother sooner than she'd expected, but a mother just the same. A mother as she'd always known she would be. And she would be married to a different man than she'd expected. But he was handsome and smart and he had a good future. Sure, he was angry now. But he'd get over it. This temper of his, it was like lightning in August or a Roman candle on the Fourth of July. A flare, a flame. Then nothing. He always got over it, always regained smooth control.

"The answer is simple," he said, finishing the length of the kidney-shaped pool. "You'll tell Lex it's his."

"No!" she blurted too quickly "I mean, ah, I can't."

"Of course you can." He looked smug, self-satisfied. He laid the skimmer down on the patio tiles and wiped his hands on white tennis shorts. He cracked his knuckles.

"You don't understand." She ran long fingers through her strawberry blond hair and tried not to cry. He hated tears. Make no mistake, if tears would have worked, Marilyn would have used them. But they were a red flag to him, and she was smart enough to know it. "I never did it with Lex."

"Oh, come on . . ." he groaned, not believing her.

"I mean it," she said, her voice starting to crack. "I thought you knew that. I told you—"

"Get off it, Marilyn. Sure you told me. We both told each other a lot of things. It doesn't mean they were true."

She stared at him wide-eyed, a sense of panic washing over her. This was impossible. He wasn't acting as if he loved her, not even a little bit. All those words about losing her to Lex and how he'd never get over it, all those words were lies.

"I love you," she said. It was her trump card, her last resort.

"Love?" His mouth twisted the word. "You were—are—going to marry Lex Simpson, remember?"

"A person can love two people at the same time," she said, crying openly now. "That's the only mistake I made."

"Well, I don't love you . . ."

Oh, he was wrong. Of course he loved her. He had to love her. Everyone loved Marilyn Collins. Everyone had always loved Marilyn Collins as long as she could remember. No, she shook her head distractedly, this simply wasn't possible. She would not let it happen.

". . . and I sure as hell hope you don't have some crazy idea that I'm going to marry you . . ."

She continued to shake her head, trying not to hear.

". . . so if what you say is true, I suggest you hustle your fanny over to Lex tonight. Yeah." He seemed to be enjoying this. "I suggest you lay a heavy line on him. Tell him you can't wait for the honeymoon. Seduce him . . ."

Like you seduced me, she thought.

". . . then tell him the baby's premature." He smiled, pleased with this logic. "Or have an abortion." He shrugged his shoulders. "I don't care. I'll even pay half." Then he laughed. She couldn't believe it. He laughed out loud. And he turned his back on her. She felt a wave of anger. She wanted *to pick up the barbecue fork and plant it between his shoulder blades.*

"I'll ruin you," she said steadily.

"What?" He whipped around. The color drained from his face. She saw anger there, but she saw something else too. Fear. And it made her bold.

"You heard me," she said. "I'm not having any abortion. I'm having this baby. Your baby. And I'll tell the world it's yours. I'll tell your family and your friends. I'll tell everyone. I'll even tell your—"

"You leave her out of this!" He raised a hand. She saw the flash of his watch. She thought he would hit her for sure. But he didn't. As quickly as it came, the storm of rage seemed to pass. He dropped his hand.

"Listen, Marilyn ..." He looked at her sheepishly. "I'm sorry. This is kind of sudden, you know? It's caught me by surprise, is all."

"I know." He hugged her close, squeezing the breath out of her. She never saw the set of his jaw, the diamond-chip glint of anger in his eyes.

"Tell you what," he said, "let me change my clothes. We'll go for a ride. Talk this thing through. Make some plans."

"Okay," she said, trying to sound grateful. She could afford to be magnanimous. She would get through this just fine, having him to lean on. It was too bad she'd had to resort to threats, but she'd never do it again. It would be forgotten. She would be a good wife.

No one ever saw Marilyn Collins again, and no one knew the whole story either. Certainly not Forrest Haggarty. Oh, he knew Marilyn was pregnant, that much he knew. Because he'd read it in her diary, a small leather-bound volume that her desperate parents finally showed him days after her disappearance. But she only referred to the father as "X," thinking she was being mysterious and romantic. Not knowing that the father would one day kill her.

Forrest questioned Lex Simpson in detail. Mildred read all that in his notes. The boy was bewildered and his pride was hurt. He never suspected that Marilyn was dead. He just assumed she'd run off with the father of her child. And everyone else did too, everyone except Forrest . . .

Thirteen years later in the fall of 1963, when Emmylou Taylor disappeared, there was no story about it in the *Raven's Wing Gazette* as there had been with Marilyn Collins. It was not the kind of story the *Gazette* published, because it was family trouble. The *Gazette* covered weddings and socials and official trouble in the Police column. But there was no column for family business, especially unpleasant family business. Of course, that didn't keep folks from gossiping about Emmylou's disappearance for weeks on end. It kept things heated up for a good long while, right up till Kennedy got shot in Dallas and they had something new to talk about.

Emmylou and Chase Taylor weren't getting along—everyone knew that. There had been a big fight at the country club dinner dance back in July, when Chase in a drunken uproar called Emmylou the slut of all time and Emmylou retaliated by shoving Chase into the pool along with a smiling maraca player from the Jamaican band. Chase hoisted himself out of the pool, mad as a raging bull. He'd landed in the shallow end and skinned his bulbous nose on the nonskid bottom. His eyes were wild, his face was bleeding, and so was his brand-new madras jacket, which was guaranteed not to run but did anyway.

Emmylou was the one who should have run, should have run right there and then. But she didn't. She was a very pretty young lady, much too young at thirty-two for Chase, who was huffing and puffing and pushing fifty. Chase had the money and Emmylou had the beauty and maybe she was overconfident. And yes, most folks agreed with Chase. She was the slut of all time. She was doing it with the golf pro, Sal Monteverde, who had a big mouth and told everyone about it one night at the Brass Bucket, a gin mill over in South Salem.

"I'll kill the bitch!" Chase cried. That's when Craig Wentworth and Jack Petersen grabbed him by the arms and said there-there-get-hold-of-yourself-Chase.

Emmylou just laughed. She thought Chase was crazy about her, thought he'd never let her go. She thought wrong.

"Chase," she said, "take a look at yourself." She whipped out a little gold compact, flipped it open, and held the tiny mirror up to his running bleeding nose. "Take a good look. You're a mess. Go on home."

People just stood there in their best semiformal dinner attire. They were horrified. Some tried to pretend it wasn't happening. A few chuckled nervously. Madge Jeffries pulled up a lounge chair, sat on the edge, propped her elbows on her knees, and watched, just as if it had been "As the World Turns" on her Zenith TV. Couples had squabbled at the Silver Spring Country Club before, especially during mixed doubles tennis tournaments, but never had there been a ruckus of this caliber.

"The slut of all time!" Chase bellowed again, seizing on the cadence of these words.

"So what?" goaded Emmylou in that southern drawl of hers. "Big deal." She looked at the horrified bystanders, took a dainty sip of her gimlet, and smashed the glass on the flagstones. This was the only indication that she was upset.

"I find you boring, Chase. And I find all your friends"— she waved an arm—"boring, too." There was a universal intake of breath, as though everyone had been simultaneously slapped. "I rue the day I agreed to marry you. I rue the day I quit flying for American—"

"A barmaid in the sky!" he yelled. "An airborne slut!"

"I was happier as a stewardess than I am with this Styrofoam collection of Barbie and Ken dolls—"

"Wait a minute," said Harvey Timlake, who was quick to take offense. "My daughter has a Barbie doll."

"Now, now, folks." Leo Martin swooped between Chase and Emmylou, spreading his hands. Leo was president of the club. Not realizing that the band's microphone hovered inches from his face, Leo tried to speak in a soothing tone that was amplified tenfold. "Why don't you two just KISS AND MAKE UP, HEH, HEH, HEH!"

"Kiss and make up?" roared Chase, shaking off Craig and Jack. "The hell I will. I want that woman out of my life. I want a divorce."

Ah, divorce. This was a word everyone could understand.

"I'll take you for everything you've got," Emmylou threatened.

"No, you won't," said Chase, cold sober now. "You won't take my money and you won't take my children, either. I'll have you declared unfit."

Everyone looking knew that Chase could do it, too. He had money and he had leverage and she was the slut of all time, after all.

"I've had a private detective on you, Emmylou. I've got pictures . . ."

At least ten men in the crowd looked down at their Weejun loafers or white bucks and coughed self-consciously.

". . . and I've got witnesses galore. Why, I'll subpoena the whole damn club!" The spectators shrank back then. Some stepped back, a few actually ran. "Horace," said Chase, "I'll be at your office in the morning." Horace Childers was an attorney. He was quick on his feet and had made it as far as the parking lot.

"Tomorrow is Sunday," Horace called out. "Bunny and I have brunch plans."

"Cancel them!" said Chase. He straightened up then,

squeezed out his sopping wet knit tie and smoothed it over his stomach. He wiped the matted hair off his florid face and almost looked like his old corporate-president self. He turned to leave.

Emmylou must have realized that the golden goose was about to truck right out of her life, because she switched gears real fast.

"Chase, honey," she said, running after him, "I didn't mean it, honest I didn't." She ran after him all the way to the Corvette, weeping and wailing and whining all the way. She could flip channels like no one else, Emmylou could. Folks figured she learned how in stewardess school.

Anyhow, everyone figured Emmylou and Chase made up, and for a while maybe they did. But then in October Chase must have had a snootful again, because he asked Horace to draw up divorce papers. Custody papers, too. Though Horace was sworn to secrecy, people said the pictures were disgusting. Lots of folks in Raven's Wing would be ruined when this case went to court, and those who wouldn't be ruined couldn't wait.

Well, it never went to court because Emmylou Taylor up and disappeared. Took the Corvette, too. She'd run off with one of her countless boyfriends, people said—with a "liaison" was the word Madge Jeffries used. People whispered and shook their heads and said Emmylou ran off, and that was that.

Except that wasn't that.

Emmylou disappeared on the night of the board of directors' meeting at the Community Center. Emmylou was social chairman on the board. She left earlier than the others, about nine o'clock, and went to her car in the parking lot. Her suitcase lay stowed in the small trunk. She fully intended to leave Raven's Wing; there was no other alternative. Maybe she would go back to flying. Maybe Chase would reconsider someday. She didn't really care. She just knew she had to get away. She was smothering here.

It was too bad about the children. She tried not to think about them or she would cry. A court case would ruin their lives and, besides, they were better off in the lap of luxury with Chase than with Emmylou, who had always been too footloose for family life.

She opened the door and climbed inside. Then she gasped.

"Jesus, you scared me," she said. "What are you doing here?"

"My car broke down," he said simply. He pointed over his shoulder at nothing in particular. "Damn engine's so fine tuned, it's always going on the fritz. I was hoping you could run me home."

Emmylou would have liked to run him over. This man had been hounding her for months. But she didn't want trouble tonight and she didn't want a scene. Besides, he seemed sincere and an emptiness inside her made her want to talk with someone. "Well . . ." She paused. "Sure. I guess so. It's on my way anyhow." This was her first mistake.

"Oh? I thought your place was on the other side of town."

"It is. Was. I'm heading over to the Merritt Parkway. I'm leaving Chase."

Chase was kicking her out was more like it. But she didn't say that.

"Well, well," he said. She could almost see him licking his chops in the darkness. This man fooled everyone. They thought he was so harmless, so respectful. Well, he didn't fool her. She knew that look. She almost told him to leave right then. She should have.

"Don't get any ideas," she said.

"Who's getting ideas? A man can hope, can't he?"

She laughed. Soon she would be gone. What did it matter? She started to drive. They were quiet for some *moments. Through the center of town, out and away from more populated streets and on quiet country roads.*

"Say, Emmylou," he said unexpectedly, "just one question."

"Yes? What's that?"

"How come you do it with everyone else and not with me?"

She felt as though she'd been slapped. She looked at him so smug and self-satisfied, and she said what she knew would hurt him most. "You really want to know?" She laughed then, her second mistake. "Because you don't appeal to me, that's why. Not in the least. You're not what people think you are. You're a sham of a man."

He wrenched the wheel from her. She'd made him madder than she intended. It was her last mistake, one she never lived to regret.

Forrest got nowhere with his investigation. Mildred could read the frustration in his notes. Leave it alone. That's what the town fathers said—along with the town mothers, brothers, and sisters. She was nothing but trouble. We're better off.

Forrest didn't leave it alone, though. He went after Chase, checked him out thoroughly. It turned out Chase had been away on a business trip in Atlanta. He was clean.

Mildred suspected that the sideways glances and innuendos about the chief started then. He was looking for crime where there wasn't any, people said. Maybe he would be happier in a bigger, more crime-ridden city like Danbury or Norwalk. Maybe he should move on. But Forrest was a stubborn man. He stayed . . .

It was different with Muriel Guthrie, who disappeared during a snowstorm in the winter of 1970.

Muriel wasn't pretty like Betty, Marilyn, and Emmylou. She was plain. She had short black hair just starting to fleck with gray, fish-white skin, and a pointy nose. She was tiny and skinny and painfully shy. In a town where the women got their clothes at the Balcony Shop on Main Street or at Saks over in Stamford, Muriel bought hers secondhand at the thrift shop.

No one knew where she came from. One November day she got off the Greyhound Bus, which stops on its route from New York City in front of Town Hall every day at noon. She waited on the curb while the driver hauled down a battered olive-green footlocker that held all her worldly possessions. She propped it against the short squat brick wall and asked Joey Warner—who always spent his mornings sitting in front of Town Hall—to please keep an eye on it for her. This simple request drained most of Muriel's courage, but she still had a little bit left.

She pulled her stretch-knit hat down tighter around her ears. It was the unfashionable kind—the kind with mirrored reflectors the size of dimes stitched all over. And she marched herself into Town Hall where she was lucky enough to bump (literally) into Anne Meskill. Anne was personnel director for the town and on her way to lunch. But she had a good heart and took the time to talk to Muriel.

"I need a job, ma'am," said Muriel straight out.

They sat in Anne's small windowless office, cups of tea between them. Muriel took a small sip of hers. Anne noticed her hand shake.

"We're such a small town," said Anne sympathetically. "I'm afraid there aren't many jobs."

"I'll take anything," said Muriel.

"Well," said Anne. "Well, well." She racked her brain. She reached over, pulled open a file drawer, and extracted a mass of papers. She spread them out on the desk.

Muriel tried to read the words upside down. Some of the papers were green forms that said JOB REQ on top. She noticed

"Accountant," "Fireman," "Medical Technician," and "Teacher's Aide." Muriel sighed a silent sigh because she had no experience with numbers, fires, medicine, or children. Then she saw another sheet.

"I could do that," she said.

"What?" said Anne hopefully. "What could you do?"

"That there." Muriel pointed. "Crossing Guard."

"Oh," said Anne, slumping back. "That. I'm afraid it's not much of a job."

"I don't care."

"It doesn't pay much."

"I don't need much."

"And it's only for a few hours a day."

"Then maybe I could get me another job on top of it. Part-time."

"In winter you'd have to stand out in the rain. Snow. Sleet."

"My skin's waterproof."

"And in the summer, well, in summer it switches from Crossing Guard to Gate Guard. You've got to sit all day at the entrance to Great Pond, checking people's beach tags."

"I could do it," said Muriel. "I know I could."

"Well . . ." said Anne, letting the word hang. She knew she would catch hell from the first selectman for hiring a stranger with sketchy references. But it was so difficult to fill the Crossing Guard position. No one in Raven's Wing wanted to do it. And the pressure was on because soon daylight saving time would be over. It would get dark earlier. Bad weather wouldn't be far behind. And children had to cross the street. Besides, Anne could see that Muriel was a poor soul, and Anne had a weakness for poor souls.

"Well," she said again, "maybe we could give it a try."

That first day Anne processed Muriel's application and took her to lunch to celebrate. They sat in a booth at the Red Lion.

"Muriel," said Anne, "tell me something."

"What's that?" Muriel tried not to wolf down her cheese-burger, the first good meal she'd had in a long time.

"What made you get off the bus here? Why Raven's Wing?"

"Well," said Muriel carefully, "it's a real pretty town." She traced her finger along the edge of the plastic place mat. "I mean, I saw that fountain as you come into town. You know, the white marble one that tilts akimbo on its base."

Anne laughed. "People are always driving into that fountain. It's never been quite right."

"Yeah," said Muriel. "Not quite right." Like me, she thought, but she didn't say that. "And then the bus drove down Main Street. I was a goner then. The driver drove real slow so everyone could take a good look. It was so pretty I almost cried. All the golden leaves coming down and the white houses and that big mansion by the square . . ."

"That's the Community Center."

"Golly, a mansion for a community center." Muriel smiled a broad smile. "If that don't beat all."

"I guess it is pretty special," said Anne, who realized right then and there how many privileged people took the beauty of the town for granted.

"Anyway, I saw all that and I just knew this was the place for me. The place I wanted to call home. I didn't see any other town near as pretty between here and New York, and I figured maybe I wouldn't get another such chance. So I told the driver to let me out."

"I see," said Anne. That night when Anne told her husband Charlie about Muriel, she cried.

Things went well for Muriel Guthrie for two months. Then on an afternoon in January the phone rang at the police station. Forrest Haggarty picked up the receiver, then held it away from his ear. An irate mother was screaming that they'd let the kids out of school early because of the snowstorm and there was no crossing guard and her little darling almost got squashed by a skidding "Vulva." That I'd like to see, thought Forrest. Yep, a skidding vulva. Outta control.

But he tried to calm her down. "Hold on," he said. "Just calm down." He promised to send an officer over to cross the rest of the children, and hung up the phone. As he did so, a queasy feeling came over him. Muriel Guthrie was an odd duck, but she was reliable. She was devoted to her job and those children. She'd never missed a day—not in rain, not in sleet, not even that time she had the flu and they had to drag her to the doctor.

Forrest was afraid it was happening. Again.

When he left the station, snow was coming down in fistfuls. He scraped crusted ice off the window of the squad car, climbed in, and drove carefully to the rooming house where Muriel Guthrie lived.

Eleanor Ventry peered out at him through a crack in the back door. Eleanor had lived alone in the farmhouse, a white frame red-roofed house squat in the middle of meadowland that now represented some of the most valuable real estate in Raven's Wing. She lived a lonely life in her isolated farmhouse and claimed she liked it that way. People suspected different, though, especially Anne Meskill, who had an eye for such things. Anne had convinced Eleanor to rent rooms to the occasional young policeman or fireman or teacher who couldn't afford Raven's Wing housing. That's why Eleanor rented to Muriel.

"Forrest?" she said, squinting into the snow. "That you?"

"Course it's me, Eleanor. For God's sake, let me in. It's freezing out here."

"Take off those boots." She opened the door and pointed to a hooked rug on the linoleum. "I don't want you tracking up my clean floor."

He stepped inside and smelled apple pie mingled with lemon oil. Eleanor was a cooker and a cleaner, and she'd been cooking and cleaning up a storm since the boarders moved in.

"Piece of pie, Forrest?" She didn't wait for an answer; already she was breaking the fluted crust with a knife.

"I don't have much time . . ."

"Aw, go on! You know you want some."

"Okay," he said.

She put the plate and a napkin before him, shoved a fork in his hand. Then she sat down to watch him eat. She'd been doing this for years. It never failed to unnerve him. Eleanor was a nice lady, but spooky.

"I'm here about Muriel," he said between mouthfuls.

"A strange bird," said Eleanor.

It takes one to know one. Forrest almost said it, but didn't.

"She never showed up for afternoon crossing duty."

"No!" Eleanor looked alarmed. "That can't be. I heard her take the call that they were letting out early. I saw her put on her coat and boots. Saw her go, too. She took that little red STOP sign with her."

"She walked?"

"She always walked. It's less than two miles." Eleanor was a country woman. If it was less than five miles, you walked. But Forrest could see she was worried now.

"Don't go getting yourself in a dither," he said with false nonchalance. "I'm sure there's a reasonable explanation."

"Maybe she met someone," said Eleanor hopefully. "A friend or something. Sure. Maybe someone gave her a ride."

And that's the way it happened, too. Muriel was walking down Silver Hill Road toward the highway that would lead her to town. Her boots were crusted with salty slush and needles of sleet stung her face.

"Hey, lady! How 'bout a ride?"

She looked at the man in the big car, amazement and

*confusion all over her face. Surely he thought she was
someone else. She'd seen him before around town. He was
important, she supposed. Someone who mattered. He doesn't
know it's me, she thought, and pushed her stretch-knit cap
back on her forehead to show her face.*

*"Thanks anyway," she said, backing away, already
expecting rejection.*

*But still he leaned across the passenger seat. He smiled
at her through the half-open window. He looked hopeful,
eager even.*

"Look," he said, "it's rotten out there . . ."

*"My boots," she stammered, "they'll get gunk in your
car. All over the carpet."*

*"So I'll have it vacuumed. Big deal. Don't be so
stubborn. I'll drive you to town. I'm going that way
anyway."*

*He answered all of her arguments so quickly. He
nudged the door open. If this don't beat all, she thought. A
man like him giving me a ride. She climbed inside. She put
the bright red sign on the floor under her frozen boots . . .*

Forrest found no trace of Muriel Guthrie. Her tracks had
vanished long ago in the fallen snow and so had she. Someone
had given her a ride, all right. He knew it. The same someone
who gave a ride to Betty Murphy, Marilyn Collins, and Emmylou
Taylor. It drove him wild.

Forrest didn't let it rest, not this time. He hounded everyone day and night. He questioned the other boarders. He questioned neighbors. He questioned teachers. He questioned
children. When questioning didn't work, he escalated the badgering.

After several days of concerted badgering, the first selectman showed up at Forrest's house.

"I've come to ask you to drop it," said the selectman.

"You're getting people all churned up. The woman took off, is all. Forget it."

"Took off? In a snowstorm?" cried Forrest, his eyes wilder than ever. He walked up close and put his nose right up to the selectman's. "The hell she took off. The hell, I say."

"Look," said the selectman, spreading his hands, "why go to all this trouble? She was just a transient. Just passing through . . ."

"She was a human being." Forrest hated himself for saying "was."

"It was a mistake for Anne Meskill to give her a job in the first place. When transients get off the bus, we give 'em a free bus ticket to move on. Anne broke the rules."

"What rules?" Forrest's eyes narrowed to slits.

"Don't give me that, Forrest. You know what rules. This is a nice town. We aim to keep it that way."

"It doesn't seem so nice now," said Forrest pointedly.

"Well, I'm sorry you feel that way." The selectman turned to leave.

"I'm not giving up," said Forrest. He said it so quietly, the selectman almost missed it. Almost.

"What?" He reeled around.

"You heard me. I'm not giving up."

"I'm not asking, Forrest. I'm telling."

"Oh, yeah? And what if I don't?"

"There are other jobs. Other towns."

"You wouldn't."

"Look, Forrest, I wouldn't want to. Don't get me wrong. Hell, you and I go way back. But I'm getting pressure from other people."

"People like who?"

"Oh you know . . ." The selectman waved his hand. "The Board of Realtors. The Jaycees . . ."

"Good Christ."

"The PTA even. You're scaring the children."

"The children should be scared. So should you."

"Drop it, Forrest. Just drop it."

It was a standoff. But Forrest was fifty-eight by then. He had to hang in for his pension. So he backed off. And he hated himself for it.

Harmony Johnson was the last straw for Forrest Haggarty. Mildred didn't find many notes about her (Forrest had destroyed most of them). She did, however, find three newspaper clippings.

The first was a small classified ad:

REWARD! $10,000 for information leading to the whereabouts of Harmony Johnson! All information held in utmost confidence! Contact: Chief Forrest T. Haggarty, Raven's Wing Police Dept. 438-0001.

The next one looked like it had been crumpled, then smoothed over:

First Selectman Ripley Crane announced on Thursday that he had regretfully accepted the resignation of Forrest Haggarty as Chief of the Raven's Wing Police Department. In a brief written statement, Crane said that Haggarty had unselfishly served the town for nearly forty years. A successor would be named within the week, Crane said. Chief Haggarty, who started on the force alone in 1944 and watched it grow to twenty men, has decided to spend time with his family.

Sources close to Crane intimated that the First Selectman was annoyed about Haggarty's preoccupation with the so-called disappearance of Harmony Johnson last March. Only last week Haggarty publicly offered a $10,000 reward for information leading to the woman's whereabouts, a move unauthorized for public funds. When confronted with this, Haggarty stated that the money would come from his pension.

Both Crane and Haggarty were unavailable for comment.

The last clipping was a section torn from a larger story:

... A brief flurry occurred during the otherwise uneventful town meeting when Forrest Haggarty of Hardscrabble Road stood up and addressed the audience.

"You're out of order," said First Selectman Crane.

Haggarty, former chief of police, replied with an expletive and proceeded to address the audience anyway. In an impassioned plea, he asked the citizens of Raven's Wing to allocate funds for an investigation into the disappearances of Betty Murphy, Marilyn Collins, Emmylou Taylor, Muriel Guthrie, and Harmony Johnson.

After several requests for order, First Selectman Crane had Haggarty forcibly evicted from the proceedings. ...

After the town meeting, everyone shook their heads sadly and said Forrest Haggarty was confused. Under too much strain, they said. Some, those less kind, said he was crazy.

* * *

When Mildred opened her eyes, the first rays of sun were coming through the kitchen curtains. Slowly she got up. There was a dent in her cheek where it had pressed against the sink and her neck was stiff. Groggily she headed upstairs, waking up a little more with each step.

She caught Forrest gazing at the salt glass. Then he realized she was there.

"Nice you should drop by," he said dryly.

"I fell asleep. How do you feel?"

"I gotta, ah . . ." He looked away from her and at the glass. "Uh, I gotta . . ."

"Oh," she said, reading his thoughts. "Here." She thrust a bedpan at him and backed away.

"Not that," he said annoyed, embarrassed, too.

"If not that, what then? You can't get up to go to the bathroom."

"Get me a plastic bag. One of those baggies on the roll. A box of Kleenex. And bring up a trash bin."

"A trash bin?"

"Preferably with a lid. Just bring 'em up. I'll take care of myself."

"I—"

"Don't argue. Just do it."

She did as she was told. She brought up a red box of baggies and a rubber trash bin with a tippy-top lid. She put the bin next to the bed and shoved the box in his hands.

"There," she said.

"Good." Deftly he ripped a baggie off the roll. "Well?" he said.

"What?"

"Don't stand there, Millie. I'd like a little privacy. That is, unless you wanna watch."

"No," she said quickly. "Of course not."

She waited outside for some moments, wishing Irene Purdy would come soon. Irene would know what to do better than she.

"Okay!" he called. "You can come in now."

"Would you like breakfast?" she said, not venturing farther than the doorway.

"Don't eat breakfast much."

"Oh."

"Maybe some toast. That'd be fine."

"Yes." She turned to leave.

"Rye, if you have it. With caraway seeds."

She stopped in midstep. "Of course."

"Some coffee too. And juice."

"Indeed," she said. She started to leave again.

"And . . ."

"What?" she said, whirling around. She felt like a waitress. She wished she had a pad.

"You got any eggs?"

"Yes!" She caught hold of herself. "Listen," she said, "I'll make you a big breakfast. Toast, juice, coffee, eggs, bacon." She ran then.

"Don't like my eggs fried," he called after her. "I like 'em scrambled. With a pinch of onion powder!"

Damnit, she thought, scrambling the eggs with a vengeance. This is a trial. But when she went back up the stairs, there were two breakfasts on the tray, his and hers. They ate side by side, talking between mouthfuls. Actually, Forrest did most of the talking.

"So you read all the notes?"

"Yes," she said.

"What'd you think?"

"Well, you had very detailed notes, you certainly did. And I certainly feel for those women. It looks suspicious, I'll say that much. Almost like people were trying to cover something up. The selectman, I mean."

"Oh, Ripley? Naw, Ripley wasn't tryin' to cover nothing up. Ripley believes I'm crazy. Tilting at windmills, those were his words. I mean," he said, staring out the window, "what'd you think about Harmony Johnson?" The question seemed to pain him.

Mildred took a sip of her coffee. "There wasn't much about her. Just some newspaper clippings. You know, the ones about—"

"I *know* what they were about. Don't you think I know?"

"Yes. Of course."

"God," he said suddenly, "I sure miss Harmony."

"You do?"

"There weren't any notes because I didn't have the heart to save them."

"You were her friend?"

"I was, ah . . ." He stopped, considering. "I was . . . Look, I never told anybody this, but Harmony and me, we were gonna . . . gonna . . . Oh, what's the use? We were gonna get married, that's what we were gonna do."

"Oh dear." She wanted to take his hand, but it was clasped now, welded to the other one on his chest.

"Funny, ain't it? Old coot like me gallivanting around with the likes of Harmony Johnson."

"No," she said, "it's not funny at all."

"Well, it wasn't then, I tell you. It wasn't. We kept it real quiet, Harmony and me. We figured if people knew, they'd wreck it. You know how people are. My kids or something, yeah, they'd wreck it. So we were real quiet about it. Discreet, Harmony called it. Turned out someone wrecked it anyway though."

"What happened?"

Forrest didn't want to talk about Harmony's disappearance as much as he wanted to talk about Harmony. It was as though the floodgates burst forth. He talked long and steadily, staring at the ceiling the whole time, letting five years' worth of hurt and anguish spill out.

"Harmony was what people called a prude. She was prim an' proper an' righteous. Inflexible, some might say." He looked at Mildred. "Sorta like you."

"Never mind that," she said.

"She was only fifty-one and I was sixty-nine, but I was a young sixty-nine. You shoulda seen me then, Millie."

"I'm sure you were grand. You're still grand."

"Oh?" He looked at her with momentary interest. "Anyhow, Queenie—that's my wife—Queenie was dead near about a year, and I never planned on meeting anyone else. I mean, sure I had needs. Like I said, I was a young sixty-nine. But I just took myself over to Rosie Dunbar's place in Danbury. Maybe you heard of it?"

"No," said Mildred. And I don't want to hear either. But she didn't say that.

"I never planned on meeting no one else. Still, being a bachelor didn't agree with me. I never did get the hang of cooking. Or cleaning neither. The kids used to come by once a week, scrape the grease off the counters and like that, but it was pretty depressing, lemme tell you. And laundry? Why the laundry used to pile up sky high." He laughed. "Still does, for that matter. Got so's I'd run outta underwear, then 'stead of washing it, I'd just buy new. Drove the kids wild, seeing their inheritance go to Fruit of the Loom."

Mildred laughed out loud.

"Course I'd known Harmony for a long time. Since she was a bitty girl. But I never looked at her *that* way, you understand."

"Right," said Mildred.

"She was a prune face, Harmony was. An old maid. Ran the switchboard at Town Hall. Had white hair piled on her head in that old-fashioned way. Went from blond to white overnight, she did."

"Some people do that."

"Well, she was a long time building her wall of prudery

75

an' it was thick as slate. Lived in Raven's Wing all her life and was always what they called overly sensitive. Delicate. Protected. She was the last kid in her class to stop believing in Santy Claus. She cried when her doll was broken. She cried when her feelings were hurt. She cried at a sad story. Come to think of it, she cried most of the time. It's no wonder folks kept their distance, she was no damn fun to be with."

"I see."

"And she cried most of all if she was lost. Go into a terrible tizzy when that happened. That's how it all started."

"What started?"

"Harmony and me. She could get lost so easy. And the town was growing, changing, so she was getting lost all the time. One day she hadda go to the shoe repair. Al had moved his shop. He left a sign in the window telling where to go, and Gene Conte at the luncheonette came out and told Harmony how to find it. I mean, he said, Turn right, turn left, you can't miss it. Well, Harmony, she missed everything. She always missed it. I found her wandering around the new shopping center, lip stuck out a mile, hair all askew, lookin' like she's gonna burst into tears. And I gave her a ride. Guess she trusted me, 'cause of my uniform an' all. Gave her a ride home, too. Door-to-door service. That's how it started."

"Yes?"

"I started dropping her here, dropping her there. We started to chat. Oh, it started, all right. One thing led to another. She started baking me cookies. Started doing my laundry. Started smiling more, too." Forrest's eyes misted at the memory. "She started *doing* for me. And me? I started getting used to it." He scratched his head. "It just sorta crept up on me."

"I see."

"On her, too. She never figured on getting married. It caught us both by surprise. But one day we looked at each other and said why not?"

"Why not indeed!" said Mildred enthusiastically, forgetting that there was a sad ending to this story.

"We were gonna elope, and we didn't tell a soul."

"How romantic."

"Then Harmony disappeared." Forrest closed his eyes. "She vanished just like them other ladies."

"Oh Forrest . . . I'm sorry. But surely people were worried this time. Surely they suspected something. This time it didn't make any sense."

"Hold on," said Forrest bleakly. "I'm afraid it did make sense, leastwise to most folks. Women like to have their secrets, and Harmony was no different. She kept her mouth shut, but only partway. They were going to modernize the phone system in the Town Hall, you see. Update it. They were going to do away with the switchboard. Harmony got all prickly and dropped broad hints that she'd be leaving anyway. Told several people when she was in a snit. Told them they could take their job and shove it. Course, Harmony didn't say exactly that, but close.

"So when she didn't show up for work one day, they figured she took off just like she said she would. Figured she went to Florida or something."

"Damn," said Mildred. "Damn."

"Yeah," said Forrest softly. "Damn." He turned to Mildred, a new intensity in his eyes. "I figure she got lost again. Got herself in a panic. And someone gave her a ride. Someone she trusted. Millie, it was someone we *knew*. Hadda be."

"You should have told people," Mildred said gently.

"Oh no. I couldn't do that, don't you see? They wouldn'ta believed me. Woulda laughed, that's what. Woulda said I was too old for Harmony. That she dumped me." He smoothed the blanket over his legs. "I won't say that the thought didn't cross my mind. But no! I know she didn't run away. We were gonna get married!"

"I'm sorry, Forrest."

"Yeah," he sighed, "so am I. But I made up my mind I'd find out what happened if it took my last breath."

"That's why you spoke up at the town meeting?"

"Right. And that's why I won't rest now. I won't!"

"Don't worry," she said. "Neither will I."

9 "Hi, honeybunch."

Mildred looked at the troll of a woman standing before her, who was peering through eyeglasses as thick as prisms, and almost slammed the door.

"I beg your pardon," said Mildred.

"Irene Purdy," the woman said by way of introduction. "I'm your new nurse." Irene didn't wait for an invitation—she barged past Mildred and into the large foyer. "Nice place you got here."

"I suppose," said Mildred.

"Suppose nothing. Why, I bet you don't even have to go outside to find the privy." Irene waited for these words to take effect. "Don't look like that, buttercup. I'm only joking."

"Indeed," said Mildred. She tried to smile. "Would you like a cup of tea?"

"Don't mind if I do." Irene set down a bulging canvas satchel and followed Mildred into the kitchen, looking this way and that as she went.

Mildred busied herself assembling the cups, the saucers, the silver spoons. She lit a flame under the kettle. She tried not to stare at Irene Purdy, who was seated—apparently content to stare into space—at one end of the long kitchen table.

Irene was not what you could call pretty. You couldn't even call her cute. She was short—came up to Mildred's shoulder —and built like a barrel. Her salt-and-pepper hair was more pepper than salt. Wiry, it was chopped into a kind of page boy cut, blunt at the chin. Or rather, where her chin should have been. Irene had a big overbite that often broke into a toothy smile, but no chin to speak of. It gave her the appearance of a woodchuck, and the plumpness of her rotund egg-shaped body reinforced this impression.

Mildred poured boiling water into delicate gold-rimmed cups. Two Red Rose tea bags floated on the surface.

"You coulda used one bag," remarked Irene. "You know —dunk it back and forth. You can save money like that. With one bag."

"There is no need," said Mildred, "to save money."

"Humph," grunted Irene. Her eyes darted around the kitchen as if it were Jupiter. They bounced from the microwave to the espresso machine to the Cuisinart. Machines. Machines that zapped and cooked, ground and brewed, chopped, diced, sliced, and mashed. You could see she didn't trust them.

"So," said Mildred, trying to make conversation, "you live in the woods."

"Uh-huh."

The woman is a real conversationalist, thought Mildred. Good company on a gloomy day. A real chatterbox, yes indeed.

"Ever since Earl died."

"Oh?" said Mildred. "Who's Earl?"

"My husband. Died in 'sixty-eight after thirty-six years of marriage."

"I'm sorry," said Mildred automatically.

Irene seemed not to hear. "That's when I sold the farm, 'cepting a small parcel on the mountain. That's where I moved. The woods."

"I see."

"No," said Irene, "you don't see."

"I beg your pardon." Mildred moved her chair a millimeter away from Irene Purdy.

"You got no idea what it's like. No offense, but it ain't at all like here." Irene waved a beefy arm. "There's no electric and no running water. Everything runs on elbow grease. No fancy machines."

Mildred wondered if she should apologize for the toast, which at that very moment popped up in the toaster. But Irene seemed lost in her own reverie.

"I like it fine up there. I got a bird feeder. I see birds of all kinds. Evening grosbeaks. Cardinals. Yellow-bellied sapsuckers. Once I even saw a pileated woodpecker. They wrote it up in the local paper. They're rare, you know."

"Oh."

"Me and Earl, we sure had a nice farm." Irene's magnified eyes turned dreamy and unfocused. "Corn and tomatoes, dairy cows and sheep. We did it all ourselves. Always hoped for children to inherit the land, but the Lord didn't see fit to bless us in that way."

"Oh."

"That all you can say? Oh?"

"Well," stammered Mildred, "I'm not used to such, ah, revelations . . ."

"Revelations! Ha, that's a good one." Irene slapped her knee. "I gotta remember that. Anyway, on our farm we had a hound dog named Luke and a tiger cat named Buster. I tended the chickens and weeded the garden and helped with birthing the lambs. That's how I took up nursing. Pretty much fell into it. Lambs and people are awful simular. Born pretty much the same way, 'cepting the way the ewe eats the afterbirth . . ."

Mildred bit down on the rim of her teacup, almost cracking a twelve hundred-dollar crown.

"Ewes are tidier than women, that's a fact. Give me a ewe any day. Neat, clean, and don't complain neither. No need for Lamaze with a ewe. Ha!" She looked at Mildred over the tops of her glasses. "Something the matter, pumpkin?"

Mildred said nothing.

"Well, you sure are the quiet one. I hope we get along, you and me."

"Maybe we should look in on Forrest," said Mildred, trying to change the subject. She moved to get up, and Irene's hand —it seemed the size of a baseball mit—shot out lightning quick and pressed her back into the chair.

"Relax, honeybunch. We got time. You city folks are a bundle of nerves, always rushing this way and that. Just set a while. Rest yourself."

"Very well," said Mildred, who wondered what choice she really had.

"I learned nursing from the animals. Then 'fore I knew what was happening, I started nursing people. During the depression poor people took to asking me, and it just sorta mushroomed. I never lost a soul neither." She stopped abruptly and blinked. " 'Cepting Earl. I lost him."

"I'm sorry," said Mildred. And suddenly she surprised herself. A wave of sympathy washed over her, sympathy for this independent squash-shaped lady who hauled her own rocks to build a fireplace and put cracked corn in the feeder for all the birds.

"Aw," said Irene, brushing it off, "it's okay. I get along okay." She seemed to brighten. "You wouldn't believe all the stuff I know. Stuff folks don't bother learning anymore. I can start a fire without a match even if the tinder's damp. I know rain's on the way when leaves on the sugar maple turn themselves upside down. I know jewel weed won't prevent poison ivy but Clorox will, that's a fact. I know enough to beach my canoe when whitecaps come up on Rainbow Lake, and I can patch a hole in that canoe with a mixture of gumsap and pine needles. I can stop the bleeding of a cut or scrape with spiderwebs. And I know a bat in broad daylight or a raccoon you can touch likely has rabies, so steer clear, wooooooo-eeee!"

Mildred sat stock still, teacup poised halfway to her lips, as this torrent of folklore poured over her.

"Ain't that something?" demanded Irene.

"Impressive," said Mildred. "Most impressive. Mark Trail is my favorite comic strip."

"Mark who?"

"Never mind."

"I buried Earl in the meadow," blurted Irene. "It was against the law, but Forrest looked the other way. Then I had to sell the land. To survive, you understand. I didn't *want* to sell it."

"Of course you didn't," said Mildred. She surprised herself again and took Irene's big hand in her two small ones. "You did what you had to do."

"Only now I get worried. They built a development there. I was nervous as a flea on a griddle every time they sank a new foundation."

"Oh dear."

"Oh dear is right, lemme tell you. I heaved a sigh of relief when they were done, yes indeed. Earl's in someone's backyard. Some family with bluebirds painted on the mailbox and china ducks on the lawn. He's right next to the barbecue. I marked the spot one night with a rock."

Mildred bit her lip to keep from smiling or, worse yet, laughing outright. "At least he's got company," she managed to say.

"I guess," said Irene. "But I still worry. I worry they might win the lottery or something. You know, come into some money. They might decide to put in a swimming pool. Above-ground would be okay, one of those circular aluminum monsters. But in-ground . . ." Irene stopped, at a loss for words. She shook her head, then sipped loudly from her cup, taking in equal amounts of tea and air.

"There, there," said Mildred, still striving for composure.

"Where the hell is everybody!" The voice boomed overhead.

"Sounds like Forrest," said Irene, breaking into a smile.

"Thank God," murmured Mildred under her breath as she scurried along behind Irene.

"Reenie!" cried Forrest, "glad to see you! What brings you to this neck of the woods?"

"Oh, I dunno, Forrest." Irene looked at him, a half smile playing on her lips. "Seems I heard someone hereabouts was ailing. Don't know who that might be, do you?"

"Nope," said Forrest. "No one's sick around here."

"Well," said Irene, "guess I was misinformed. But since I'm here, we might as well play a hand of rummy. What do you say?"

"Might as well," said Forrest happily.

Mildred felt momentarily displaced. Preempted. Then she remembered she had important business to tend to. She said her goodbyes and edged out the door. The last thing she heard before she left the house was the snap of shuffling cards.

It was a beautiful day. Mildred drove her emerald green Jaguar through the center of Raven's Wing, taking her time along Main Street. She was surprised to find the town much more crowded than she remembered. She saw lots of BMWs, Volvos, and Saabs. Yuppie heaven, it looked like. What had happened to the old Connecticut Yankees she remembered—the Wasps with their old money and the Italians with their sweat and passion that made the town alive and real? Settled in 1708, Raven's Wing had been a small farm town until the turn of the century when it was discovered by wealthy New Yorkers as a place more accessible—and less pretentious—than Newport. The governor of Connecticut built his summer home there (it was now the Community Center). He was followed by other out-of-towners who built palatial vacation homes and retreats. Along with the wealthy came Italian immigrants. The two formed a symbiotic relationship of sorts. The New Yorkers came on weekends and for summers. The Italians took care of them—tending their estates, building rock walls, planting flowers. It was the Italians who made the once sleepy farm town a place of beauty. The Italians were enterprising, too. They moved on from masonry and gardening to establish small businesses. Plumbing. Fuel oil. Electrical. Contracting. Soon they had money of their own. Some belonged to the Italian American Mutual Aid Society *and* the Country Club. The walls came crumbling— if not tumbling—down.

But now Raven's Wing seemed dominated by a different breed, and Mildred was not sure it was a change for the better. They wore bright pastel sweatsuits, though it looked like they never sweat a drop. She noticed stickers on the windows of their imported cars. Middlebury. Williams. Colby. Preppy schools. Most possessions, she observed, were displayed as prominently as those stickers. Tennis racquets. Afghan hounds. Rolex watches.

Still, she considered, maybe I'll stay here. It's not the same as I remember, but there are still some real people. People like Forrest and Trevor and Irene. Yes, even Irene.

10 The Ballard Green complex was tucked behind Ballard Park. The connected units were neat and tidy but not plush by any means. Mildred turned into a cracked macadam driveway and eased the Jag into a spot marked VISITORS. It was a parking lot full of old Chevys and Fords. The fanciest car was a Cutlass Supreme. She felt a twinge of embarrassment about her own car, so much so that she reparked in a more obscure spot.

Ballard Green was a town-sponsored apartment complex for people of sixty-five or over living on limited incomes. The tenants were people who had lived in Raven's Wing all their lives. Oldtimers. As the town changed, as waves of newcomers and corporate transferees moved in, property values skyrocketed. Suddenly older people found themselves priced right out of the small rental market. Ballard Green was created to solve this problem. There was a waiting list a mile long to get in. Long-term residents had first chance. Relatives of residents had second chance. Nonresidents had no chance at all. Raven's Wing took care of its own, and that's as far as it went.

Mildred walked up to an end unit. Number 18 in the Fox Run section. A ground-floor apartment, it was the unit that Agnes Peabody had occupied until her last night on this earth.

Her intention was to look in the window quickly, then leave. She didn't know what she might see. If the police were there, she would flee. She didn't like snooping—it went against her grain. But she had promised Forrest. Okay, she had said. I'll look in on the apartment. She'd said she'd look, and that's what she would do. That's all she would do, too.

The curtains were drawn, and she couldn't see a thing through the wall of white lining. So much for that, she thought. Just as well. But then she found a crack, a space where the curtains didn't quite meet. The room inside was dark and it took a moment for her eyes to adjust. She saw a sparsely furnished room—the living room—in vivid Florida-style colors. An overstuffed armchair. A small Formica dinette table with two chairs covered in flowered vinyl. A sofa with loose cushions along the back. A person in the middle of the sofa. A person? It took some seconds for this to register. The person was motionless, like the furniture. Hunched over, her head—yes, it was a woman—in her hands. What Mildred saw was a person consumed by grief.

Oh dear, thought Mildred. It was someone from the family. She would leave immediately. Her sense of decency, propriety, dictated that she do so. Then, much to her alarm, the head tilted up and a tear-streaked face looked right into Mildred's eyes. Mildred was horrified, caught in this act of voyeurism. But the tormented face looked almost relieved. The woman stood up and pointed to the door. Then she walked over to it and came out on the landing.

"I'm sorry," said Mildred. "I didn't mean to spy."

"Please," said the woman, "come inside. Him too." She pointed to Winston.

The woman looked like a throwback to the days of Lenny Bruce. The days of coffeehouses and white nail polish and no makeup. Her long hair hung in a black rope down her back. She wore paint-spattered dungarees and a black T-shirt stretched over huge braless breasts. Mildred expected to see bare feet, but saw sandals instead. She judged the woman to be in her late forties, early fifties.

They sat opposite each other at the dinette table. It was hot in the apartment and the air was stale. No ventilation, Mildred realized. The windows were sealed shut. The place was like a crypt. The woman fished a crushed pack of Virginia Slims from her back pocket and inserted a flattened cigarette in her mouth. Mildred noticed the flame waver as she lit the cigarette.

"Want one?" the woman offered.

"No. Thank you."

"Are you a friend of Agnes?"

"In a way," said Mildred.

"Agnes didn't have a whole lot of friends," said the woman. "She was quiet, Agnes was."

"So I understand."

"Jeez," the woman hooted abruptly, exhaling a stream of blue smoke. "I don't even know who you are, and here we are talking. For all I know you could be selling Girl Scout cookies. Or Amway." She narrowed her eyes suspiciously. "You're not from Amway, are you?"

"No," said Mildred. "I'm Mildred Bennett. I heard about Agnes, and I thought I'd come over. To see if I could help." It wasn't a lie, not exactly.

"No one can help Agnes," said the woman angrily. She looked at Mildred, and her face softened. "Sorry," she said. "It's nice of you to come. Not too many people know about Agnes yet."

"I have a friend in the police department," said Mildred, stretching the truth again.

"The police," the woman snorted. "They're good for nothing. What'd they do? Send you over to counsel the family?" She didn't wait for an answer. "Well, the family's not here. I'm Hermine Goldman. Agnes was my friend."

"I'm sorry," said Mildred.

"The family's on the way. They live in Cleveland. They asked me would I sort through her stuff. Organize it. Pack it up. Give it to Goodwill."

"That's nice of you."

"Kind of soon to be shipping her stuff off to Goodwill, if you ask me. But no one asks me. I'm doing this for Agnes, not for them." Hermine sniffed deeply through a reddened nose. "I just can't believe this has happened," she said, her eyes filling.

"It must be a terrible shock." Mildred handed her a Kleenex.

"I tried to talk to the police," Hermine went on, "but they're busy studying bits of fabric. Matching some rock to her skull. My God, they're looking for skin under her nails." She wept, covering her face with her hands. "To die is bad enough," she said into her palms, "but to die like that . . . Violently." She drew a breath, forcing herself to go on. "They said they'd call me. They're hopelessly understaffed, that's what they said. Don't call us, we'll call you. I bet they never call. Screw them anyway."

"Did you have something to tell them?" Mildred asked the question gently, nudging ever so slightly.

"Maybe I should forget it, you know? Not get involved. But I keep thinking it's my fault. If I'd left her alone, if I hadn't pushed her. Some people should be left alone."

"No one," said Mildred, "wants to be left alone. No one."

"I mean, it seemed like a good idea at the time." Hermine went on, oblivious to Mildred. "Everyone's doing it. What's the big deal?"

"Doing what?"

"And Agnes was such a mouse. Ever since Clarence died. Of course, her friends were no help at all. A single woman in this town, are you kidding? They treat you like a pariah."

"Just what did—"

"It started as sort of a lark, that's all. A joke, you know? Why she was friends with me, I'll never know. We're so different, Agnes and me ..."

Mildred wondered if she would ever manage to extract any useful information from Hermine Goldman. "Tell me about it," she said.

"I'm an artist," said Hermine, dabbing her eyes with the Kleenex. "I had an exhibit at the Village Bank a while back. Maybe you saw it?"

"Afraid I missed it."

"I do three-dimensional objects. Mostly masks. I carve them. I paint them. I varnish them. I don't even know how I met Agnes." She crushed out the stub of her Virginia Slim. She made swirls in the ashes with the filter. "Oh yes, I do remember. It was at the greenhouse. We both like to garden. You saw all those roses when you drove in? Well, Agnes planted them. And she did volunteer work at Ballard Greenhouse too. Taught a class there. Agnes had a real green thumb. I took the class, and we got to know each other."

"I see."

"An unlikely pair, I know. But Clarence had just died, and I was going through a divorce. You know how it is."

No, I don't know how it is, thought Mildred. But I'm sure finding out. She remembered Connor and flipped him from her mind like last year's birthday card.

"We'd have coffee. Chat." Hermine looked at the ceiling and almost smiled. She looked mischievous for the barest instant. "I'd tell her about my boyfriends," she said shyly. "At first Agnes was shocked. Listen, there was a whole world out there, and Agnes was missing it. She was afraid. She couldn't believe I met my boyfriends through the newspaper."

"The newspaper?"

"Right. The *Raven's Wing Gazette*." She saw Mildred's surprised expression and went on. "Used to be the only personals column around here was in *Connecticut Life*, the monthly magazine."

"I see," said Mildred. Yes. Sometimes she herself read the personals in *New York* magazine just for entertainment. Little square boxes. People seeking companionship, some openly seeking marriage, a few openly seeking money. She had laughed at them. Had felt superior to them, too.

"Then the *Gazette* started running them. Personals. This town is a little slow on the uptake, if you know what I mean. But the column took off like a rocket. I met some nice guys through that methodology. Real nice guys. A little stuffy, maybe. A little too straight. Businessmen mostly. Divorced guys. Widowers. Nice. Boring, but nice."

"I see," said Mildred. "Or I'm trying to. What exactly did this have to do with Agnes?"

"Oh." Hermine shook her head miserably. "Don't you understand? I put an ad in the paper for Agnes."

"What?!"

"She was hiding her light under a bushel," Hermine rushed to explain. "The world was passing her by. It was such a waste. So I placed the ad."

You didn't, Mildred wanted to scream. How could you! But she said nothing.

"Agnes was furious when I told her. She carried on like you wouldn't believe. She said awful things to me. Called me a meddler. Told me to leave her alone. I still remember how she said it. 'Leave. Me. Alone!' " Hermine started crying fresh tears.

"There, there," said Mildred. "You thought you were doing the right thing." But inside, Mildred was horrified.

"We had words," Hermine went on. "A terrible fight really. I told her she was one of the living dead. One of the pod people. And, my God, now she *is* d-d-d-dead." Hermine grabbed two fresh fistfuls of Kleenex and thrust one wad onto each eye. The wetness of her tears held the wads in place, and when she looked at Mildred there were white balls where her eyes should have been. Like a mummy. The effect was bizarre.

"So what happened?" said Mildred to the mummy.

"I lost my temper." The wads fell. "I told her the replies could rot in the box at the *Gazette* for all I cared. I told her I wasn't going to pick them up. The poor lonely hearts who responded to her ad would go on being just that. Lonely hearts. And so would she. That's what I told her. Because she was a pod person."

"Oh," said Mildred, feeling slightly like a pod person herself.

"I assumed she never went to pick up the replies. We made up the next day, and it was never mentioned again. I never dreamed she'd pursue the matter further. Never dreamed she'd contact any men without consulting me. For guidance, you know. I've been through all this before, and I know how to cull the weirdos from the nice guys."

"You mustn't feel guilt over this," said Mildred with as much conviction as she could muster. "I'm sure Agnes never followed up on this ad of yours."

"I'm not so sure," whispered Hermine.

"You're not?"

"Well . . ." The words came out slowly, agonizingly. "I was going through her things." Sniff.

"And?"

"And I figured I'd start with the food. I mean, food's not so personal. I could deal with it. And people in this complex can use food . . ."

"Yes?"

"So I'm going through the cabinets, the refrigerator, the canisters . . ."

"And?"

"And there they were in the coffee canister." Hermine pointed to a set of Victorian-style tins on the counter. Fluffy Flour. Brite White Sugar. Sunshine Coffee. Golden Leaf Tea.

"There was what?"

"In the coffee canister. The letters."

Mildred stared at the canister.

"Agnes never drank coffee. So the canister was empty, or so I thought. But something shuffled inside. Recipes, I thought. Only they weren't recipes. They were letters. Five of them. To the ad."

"Good Lord! Did you read them?"

"No." Hermine recoiled. "I figured they might be evidence. And I didn't want to know what's in them anyway. I still don't!"

"Okay, okay," said Mildred.

"So I left them in there."

Mildred tried not to lunge, but she couldn't help it. She snatched the canister from the counter and clutched it to her breast. Gingerly she removed the lid and looked inside. She saw a small stack of differently shaped envelopes, some folded, some flat, all clumped together with a single red rubber band. She also saw a torn scrap of newspaper. She extracted that scrap.

> Widowed female, age 57, fit and trim. Enjoys gardening and candlelight dinners. Seeking considerate male 50s or 60s for conversation and companionship. Reply with letter and photo. Gazette Box P56.

"I hate myself," said Hermine.

"Don't say that," said Mildred, taking the woman's hand. "We don't even know for sure that one of these was the one. Besides, if it hadn't been Agnes, it would have been somebody else."

"I suppose," said Hermine hollowly, "but at least I wouldn't have known her, whoever it was."

It might have been you. Mildred almost said it but didn't. "May I take these?" she asked.

"Why not?" said Hermine. "That friend of yours in the police department? Maybe you'll have more luck getting through to him than I did."

11 Mildred smoothed out a bubble in the strip of Magic Mending Tape and stood back from the wall surveying the row of five photographs. They hung there like little multicolored flags, the bottom edges curling ever so slightly, as if pulling away from the faded flowered wallpaper. A rogues' gallery, she supposed, but such a harmless-looking one at that. The faces were plain-featured men in their late fifties, early sixties, oldtimers all of them. Respected people. Neighbors. Men who had lived in the town all their lives. She remembered them from high school. They were achievers even then. Loomis Brewster. Noah Lockwood. Spencer McCloud. Marcel Wintermute. And Ripley Crane, yes, even Ripley.

Mildred turned away from those flat faces and looked to her audience, waiting for the reaction she knew would come.

"Jesus Night," breathed Forrest. "If I didn't see it with my own eyes, I wouldn't believe it. Not in a million years." He looked at the wall as if it were ablaze. He blinked hard, half expecting the faces to disappear or at the very least transform themselves into less unlikely suspects.

"Take 'em down, honey." Irene Purdy said it flatly. She hunkered down tight in the rocking chair, looking ever more like a jack-in-the-box ready to spring. "Take 'em down an' put 'em away. Or better yet, rip 'em up."

"She can't do that, Reenie." Trevor Bradford shifted uncomfortably on the broad windowsill. He wondered for the life of him how he'd gotten involved in this. A routine visit to check on Forrest, that's all it had been. Maybe, maybe not. If pressed, he'd admit the visit was born in the hope of a dinner with friends. A flight from loneliness. The invitation had been forthcoming, and he was so pleased. But afterward . . . well, then they assembled up here in this boxy high-ceilinged room that smelled of liniment or maybe (he hoped not) bourbon. For a parlor game, he thought. Charades maybe. But it was no parlor game now, not by a long shot.

"It's evidence," Trevor went on. "She can't destroy evidence. It was a mistake to take it in the first place." He paused, considering. "Well, what's done is done. We'll just turn it all over to the police."

"The hell we will!" boomed Forrest. "The police had their chance when this happened with Agnes. And they blew it. Now I'm taking over."

"Forrest . . ." Trevor spread his hands, appealing for reason. "Please. Please don't do this. Drop it, okay? Just let it go."

Irene Purdy became nervous then and started to rock mechanically. Boinka, boinka, boinka.

"No. I'm not letting it go. Not no more. No sir."

"Forrest, I hardly think you're in any condition to—"

"I'm gettin' stronger by the minute." Forrest shot up on his elbows to prove this point. "And besides . . ." He let the word dangle.

"Besides what?"

"Besides, I got help, that's what."

"Help?" said Trevor. "Help from whom?"

"From me," Mildred said.

"Millie, don't be ridiculous."

"I'm not ridiculous," she said hotly. "What's the harm?"

"The harm," Trevor sputtered, "the harm . . . Lord, I don't believe this . . . the harm is that this is no time for amateurs. You could get hurt. At the very least, you'll get yourself in serious trouble. You're breaking the law. Right now." Trevor shot up and raised his fist like a New England preacher. He faced them all, his face slightly pink. "That's what we're all doing. Breaking the law. Obstructing justice!"

Still Irene rocked. Boinka boinka boinka, faster now. "Some justice," she muttered under her breath.

"It's a risk I'm willing to take," said Mildred. "Someone should do something. All those women—"

" 'Sides," broke in Forrest, "you know what the police will do if we turn over this stuff. These faces. You know, don't you, Trevor? Well, don't you? They'll *lose* it, that's what they'll do."

"Oh no they won't."

"Oh yes they will," Forrest said, not even arguing but disgusted now. Disgusted with the police, disgusted with his own infirmity, and disgusted with the relentless passage of critical time. "They'll lose these pictures accidentally on purpose. And, oh sure, everybody'll be sorry as can be. They'll be embarrassed, too. Someone might even get fired for such carelessness. But it won't matter none, because our chance will be gone. Our one chance right here and now. Maybe our last chance."

"That's nonsense," said Trevor. "Stop with this talk of last chances."

"Well, I don't know about you, old buddy, but I'm seventy-six—"

"Not so old," said Trevor quickly. He himself was seventy-three.

"—and sometimes I wake up in the middle of the night. And I'm scared. I thought I was scared of dyin', for a long time I thought it was that. But it ain't that, Trevor. I'm scared of coming to the end of the line and having done nothin'. Having it all add up to a great big zero. My whole life, Trevor. My whole goddamn life."

"Zero," repeated Irene. Boinka boinka boinka. Irene knew from zero.

"Stop with that, I tell you. Stop with that!" Trevor looked

at Irene Purdy with fire in his eyes. He didn't like this talk about nothingness, didn't like it at all. His hand shot out and clamped over the back of the rocker. He dug rounded fingernails into the burlap cushion that was tied to the spindly back. "Just stop it, Irene. Please. Let us think."

Irene switched from rocking to clicking. Her dentures went clicka clicka clicka. It was her way during times of contemplation. Sometimes she even did it in church. Then she looked sharply at Forrest and clicked the dentures decisively back into their gum nest. She seemed to make up her mind right then.

"Shhhhhh," she whispered, "it's a secret."

"What the hell're you talking about, Reenie?"

"We'll investigate these men. But it's a secret."

"Oh," said Forrest. "Right. We tell no one outside this room. No one. We'll conduct our own private investigation. Just us four."

Trevor sagged visibly. He couldn't fight all three of them.

"I don't know about this, Forrest. I just don't know . . ."

"You want out, Trevor?" asked Forrest gently. "Just say the word. You can leave now. No hard feelings neither."

Trevor looked at the other three and knew for sure he didn't want to leave. That much he knew. It was stupid, it was crazy, this thing they were planning. Maybe it was dangerous too. But he didn't want to leave. Where would he go, after all? Home? Home to the blunted grayness of days that blended one into the other. Home to poor Mary Margaret, who was only a shell of the lovely girl she had once been. Mary Margaret, who hardly even knew him anymore. No. Not home.

"I'm in," he said with resignation.

Mildred sat quietly, holding a yearbook in her lap. Raven's Wing High School. 1944. Some of the pages in the back—pages where the seniors were—were dog-eared. She'd spent an hour that afternoon matching the faces on the wall to faces in the book. They were all there, of course, just as she knew they would be. And Betty Murphy, she was there, too. That bothered

Mildred most of all. Under Betty's posed picture there weren't any clubs or prizes or shining achievements. There was only an ambition. To see the world, it said. Mildred wondered if Betty ever got to. She thought not. Mildred traced the gold seal on the cover of the book with her fingertip and tried not to think about Betty.

"... still," Trevor Bradford was saying, "I've known these boys since they were in grade school. Loomis Brewster and Noah Lockwood—I patched them up after a fight in the school-yard. It was me who set Spencer McCloud's arm when he fell off the railroad trestle. Ripley Crane walked my dog when Mary Margaret and I went to Europe that summer. And it was me who diagnosed Marcel Wintermute's rheumatic fever and made him stay in bed for a year. Me! I tell you, Forrest, I know these fellows. And nothing you can say will make me believe any one of them would have done the things you're talking about. Nothing."

Mildred listened with half an ear while the two old friends went around and around. She listened to a litany of achievements and accomplishments, of good deeds and generosity. She listened to it all, but she wasn't sure she believed.

Someone wasn't who he seemed to be ...

Ripley Crane, respected first selectman, started off his political career at Raven's Wing High School as president of the senior class. He went on to Hamilton College, then New England Law School, where he graduated—just barely. He married a local Raven's Wing girl, Sally Wilkins, who had an open, welcoming smile and whose intellect was no threat to his own.

People liked Sally. She was uncomplicated and volunteered enthusiastically for every committee, no matter how dreary. Ripley figured Sally would be an asset to his career, and he was right. At the tender age of twenty-four, he ran for state assembly, winning handily. During the next four years, Ripley fathered three children and divided his time betwween Hartford and Raven's Wing. His work was uninspired, but conscientious and predictable. People—those who counted—saw the governorship as his next step.

Then, tragically, Sally was struck by polio. It didn't kill her, but folks agreed it might have been kinder if it had. Sally couldn't even breathe on her own and had to live in an iron lung. Valiantly she smiled, kept her spirits up, and read bedtime stories to her children, as a stony-faced nurse stood by her side flipping pages of *Peter Pan* or *The Little Engine That Could*.

Then one summer day, while the nurse was downstairs in the kitchen and Ripley was holed up in his study, three-year-old Huey Crane (*Don't*) pulled (*Don't!*) the big gray plug (*Huey, honey!*) of the iron lung (*Come to*) from the wall socket (*Mama!*), thereby killing his own mother. Grief-stricken, Ripley announced that he was renouncing his seat in the legislature and would devote himself to raising his children and to the town he loved, if they would have him. Riddled with sympathy and compassion, the town did better than that. At a special town meeting, they elected Ripley first selectman, their first-ever full-time official outside of Forrest Haggarty. The vote would be reaffirmed by general election every four years thereafter.

By 1989 not too many people remembered Ripley's earlier tragedy. He had three grown children and profitable interests in construction, banking, and real estate. If anyone thought these sidelines suggested a conflict of interest, they had the good sense not to say so . . .

Of the five faces on the bedroom wall, Loomis Brewster was the only one who started out poor. As a youngster he didn't—as they say—have a pot to piss in. The oldest of seven children, Loomis was always barefoot in summer and usually walking on soggy cardboard inserts in his shoes during the winter. But Loomis was smart, enterprising, and energetic. He worked a never-ending string of odd jobs, including delivering newspapers, cleaning out the mung pit at the dry cleaners (by far the most disgusting) and hauling sacks of de-icing salt at Young's Feed Store.

Loomis had a knack for making friends with all kinds of people—everyone from Ripley Crane, a rich kid, to Sonny Joiner, a no-count foul-smelling bum. Loomis used to regale his friends with stories about Sonny: like the time they were sitting in the cab of Young's pickup and Sonny gummed down an entire brick of Velveeta he'd stolen from the 7-Eleven. (Sonny had no teeth, leastwise not up front where you could see them.) Loomis took particular delight in the fact that when Sonny started his repast, his fingernails were crusted with grime. And when he finished, well, they were clean as a whistle. Everyone was disgusted by this story, but they laughed like hell.

One summer Loomis was caddying for Herb Palmer, a millionaire investment banker. Herb admired the boy's energy and spirit as he carried the heavy bag in ninety-degree heat without complaining. When Herb shot the one and only hole-in-one of his life, he was moved to tears and three double martinis. He was also moved to offer to finance Loomis's education at his alma mater, Cornell. Loomis wanted only to be a builder and said so. Fine, said Herb. I'll set you up in that. But first you'll get an education.

From that day on Herb coached Loomis. He bought him Ivy League clothes, saw that he got a haircut, corrected his grammar, and taught him which fork to use at dinner. Loomis finished his senior year in high school in style. He went through Cornell, where he joined exactly the right fraternity, in three years. He became a contractor in the right town at the right time. And he was never pisspot poor again.

Plenty of women wanted to marry Loomis Brewster. Plenty. But marriage was not in his plans. He already had a family to take care of—a mother and six brothers and sisters. Oh, Loomis dated, mind you. He even came close to marriage a couple of times. But family responsibilities always got in the way. People liked Loomis Brewster. He was a man, they said, who didn't forget his roots. A man with a sense of duty . . .

Some people made fun of Spencer McCloud. He wore madras Bermuda shorts and knee socks and loafers with tassels as he strolled up Main Street in summer. Spencer had plenty of time to stroll too, because he derived a hefty income from appearances in television commercials, which required working only ten, maybe twelve, days a year. In the Fifties Spencer was the man who appeared on TV between "Disneyland" and "Maverick" saying "Hi, I'm Spencer McCloud from Tacoma Securities." In the Seventies, when Spencer developed crow's-feet and wattles, he switched to voice-overs for such companies as IBM, Xerox, and Johnson & Johnson. Spencer had it made in the shade, everyone said so.

He was married to Leslie Hollister, a tight-assed woman from one of Raven's Wing's old families. Leslie was known for prize-winning dried floral arrangements that always took blue ribbons at garden club shows and for a truly remarkable set of tits that jutted out like two parallel bars. Some folks swore they were falsies, but no one knew for sure, maybe not even Spencer.

Theirs was not a match made in heaven. Early on Leslie and Spencer discovered they could not have children, so they gave up on sex altogether. Mind you, Spencer did keep a packet of ribbed Trojans in the medicine cabinet, but it was mostly for show—something to satisfy nosy cocktail party guests. Spencer and Leslie adopted three babies—a boy and two girls—all blond, blue-eyed, and appropriately angelic. Under Spencer and Leslie's influence these babies developed into thoroughly obnoxious children and ultimately into even more disagreeable adults.

For a long time Leslie busied herself with the garden club, tennis, and perfecting the fine art of swilling down vodka gimlets at two in the afternoon. Spencer did commercials and club work. He was generous with his time, volunteering at the Community Center, the District Nursing Association, and Meals on Wheels. Often he was the only man serving on any given committee, a situation he liked just fine. There was talk that Spencer was a ladies' man, but that's all it ever amounted to. Talk. Leslie stayed with him all those years, at least until 1978.

That was the year Leslie was committed to Silver Glen, a private sanitarium, for treatment of acute alcoholism. After many relapses and trips back and forth, Leslie got tired of packing and unpacking. Maybe she got tired of Spencer, too. In any event, she stayed at Silver Glen. Permanently. She said she couldn't stop drinking on the outside, so she might as well stay in. If Spencer minded, he didn't say so. Everyone said he was a saint . . .

Mildred, Forrest, Trevor, and Irene were perhaps surprised most of all that Marcel Wintermute had responded to Agnes Peabody's ad. Surprised because he was mild-mannered and at times even painfully shy. Surprised because, though Marcel dated conspicuously on occasion, people suspected he was homosexual.

The wealthiest man on the wall by far, Marcel was heir to a vast apparel fortune amassed by his paternal grandfather, Silas. The business, which started with simple children's pajamas called Wintermutes, exploded into a clothing empire that included adult evening wear, women's classic casuals, and cruise wear. After Silas died, Marcel's mother, Beatrice, shrewdly sold off the business piece by piece, then promptly died herself. This made Marcel a very wealthy young man indeed.

Although he had been a quiet shadow of a boy in high school, Marcel ran rather wild after escaping from under Beatrice's thumb. Rumor had it that he sometimes tried to pick up caddies at the country club. More than once people spotted

Marcel in his Bentley chauffeuring young men—hardly more than boys—from the train station to his estate on Juniper Hill. Folks started whispering that he should move to New York, where others of his kind lived.

A turning point seemed to come one night when Marcel picked up a hitchhiker on Route 7. He was beaten up. Brutally. Badly frightened, he seemed to turn over a new leaf. He started to be seen in public with beautiful women, women who were only too happy to be seen with him. People started to change their minds about Marcel. It had been a passing phase, they decided.

Then Jimmy Perkins moved in, and people changed their minds back. Jimmy was bad news. He had just flunked eleventh grade for the second time. He had been arrested on various occasions for shoplifting, passing bad checks, and selling liquor to boys in the junior high. Finally, washing their hands of this son they couldn't understand, Jimmy's folks threw him out. Jimmy was bad news, everyone said so, but Jimmy's biggest asset was his good looks and he used these to his advantage. When his folks threw him out, Jimmy Perkins sashayed himself over to Marcel Wintermute's, moved in, and never moved out.

Officially, Jimmy was head groundsman on the Wintermute estate. Ha, everybody said. Sure. But surprisingly Jimmy worked miracles with the neglected place. He trimmed the shrubs, tended the roses, and pushed back encroaching brush with a monstrous Weed-Whacker. He created a wildlife refuge and became licensed by the state as a certified wildlife rehabilitator.

Marcel dressed Jimmy up, taught him manners, and took him to parties. People were scandalized. Then the next time the two men would come with two women, sometimes famous, always different and always out-of-towners who kept their mouths shut. It kept people in a constant state of confusion, a fire fanned by Jimmy's voracious womanizing, which took on legendary proportions.

Over the years Marcel left the day-to-day operation of the

estate to Jimmy. He himself turned more and more to his creative talent, which was considerable. He wrote and illustrated a series of children's books. Marcel's rhymes and pictures were startling and fantastical, featuring brilliantly colored dinosaurs with friendly faces. Adults (if not children) loved them. Amazingly, Marcel Wintermute's work became "in." He wrote a bestseller that won an international literary prize. He started doing more and more books, naming his own terms. Then he did some movies, doing the sets for such flamboyant stars as Bette Midler and creating backdrops for a series of Broadway shows.

By the time he was fifty, Marcel Wintermute had almost everything anybody could want. He had money. He had artistic recognition. He even had acceptance—acceptance hard won but finally achieved when Marcel figured out that it could be bought, plain and simple. He started off by giving the town a much needed ambulance. Then he bought new uniforms for the high school band. He put a new roof on Town Hall and added a children's wing to the library. When the Women's Club needed a place for the annual Christmas ball, Marcel gave his whole house. As well as the hors d'oeuvres, cocktails, and buffet dinner. He gave and he gave and he gave. He was an easy touch.

But it worked. Over time, Marcel eased into Raven's Wing society. He began to be invited to exclusive social functions, benefits, and cocktail parties. Invitations were vaguely worded and deliberately flexible, allowing him to bring any guest his heart desired. He could have brought Big Bird or Miss Piggy, and people wouldn't have batted an eye. As it was, he usually brought Jimmy.

So by 1989 folks assumed Marcel Wintermute had come out of the closet and were even starting to accept it. Why then, wondered the people in Forrest's bedroom, had Marcel sent his picture to Agnes Peabody?

* * *

The appearance of Noah Lockwood on the wall was almost as much of a surprise as Marcel Wintermute.

For one thing, Noah was a judge in the superior court of appeals. He had his dignity to maintain, and maintain it he did. With a vengeance. Noah had a long hatchet face and flinty unforgiving eyes. His bloodless lips were pressed into a permanent horizontal line. His skin was the color of feta cheese and covered with a fine network of wrinkles like a cracked china plate.

He lived alone in a big gambrel-roofed colonial on Main Street behind a solid eight-foot dry-rock wall. The heavy wooden gate was always closed except when a boy from Gristede's delivered the groceries. If Noah Lockwood ever did anything for fun, no one could guess what it was, unless maybe denying someone's appeal.

Most people didn't remember Noah ever being any different than he was now, but Forrest remembered Noah the boy. He remembered a tall skinny kid who delivered the valedictory speech at the high school. He remembered a studious boy, an all-too-serious boy, but a boy not yet quite so dour and unyielding and full of the sour sap of criticism. Nothing was ever right for Noah Lockwood, and if you had to place blame, it might have been the thing that happened with his wife Jessica.

Noah married Jessica late, long after he finished school. He came back to Raven's Wing and hung out his shingle. A master of self-discipline, Noah allowed himself no female companionship until his firm had prospered to the point where he was able to comfortably support a wife. It took a long time. By the time Noah decided he had enough money, by the time he looked around, there was no one left who wanted him. Except Jessica Houston.

Jessica was thin and spiky, just like Noah. She had a fanny like the shingle he'd hung out so many years before. People snickered behind their backs and said they made a perfect pair. Two broomsticks.

People couldn't imagine that Noah Lockwood could love

anybody, but he did seem to brighten when Jessica entered his life. He threw the biggest wedding party in the history of Raven's Wing and invited everybody, even people he didn't know. He invited the fire department, the police department, and all the school teachers. He invited the boys at the Texaco station and Scotty who tended the grounds of the Community Center. He even invited Sonny Joiner. (Loomis Brewster told Noah to be sure to put out a hunk of Velveeta, a suggestion Noah did not find amusing.)

When Noah and Jessica went on their honeymoon trip to Mexico, Noah was lit up like a Roman candle. It was amazing to see him so happy. Three months later he proudly announced that Jessica was pregnant. Then seven months after that Jessica gave birth to a stillborn baby. People sympathized and told her she would have another. Jessica had always been emotionally fragile but seemed to bear up. Then one night she left the house in her nightgown, headed straight for Duck Pond, tied cinder blocks to her spindly ankles, and pitched herself off the dock. It took three days to dredge her up.

Noah went completely to pieces after that. He disappeared behind his wooden gate. He stopped going to the office. When his assistants came running, asking him to sign some papers *please*, he threw them out. Finally Forrest intervened. People were complaining. People who were waiting for divorces, probates, real estate closings, and bankruptcies. Town Hall was in a paper tangle because so many deeds and such were piling sky high. Things were going to hell in a handbasket everywhere, all because Noah Lockwood was in a depression.

Forrest climbed over the fence and walked to the back door. He didn't bother to knock. He went right inside. And what he saw was a disgusting sight to see. Noah Lockwood was slumped dead drunk on the pine table in the kitchen, surrounded by old cartons of Roma pizza and Chicken Delight. He had thrown up on himself, more than once, it looked like.

Trying not to gag, Forrest hauled Noah upstairs. He washed

him, dried him, and put him to bed. He forced him to drink some Campbell's chicken noodle soup. Then he left. When he came back the next day, Noah had one helluva hangover, but said he would go back to work. He thanked Forrest gruffly, showed him the door, and never spoke to him again. It was nothing personal—Noah treated everybody the same way after that.

Noah Lockwood not only went back to work, he became a successful (some said cruel) judge. Forrest never thought much about him again. Until now . . .

"We can solve this case, I know we can." Forrest shot up on both elbows and looked at the others gathered around his bed. The gleam in his eyes was almost maniacal. Mildred found herself caught between a cold shiver of fear and a compelling urge to laugh out loud, denying the reality of it all.

"I don't know," she said carefully. "We've got five faces and five letters, but we're all such neophytes."

"Never mind that," said Forrest. "I've given this a lot of thought. More than forty years' worth of thought. I'm an expert. I can put you on the right track, don't you worry."

"How?" asked Irene Purdy, who didn't know what a neophyte was but didn't want to be one just the same.

Forrest's demeanor changed, his pattern of speech, too. He was the expert now. "First," he said, "we make some assumptions. All of us." He glared pointedly at Trevor, challenging his friend's skeptical look. "One: We assume that the missing ladies—Betty Murphy, Marilyn Collins, Emmylou Taylor, Muriel Guthrie, and Harmony Johnson—were, in fact, murdered. Just like Agnes Peabody. Okay?"

Everyone nodded in agreement. Trevor nodded last, one small, almost imperceptible, grudging nod.

"Two: We assume that the murders were done by the same

person. That's no great leap of logic, because everything here points to a serial killer."

"A what?" said Irene.

"A serial killer." Forrest recited as if by rote: "A man who kills intermittently, often over the course of many years."

"Much as I hate to admit it," said Trevor, "what Forrest says makes some sense. I did part of my medical training with the criminally insane. It's a part I'd rather forget. But the most successful—if you want to call them that—violent criminals are not crazies. The majority of them are intelligent—at least average intelligence, often above average. They are socially and sexually competent. Not outwardly bizarre."

"Normal looking. Like the men on the wall." Mildred pointed.

"Exactly."

"Right!" cried Forrest. "I've done a lot of research on serial killers. A lot of reading. And the way I figure it our boy's first crime may have been spontaneous. Accidental even. He lost his temper. He hit and didn't mean to kill. Whatever. You see, case histories show that if such a killer gets away with that first crime, his method in subsequent crimes is more refined. More organized, so they say."

"Organized?" Mildred couldn't imagine murder by method. Murder by madness, yes. Murder by passion, that too. But a cold, calculated, organized approach? It wasn't human.

"Yes, organized. Serial killers break into two distinct types. Organized offenders and disorganized. The disorganized offender doesn't last long. He's usually what they call 'overtly inadequate.' Stupid is more like it. He's a loser. A loner. He'd stick out like a sore thumb in Raven's Wing. He kills on the spur of the moment with very little thought about hiding his act. He's easy—or easier—to catch."

"And the organized one?" said Mildred. "What about him?"

"He's methodical," Forrest said. "Usually he commits his crime after some stressful event. He has a fight with his girlfriend or something, and he takes it out on someone else. He has an absolute need for mastery. He will panic when he loses control. He habitually uses his own vehicle. What's more, he knows of a convenient place to carry out the crime. Mildred, your house had been vacant for some weeks, no?"

"Yes," she said, shaken. It had been vacant and remote and beyond shouting distance. The house and me, too, she thought, but she shoved the thought away.

Forrest nodded, almost smugly, and rattled off still more characteristic details: "The organized serial killer chooses his victims. They often conform to a type. As I said, he's very controlled. He doesn't leave incriminating evidence behind. He often takes souvenirs—pieces of clothing, jewelry, body parts—but he takes special care to hide his victim's body."

Mildred and Irene sat silently, both reeling from the reference to body parts. But Trevor became agitated.

"That's how it could happen," he said, almost talking to himself. "That's how such crimes could be committed for years, decades even."

"My God," breathed Mildred.

Forrest wasn't through yet, though. "Now," he said, "let's assume our serial killer is someone who wrote Agnes Peabody a letter. One of our five on the wall there. It fits. Because it's methodical. It's calculating. But now it's more than that. He's playing games now. Remember, he's been doing this for years. He's getting older. I figure he's between fifty-eight and seventy-five. And now he's bored maybe. So he plays this little game. Who did it, which one who answered the ad? Come and catch me, you jerks. He knows someone will be looking for him. Maybe he even knows it'll be me. And he's enjoying himself immensely."

"You said he was between fifty-eight and seventy-five," Mildred broke in. "How do you know that?"

"By simple deduction. I figure he wasn't younger than sixteen when he killed Betty Murphy, and he's probably not older than seventy-five when he kills Agnes Peabody. 'Sides, it strikes me as more than coincidental that we have an orderly progression of age in the victims. Almost like they were growing old with him. Other than that, I don't have any magic answers. Only what's obvious: he's probably a white male. Someone who's been around Raven's Wing for forty years. Someone people respect. Someone people trust. Someone whose car you'd get into."

"There's more," said Trevor quietly. "I don't know if you want to hear it, but there's more."

"What?" said Mildred, not wanting to hear but needing to.

"We're all acting like this is some sort of game. It's not, you know. If we go on Forrest's assumptions—and okay, maybe I believe them—well then, what we're dealing with here is a psychopath. And that's no game at all."

"What's a psychopath?" blurted Irene.

"Oh boy," sighed Trevor, running a hand through his silver hair. "Where do I begin?"

"Tell us something," urged Mildred. "Anything. It might help—knowing what kind of person we're up against."

"Well . . ." Trevor stood up and walked to the wall, turning his back on the row of five faces. He took a deep breath and told them what he knew: "Psychopaths consider themselves superior to the rest of us. They show a degree of arrogance that borders on contempt for other people. Combined with this grandiosity, this extreme self-centeredness, is a rather remarkable absence of interest or empathy in others."

"Sounds like a lotta people," remarked Irene dryly.

"True, Reenie. In fact, many psychopaths function quite well. Like Forrest said, they are not necessarily what society calls 'losers.' They can be brilliant, remorseless people with icy intelligence."

"Politicians," said Forrest.

"Company presidents," said Mildred.

"Yes," said Trevor. "But there's more. A particularly grisly characteristic of the psychopath is the tendency to act out, often in antisocial ways."

"Act out?" Irene Purdy shrank back into her rocker.

"Lie, cheat, steal, even kill—without guilt or remorse. Let me repeat, there is an extreme lack of feeling. These people demand instant gratification. They have a marked inability to contain desire or tolerate frustration. The theory—one I believe—is that they contain a boundless repressed rage. Because of this rage, there can be explosive outbursts. Quick. Unpredictable. Deadly."

"Lord help us," whispered Irene.

"Remember one thing," said Trevor. "Psychopaths are manipulative, controlling people. They are exploiters. Under a veneer of charm, that's really what they are. They surround themselves with admirers. They bask in attention, adoration even. So be an admirer with these men. It's the safest bet. They are most fearful of being dependent in any way. Do not, I repeat, *do not* try to trap a psychopath. If you think you're onto something, if you have a hunch—no matter how slight—come back here and we'll decide what to do. Get away as fast as you can, okay?"

"Okay," said Irene.

"Okay," said Mildred.

They were silent for some moments. Suddenly Irene spoke out. "Can he help it?" she asked Trevor.

"What, Irene?"

"You know. Can he stop himself? Should we oughta feel any sadness for him at all?"

"Oh Christ," fumed Forrest, "don't be a bleeding heart."

But Trevor seemed lost in thought. "Well," he said carefully, "experts have argued that back and forth—what makes a person do these things? Can a person stop? I don't know. You're talking another language here. You see, the person who does these things doesn't think they're wrong. Wrong isn't in his vocabulary. And he doesn't kill because he hates his victims per

109

se. There's no motive like that. He kills because he *likes it*. It's that simple."

Forrest didn't say anything. He remembered the theory about boundless rage from the criminology textbooks he'd read so long ago. And he remembered something else, too, something that bothered him even more: psychopaths who kill without motive are almost impossible to catch. Unless they are caught in the act. He almost spoke up then, almost told them to forget the whole thing. It was a dangerous business, he almost said. But Mildred spoke first, and the moment was lost.

"Well," she said, standing up, "it's getting late. And we've got work to do tomorrow." She fanned out the five letters in her right hand, some neatly typed, others written in script. She closed her eyes and plucked two of the five from her left hand. Then, without being asked, Irene Purdy came forth and snatched two more, one with each hand.

"There's one left," said Mildred, looking at Trevor. "What do you say?"

Trevor took it slowly, pinching it between his fingers as though it were a death warrant. He shoved it into his jacket pocket, still folded and unread. "I just don't think it will do any good," he muttered.

"Okay," said Mildred, ignoring his pessimism. "We've got our assignments. We start tomorrow."

12 At seven o'clock the next morning Mildred was sitting on a stool at the counter of Richie's Luncheonette. The place had been there as long as she could remember, plain and simple with a yellowed plastic counter and whirling Casablanca fans overhead. Nothing had changed. She sneaked a peek under the counter. Sure enough, it was still riddled with hundreds of wads

110

of chewing gum placed there by Raven's Wing High School students when they'd hung out at Richie's after school. She smiled, remembering the time Richie Senior had threatened to rip the counter out and hang it at the Aldrich Museum of Modern Art as an example of modern artistic expression.

This morning the luncheonette was a place of refuge. Forrest and Irene had kept her up half the night. Her room was across the hall from Forrest's, but all night long she could hear the snap of cards as they played yet another game of rummy. And she heard more than that, too. She heard chuckles and tee-hee-heeing until she thought she would go out of her mind. They certainly seemed to be getting friendly. She must have drifted off to sleep after two. When she woke up both of their doors were closed, and she couldn't hear a sound. This silence, when she didn't need it, infuriated her all the more.

Fine, she thought. Fine. Let them sleep away the day. Let them be layabouts. Suddenly she found the house oppressive. She found their constant companionship oppressive, too. So she put Winston on his run and escaped to the luncheonette, a place that never changed, a place that was plain and simple, a place that served the best cup of coffee in town.

Richie Junior was so busy handing out Styrofoam cups of coffee to hurried commuters that it took him a while to get to Mildred.

"What'll it be, ma'am?"

"Just coffee, Richie. And maybe one of those marvelous homemade jelly doughnuts, if your mother's still making them."

He looked at her surprised, his eyebrows arching like question marks. She wondered how she knew him. And looking back at Richie Junior, Mildred's memory flashed to his father. Why, the young man was his spitting image.

"I knew your father," she said. "I used to come in here all the time after school. Oh, it was *way* before your time."

"No kidding?"

111

"No kidding. How is your father anyway?"

"Pretty good. It was touch and go for a while. He had a stroke, you know."

"Yes, I heard. Well, you tell him Mildred Bennett was asking for him. And tell him I love the luncheonette. It's just the same."

"Sure," he said. "You bet." He would tell his father that Mildred Bennett was asking, all right, but he wouldn't tell the part about the luncheonette. Cathy, Richie Junior's wife, had been after him to modernize the place. To change it into a stylish bistro or perhaps an art deco eatery with black lacquer furniture and White Rock girls supporting frosted glass lamp shades. The town was changing, Cathy said, and the luncheonette should change with it. Richie Junior supposed she was right.

Mildred was about to bite into a gooey doughnut overflowing with strawberry jam when two hands reached in front of her face and covered her eyes.

"Guess who."

No, she thought, it can't be. But she would know that voice anywhere.

"Clyde?" she gasped. "Clyde Thompson? Is it really you?"

"You bet it's me!" He spun the stool around and enveloped her in a spontaneous hug, almost knocking her off.

She couldn't believe it. She was at a loss for words. Clyde Thompson had been the one she almost married. If the truth be told, the one she probably should have married. She looked at him now and felt a flood of conflicting emotions.

He was a man you wouldn't look at twice on the street. Paunchy. Rumpled. Wearing a linty plaid jacket and old twill hat. Everything about him was small town. But his grin was open and welcoming, and Mildred felt her usual reserve melt away.

"I didn't know you were still here," she said, trying to dismiss the feelings inside her. "I thought you'd be off lawyering somewhere. Or maybe a senator by now."

112

He laughed, an uninhibited, hearty laugh. His face broke into a network of lines and she realized he looked nice when he smiled. Mildred took in the clear blue eyes, the curly blond hair (turning ever so slightly white), the bushy eyebrows. He's really not bad-looking, she realized. In fact, he's rather handsome.

"Oh," Clyde said, shaking his head, "that wasn't for me. I dropped out of law school and came back home. Lucky thing for our judicial process. When the chips were down, I just wanted to stay right here. This town has its quirks, but it's home to me."

Impulsively he picked up her coffee mug, her plate, and her napkin. "Come on," he said, "you're having breakfast with me."

Flustered and flattered at the same time, Mildred grabbed her patent leather handbag and followed Clyde. They slid into a red vinyl booth in back, and sat facing each other.

"So," she said, "tell me what you've been up to. Tell me everything."

"Oh God," he smiled, "how long has it been? Forty years?"

"Don't remind me," said Mildred good-naturedly.

"Well . . ." Clyde propped his elbows on the Formica table, thinking. He leaned toward her. "Let's see. There's not much to tell, really. I came back to Raven's Wing after a year of law school. The newspaper was for sale, and my mother was good enough to help with the financing."

"How is your mother?" Mildred asked.

"She died several years back."

"I'm sorry," said Mildred quickly.

"Oh . . ." He waved it off. "She hadn't been well for a long time. It was a blessing really. Anyway, where was I?"

"You bought the paper."

"Right. I bought the paper. Just like that. I was either incredibly stupid or totally crazy, because I had no experience and no idea of the amount of work involved."

113

"If anyone could make it work," put in Mildred, "you could."

"You're too kind. I made a lot of mistakes, Mildred, but somehow the paper prospers in spite of them."

"I've been so out of touch," said Mildred. "I'll have to start reading it."

"Well," he said grinning, "now you've got a free subscription. On me. Anyway, sometimes I still can't believe it, even at this late date—me owning a paper. I did lousy in English composition in high school, and now here I am doing everything. I'm the owner, the publisher, the managing editor. Everything. Oh, I had a string of editors for a while, but none of them lasted. I'm not a delegator, so I guess they got frustrated. I finally made a management decision to do it all myself. And that's what I'm doing. Loving every minute of it, too."

"Wonderful," said Mildred. He looked so thoroughly satisfied with his life. For a split second she was almost envious. "I'm glad it turned out so well for you, Clyde. You deserve it. And I suppose you've got a wonderful family, too. Children. Maybe even grandchildren?"

His face clouded. "I guess you never heard. I lost my wife last year. It was a freak thing. An aneurysm, they said. Happened in her sleep."

"Oh," said Mildred. "I'm so sorry."

He remembered how it had been when Paula died. How he had awakened one morning and reached to touch her as he had done a thousand times before. Only she didn't wake up. Sometime during the night, as he slept peacefully at her side, she had died. Just like that. And just like that his world turned upside down and inside out. For weeks he went through the motions, accepting dinner invitations and sympathy from friends, eating food he couldn't even taste, putting himself to sleep with half a bottle of numbing scotch every night. He started smoking again, something he'd given up thirty years earlier. Tumbleweeds of dust grew under the furniture and cheese grew moldy in the refrigerator. He got teary-eyed at odd moments, then gruffly claimed it was hay fever when anyone tried to sympathize.

"We never had children," he said, "so I suppose we were closer than most couples. Anyway, I'm okay now." He saw her skepticism. "Well, mostly I'm okay. I have my moments, I admit. We had a good marriage, for which I'm glad. I'd seen the other side of the coin with my folks."

"Oh," said Mildred, veering away from a sore subject, "no one's parents were perfect."

"Anyway"—Clyde straightened up—"basically I'm fine. I guess you'd call me a workaholic. I'm always at the paper. My accountant tells me I should modernize it. You know, put in computer type and whatnot. But I just love the clang-clang of the old linotype machines." He smiled again. "I've probably got the only paper in the country that still uses linotype."

They were quiet for a moment. "Gosh," she said impulsively, "it's so good to be talking with someone my own age again."

"Huh? Who've you been talking to? Babies?"

"No one," she said quickly. As much as she wanted to confide in him, she remembered Irene's whisper: *Shhhhh. It's a secret.* "I've been talking to no one really. I'm here because my mother died and I'm working on the house. Getting ready to sell it." Or maybe to stay, but she didn't say that.

"That right?"

"Yes. And I'm here because my marriage has fallen apart." There. She'd said it.

"Now it's my turn to be sorry," he said. "That's a shame."

"I'm sorry too," she said, admitting it for the first time. She smiled a small smile. "But I'll get over it. Anyway, as long as I'm here, I thought I'd look up some old friends."

"Starting with me." He put his hand over hers.

"Yes," she said, delighted. "Most of all you."

"And who else would you be considering?" asked Clyde. "Maybe I should be jealous."

"Oh you!" she laughed. "It's not like that. I'm just getting nostalgic, I guess. Soft in my old age. I got out the yearbook the other day—"

"Oh Lord, not that!"

"Yes, and I was looking through our class—"

"A lot of our friends are still here," put in Clyde. "You'd be surprised."

"I know," said Mildred. "Dolly Church is still working in the photo shop and Phil Keeger's got a real estate business. And Seymour Henning is an accountant over at Benrus—"

"Sounds like you've tracked everyone down," he said, smiling.

"—and Marcel Wintermute is a famous writer now . . ."

The smile faded. "Oh, Marcel and his kiddie books. He's one of the more visible members of our class. Quite the social butterfly."

Mildred detected a sneer in Clyde's voice. She looked at him in surprise.

"Forgive me," said Clyde. "I shouldn't be so stiff-necked. Marcel's done a lot of good for this town. He's very generous. It's just that he tends to flaunt his success, and he tries to buy friendship, too. Yet even with all his efforts, I still get the feeling he's laughing in everyone's face."

"Is he still living over on Juniper Hill?"

"Yes. It's quite the place now. Breathtaking, so I hear. But never mind Marcel. Never mind any of them. What about us? What about going to dinner with me tonight?"

"Dinner?"

"You do eat dinner, don't you?"

"Well, yes. I mean, of course. Dinner." She was blushing like a schoolgirl.

"So will you go? With me?"

"Of course." Her voice sounded very far away. She thought maybe it squeaked.

"Good." He stood up abruptly. "Listen, I've got to get to the paper. Open up and all that. I'll pick you up at seven. Dress up. I want it to be special."

"Wait," she called after him. You can't pick me up, she wanted to say. But she couldn't think of a reason why not. Damn, she thought. She'd just have to hide Irene and Forrest. Besides, it shouldn't be too much of a problem anyway. If they kept their mouths shut.

"What?" He cocked his head.

"Never mind," she said. "I'll see you then. At seven."

13 Irene Purdy opened one eye, not knowing exactly where she was. She clutched her breasts under the covers and discovered she was nude. Then she spied an old Westclox wind-up alarm on the night table. She could read the time just barely between two shot glasses. Nine thirty-four.

"Mother of God," she breathed. Gingerly, ever so carefully, she eased out of bed. She did not want to wake the other occupant.

"Where you goin', Reenie?" Forrest Haggarty thrust his head high off the pillow, looking like a long-necked chicken or maybe Frank Perdue with hair.

She mumbled while she gathered her clothes. Mostly she spoke to her feet. "Gotta get dressed. Gotta feed you breakfast. Gotta get you shaved. Gotta see Hattie Brewster and Huey Crane. Gotta, gotta, gotta . . ."

He watched her pull on large apricot-colored nylon panties with undisguised interest. She yanked up a pair of red knee socks, her breasts swinging this way and that. She never once looked at Forrest.

"You seem outta sorts," he said.

Irene said nothing.

"I'd think you'd be in a better mood. After last night."

She zipped up the fly on her dungarees with such force the zipper snagged on the denim. There was a brief struggle while she tried to rip it free. Huffing and puffing and more exasperated by the minute, Irene gave up on the zipper, sucked in her stomach and buttoned the pants closed. She untangled a knotted bra with trembling hands, put it on, followed by a red plaid flannel shirt.

"Is it Earl, Reenie? You feelin' badly about Earl?"

"No," she said. "Earl's dead a long time. It ain't that."

"What then? I thought last night was . . ." He groped for a word. ". . . nice. Real nice."

"It's your back," she said, telling only part of the truth. "I never should of done it. I don't know what got into me."

"Reenie," he said softly, "come here." He patted the bed. She went to him and he took her hand in his. "You were, ah . . ." He searched for a way to say this that wouldn't embarrass her. ". . . real gentle. Honest."

Irene looked thoughtful.

"Yep, real gentle. Why, Reenie, I hardly had to move a muscle. That position you showed me, well, it was real nice."

Now Irene looked like she would die. Her face flushed beet red.

"I mean it was great," he assured her. "And you know what? I think it helped my back, too. I think maybe my back went out because it had been so long since, well, you know. You'd be amazed how that tension can build. Like a boiler ready to blow."

Irene started to jiggle, and Forrest was afraid she was

crying. He saw tears in her eyes. Then he realized she was laughing. His gladness that she wasn't crying flip-flopped to an embarrassment of his own.

"It ain't funny, Reenie. You shouldn't oughta laugh like that. You don't understand. A man has needs."

"Oh Forrest, you're too much." She wound down slowly, jiggling less and less. As he watched the subsiding jiggles, Forrest found himself wishing that she hadn't put on the shirt and bra. "Women got needs too, Forrest. Jeesum. A boiler, oh, I like that."

"Women got needs?" Forrest wasn't sure he believed it. Queenie never seemed to have needs. Queenie never got on top, either.

"Well, yeah. Sure."

"Even at our age?"

"Oh Lordy, Forrest. You got a lot to learn."

She went to get his breakfast. He leaned back contentedly. His back felt much better, yes indeed. He wondered what Trevor would say if he knew about this home remedy. Of course, they'd never tell Trevor and not Mildred, either. For now, he would enjoy himself. He looked forward to ten days, maybe two weeks if he could stretch it, with Irene Purdy. Maybe he did have a lot to learn. And maybe she would teach him.

14 Sometime before sunrise Trevor Bradford rolled over into the space on the bed where Mary Margaret should have been. The alarm in his head didn't go off right away. It wasn't until the Dickree Dairy milk truck clattered down Spring Street, when he slipped across the edge of deep sleep into half sleep, that he reached over reflexively to take hold of Mary Margaret's hand. And she wasn't there.

Trevor sat bolt upright in bed. He tried to swallow down

the small bubble of anxiety that lodged in his throat. Maybe she had just gone to the bathroom. He cocked his head, listening. He couldn't hear the water running or the toilet flushing, but then sometimes she forgot to flush. Sometimes she forgot a lot of things.

He allowed himself another thirty seconds to listen. Please, he thought. Please, Mary Margaret. I don't have time to search all over town for you this morning. Not today. Please. And he felt ashamed inside that he was thinking of his own agenda. His own priorities. Instead of her safety.

God protects children and crazy people, he reminded himself. She's all right. Sure, she's all right. Of course Mary Margaret wasn't crazy, not really. She was just getting on in years. A little forgetful sometimes. It wasn't anything serious, not anything debilitating and progressive like Alzheimer's. Thank God for that. No, it was just a slight hardening of the arteries—all that butter she'd used in her cooking for all those years, you know. It had to congeal somewhere, but why it congealed in Mary Margaret's pipes and not in his was a mystery.

God protects children and crazy people. And *old* people, he told himself.

Trevor threw on a pair of corduroys over his long johns. He'd done this before. He slipped sockless feet into leather slippers and pulled on yesterday's Viyella shirt. Quick as a fireman, he raced out the bedroom door and down the stairs. Maybe she hadn't wandered far yet. He hoped not.

Trevor got as far as the front porch. There she was, bundled in a quilted Snug Sack against the autumn chill. She sat in an old swing seat with a mildewed cushion. It groaned softly as she swung ever so slightly back and forth. She had her glasses on and she was looking, staring really, at the top of the Rockwells' barn across the street. The rooster weathervane looked black against the sun's first rays.

Don't look into the sun like that! he wanted to shout. You'll go blind! Your eyes won't work anymore! Is that what you want?

Is it? You scared me again, Mary Margaret! I want you to stop running off like that, do you hear?

"Good morning, honey," is what he said.

"Oh," she said, turning to him. "You startled me."

I startled you? he wanted to shout. Me! But he said nothing.

"I woke up early," she said. "I wanted to see the sun rise."

"That's nice," he said, breathing a little easier. "You just stay there." He pictured himself in his mind chaining her to that swing seat, and he shoved the thought away. "I'll get you breakfast. We'll eat out here, okay?"

"I'd love that."

He went to the kitchen and fixed her usual breakfast: black coffee, fresh-squeezed orange juice, and a big slab of rye toast with strawberry preserves—no butter—spread on. Sometimes a caraway seed lodged under her dentures, and that was painful. But that was only when she remembered to wear her dentures. He cocked his head momentarily. Yes, this morning she was wearing them. He was glad about that because it unnerved him when she forgot. It made him feel like he was living with another person. A stranger. An old person.

Why, he wondered, had she grown old when he hadn't? Let us grow old together, that's what the poem said and that was the way it was supposed to be. But somehow she'd slipped ahead of him, and he'd been transformed from companion to caretaker. She developed mysterious aches and pains, which she talked about incessantly. She stockpiled medications. Their medicine cabinet looked like Drug Fair, crammed as it was with Ex-Lax, Sleep-Eze, Tylenol (the old variety in capsules), Anacin Three, Pepto-Bismol, Dr. Scholl's Corn Pads, Preparation H, and Midol (which she didn't even need anymore but which, she insisted, eased lower back pain).

Doctor though he was, Trevor was also a man of the Stiff Upper Lip school. He believed in medicines only as a last resort. It drove him wild every time he opened the bathroom cabinet and saw such blatant evidence of Mary Margaret's never-ending quest to ease pains that really weren't there. It seemed almost selfish somehow.

You want sick, Mary Margaret? You want sick? I'll show you sick. Come with me to Ballard Green. Take a look at old Gene Valente. A man whose heart looks like a pulsating network of Swiss cheese. A man with a time bomb in his chest. A man with a month left, two if he's lucky. And I don't have the nerve to tell him. I don't have the *heart*, you see. Or take a look at Emma Olmstead, her hands so crippled with arthritis she can't embroider anymore. Can hardly get dressed even. And then there's Forrest Haggarty, laid up with excruciating back pain, one step away from enforced incarceration in a rest home. Oh no, Mary Margaret, you're not sick. You're just getting old. So am I. It happens to everyone. It's natural. We're all going to die. That's natural, too.

But he couldn't say it. He just couldn't. Because despite her complaints, despite her medicines, despite her stubborn insistence on spending her days in front of the television set with "One Life to Live" (she had three years' worth taped on videocassette), despite all that, he loved her very much. He loved the person she used to be and, yes, he even loved the person she was now. But sometimes he felt so all alone.

"Ah, Mary Margaret," he sighed as he set plates down on a wicker table before her, "where did you go? When did you leave me?"

"What?" she said. "I've been right here."

"Nothing," he said. "Never mind."

They ate silently as the sunrise washed over them. It would be an Indian summer day. The rays felt warm against his skin.

"I've been thinking," he said carefully.

"Yes?" She looked at him hopefully. Like she wanted him to do something. He was so frustrated by that look. He looked away and pressed on.

"You know Penelope?" he said, turning a statement into a question, which was ridiculous.

"Penelope? Our daughter? Of course I know Penelope."
Her tone edged up shrilly, as it was prone to do when she was
frustrated or when he spoke to her like a child or both.

"I think you should go visit her." He held his breath.

"Alone?"

"I have some business to take care of here. A patient . . ."
He groped for words, avoiding the simple one: yes.

"Okay."

Trevor stared at Mary Margaret dumbfounded. He had
expected an argument at the very least. Or tears and weeping,
promises to be a better wife. Oh, those were the worst, those
promises. As if she could help the way things were. He had
a mental list of reasons for the trip at the ready. Penelope had
been begging Mary Margaret to visit. Mary Margaret had a
new grandchild she'd never even seen. The plane ride to San
Jose would be thrilling. They have oxygen on the plane, if
you need it. You could see the whole country in five hours,
Mary Margaret. You could fly first class. You could . . . go, Mary
Margaret. Go!

"Okay?" he repeated in amazement.

"Yes. Okay. Relax, Trevor. You're all set for an argument,
I can see that."

He looked at her closely, searching for signs of dementia.
Instead he saw sly, piercing eyes that held his gaze. She reached
out with chilled fingers and held his hand too tightly.

"You scare me sometimes, Trevor."

"What?" The word came out a whisper. She had flipped off
the track, he could see it in the intensity of her gaze, feel it,
too, in the tightness of her grip.

"The secrets you have."

Trevor Bradford swallowed hard and felt a tremor of panic.

"Don't think I don't know," she said, leaning close to him
now.

"Know what?" he said desperately.

"All these years," she said in a singsong voice. "All these

123

years, you and your secrets. Your disappearances. You want me to go on?"

"Patients," he offered, hating himself for making excuses, wanting at the same time to scream, yes, to scream. *Haven't I done enough! You with your wanting! You with your demands!* But he said none of this. "Patients," he repeated woodenly.

"Bah," she spat out. "I'm fresh out of patience."

"You don't understand," he said hopelessly. "I mean *my* patients. I have responsibilities."

"Don't lie to me, Trevor. Not after so many years." She looked away.

"It was nothing, Mary Margaret." There it was. The barest admission.

"I'll go to California," she said decisively. "I'll go and be glad."

He put his face in his hands. "Oh God, Mary Margaret . . ." I love you, he wanted to say. Believe me. But the words were lost in the folds of closed fingers, and Mary Margaret never heard him.

15 The Wintermute estate on Juniper Hill was more imposing than Mildred expected. She eased the Jaguar along a lengthy driveway of sparkling white crushed stone. Massive hedges flanked each side, creating the sensation that she was navigating through a bushy green tunnel. The hedges soon gave way to towering sugar maples, their leaves crimson and orange and yellow-green in the morning light. They cascaded around the car in a spray of firefall, then skittered in windy whirlpools along the frosted ground.

She passed over a narrow one-lane bridge. The terrain here was unclipped and tangled—a hairy mustard yellow meadow, an occasional stooped cedar, and knots of gnarled blueberry bushes. The bushes were woody, hard as ironwood and just as barren. It had been years since the young Marcel had picked any berries from these twisted branches.

Suddenly the environment transformed itself from untamed to elegant. Scrub brush gave way to manicured lawn. Thistles were replaced by formal gardens of precise geometric symmetry. Blue-green fields were neatly compartmentalized by a network of split-rail fences, bleached white by the relentless passage of countless New England winters. Over by a pristine white barn Mildred saw row upon row of animal runs for recuperating wildlife—beaver, raccoon, fox, and deer.

A thought crossed her mind like a shadow. Everything was so picturesque. So perfect. It didn't seem real.

She parked the car in front of the sprawling main house, walked up brick steps, passed between two fluted pillars, and gingerly lifted a heavy brass knocker. She let it fall, then unexpectedly stepped back into a man standing directly behind her.

"Oh!" she cried.

"Sorry to scare you."

Mildred whirled around and came face to face with one of the most handsome men she had ever seen. He belonged on television, this man, or in Arrow collar ads. Even in work clothes he looked elegant. Now he backed away, leaned against a pillar, and crossed one foot over the other. He looked her up and down with blatant interest. She felt herself flush.

"James Perkins, at your service." He wiped his hand on his khaki pants and offered it.

He was trying to be friendly, she could see that. But she also detected the barest hint of a smirk on his lips. When he smiled, he exposed a row of perfectly white, professionally capped teeth.

"Mildred Bennett," she said somewhat stiffly. "I remember you. You went to Raven's Wing High."

"I started off in the class ahead of yours," he said through

his smile, "but ended up finishing a year later. I was in voca-
tional ed some of the time and detention most of the time. Our
paths didn't cross."

"I suppose not," she said, thinking, Thank God for that.
Now it all came back to her. Jimmy Perkins, the worst boy in
school. A boy destined, if anyone was, for prison or the state
hospital. He'd done horrible things, cruel things. She remembered the time he stuffed fat Chucky Thomas in a locker and
it took the boys from metal shop four hours to cut him out.
Chucky wet his pants in there and left school in humiliation.
Another time, Perkins overpowered Justin Wentworth (who was
acne-scarred and had arms like pipe cleaners) in the boys'
locker room, wrapped him in adhesive tape like a mummy, and
left him there overnight. When they took off the tape, Justin's
skin came off with it. Then there was the time he set off an
explosion in the chemistry lab that did five thousand dollars'
worth of damage and triggered an asthma attack in Robert Stein,
an attack that almost cost him his life.

Invariably the victims were too terrified of their tormentor
to say who'd done it. People in power suspected, of course,
but no one could prove anything. And if the boys were frightened of him, the girls—who certainly should have been—
weren't, not by a long shot. Many—the gum-snapping, wise-
cracking streetwise variety to be sure—flocked to Jimmy Perkins.
With almost predictable regularity these girls would disappear
from school, usually going to "visit their aunts" because Jimmy
had gotten them pregnant.

He must have read these thoughts in her face.

"Look," he said, "that was a long time ago. I've changed."

"That's nice," she said smoothly, thinking, Some people
never change.

"No. Really. I have." He straightened up. He almost seemed
to preen. "See this place?" He waved his hand, lord of the manor
now. "Impressive, huh? Well, I did it. Every blade of grass, every
shrub—and some of them are pretty exotic, I can tell you—

every flower in that garden." He gestured at a formal garden, a remarkable geometric pattern spanning most of the open space in front of the house. "Course, the last flowers are dying now. It's the season. But when they bloom, well, I've got it timed perfectly, see? They're perennials. You've got your crocus, your azaleas, your tulips, your daffodils—they all go in perfect sequence."

Mildred felt a chill and pulled her sweater more tightly around her. What about the last flowers? she wanted to say. It's the season for dying. But she didn't. "Mr. Perkins—"

"Jim," he said.

"Jim. As interested as I am in horticulture—and I am, you may be sure—we'll have to continue this conversation some other time. I've really got to see Mr. Wintermute."

"Oh?" he said carefully. "How come?"

The lie came easily, since she had already practiced it once on the phone when she made the appointment. "I'm visiting some of my old classmates. Trying to find out if there's any interest in a reunion."

"Oh," he said. "Well, Marcel's the man to see, all right. He loves a party. And if you need funding, he's very generous." Jim's face darkened. "If you ask me, sometimes he's too generous. Always giving money away. People take advantage."

People like you, thought Mildred to herself.

"Well, Mildred, I'd like to continue our conversation, too. Maybe we could go out sometime."

She hated it when someone she didn't know—and a handyman at that—called her by her first name without permission. She felt her hackles rise, but bit her tongue. "That's most kind of you, Mr. Perkins—"

"Jim."

"Jim. But I'm only in town a short while, and my calendar is already full."

"I see," he said, stiffening. And he did, too. She could see that. "I'll take you to Marcel. He's in his studio."

She followed him up a palatial circular staircase, through a series of interconnecting hallways on the second floor, into what seemed to be a wing at the back of the house. Jim Perkins rapped twice on a white enameled door, opened it, and motioned for her to step inside, which she did. He sullenly closed the door behind her and left soundlessly.

Mildred stood on the periphery of a cavernous room with a cathedral ceiling and massive overhead rafters. Sunlight cascaded into a jungle of hanging ferns. At the far end of the room, next to a solid wall of glass overlooking a pond outside, Marcel Wintermute worked hunched over an enormous drawing board that seemed as tall as he was. He didn't look up.

Nervously Mildred twisted her handbag in her hands. She took a few tentative steps closer.

"So," he said, his unexpectedly loud voice reverberating through the rafters, "you're here to talk *reunions*."

"In a way," she said hesitantly.

"What?"

Mildred felt like Dorothy confronting the great and powerful Wizard of Oz. She wished she had a telescope so she could see him better. She fumbled for her glasses and scolded herself for being so jittery.

"You'll have to shout!" he shouted. "Or come closer. This is a damned inconvenient way to have a conversation."

Swallowing her jitters, Mildred crossed the room, brushing ferns from her face as she went. Even hunched over his board, his nose practically touching the paper, she recognized Marcel Wintermute from high school long ago and from recent photos she'd seen on the jackets of his books and in the society pages of *Town and Country*. It occurred to her that Marcel Wintermute resembled the creatures he drew. For one thing, he was smaller than small. He was elfin. His sandy brown hair was cropped close on top in an old-fashioned crew cut. The beard on his chin was neatly trimmed. His brown eyes were more amber than brown. They looked like lanterns. And when he smiled, which was often, he exposed a row of white teeth dominated by two unusually large canines. Bigger boys who had bullied him as a child pointed to those distinctive teeth and called him "vampire boy." He survived this insult (and others much worse later) with his sense of humor intact.

"There!" he said, throwing down a color pencil. "He's done!"

She looked down and saw a turquoise brontosaurus. "Very nice," she said politely.

"What?" he blurted. "Nice? You look at my masterpiece, my labor of love, and that's all you can say? *Very nice?*"

"Well," she stammered, "I—"

"Never mind," he sniffed, feigning hurt feelings. "Never mind. I'll get over it."

A smile broke out on her face as she realized he was kidding.

"Come. Let's sit over here." He led her to a voluminous white couch that looked like a leather marshmallow. She'd worn a skirt that day in deference to seeing a semifamous person, and her legs sprawled every which way despite her best efforts to weld her knees together.

He poured coffee into translucent porcelain cups. "I must say, I am honored to have Mildred Bennett née Schroeder visit my domicile. You who were so popular. A cheerleader, no less."

"I peaked early," she smiled.

"I don't think so. You look marvelous. You said something about a reunion," he went on. "Of course, I won't be able to make it. I'm booked up for the next three years. High school wasn't the best time of my life. I'm into a lot of bizarre things," he winked, "but masochism isn't one of them. I have no desire to be kaboomed again."

"Kaboomed?" He was a strange man who drew strange pictures and talked a strange language, too.

"A lovely little ritual, I assure you. Boys do it mostly." He noted her expression. "Oh, I don't mean"—he tried to think of another word for "buggering"—"I don't mean—"

"I know," she said quickly, "what you don't mean."

"Yes. Well. Kabooming is done when large boys grab a little kid by the ankles. They hold him upside down. They chant 'Ka-boom, ka-boom!' And they dunk his head in the toilet. The little kid was usually me and the toilet usually wasn't flushed. Sorry to be so gross, but that's the way it was." He ran a hand over the stubble of his crew cut. "Funny how things turn out. The one who kaboomed me the most was Jimmy."

Now you're kabooming him, thought Mildred and tried to push that somewhat obscene thought away.

"Is that why you started drawing those?" She pointed at the tilted drawing board—the dinosaur with the enormous leering grin and pink pointed nails growing from his feet. Not quite animal, not quite human, the dinosaur was endearing and unthreatening in a bizarre way.

"Oh, I suppose that's the book on me. That I started drawing to create friends when I didn't have any of my own. You like him?"

"Very much," she said.

"Wait," he said, springing from the couch. He ripped the sheet from the pad, and handed the drawing to her.

"Oh, I couldn't . . ."

"Yes you can. And you will. Come on, take it or my feelings will be hurt. Besides"—he waved at a wall papered with other similar drawings—"I've got lots more."

Guiltily, Mildred accepted the offering. He seemed like a nice man, a harmless man, and now she was about to turn his world upside down.

"Marcel," she began tentatively, "I'm not here about any reunion."

"Oh?"

She took a deep breath. "I suppose I should get right to the point."

Marcel said nothing. His eyebrows knitted together apprehensively. Whenever anyone said they were getting to the point, the point was bound to be bad.

Mildred zipped open her large leather handbag and rummaged inside. Out came a bulging wallet stuffed with money, credit cards, and pictures of her family. Somehow she couldn't quite bring herself to discard Connor's picture. Out came a lipstick. A checkbook. A bottle of nail polish. And finally, the letter. She placed it on the smooth arm of the couch and laid her hand gingerly on top.

Marcel looked at the letter as though it were a bomb ready to explode. "What's that?" he blurted.

"I think you know what it is, Marcel."

"It's the letter I wrote to the personal ad. The letter to Agnes Peabody. So? I never expected her to respond."

"But she did?"

"Yes." Marcel started to unravel before Mildred's very eyes. "It was a daring notion. Writing that letter."

"Why did you do it?"

He leaned back in the couch and stared up through the skylight at the day outside. "I don't know. Maybe I was lonely." He lowered his voice, so low she had to strain to hear. "I am very social, of course. I suppose you've heard. Always out and about. But my circle of, shall we say 'intimate' friends is severely restricted. Jimmy's wonderful company, don't get me wrong, but he can be possessive at times. And our conversations are somewhat limited. Besides, I enjoy the company of women on occasion. I really do."

He seemed to be trying awfully hard to convince her.

"I'm getting older," he went on in a whisper. "For a long time I'd been thinking. About my situation, you know? And I guess I had some crazy idea. That it's not too late . . ."

"Too late for what?"

"Promise you won't laugh."

"Promise."

"To get married or something."

"Married?" she said in amazement.

"I know it sounds crazy. At my age. And everyone thinks I'm not 'that way,' don't think I don't know it. But I could be happy with a woman—with the *right* woman, you understand. I know it. And it makes perfect sense really." Marcel's voice escalated with excitement. "I mean, here I am with all this"— he waved his arms—"all of this and no one to share it with. Agnes has nothing. I could share it all with her. And I even harbor the dream that we might"—he seemed afraid to say it but forced himself to go on—"adopt a child. Not a white baby, of course, they'd never give us one of those. But there are so many older children who need homes. Handicapped children. Racially mixed children. Lost children. This house is so big. There's lots of room . . ."

Mildred felt like crying. She felt like tearing up the letter.

"Well," he said abruptly. "I don't know why I'm telling you this. It's no big deal. I wrote Agnes. I took her to the dinner theater in Westport. We had a very nice time, thank you. And I intend to see her again. I have no idea how you got my letter, but it's my private business, Mildred. The more I think about this, the more annoyed I get, I must say."

"Agnes is dead, Marcel."

"What?" The color drained from his face.

"It's true. Didn't you know?"

"No, I didn't know! Good God. I hate it when someone dies! Hate it, you understand?" He bolted from the couch. At first she thought he would be sick. But he stumbled over to a tea cart in the corner. He pulled one of many bottles from the bottom shelf and poured a good six ounces of Four Roses into a tumbler. He took a shaky sip.

"You want one?" he asked hoarsely.

"No thank you."

Marcel turned to her. He grabbed the bottle almost as an afterthought, walked jerkily back to the couch and sank down beside Mildred.

"When did it happen?" he asked hollowly.

"The day before yesterday. Saturday."

"But I saw her only last week. She seemed in perfect health."

"She was murdered—"

"Stop! I don't believe you."

"—on Saturday night," she pressed on. "They found her body in the woods on my property. Apparently she put up quite a struggle. Someone hit her on the head with a—"

"I don't want to hear!" He pressed his hands to his ears. "Not another word! It's vile. It's sick, that's what it is."

"She was dressed up. Like she was going on a date, Marcel. A date."

Marcel looked at her wild-eyed. He let his hands drop. "Wait a minute. You don't think I had anything to do with this?"

There was something new in his voice. An element of anger, a tone of outrage. It made Mildred wary. "I don't know what to think," she said carefully.

"Well, I didn't, you hear? I didn't!"

"Then you won't mind telling me where you were on Saturday night."

"I most certainly do mind. This is a monstrous invasion of my privacy. You may leave this instant."

"Fine." She picked up the letter and stood up. "Then I'll just turn this over to the police." She hoped he wouldn't call her bluff.

Marcel sagged deeper into the couch. "What is it you want from me?" he asked quietly. "Money?"

"The truth, Marcel. That's all I want."

He laughed then. It was a sudden desperate outburst. "The truth," he said wretchedly. "You make it sound so simple. The simple fact is that I can't account for my whereabouts that night."

"Oh?"

"Jimmy and I had a fight. A bad one."

"A fight?" *Usually he commits his crime after some stressful event.* Mildred remembered Forrest's words.

"We've been together a long time, Jimmy and I. But he's running my life. He decides where we go, when we eat, whom we see. I can't even negotiate the terms on my books anymore. I've become a prisoner in my own house. I took it and I took it and I took it. For years I took it. Basically I'm a mouse. But finally I had the temerity to speak up. I told him to back off. Told him I needed space. It was awful. We had a frightful row."

"I see. Did you tell Jimmy about Agnes?"

"I don't know. I suppose."

For the barest instant his eyes widened in horror. But neither said anything.

"I went out driving that night," said Marcel doggedly. "I went to see a movie at Six Cinemas in Danbury. *Rain Man.*"

"Maybe they'll remember you," she said.

"Yeah, sure. And maybe dinosaurs will grow wings."

"Yours can," she said, trying in some small way to cheer him up.

He looked at her hopelessly, his face slick with perspiration. "So what are you going to do?"

"I don't know," she said.

"Maybe the ticket man at the theater will remember me."

"Maybe." She felt she couldn't leave him like this, as if she had to offer him something. "I won't go to the police," she said. "Not yet."

"You won't?" He was pathetically grateful.

"No. But I think you should know that I've got all this written down. Hidden. If anything happens to me . . ." She let the sentence hang unfinished.

134

"Oh Christ!" he wailed. "You think I'm going to *do* something? To you? Oh Christ!" He buried his face in his hands.

She got up to leave then, got up to leave the broken little man with his tumbler and his bottle. And she tried not to hate herself for what she had done.

16 Irene Purdy clomped her hiking boots against the cement sidewalk, trying to rid them of clots of mud that clung to the waffled soles. The last thing she wanted to do was track crud all over Ripley Crane's immaculate Oriental rugs. She had timed her visit to coincide with Ripley's lunch. He always walked the five blocks from Town Hall to his Victorian house on Main Street for his midday meal. It was part of his daily routine.

So Irene Purdy was surprised when Huey Crane opened the front door instead of his father. She could tell it was Huey right off—the same wide-mouth grin, the full face with cheeks that looked like they were stuffed with crab apples, the shaggy blond hair that fell into his eyes.

Huey hadn't turned out as Ripley had hoped, and the older man made no bones about it. Huey didn't own a suit and rarely wore a tie. His favorite outfit was a pair of denim overalls, washed so much they were more white than blue, and an open-necked plaid work shirt with patches sewn on the elbows. It embarrassed Ripley that Huey went around town like that, and it embarrassed him even more that Huey made his living driving a septic cleaning truck. Huey called it "the honeybucket" and took special delight in blowing the screaming claxon horn every time he drove through the center of town.

It amazed Irene that two people as different as Huey and Ripley could live in the same house. Ripley's other two children had gone off to college and careers and marriage. But not Huey.

135

Huey stayed put. Huey would be the first to tell you that he was not overly ambitious. He knew a good thing when he saw it. And if living with a few creature comforts meant listening to a steady flow of complaints and insults from his father, well, that was okay. Basically Huey was very good-natured. He knew how to turn a deaf ear.

"Ma'am?" said Huey.

Long ago Irene might have decided like the rest of the people in Raven's Wing that Huey Crane was slow in the head. She might have decided this had she not stumbled upon a collection of intricately carved wooden birds while baby-sitting with Huey and his sisters. Even though he had painted them with flat water-based paints from his model airplane kit, the birds were so lifelike they gave her a start. She couldn't believe a ten-year-old boy could create such beauty. He hadn't lived long enough. His hands weren't skilled enough, his eye for observation not developed enough.

Irene confronted Huey about the birds, wanting to know where he got them. She didn't say "stole" them.

It was me, he said. I made them.

Huey, she said, don't lie to me.

I'm not lying neither, he said. And to prove his point he opened the door to his walk-in closet. He yanked the string to turn on the light overhead. Irene gasped. She was overwhelmed. There on the shelves were birds, all kinds of birds. Owls, tanagers, blue jays. Robins, catbirds, and mourning doves. They were crammed together all chockablock. The floor was covered with shavings. An unfinished bird—one just emerging from a small brick of pine—sat on a chair in the center.

It almost blew Irene away, it was so unexpected. She apologized for doubting his word, and Huey gave her a bird from his collection. They became friends from then on. But that was a long time ago.

"Huey, it's me."

"Pardon?"

"Reenie. Remember? I used to baby-sit you when you were a . . ."

Baby! Well, maybe not a baby exactly, but a little boy. Huey Crane remembered Irene Purdy with warm affection. She was the only one who didn't look at him funny after the accident happened with his mother. Lots of folks made a big deal about saying he was only a baby. Boys will be boys, they said, and boys play with plugs. It was the nurse's fault for being downstairs and not where she belonged. That's what they said, but it wasn't how they acted. They looked at him like he was a monster. Everyone except Reenie. She gave him hugs and cookies and tucked him into bed at night. She listened to his prayers, to his pitiful requests that God should, please, send back his mother before she forgot him. Irene never said this was impossible, never said that dead is forever. And one day, when Huey was finally ready, he looked at Reenie sideways, then away real quick. He said, "She's not coming back, is she? Not never." Reenie looked him full in the face and said, "That's right. Now let's go fishing."

"Sure, Reenie! I remember you." He opened the door all the way and grabbed her to his chest in a big bear hug. The buttons on his shirt mashed against her dentures. "I ain't seen you in a coon's age," he said. "How you been?"

"Fine," she gasped.

He set her free. "I'm just home for a sandwich and a beer. Want one?"

"No thanks. I stopped by hoping I might see Ripley." Irene glanced out the window nervously. She didn't want to confront Ripley while Huey was there.

"Oh. Pop'll be along soon." Huey took a mouthful of liverwurst on rye with ketchup. "Dunno what's keeping him. He's usually here by now."

"I'll wait. If it's okay."

"Sure it's okay. Sure. Set yourself." He waved at an imitation French provincial Stratolounger. He took a pull on the beer and burped.

"Still carvin' those birds?" asked Irene.

"Naw. That was kid stuff. I gave it up."

"Too bad. You were good."

"I guess." He looked thoughtful for a moment. "You know, Reenie, I never told you this ..." He considered his words carefully. ". . . but I really 'preciate what you did for me."

"I didn't do anything for you, Huey. Not really."

"Oh, you did a lot. You didn't know it maybe, but you did. You treated me nice. With respect. Like a human being, not like some kind of monster."

"You were never a monster," she said flatly, almost angrily. "It was an accident, God knows."

"I guess that's the way it looked."

He said it so quietly, she almost missed it. Almost.

"What do you mean, Huey?"

"Nothing. Forget it."

Irene tensed in the recliner. She looked at Huey and noticed his face was a little flushed. She wondered how many beers he'd put away in the past hour. Now he seemed nervous. Wired almost. She eyed him silently as he rearranged knickknacks on the coffee table that didn't need rearranging.

"Well," he said all at once, "I gotta go." But he made no move to leave.

"Don't go, Huey. Set a spell. We'll talk about old times."

"Old times are over and done," he said pointedly. "Can't do anything about them now."

"Sometimes trouble never rests," Irene said quietly. "Come on. Talk to me, Huey. Humor an old lady."

Obediently, he sat across from her, his mouth set in a grim

line. "I promised myself a long time ago I wouldn't torment myself about it anymore."

"Break your promise and the torment will stop. That's the way it works."

"Great," he hooted. "A shrink I don't need."

"You watch your smart mouth, sonny. I can still take you over my knee."

The thought of it was so ridiculous, he had to smile.

"So it wasn't an accident," she stated flat out. "What you did."

"I didn't say that," he said.

"Huey, what are you trying to tell me?"

"Promise you won't tell."

"Nope," she said truthfully. "I don't promise nothing. I might tell someone."

"Oh, what the hell," he said sullenly, "no one would believe you anyway." There was the slightest pause. "He made me do it."

"He who?" whispered Irene.

"My father, that's who."

"Oh no, Huey. It was a long time ago. No one remembers what happened when they were three. Your mind's playing tricks."

"I remember." The way he said it, so calm, so matter-of-fact, gave Irene a chill. "You'd be amazed what I remember. What I can't forget. I remember the sound of that machine. Hiss, sputter," he chanted, "hiss, sputter, hiss—"

"Huey, don't go talking like this. You're gonna get yourself all upset."

"—and I remember her crying, *'Don't!'* And I remember someone—*him*—grabbing my hands. I was playing with Lincoln Logs on the floor. I remember the plug. The thick gray cord. Thick as a snake, it was."

Nervously, Irene looked to the door. She prayed Ripley Crane would be delayed a while longer.

" '*Don't*,' she said." Huey's words came in a rush now. " '*Don't!*' Said it to him, not me, see? '*Come to Mama!*' she said. But I couldn't, because he was holding my hands, holding them to the snake plug, squeezing. And I remember the cord in my hands, how my nails dug into my palms. '*Don't!*' Hiss, sputter, hiss. And the plug came out and she was choking and he left. Left me with the plug and her dying. I tried to put it back but it wouldn't go. The prongs went every which way. She was choking, see. Gasping. Kind of a gargling sound. And then it was quiet. So awful quiet."

"Oh God."

"Right," said Huey. "Jesus H. Christ."

"Huey, why didn't you tell anybody?"

"Because I was three years old. Because he was my father. Because he was all I had left."

"I can't think of much worse than having a father like that."

"Because I was afraid of him. How's that?"

"Oh."

"He never really talked about it after, but would hint in a roundabout kind of way. Hint that it was the best thing. You know. Said stuff like, She was in misery anyway. Like, It was a blessing in disguise. Can you believe it? I didn't buy that back then and I don't buy it now. And, of course, he said one other thing."

"What's that?"

"He said if I told, he'd deny it. He'd let them take me away. Put me someplace. A place for crazy children."

"Oh Huey." She wanted to ask another question but didn't. She wanted to ask why he didn't kill Ripley when he grew up.

"You must hate him awful bad," she said.

"Nah," he lied. He leaned back and looked at her. "You're probably wondering how I can live here. With him."

"Well, yes. I'm wondering that."

"He takes care of me," said Huey simply. "Food. Money. Whatever. He owes me, see? And there's another thing—the real kicker: as much as I hated him all these years, I hated her, too. My mother. Because helpless or not, she let it happen. And she left me with him. Course, I'm over that part."

Irene looked hard at Huey Crane, and knew he'd never be over it. She knew, too, that some day he might well go to any lengths to extract vengeance from his father. A sadness washed over her. The little boy inside the man was gone. Disappeared. Destroyed.

"Don't tell anyone, Reenie. If you do, I'll deny it. It's too late to do anything about it now and, 'sides, no one would believe me."

She nodded numbly. He was right.

"Now I do hafta go," he said abruptly. He ran a sleeve across foamy lips and turned to go. Then he stopped at the door and seemed to turn a thought over in his mind. "Listen," he said, "I just thought you should know what you're dealing with. 'Cause I owe you, see?"

"No one owes nobody!" she snapped.

"Just be careful, Reenie." He turned to leave.

"Wait!" she cried. "Boy! Come back here!" But the only reply was the slam of the kitchen door.

Irene Purdy sat there with her thoughts for a good ten minutes, getting more and more upset. Never one to mince words, by the time Ripley Crane walked in she let tact fly out the window.

"Did you kill Agnes Peabody?" she blurted.

"What?" Ripley looked at Irene as though she were cheese gone bad. He took off his hat and made a production of hanging it on a peg by the door. He took off his overcoat and hung it up too. When he swung around, his face was pinched and pink.

"I must say I don't know what you're doing in my living room, Irene. My door is always open to the citizens of Raven's Wing, but you might at least have had the courtesy to wait outside until I got home."

"Huey let me in," she said sullenly.

"I see." He looked at her as though gauging her sanity.

"Sit yourself down, Ripley. We need to talk."

"Of course, Irene, of course. But you'd better get hold of yourself. Agnes Peabody, you say?" He shook his head sadly. "I only heard the news today. Horrible, just horrible. Obviously the work of some drifter. Or an escapee from the state hospital. I myself didn't know the woman." He sat down across from her. "Now, what's all this nonsense you're talking?"

"You knew her all right," Irene shot back. "You sent her a letter."

The barest hint of color tinged Ripley's cheeks. "I can assure you, Irene, I know nothing of any letter."

"Sure you do. Here's your picture." She withdrew the Polaroid from the pocket of her shirt and waved his face before him.

"What on earth . . ." But the question died in his throat as recognition hit. "Oh, *that* letter." He made a dismissive gesture. "I was wondering if it would turn up anywhere." Then his eyes widened slightly. For the first time Irene thought she saw fear. "You mean the letter I sent to the personals, *that* letter went to Agnes Peabody?"

"Yep."

He sank into a chair. "Well, I never knew that. I swear."

"Humph," grunted Irene skeptically.

For some moments Ripley seemed lost in thought. "Surely there were other letters," he said at last. "Mine wasn't the only one."

If Irene had a fault, it was that she had great difficulty keeping a secret of any kind, let alone one so monumental. This natural openness on her part was now compounded by the fact that she wanted to make Ripley Crane squirm.

"So what if there were?" she said hotly. "The others are solid respectable citizens. Not the type to murder a defenseless woman."

For the moment Ripley chose to ignore this slur on his

character. "Ah," he said with relief, "I understand. You have numerous letters, all, I'd venture to say, written by more likely candidates than the first selectman of Raven's Wing."

"They are not neither! They're people like Noah Lockwood an' Spencer McCloud an' Loomis Brewster! People like Marcel Wintermute, too! If you could ever in your wildest imaginings imagine someone like Marcel doing such a thing it's you who's sprung a sprocket, not me."

Ripley was stunned. But his face remained impassive.

"There," he said heartily. "You see? Solid citizens every one. Citizens, I might add, entitled to engage in a little harmless socializing via the personal ads. Citizens entitled to their privacy too, Irene."

Goaded by Ripley's smugness, Irene spoke boldly, forgetting all of Trevor's and Forrest's words of warning. "We'll get you dead to rights," she said quietly. "Considering your history."

The words struck a nerve. Ripley sat bolt upright, every muscle in his body taut. "And just what do you mean by that?" he asked.

"Never mind."

"Now look, Irene . . ." His voice sounded suddenly weary. He held his hands out as if appealing to reason. "I don't *have* any 'history.' And if you're being heartless enough to refer however obliquely to the tragedy of my wife"—he gazed sadly at Sally Crane's portrait over the mantel—"let me remind you that her death was investigated and deemed accidental more than thirty years ago. Thoroughly investigated by someone I happen to admire and respect. Forrest Haggarty."

"Oh," she said uncomfortably, her loyalties torn.

Ripley watched as these words struck home and guessed Forrest Haggarty was involved. Haggarty and Irene Purdy went way back.

"And another thing . . . If you've been listening to my son, Huey, there's something else you should know. Don't put too much stock in his ramblings. The boy's unbalanced. Everyone in town knows it. Why do you think I allow him to live with me at his age? Because we enjoy each other's company? No, Irene. For some reason the boy has always resented me, I know that. Living under the same roof is no picnic for me, I assure you. But if Huey couldn't live here, he'd be in the state hospital. He came unhinged when his mother died, and he's never been right since." With that, Ripley removed a handkerchief from his pocket and mopped his brow.

Irene looked at him hard. His face was open and pained. He seemed to believe what he was saying. She couldn't help but wonder if it could be true—if possibly Huey could have hallucinated the events he'd related to her so vividly.

"Not many people know it, Irene, but Sally begged me to end her life. *Begged* me, you hear? And I couldn't do it. Wouldn't do it."

"But Huey could?" she asked in disbelief.

"Yes," he said flatly. "I'm afraid Huey could."

"He was only a child," she protested.

"I know. I told myself so at the time. Over and over, I told myself. It was an accident, I told myself. Unintentional. But the boy scares me, Irene. To this day he scares me."

"Why?"

"He hasn't got any feelings. No regret. No remorse. No tears. No nothing."

Irene said nothing.

"All I'm asking is that you think about what you're doing before you damage the reputations of individuals who have served this town selflessly. Think before you start pointing your finger."

"All right," she said quietly. "I will." That much, at least, she could promise.

17 Ripley Crane watched as Irene Purdy trundled down the front steps and along the sidewalk down Main Street. He blinked several times in quick succession, as though by wishing it so he could make her disappear from the face of the earth.

Though outwardly calm and controlled during Irene's visit, Ripley was badly shaken. There was no telling how much damage she might do with her gossip. Here he had tried to do the right thing, for years he'd tried so hard. And now the trouble would be stirred up all over again. Old trouble with new trouble mixed in for good measure.

Ripley went to the kitchen and dropped two Alka-Seltzer tablets in a glass. He tried to think. Plop-plop-fizz-fizz-oh-what-a-relief-it-is ... The jingle danced in his head. Answering the personal had been so unlike him. How the hell could he have done such a stupid thing?

The answer was simple, he knew it. He'd been avoiding the truth for some time now. As was increasingly the case, he'd had too much to drink. He'd had a snootful, then had written the letter, sealed it, and mailed it in the postbox right there on Main Street before he sobered up. Hell, he was human, wasn't he? He was entitled to a taste of the grape now and then. He was entitled to a little female companionship, too. What was the harm?

The harm was that now he was in deep shit. People would start asking questions. They'd start wondering where he was. And they'd want to know where he was last Saturday night in particular.

The world, he thought with increasing agitation, was going to hell on greased skids. Nothing's worth a rat's ass anymore.

Easy, Ripley. It's no big deal. A few old farts playing detective. Why the very idea is laughable. No one will listen to them. Don't you worry, Ripley, don't you worry.

Ripley felt a rumble as the Alka-Seltzer sloshed around in his empty stomach. It erupted with a monumental belch. All these years, he thought grimly, all these years I've watched what's going on. I should have let Haggarty have his way back then, let him go off on his tangents before he ricocheted back and bit me on the ass.

Shit. It was so fucking unfair.

Angrily he swiped a black wall-phone receiver, heavy as stone, from its hook. He'd had that phone since 1955—it was the same one he'd used to report Sally's death. He dialed some numbers, then waited with mounting frustration as the rotary dial made laborious revolutions. Touch-tone, goddammit, touch-tone. Everyone in the world has touch-tone, but not me. Oh no, not Ripley T. Crane. I wouldn't have it, called it another phone company rip-off.

The person at the other end hardly had time to say hello before Ripley blurted, "Noah?"

"Yes, Ripley." In his duties as first selectman, Ripley Crane often called Noah Lockwood on his private line during the lunch hour, so Noah was not unduly surprised.

"Are you sitting down, Noah?"

"No, Ripley, I'm hanging by my heels here in chambers. Of course I'm sitting down. Don't be melodramatic. We're not at Town Meeting, okay?"

"You won't think I'm so melodramatic when I tell you what's happened."

Noah Lockwood swallowed the last of his American cheese on whole wheat and listened as Ripley told his story. At one point he felt the sandwich return up his throat but forced it right back down.

"Don't go getting excited," he said, with a conviction he didn't feel.

"Noah, I think there's others beside Irene Purdy involved. She said 'we,' Noah. '*We*.'"

"I heard you the first time, Ripley."

"I think Haggarty's in on this."

"Most likely," agreed Noah, making a grimace Ripley couldn't see.

"So what are we gonna do?"

What do you mean *we*, Noah wanted to scream. Ripley Crane was a pompous ass with plenty of dirty laundry to go all around town. Noah himself was clean, clean, clean. Still, a thought crossed Noah's mind that caused his bowels to loosen.

"I don't know," he said evenly. "I have to think."

"Oh, I see," said Ripley, his voice dripping with sarcasm. "You have to think. And while you think we're just going to sit back. Just going to let those people tear our reputations to smithereens."

"For now, Ripley, that's exactly what we're going to do. Sit back. Bide our time."

"Maybe you can afford this, Noah, but I can't."

"I *told* you I have to think!" cried Noah, losing patience now. "Just go about your business. All they've got is a bunch of letters that don't amount to squat."

"But—"

"But nothing. I've got to go, Ripley. Give it some time. I'll call you."

Noah Lockwood dropped the receiver as though it were on fire. No, he thought. Please. Not again. It can't be happening again.

18 Trevor Bradford turned the Lincoln between the twin pillars that marked the entrance to Silver Glen. Badly shaken by his conversation with Mary Margaret, he tried to concentrate on his driving. He gripped the wheel tightly to steady his trembling hands.

After Mary Margaret agreed to visit Penelope, things moved quickly. Trevor telephoned his daughter in California and explained the situation. It was four A.M. Penelope's time, so it took some moments for her to understand. Once she did, she urged that her mother should come right away. Today, if possible. Before she changed her mind, which Mary Margaret was prone to do.

Trevor managed to get a seat on United, and by noon Mary Margaret was winging her way across Pennsylvania, champagne glass in one hand, an outdated passport in the other, which she was certain was required for a cross-country trip.

The Lincoln rolled on. Past clay tennis courts that were never used. Past a greenhouse. Past an indoor swimming pool. To the casual observer, Silver Glen appeared more like an expensive resort than a private mental institution. In a way, it was the ultimate resort, promising individual attention in the form of daily private therapy sessions, exercise classes, art classes, and gourmet meals. The tab for his individual attention was steep—averaging $21,000 per month—but there was a waiting list to get in.

Trevor parked the Lincoln in front of the main building, a Georgian-style brick manor house called Twelve Chimneys because there were, in fact, twelve chimneys. He went inside, nodded to the nurse at the reception desk, and passed unobtrusively through ornate mahogany doors that led to the patients' private rooms. No one stopped him. He was, after all, a physician and, as such, exempt from normal security procedures.

The sound of his footsteps was muffled by thick carpeting. He followed this wine red pathway down cream-colored halls, through a series of interconnecting passages, all flanked by private rooms, some of them occupied by famous people. Every so often he passed through a sort of living room. These large vaulted chambers were furnished with tasteful traditional pieces, some of them valuable antiques. The effect was elegant, even ponderous, and definitely noninstitutional. If a patient arrived convinced that he didn't need help, the surroundings certainly reinforced this delusion.

Finally Trevor came to the room he was looking for. A brass plate on the door bore the name MCCLOUD. She's been here so long she gets her name on the door, thought Trevor. In brass.

He tapped on the door, which was ajar.

"Leslie?"

"Come in."

She looked up from a book she was reading. She was sitting by a bay window. Sunlight streamed over her shoulder, catching her hair, spilling onto the pages in her lap. He had forgotten how pretty she was. Yes, she had been pretty once—when she was sober. It was common knowledge that anyone who wanted any kind of contraband and was willing to pay for it could get it at Silver Glen. The staff was notoriously corrupt. Trevor was happy to see that from the looks of things Leslie McCloud hadn't been buying bootleg booze. Her complexion was creamy, her eyes bright and alert, and her hair lustrous. It was tied back in a ponytail that made her look younger than her fifty-four years.

"Trevor! If you aren't a sight for sore eyes."

"No," he laughed, sitting on a small love seat opposite her, "you've got it backward. You're the sight. You look great, Leslie. Just great."

"It's all this clean living. If I don't watch out, they might kick me out of this place."

"Would that be so bad?"

She looked away. "I don't know. I've been thinking about it. The doctors say I'm ready . . ."

"So what's keeping you?"

"Spencer thinks it may be premature."

"Oh?"

"Don't misunderstand," she said hastily. "Spencer has my best interests at heart."

"Um-hm," said Trevor, unconvinced. Spencer McCloud had his wife's money at heart, was more likely the case. Leslie was the one in the family with real money. Inherited money. With Leslie "away," Spencer could live a life of luxury without encumbrances. If Leslie got out, she might have a mind of her own. She might realize there was more to life than Spencer McCloud. And she might leave him.

"He does, you know. He's stood by me all these years. He visits every day. He's a saint, Spencer is." She closed her book decisively. "But never mind Spencer. Sit down. I'm so glad you stuck your head in here. I didn't know you had any patients in Silver Glen."

"I don't," said Trevor, taking a seat in a mauve velvet armchair. "I came to see you."

"Oh?" said Leslie.

"Actually it's rather a delicate situation. I've got to talk to Spencer about something, and frankly I wanted to talk with you first. You may be able to clear everything up, and then my chat with Spencer will be entirely unnecessary."

"I don't understand."

"Bear with me. You said Spencer visits you every day?"

"Yes," she said carefully.

"What time?"

"It varies," she said, looking perplexed. "Usually in the evening. He comes at six o'clock. We watch the news. We eat dinner. We read. Just like any old married couple. Except we don't live together. He goes home at about ten or eleven."

"And this past Saturday—was he with you as usual?"

Leslie McCloud inclined her head slightly as she thought. "No," she said slowly. "I don't think so. Saturday was one of the times he didn't come. Sometimes he doesn't." She shrugged her shoulders, then looked at Trevor sharply. "What's this all about, Trevor?"

"A woman was killed Saturday night," he said gently. "Agnes Peabody. Maybe you heard."

"Yes," she said, shuddering. "The staff was talking about it. But I don't see what that's got to do with Spencer. So he wasn't here? That doesn't make him a murderer."

Reluctantly, Trevor told her about the letters.

"I see," she said. Leslie McCloud was shaken, Trevor could see that, but valiantly she maintained her composure. "Well," she said finally, "ours isn't much of a marriage, is it? Not in the traditional sense. I suppose Spencer is entitled—"

"Leslie, for God's sake, when are you going to get angry?"

"Angry?" she repeated, as though the word were totally foreign to her.

"Yes. At the very least, the man is making a sham of your marriage. And"—he hestitated—"at the very most, Spencer may be the one—"

"I don't like what you're implying, Trevor."

"Look, Leslie, it's none of my business maybe, but I always worried about your marriage to Spencer. I mean, you were so young and naive when you married him. So full of life and happiness too—"

She shook her head, indicating that he should stop this talk.

"—and afterward, over the years, well, you seemed to unravel. He chipped away at you bit by bit."

"No," she said quietly. "No."

"You can blame it on a drinking problem, if you wish," he pressed on, "but I saw the drinking as an effect. Not a cause."

"Please," she said, closing her eyes. "Don't."

"I suspected abuse, Leslie. And I'm sorry. Sorry I didn't do anything."

"What could you have done?" she said, turning her face to the window. "What could anyone have done?"

"Would you like to tell me about it?"

"It wasn't Spencer's fault," she said all at once. "I had been overprotected. As you say, I was naive. I had trouble . . ." She stopped and gazed out the window.

"Trouble what?" he asked softly.

"Touble accommodating his needs." She looked Trevor in the face now, her eyes almost accusing. "That's what a wife is supposed to do, isn't she? Accommodate her husband's needs."

"Leslie, do you really believe that?"

"I didn't like sex, Trevor. Does that shock you?"

"You were young, Leslie. Sometimes when people are young it takes a little time. A little gentleness, too."

"Spencer was patient for a while," she said woodenly. "Then he wasn't anymore. His demands escalated."

Leslie McCloud was flushed and trembling. Nervously Trevor glanced at the door. "You don't have to talk about this if you don't want to, Leslie."

"You asked, Trevor. Now I'm going to tell you." She took a deep breath and went on as though by rote. "He asked me to lie in a tub of ice cubes. I thought he was joking. I said no, of course, but he turned so nasty, so mean, that, well, it seemed easier to do what he wanted. It seemed harmless enough."

Trevor nodded.

"And then, after I'd lain in the ice cubes, when I was chilled to the bone, he made me lie on the bed very still. I wasn't allowed to move while he ... he ..."

"Made love to you?"

"Yes." She shuddered.

Disturbed as he was by Spencer McCloud's obvious need to humiliate his wife, Trevor was reluctant to frighten her further. "Leslie," said Trevor gently. "It's all right. You didn't break any laws. You agreed to please your husband in a way that's unusual, I'll admit, a way that you clearly found distasteful. The only tragedy here is that you felt you had to do something you basically didn't want to do." And that your husband would dominate you in such a perverted manner, but Trevor didn't say that.

"For a while that was the only way it worked with Spencer.

The only way he could get an"—she gulped convulsively—
"erection. But then even that didn't work anymore. So he tried
other ... methods. Other things ..." She cried openly now,
never looking at Trevor and not bothering to wipe away the
tears. "He used to tie me up. And he hurt me. He cut me. He
put things there. Inside me."

Trevor felt the room getting smaller. He fought the urge
to fling open the window. He thought he might be sick.

"Things," she repeated dully. "A coat hanger. An ice pick.
A, uh ..." She broke down entirely then, burying her face in
her hands. "I was scarred. I could never have children."

"Leslie, Leslie," he said. He moved next to her and put an
arm around her shoulders. He drew her close. "Did you tell
anybody about this?"

"No," she sobbed. "Here I was a grown woman, allowing
this ... this ..."

"Torture," he spit out.

"I was so ashamed. I told nobody. I drank instead."

"I see," said Trevor sadly.

"It wasn't all his fault, of course." She turned her tear-
streaked face to Trevor, her eyes begging his to believe this.
"It was my fault as much as his."

"It was not your fault, Leslie. You must believe that."

"I went along with it," she said doggedly. "I thought it
would get better, but it got worse. And I was a bad wife. I turned
away from my husband. I neglected my children."

"You ran the only way you knew how," offered Trevor.

"Despite what I told you," said Leslie, dabbing her eyes
with a handkerchief, "Spencer isn't all bad."

A monster, thought Trevor. An abomination.

"He stood by me all this time, through all my bouts of
alcoholism, through my trips back and forth here. He never left
me. He visits. He's the only one who does."

"Did you ever think," said Trevor gently, "that maybe he
didn't leave because of your money?"

"I try not to think about that," she said softly. "Somehow that would make it even worse."

Trevor made a concerted effort to talk about other things then. She had had enough, and so had he. He waited while Leslie went to the bathroom to blot her face with a cool washcloth. He watched her untie the ponytail and brush her long hair. She seemed to pull herself together.

They sat for an hour, making small talk. Talk about goings-on in town. About their children. About books. About art.

"There's a new exhibit at the Metropolitan," said Trevor impulsively. "Impressionists. Maybe you and some of the others would like to go sometime. My car seats six."

"Oh," she said, "that's so thoughtful. But I couldn't."

"Think about it. It's just a first step. See how you like it out there."

"Well, maybe."

All too soon they heard Spencer McCloud's booming announcer voice reverberating off the walls down the hall. Spencer liked to make an entrance. He enjoyed being recognized and made sure everyone knew who he was. Leslie stiffened visibly.

"Don't tell," she whispered.

"I won't. I promise."

"You'll come back?" her eyes pleaded.

"Soon," he said. "Tomorrow if I can."

Trevor ran into Spencer McCloud in the carpeted hallway. He had to stop himself from slugging him. It most definitely would not have been a fair fight. Spencer was six-two, barrel-chested, and in excellent physical condition for a man of fifty-eight. He considered the preservation of his body to be of utmost importance. Even though he did a steady stream of voice-overs for commercials, Spencer much preferred to be in front of a camera. Recently his agent had assured him that the mature look was "in" and that more work would be coming his way. Spencer hoped the little prick was right.

"Trevor," he said, extending his hand, "fancy meeting you here. How're you doing?"

Trevor didn't shake Spencer's hand. He simply could not. Instead he stared down at it as though it were a piece of toxic waste. "There's something I have to discuss with you, Spencer."

Spencer retracted the hand and narrowed his eyes suspiciously. "What is it? Something about Leslie? Did someone give her a drink? The woman has no willpower, you know, none at all." A new realization flashed into his mind. "Wait a minute. You're not her doctor. What are you doing here?"

"This is between you and me, Spencer. Come on."

Trevor led Spencer McCloud into a small conference room, one of several used for group therapy sessions. He closed the door.

"Okay," said Spencer, dropping all pretense of cordiality, "cut the crap. What's all this about?"

"It's about this, Spencer." Trevor extracted a Xerox copy of Spencer's letter from his breast pocket and gave it to him. He had to hand it to Spencer. The man didn't move a muscle. Didn't flinch. Didn't show surprise. Cool, he was, real cool. Not batting an eye, Spencer handed the letter back to Trevor.

"Look, Trevor ..." Spencer leaned forward and pressed his surgically straightened nose up to Trevor's crooked one. "I don't know how you got a copy of that letter, and I don't really care. I answered one of the personal ads. So what? People do that every day. My wife is a bit incapacitated, in case you haven't noticed. We haven't lived as man and wife for a long time. Years. So I sought a little female companionship. Is that a crime?"

"It's a crime that the woman who placed the ad is dead."

"What?"

"Agnes Peabody. Maybe you heard. She's dead."

"Agnes Peabody wrote that ad? You're kidding!"

"Do I look like I'm kidding?" said Trevor grimly.

"Now wait a minute here." Spencer spread his hands in a

gesture of apology. "I'm sorry about Agnes Peabody. It's a pity and all that. But just because I sent her a letter doesn't mean I killed her."

"She never contacted you?"

"Hell no."

"And you weren't with her on Saturday night?"

"Of course not."

"So where were you?"

"That's none of your goddamn business."

"Oh yes it is. You'll tell me, or I go to the police."

"And I'll have your ass in court for harassment!" snapped Spencer. But Trevor could see he was worried. "What the hell," he shrugged. "It's no big deal. I was here on Saturday night. With Leslie."

"That's not what she remembers," said Trevor evenly.

"Why you son of a bitch," exploded Spencer. "You've been talking to my wife behind my back. You leave her out of this, you understand? She's delicate, see? If she goes off the deep end again, I'm holding you responsible."

"I think you're the one who pushed her off the deep end in the first place," said Trevor, "and you're the one who keeps her there too."

Again Spencer didn't bat an eye. He studied the face of his Rolex. "So what is it you want from me? You want to ruin me, is that it? You want to ruin her?" He jerked his head toward Leslie's room. "Because you will, you know. I'm all she has. She needs me."

"I don't want to ruin anybody." That was a lie, of course. Trevor would have liked nothing better than to ruin Spencer McCloud. "Right now I just want to know where you were on Saturday night."

"Christ, I can't believe this. You're actually serious, aren't you?"

"Dead serious."

Spencer McCloud turned and went to his wife's room. Too

late Trevor tried to follow. When he got there, the door was closed. Locked, too. He had no choice but to wait outside. He heard muffled words inside. When the door finally opened, Leslie and Spencer stood before him.

"Tell him," said Spencer brusquely.

Leslie McCloud stood next to her husband, her eyes fixed on the floor.

"Go on, Leslie." He gave her a nudge. "Tell him."

"I must have been confused," she said woodenly. "Spencer was here with me on Saturday night."

Trevor drove away feeling convinced she'd been forced to lie and more than a little depressed. As soon as he got home, he placed a call to Leslie McCloud at Silver Glen.

"This is Dr. Warren," a deep voice said. "I'm sorry, Dr. Bradford, but Mrs. McCloud was greatly disturbed by your visit. She's under sedation."

"I'm sorry," said Trevor. "I'll call back in the morning."

"I wouldn't bother, Doctor."

"Oh?"

"You're not on her approved list of visitors, and we have instructions not to put your calls through."

"Instructions from whom? Her husband?"

"Well, yes."

"Listen, Dr. Warren, I don't know you. I don't know how familiar you are with Mrs. McCloud's condition. But if you examine her—a pelvic exam, I mean—you'll find damage there. Wounds."

"Self-inflicted wounds," said Dr. Warren smoothly.

"The hell they are! If you've observed Mrs. McCloud for any length of time, if you've talked to her at all, then you have to know that her husband is contributing to her illness, not helping it."

"Our policy is to work within the framework of the family," said Dr. Warren. He sounded almost bored. "It's best for the patient. It's best for the—"

"For the institution!" said Trevor hotly. "Best for Silver Glen because he pays you!"

"Dr. Bradford, I really cannot continue this line of conversation. But I strongly suggest you avoid further embarrassment. And I suggest you leave Mrs. McCloud alone."

Ever so gently, Dr. Warren hung up the phone.

19 Leslie McCloud lay in her bed. She was vaguely aware that she had missed dinner. (If today was the second Monday of the month, and she thought it was, that meant she'd missed lobster Newburg, one of her least favorite meals.) Someone had given her a shot, she remembered that. Something to calm her nerves. She was too foggy to be angry, but nonetheless a small voice within her cried out, "Medication? Alcohol? What's the difference?"

She remembered seeing kindness in Trevor Bradford's eyes. His eyes were accepting, not cold and calculating like eyes in the heads of doctors on staff here. Sometimes she felt like a bug under a magnifying glass, the way those eyes looked at her this way and that, studying her, trying to unravel why something had gone wrong when everything should have gone right. She could never think of an answer, though she would have liked to give them one. So for a long time—years even—they entertained themselves by turning the magnifier, intensifying the beam into a single point of burning light. Then abruptly they stopped. Perhaps they came to realize that if they persisted she would be burned to a hollow crisp. Perhaps they merely got bored. In any case, they seemed to give up. And now, mostly, they left her alone.

Trevor's questions had rekindled unpleasant memories. Even lying here as she did in a cocoon of half sleep Leslie's mind wandered to a time way back. A time when she was young. The time when she and Spencer were first married.

He was considered quite a catch, Spencer was. He was polished, he was poised, he was beautiful to look at. He was, Leslie believed, everything she wasn't. But more than that, he had things she didn't. For one thing, Spencer had a family. It was a close family, the men always slapping each other's backs and the women giving quick clutching little hugs filled with implied love and understanding. Spencer and his father never kissed, of course, but they shook hands a lot. They shook hands every time they met and kept on shaking. Shaking and smiling as though they were the greatest buddies in the world. Later Leslie found out that they were indeed the greatest buddies— until one might fall sick or the other might need money or one might commit an unforgivable faux pas such as crying in public. Until one might need the other. But that was later, much later.

Leslie didn't have a family, not really. Her parents died in an airplane crash when she was three. As soon as Leslie was old enough to read the press clippings, she pointed out to her grandmother that her parents would have been better off flying coach. After all, she said, it was first class that hit the ground first. Her grandmother (who was raising Leslie) ignored this observation. She was sophisticated and worldly-wise, but not in the ways of children. She had no idea that such an apparently callous comment from an eight-year-old child masked the horrified realization that money and limousines and even a fistful of first-class tickets could not protect one against horrors of happenstance.

When you fall off a horse, you get back on. That was Grandmother's motto. She and Leslie traveled around the world many times, and they always flew first class. Leslie never mentioned her fear; she just clutched the arms of the seat with white knuckles. When she was fifteen, Grandmother allowed her to have a drink on the plane, and Leslie discovered that it helped quite a lot.

Anyway, Spencer's big family appealed to Leslie and they seemed to accept her, too. (One day Spencer's mother, Marjorie, hugged Leslie in a loving little clutch and whispered that she was "so relieved Spencer had finally settled down with a nice girl.")

If I'm anything, thought Leslie back then, I'm a nice girl.

After a while, the closeness of Spencer's family got on Leslie's nerves, and after a while they stopped being so accepting, especially Spencer's mother. Marjorie had a suggestion for everything. "Not the gold chain with that outfit, Leslie. Wear the pearls." "Really, Leslie, I think a needlepoint fabric on that love seat would be ever so much nicer than velvet. Don't you?" "I know you mean well, dear, but Spencer likes his shirts from Dunhill. Fifteen-and-a-half-thirty-six. They've got a file on him. I'm sure you can return these before Christmas. Oh, they're monogrammed? That *is* a shame."

It's my money, Leslie wanted to scream. Can't I spend it the way I want? But she said nothing.

She hoped things would improve after they adopted the children, and for a while they did. Marjorie didn't like babies and diapers and spit-up, so she left Leslie alone. But as soon as Alicia and Mark were old enough to walk and talk, Marjorie took over. "She's only trying to help," said Spencer soothingly. "And she has a way with kids." He winked. "Look at how I turned out." Leslie looked at him and said nothing.

In no time the children joined the McClouds, the enemy camp as Leslie saw it. They saw their mother for what she was. A mouse. A frump. A drinker. She was more alone than ever.

Leslie felt guilty when Marjorie finally died because she was so relieved. Now, she believed, things would finally get better. She would have her family. But Spencer was so grief-stricken he hardly spoke to her for weeks. Once she found him weeping into Marjorie's Icelandic sweater. When she touched his shoulder in a gesture of sympathy, he recoiled. He looked up at her with a face full of rage. Leslie was so taken aback she almost fled. "What do you know about it?" he sneered. "You weren't fit to lick her shoes."

She could still remember the curl of his lip.

After that they hardly spoke. Leslie drank more. When she found Spencer wearing Marjorie's sweater one day, he looked at her coldly, as though daring her to say something. She didn't. Later, when she happened on him wearing Marjorie's other clothes as well, she looked the other way.

Yes, she thought, as she slipped into sleep, here is better. Definitely better. Better than out there. But a little part of her, that same small voice, said maybe, just maybe, Trevor Bradford would call.

20 By late morning of that same day the warm afterglow of sex with Irene Purdy had already faded as Forrest Haggarty flipped with consternation from channel to channel on the TV set. He was so aggravated he almost cracked the remote control handset. Already he had been subjected to more senseless crap than any human being should endure in a lifetime: Phil Donahue (a man who, it seemed to Forrest, spent an inordinate amount of time discussing inconsequential drivel), Geraldo Rivera (a video vampire if ever there was one), "$25,000 Pyramid," and a rerun of "F Troop." As he flipped from channel to channel, he found that his choices now consisted of "The Price Is Right," "Wheel of Fortune," "The New Brady Bunch," and "Alf."

"This is shit," said Forrest to no one in particular. "I don't think I can take it."

Slowly, painfully, he eased himself out of bed and onto a small braided rug. He positioned himself belly-flop style, his arms and hands reaching over the sides of this little rug raft. By pulling with his palms and pushing with the balls of his feet, he found that he could move without pain inch by inch across the waxed hardwood floor. His intention was to find a telephone, which he did, in Mildred's room across the hall. He reached up to the nightstand, dragged down a pink Princess phone, and punched out a number. The receiver looked like a toy in his big hand.

"Raven's Wing Police Department," said a weary voice on the other end of the line.

Thank God, thought Forrest. It was Lenny Pulaski. He wasn't sure he had the duty roster straight in his head anymore, wasn't sure Lenny would be the one on the desk. But he was.

"Turn off the recorder, Lenny," said Forrest immediately. The station recorded all incoming calls, and Forrest could ill afford to have anyone else hear this conversation.

"Huh?"

"The recorder, Len. Turn it off."

"Forrest?" blurted Lenny. "Is that you?"

"Jesus Christ, Lenny! Will you turn the damn thing off!"

"Oh. Right." The faint beeps that signaled the presence of the recorder died. "There," said Lenny.

"And erase it, Lenny. Don't forget that."

"I won't," said Lenny in a hurt voice. Lately everyone treated Lenny as if he were stupid. Ever since a year ago when his then girlfriend stole his revolver and shot her cancer-ridden father with it. Ever since, he'd been taken off the beat and relegated to desk duty. "Jesus, Forrest, where are you? Your kids are going crazy with worry."

"I'm sure," said Forrest dryly. "Look, Lenny," said Forrest, getting right to the point, "I need your help."

"Oh?" said Lenny, immediately wary but flattered, too, that a man like Forrest Haggarty would be asking for his help.

"Yeah. I need to know whatever you've got on the Agnes Peabody case."

"Oh jeez, Forrest, I don't know . . ."

"Come on, Lenny. I'm not asking you to give me any files or anything. I'm just asking you to tell me what you know." Forrest knew Lenny wasn't stupid. He was a good cop. What's more, he had a mind like a Xerox machine. Any conversation, no matter how seemingly trivial, could be repeated later verbatim; the most obscure portion of the most deadly dull written report could be recalled with ease. "That is," said Forrest, "if you know anything about the case." He knew this was a challenge Lenny would be unable to resist.

"Course I know about it. Hell, it's all people are talking about down here. They're all out running around, chasing for leads. Me, I'm at this desk. I got nothing to do all day but sit and wait for the phone to ring. Which it doesn't. So I study the case. I think on it. I read the reports." He inhaled heavily. "Christ, I'm so fucking bored."

"So why don't you come over and tell me about it? You'll be on lunch soon."

"Where are you?" said Lenny, momentarily forgetting his own misery.

"Swear you won't tell," said Forrest.

"Right. I swear. If you don't want to be found, Forrest, I don't see where other people get off trying to find you."

"Okay. I'm over at Mildred Bennett's. You remember. The Schroeder place over on High Ridge."

"Jeez, Forrest, you're hitting the big time. I heard Mildred Schroeder was back in town. But you and her? I never woulda guessed it."

Forrest started to say, It's not like you think. But his pride stopped him. Let him think it, he decided. Let him. "How soon can you be here?" he asked.

"Give me twenty minutes."

Lenny was there in ten, knocking respectfully, daintily almost, on the front door.

"Door's open!" bellowed Forrest out an open window. "Come on up."

Lenny was a big man who had seen a lot in nearly thirty years of police work, but he stepped into the enormous foyer of Mildred's house with a sense of wonder on his face. He'd seen houses like this before, of course, plenty of times. Over the years he'd been hired from time to time to supervise local boys as they parked cars at one big party or another at these houses on High Ridge. And he'd stood by on the sidelines at more than one sweet-sixteen party, a visible deterrent in his blue uniform, window dressing designed to keep crashers out or to intimidate any unruly kids who might have had one too many chug-a-lugs from a hip flask. His job was to keep order. To keep things from getting ugly. Because ugliness didn't belong, not at places like this. Yes, he'd been on the outside of these houses plenty of times. But never inside.

"Anybody home?" he said tentatively. "Mrs. Bennett?"

"Lenny, get your butt up here." A voice echoed down the stairs. "There's no one here but me."

He shouldn't oughta talk like that, thought Lenny, not in a place like this. Probably no one even takes a crap in a place like this, thought Lenny further. He stepped carefully up the sweeping center staircase, placing one large shoe, then the other on the emerald green Oriental runner. His eyes drank in silk wallpaper, the prismed chandelier, and mahogany woodwork. He looked for the life of him like a stocky scarecrow who has just arrived at Oz.

"What took you so long?" said Forrest, half joking.

"Forrest?" said Lenny, looking around. He walked past room after room, his head swiveling from side to side as he went. In one room he noticed an unmade bed. Empty. It was here that he stopped. "Forrest?"

"Down here," said Forrest from the floor.

"What are you doing down there?"

"Hunting cockroaches," said Forrest.

"Oh, I don't think a place like this has cockroaches, Forrest."

"Will you kindly help me back to bed?" said Forrest, losing patience. He hated to appear infirm in front of one of his men. "It's my back. You know how it goes out every now and again."

"Oh," said Lenny, springing to motion. "Sure. Why didn't you say so?" He scooped Forrest up as if it were the most natural thing in the world, did it quickly and painlessly, with a deftness that belied his massive size. Then he pulled up a chair and looked at his former boss with concern. "So you want to know about the Peabody case," he said.

"Right," said Forrest with a nod of his head.

"Why?"

"Call it a hobby," said Forrest cryptically. "Something to pass the time while I lie here in my sickbed."

"Oh. I see." Lenny hesitated. "You wouldn't," he said carefully, "be getting on that jag again ..."

"Jag!" Forrest shot back. "Jag?"

"You know, Forrest. Trying to connect this case with those others you always used to talk about. Those ladies."

"Oh," said Forrest in a dismissive tone. "Those."

"Well?" said Lenny, not relenting.

"Lenny," said Forrest impulsively, "you were always on my side. You didn't think I was ... well, you know." He couldn't bring himself to say crazy.

"No," said Lenny quickly. "I never thought that."

"You weren't like the others."

"No." It was true. Lenny hadn't participated in the whispering campaign and hadn't joined in when the whispers turned to snickers either. In his heart he conceded that maybe, just maybe, the chief was right. But it was a big maybe, and he kept his thoughts to himself. To do otherwise, to grandstand on Chief Haggarty's behalf, would have been professional suicide. Fat lot of good it did me, thought Lenny now, deskbound as I am. But he said, "Look, Forrest, it caused you nothing but grief. You set up an impossible task for yourself. Some cases are unsolvable. You know it. I know it."

"I know no such thing."

"Sometimes I thought it was almost like you had a death wish. And now, Forrest, you got to let it go. You got to."

"Sure," said Forrest grimly.

"So tell me right now you're just concerned about Agnes. A nice lady. Everyone liked her. Tell me you're not trying to make this thing into more than it is."

"Okay. I'm not trying to make this thing into more than it is."

"Shit," said Lenny. "You're going off on this again. I can see it plain as day."

Forrest flashed a spontaneous, devilish smile.

"Damn," said Lenny. "I should get up and leave right now."

"But you won't," said Forrest. "Because you think I might be right."

"And I'm s'posed to break departmental rules, give you all kinds of confidential information, on the basis of some crazy long shot?"

"No," said Lenny simply. "On the basis of friendship."

"Oh, you slay me, Forrest. You really do."

"What the hell, Lenny. You're already up shit creek."

"You got a point," said Lenny morosely. "Okay. I'll tell you what we know. But don't get your hopes up. We don't know a whole lot."

Lenny plunged ahead. They would talk well into the afternoon . . .

"The last time anyone saw Agnes Peabody was at a plant sale at the Community Center. Run by the Owls, of which Agnes was a member." The Owls stood for Older Wiser Livelier Set, an organization of mostly retired people. At fifty-eight, Agnes Peabody would have been one of the youngest members. "People we questioned said she was more dressed up than usual. And more nervous too. Fidgety was the word one woman used. In retrospect it seems she may have been planning to meet someone, although her friends said she never dated. There was no love life for this woman, as far as we can ascertain. In any case, though, she did have dinner. Somewhere. There was lobster in her stomach. And wine."

"Are area restaurants being questioned?"

"Yeah. We're as far as Westport, and pushing out the radius. So far zilch."

"Go on."

"Anyhow, the lady leaves the plant sale about five-thirty. And no one saw her again. Not her neighbors. Not her friends. Her car turned up in the center of town." Lenny saw Forrest about to interrupt and answered his question before he asked it. "No prints on the car except hers. We checked."

"Okay."

"This morning the pathologist's report came in . . ."

"Who did the work, Bloomberg or Cuddahey?" Forrest prayed it was Bloomberg. Though the man had the personality of a phlegmatic flounder and could be maddeningly slow on occasion, Bloomberg was thorough. Cuddahey drank and his work was often slipshod. His sense of humor, which was decidedly juvenile, grated against Forrest, too. Cuddahey often joked to friends that, as a pathologist, he did not have to worry about malpractice insurance, which was a good thing since most of his patients were deadbeats about paying their bills. He was as funny as a crutch, Cuddahey was.

"Bloomberg was on vacation."

"Shit," said Forrest. "If I'd been in charge, I'd have hauled Bloomberg's ass back from vacation. That little nebbish never goes anywhere but the Catskills anyway."

"Cuddahey was sober," said Lenny. "That's the word I got. And he was willing to work on Sunday."

"He always was a prince."

"So anyway, the time of death is fixed between eleven and twelve on Saturday night. The victim died of strangulation."

"Wait a minute. What about the rock?"

"Whoever it was bashed her one, too, but the way Cuddahey figures it, that was for good measure. There wasn't much bleeding from the wound, and the bruises on her neck, the crushed larynx, the broken capillaries under the eyelids, too, indicate she was strangled first."

"Which may have been his immediate impulse if she was crying for help."

"Right. The rock, well, I dunno. You and I both know how long it takes to strangle someone. He mighta got impatient."

"True," said Forrest. He tried to keep his face an impassive mask. Tried not to show that this talk was, all of a sudden, bothering him. I must be losing my grip, he told himself. Getting soft in my old age. He tried to toughen up, but the fact that death by strangulation, clinical brain-dead death, takes a full six minutes combined with the fact that the murderer may have lost patience as he squeezed the life out of Agnes Peabody and bashed her head with a rock for good measure, yes, those facts bothered him a lot. But Forrest forced himself to go on, to proceed with these most intrusive questions. This is my last case, he told himself. My last case. "There was evidence," he said woodenly, "as I understand it, of rape."

"Right," said Lenny. "Anal and oral."

"Christ," said Forrest. But still he went on. "Did the rape happen before or after the time of death?"

"The way Cuddahey figures it, the anal occurred before death . . ."

Forrest experienced a wave of sadness. He had hoped that Agnes Peabody might have been spared some measure of humiliation, even if death had been the savior.

". . . There was tearing, evidence of blood—her blood. But no sperm."

Forrest could now picture the death of Agnes Peabody. It played in his mind like some crazy movie. She had, somehow, escaped her captor. Run from his car as it was parked in the very same clearing where he'd had his pickup. (Forrest hoped the guys in the department had the good sense to take tire impressions before every curiosity seeker flattened the location.) She ran. The murderer followed, catching up easily. *I won't hurt you*, he probably promised with his forearm braced across her throat from behind. *Not if you're quiet. Not if you just let me . . . just let me do . . .* And he did. But he hurt her. Intimately. Brutally. And she screamed. And he tightened his viselike grip on her throat, crushing her larynx. This alone would have killed her. But still unspent, he turned her around. Finished the job in her lifeless mouth as she watched with sightless eyes. Maybe it bothered him that she could feel no pain. So he bashed her head with the rock. Maybe that was it. And because she was already dead—because her throat was constricted—the autopsy would detect ejaculate in her mouth but none in her stomach.

"He did that," said Lenny mechanically. "Killed her in the midst of the first intrusion. Probably she screamed, but we both know even if she hadn't, odds are he would have killed her anyway, this kind of sicko. He breaks her larynx, flips her over, then strangles her again in the more conventional manner . . ."

The more conventional manner, Forrest's mind echoed. My God, what does this business do to us? "I get the picture," he snapped.

Lenny failed to read Forrest's display of outrage. They had become deadened to things like this a long time ago. "Cuddahey speculates the guy was angry. Real angry. That's why the rock. I mean, why kill someone twice?"

"Did you know her?" asked Forrest suddenly, almost angrily.

"Huh?" Lenny looked at Forrest carefully. "Forrest, are you all right?"

"Did you, Lenny? Did you know the woman? The victim. The person, Lenny. Agnes Peabody."

Confusion flickered across Lenny's face, followed quickly by anger of his own. "Yeah, Forrest. I knew her. Not well, but I did. And I don't want to think about it. You know why? Because thinking about it won't help. It won't help her, and it most certainly won't help me."

"Well, it will help me," said Forrest fiercely. "It'll help me get the son of a bitch that did this. Fuel for the fire, Lenny. Fuel for the fire."

"Forrest, I think you oughta take it easy."

"Tell me," demanded Forrest. "Tell me about Agnes Peabody."

"It was nothing, really. She put up those flower boxes along Main Street. You know, the ones attached to the fancy trash bins that are so fancy they don't even look like trash bins. She had a couple left over, so she came to the station. Asked could she put them on our windows. I couldn't believe it. No one seems to give a shit about cops around here. Most of us can't even afford to live in this town. They stick us in a leaky buncha cramped rooms under Town Hall, and they pray to God we don't uncover anything really wrong. Or, God forbid, embarrassing. That no one's little snotnosed darling is dealing coke or no upstanding Little League coach is forcing himself on his daughter ..."

Now it was Forrest's turn to be surprised, for this outpouring of bitterness was totally unlike Lenny. Lenny loved Raven's Wing. He'd said so more than once. He'd do anything to keep the town a safe place. But maybe for Lenny, like many of the other officers, it was a love-hate relationship. Police in Raven's Wing were a necessary evil, and they were treated as such. Many townspeople put policemen in the same general category as other servants—a category that lumped together teachers, garbage men, and household help. It was not a pleasant category to be in, and it could get to you. Sometimes.

"... and here's this nice lady wanting to put up flower boxes." He shook his head. "You know, Boyle said she couldn't do it."

"That sounds like Boyle." Boyle was the new chief and a real hardass. By-the-Book Boyle, that's what they called him.

"He said none of his people could take time from their busy schedules to water flowers. I said I could, and he gives me a look that says shut-the-hell-up. Agnes though, she straightened up right and proper and says she thinks the windows need flowers. They're so drab, she says. They're s'posed to be drab, Boyle says. It's parta the atmosphere. I'll water them, she says. Finally, the phone rings or someone comes in. Boyle gives up. Tells her to do whatever she wants. So she planted them." Lenny looked to the ceiling. "They'll probably die now."

"Oh go on, Pulaski. You know you'll be out there at midnight with a watering can in your hand."

"I guess," he laughed. "I can see it now: 'Cop Brought Up on Charges for Unauthorized Watering.' Ha, ha!"

"Yeah," smiled Forrest. He forced his mind back to the business at hand. "Okay. So that's Cuddahey. Did the report come in from the guys in the lab?"

"Wait," said Lenny. "I'm not finished with Cuddahey. There was one other thing. Probably nothing."

"What's that?"

"She had something in her hand. A piece of candy."

"Candy?"

"Yeah. You know, one of those candies ... A Life Saver. Yeah, that's what it was. A white Life Saver."

The irony of it was almost too much. "A white Life Saver?" Forrest repeated.

"Yeah. They hadda pry it out of her hand."

"Interesting," said Forrest, almost to himself.

"Yeah," said Lenny, already dismissing the bit of information.

"What flavor was it?"

"Flavor? Hell, I don't know."

"You mean no one checked?"

"Forrest, we didn't taste the damn thing."

"Well, it should be checked. Checked to see if it's winter-

171

green or spearmint or whatever the hell flavor Life Savers come in."

Lenny looked at Forrest like he was crazy.

"Listen, Lenny, it's a small thing. I'll grant you that. Not much. But who knows? Maybe some guy's walking around offering candies to little old ladies. I don't know. Maybe he sucks on them all the time. Only one brand. Only one flavor. It's remote, I know, but it's something. It shouldn't be ignored."

"Okay," said Lenny. "Okay." But he didn't sound convinced.

Lenny then proceeded to elaborate on the findings (or, more accurately, the lack thereof) by the men in the crime lab. Forrest listened with increasing frustration because so far that part of the investigation had produced nothing. According to textbook criminology, every perpetrator leaves something of himself at the scene of a crime. Sometimes it's an obvious thing. A button. A crushed-out cigarette. A footprint. More often it's not. There may be part of a smudged fingerprint. Fibers. A hair. But this time the crime was committed in the woods, which would have made laboratory analysis difficult under the best of circumstances. And the fact that Agnes Peabody was killed during a drizzle, which was followed by a downpour, made the search for clues all but hopeless.

They had five suspects. Five at least. But the possibility of determining which one had committed the murder was, Forrest knew, looking pretty remote.

21 By the time Mildred came home it was late afternoon. She had driven over to Danbury—to Six Cinemas—and the traffic on Route 7 was horrendous. It was a discouraging, but not wasted, trip. Discouraging because she wanted to believe Marcel Wintermute, and she still had no positive proof that she could do so. Not wasted because she'd been lucky enough to

find exactly the same ticket man who had been on duty the previous Saturday night. Yes, he said, *Rain Man* had been playing. It was still playing. It's a big picture, lady, they'll probably hold it over. But no, he couldn't remember any little guy with a beard buying a ticket to the seven o'clock show. Sorry, lady. It was crowded. Date night, and all that. Yeah, I'll think on it. Sure, I'll give you a call if I remember anything. Yeah, yeah, yeah.

At home she found a red Ford Escort parked in the driveway. For a moment she was afraid that maybe Clyde had shown up two hours early. Then she noted the New York plates and a Hertz sticker on the window. Mildred grabbed briefly at the thought that maybe it was Connor. Maybe he'd come after her. Tracked her down. But no, Connor would never rent an Escort.

"Mother." She heard the word the minute she opened the door. "I thought you'd never get here."

"Molly?" Mildred pulled the girl to her in a brief hug. Molly seemed even thinner than before, if that was possible. Her clothes swam on her—a billowing man-styled shirt, a baggy sweater vest, and shapeless corduroy pants cinched at the waist with—of all things—a piece of rope. "Goodness, Molly, this is a surprise. I hope nothing's wrong." She looked at her daughter with concern. "You look tired. Are you sick? There's a doctor here. An older man. Experienced. Competent. Maybe he should have a look at you."

"Mother, relax. There's nothing wrong with me. Can we talk?"

"Of course."

They went into the living room and sat in twin velvet wing chairs, their knees almost touching.

"Mother," Molly whispered conspiratorially, "there are strange people in this house." She rolled her eyes upward. "And I think they're screwing in Grandma's guest room."

"I'll thank you to clean up your trashy mouth, young lady." Mildred's worst suspicions were confirmed.

"All right, then. Copulating. Is that better? I think they're copulating in Grandma's guest room."

"Don't be smart with me," said Mildred. "What they choose to do is their business. They're free, white, and twenty-one."

Molly looked at Mildred as though she were crazy.

"Besides," Mildred went on, "they're not strange. They're my friends."

"Your friends?"

"Yes. What's so bizarre about that? Can't I have friends?"

"Yes. Of course. It's just that one of them looks like a gargoyle and the other—"

"They're my friends," repeated Mildred. "I expect you to speak charitably about them. And I expect you to mind your own business."

"Mother, you're acting very weird. I think you should come home."

"I am home."

"I mean to West Twelfth Street."

"I put the apartment on the market."

"You didn't!"

"I most certainly did."

"You didn't even ask Daddy. The apartment's half his."

"I'm sure *Daddy*"—Mildred spit out the word—"will manage just fine. He'll have no trouble finding a bed."

"Mother, he'll snap out of this."

"Well, I won't. Not anymore."

"He needs you."

"In a pig's eye." She said a silent thank-you to Forrest for giving her this most perfect expression.

"What's gotten into you, Mother? I've never heard you so bitter."

"Well, there's a lot you don't know, Molly. A lot you haven't known."

"Oh, right. I forgot. You always protected me. You did me that favor. Never told me anything. Never talked."

"That's enough."

"Even when Sam died—"

"Never mind Sam!"

"Even when Sam died," Molly pressed on, "you never talked about it."

"Not everyone likes to air their most intimate feelings, Molly. Not everyone likes to wave their grief like a flag for all the world to see."

"I'm not talking about all the world, Mother. I'm talking about family. After Sam died, you shut us out. Daddy and me both."

"Stop!"

"It's true. You sent me away."

"To a fine boarding school. Other girls would have given their eye teeth to attend such a school."

"Well, I wasn't other girls. I was me. And I hated Saint Margaret's with its cliques and field hockey and designer labels. I wanted to go to the Little Red Schoolhouse right in the Village."

"A Communist school."

"Oh sure. A bunch of flaming liberals—I believe those were your words. But the reason, the real reason, I didn't go there was that I could have walked there. I could have lived at home. And you wanted me away."

"That's not true," blurted Mildred. "Not entirely true, anyway. There were things going on, things with your father. I won't cast stones at him, not when he can't defend himself. But the marriage was falling apart, Molly. *I* was falling apart . . ."

"Why didn't you tell me?"

". . . and I simply couldn't cope with the marriage and you at the same time. Maybe that means I'm a weak person. If it does, I'm sorry. But I had to be sure you were all right. Safe. The city is dangerous. It's no place for a young girl."

"Oh come on, Mother. Already you sound like an out-of-towner. You lived there. The city's safe enough."

"It is not. Why just a few years ago a girl—a lovely girl—

was murdered behind the Metropolitan Museum. Strangled. By a nice boy. It's not safe. I didn't want you to die, too."

"Mother," Molly said not unkindly, "I wouldn't have killed myself."

"Hush!"

"Still you won't admit it."

"Molly, I'm still your mother and if you care for me at all, even a little bit, you'll stop with this line of nonsense. It's over. It's done. It was a long time ago. Please."

"Okay," said Molly wearily. "I didn't come here to fight. Honest. I came here because I saw Daddy."

"Oh?" Mildred tried to filter curiosity from her voice and failed.

"Yes. I had dinner with them at an Indian restaurant. The Tandoor."

"With them?"

"With Daddy and Heather. She's—"

"I know who she is. God, even her name sounds like a centerfold."

"She's okay."

"Spare me the sordid details."

"Anyway, Daddy didn't look so good. Pale and puffy. And you know how he hates Indian food. He always refused to eat it."

"With me he refused," sniffed Mildred.

"That's just it. I think he's knocking himself out to be what he thinks this Heather person wants him to be. You know, eating Indian food, staying up late—"

"Forgive me if I'm not sympathetic."

"—seeing arty movies, going to parties in drafty lofts, doing drugs—"

"No," gasped Mildred. "Not Connor."

"Well, maybe not drugs. But he did look a little desperate. And he kept asking about you."

"He did?"

"Yes. I could tell it drove Heather wild."

"Really?" This made Mildred feel wonderful.

"Yes. He wanted to know where you were. He followed me into the ladies' room and asked. Can you imagine?"

"No." Mildred almost laughed out loud. Not in a million years could she imagine Connor walking into a ladies' room —even dead drunk she could not imagine him doing it.

"Yes. He cornered me in one of the stalls. He closed the door so we'd have privacy. It was awful."

"You didn't tell him, did you? You promised."

"I know, I know. But I think you should come home. I think if you were there, he'd come back."

"Home is for sale. It's too late. He made his bed."

"I never thought you were vindictive, Mother. You could talk to him at least."

"I'm not ready, Molly."

"Then think about it. At least do that."

"All right."

"Well," said Molly lamely, "I've got to go." She waited for the dinner invitation she knew would be forthcoming.

"I'd invite you to dinner," said Mildred, "but I can't."

"You can't?"

"I have plans."

"Plans?"

Oh, why was Molly making this so impossible? Mildred tried to think of a word that wouldn't sound ridiculous and came up empty-handed. "I have a date."

"A date?"

"Will you kindly stop repeating me! Is that so amazing? A date? For me?"

"Yes. I mean no. It's just that, well, I thought, I hoped, that maybe you and Daddy . . ." Molly let the words hang. "I mean, you both had a lot going for you. Maybe you didn't know it, but you did. And now . . ." She looked on the verge of tears. ". . . well, if you're going to start sleeping around—"

"I am not, as you say, planning to sleep around."

"I hope not."

"Molly, I just need a little time. Time to think. Time for a little excitement. Time to feel desirable, a little bit at least. Can't you understand that?"

"I don't know." She looked at Mildred, looked at her in a new light. "I'll try, Mother."

They walked slowly to Molly's car. It wasn't until her daughter had turned on the ignition that she asked Mildred if she could stay in the apartment on Twelfth Street.

"But what about"—Mildred ransacked her memory for the name of Molly's live-in boyfriend—"Larry?"

"Barry, Mom. His name's Barry. We broke up. I need a place. Just for a while. Until I get myself together."

Mildred tried not to look jubilant. Larry, Barry, or whoever he was had departed. Hallelujah! "Of course," said Mildred quickly. "Use the apartment. Take as long as you like."

"I'll move out as soon as you sell it."

"Oh never mind that," said Mildred. "I'll take it off the market."

"You will?"

"Yes." She had just this minute decided.

"You think maybe you'll come back?"

"Let's just say I'm hedging my bets."

22 "You can't go out tonight."

Irene Purdy stood on the dry side of the shower curtain with hands as big as oven mitts on ample hips.

"I most certainly can," said Mildred through a haze of shampoo suds. "Can't a person have any privacy around here? Five bathrooms in this house, and you have to follow me into this one." She rinsed herself off, snapped open the curtain, reached for a large white towel and wrapped it around herself. "For heaven's sakes, even the dog is in here." Carefully she stepped over Winston, who lay deep in sleep on the bath mat.

Irene looked at Winston with concern. "The hot steam is good for his arthritis. Poor thing's joints are seizing up with the cool weather coming. But never mind that. What about the meeting we're s'posed to have tonight? You can't just sashay off. We all had an agreement." Irene hurled down the word like a gauntlet.

"Oh? Well, count me out."

"Why are you so testy all of a sudden?"

"I'm not testy." Mildred reached for a hand towel and concentrated on drying her hair. I'm nervous, that's what I am. Nervous as hell because I'm going on my first date in more than three decades. But she said none of this to Irene.

"You are too testy. I thought you had a nice visit with your daughter. But no, you've had a burr up your ass ever since you walked in the door."

"That," said Mildred hotly, "is a disgusting, crude thing to say. It matches your behavior."

Irene's eyes narrowed to slits. "What's that s'posed to mean?"

"It means," said Mildred, "I'm sure I don't know how we have time to investigate any murder. What with the way you and Forrest are carrying on."

"Carrying on?" For a moment—only a moment—Irene was mystified by Mildred's remark. "So that's it!" she exclaimed. "You're jealous! The green-eyed monster's gotcha."

"That's perfectly ridiculous."

"Well, you listen here, girl—"

"Don't call me girl."

"You listen here. You got a family, see? You got a daughter and you got a husband." She waved her hand, anticipating Mildred's protests. "Oh sure, maybe he's catting around a little. But lotsa husbands cat around."

"Hush!" cried Mildred. She pressed her hands to her ears.

"Still an' all, you got a husband. You got a family. Me an' Forrest, we don't got nobody. An' here you are holding a little human affection against us, acting like . . . like . . ."

"Like what?" said Mildred, daring her to finish.

"Like a shriveled up old bitch."

Mildred flinched. Then, without warning, she was overcome by tears. She, who hadn't cried in years. Beside herself, she turned her back on Irene and pressed her flushed face against the cool tile as silent tears streamed down her cheeks.

"Millie? Millie . . ." Irene was totally astounded by this reaction. She reached out a tentative finger and touched Mildred's shoulder. "I didn't mean it. Honest."

"No," sobbed Mildred. "You're right. Maybe I am jealous. Not of Forrest exactly, but of the closeness you two have. Of the c-c-c-companionship." She let fly a fresh torrent of tears.

"Aw honey . . . don't." Irene put a comforting arm around Mildred's waist. "There, there," she said. "You've got companionship. We're your friends, you know."

"I know."

"We'd do anything for you." Mildred's tears subsided. "Tell you what. Why don't you just get yourself dressed? I'll even help you fix your hair."

At the thought of Irene Purdy fixing her hair, Mildred pictured a disastrous result and almost started crying anew. "That's sweet of you, Irene, but I'll be fine. Really. I'm just a little edgy, what with this awful business about Agnes Peabody and Molly's unexpected visit and going out on a date."

"You'll do just fine," Irene assured her. "And don't you worry about the meeting either. Put it right out of your mind. We'll just hold up on things until you get back. There's a movie on TV tonight. Me an' Forrest an' Trevor, we'll order out for pizza. We'll save you a slice, too."

When Irene returned to Forrest's room, her report was short and to the point.

"She's got a date," said Irene. "An' I don't want to hear any yammering about it. The poor girl needs a little fun. We can hold our meeting later as well as sooner."

"Humph," grunted Forrest. He didn't like it, not at all. Women couldn't keep secrets worth a damn, and he was afraid Mildred might open up the circle.

23 As it turned out, Forrest was right. Mildred did break the circle. It happened for the simplest and the oldest of reasons. She was lonely. She wanted to have a good time. And she couldn't hold her liquor.

Clyde Thompson showed up at seven o'clock on the dot. She met him at the door, easing outside quickly so he wouldn't happen to overhear Irene and Forrest upstairs. It had grown chilly. A light drizzle was falling that verged on sleet. At the last moment, Mildred decided to wear her mink coat. It would keep her warm, she rationalized. Actually, she hoped it would give her confidence. Clyde gave her a peck on the cheek, hooked his arm in hers, and snapped open a large black push-button umbrella.

"You look lovely," he said.

"And you," said Mildred, "look dashing." It was true too. He wore a button-down shirt with a faint red stripe, a rep tie, a blue blazer with brass buttons, and charcoal gray slacks. His wing-tip shoes were freshly polished and his unruly blond curls combed for the moment into some semblance of order.

"For me this is pretty formal," he admitted. "But I sure don't do justice to your mink."

Oh dear, she thought. Maybe she'd overdressed. She didn't want him to feel inadequate. There was a perfectly good navy blue cloth coat hanging in the hall closet.

"I could go back," she said. "I could change coats."

"Don't change a thing," he said, smiling. "I'm proud to be seen with you."

"Oh." She stood a little taller, leaned ever so slightly closer to him under the umbrella. Proud. He said he was proud. Of her.

Clyde took her to the Elms Inn, a fine gourmet restaurant in town. The inn was an elegant establishment consisting of a warren of small, intimate rooms with low ceilings supported by heavy oak crossbeams. An expressionless waiter led them to a room that they could have to themselves. He seated them by the window, snapped open starched pink napkins, and placed the napkins in their laps. He lit a small pink candle in the center of the table.

"Would madam care for a cocktail?"

"I think madam would," said Clyde. "What'll it be, Mildred?"

A Shirley Temple, she almost blurted. She was getting intoxicated on all this attention alone. It made her feel giddy and relaxed. As if she could just float along and leave everything to Clyde. It had been so long since she'd felt like that. Connor and Molly seemed very far away.

"An extra dry martini with a twist," she said.

"Make it two."

By the second martini, Mildred had told Clyde all about Connor and Molly and Sam. Yes, even Sam. The words seemed to fly from her mouth, unbidden and unconsidered. It was as though she'd popped open the little wire door on a cage full of parakeets.

"I had reservations about that car," she said. "He had always been somewhat reckless. Accident prone. But he was past the age when you could give him a Tonka truck and expect him to play in the sandbox."

"Stop blaming yourself, Mildred. Boys are all crazy. They think they're immortal. Indestructible. Most of them grow up in spite of it. A few, sad to say, don't."

"I'm glad you did, Clyde." Impulsively, she reached across the linen tablecloth and gave his hand a squeeze.

"Yeah," he laughed. "I had some close calls of my own. I was the one who parachuted onto the forty yard line during the homecoming game. Who would have thought I'd grow up to be a boring old widower?"

"You are not boring!"

"Yes I am, Mildred. I don't try to kid myself. The other day I found myself in the pharmacy buying a can of Metamucil. Me! It seems like only yesterday I was a kid sneaking in there to filch Trojans. And last week, well, last week I ran into this kid on the sidewalk. I was jogging, trying to lose some of the paunch." Clyde patted his stomach. "He had a skateboard, and I offered him a quarter if he'd let me ride it. The kid thought I was nuts, but I guess he knew a good deal when he saw one."

"You didn't!"

"I most certainly did. Damn near broke my leg, too."

"Oh, Clyde!"

"I just don't know what's got into me. Sure, I live a nice comfortable life in a town where everyone knows me. It's sort of a family, I suppose. But at night when I finally go home, no one's there saying 'How was your day?' It gets to me sometimes. I sit in front of the tube with my drink and my TV dinner, and it gets to me. Kate and Allie are my girlfriends." He laughed, but it sounded forced. He looked Mildred full in the face and spoke without thinking. "Oh Mildred, why did I ever let you get away?"

Mildred was caught so off guard she almost spit out her drink. She liked him very much. And she too was lonely. But it was going so fast. We must, she thought in a kind of knee-jerk reaction, maintain perspective. Yes. Perspective.

"We were kids, Clyde. Children."

"Not so young," he said wistfully. "You remember the time out on the lake?"

"Hush," she whispered, though no one could hear. She had lost her virginity out on the lake. On an August night between her junior and senior years. They had swum out to the float. The air was chilly against her scratchy one-piece swimsuit. The float rocked gently. She could hear the soothing lap-lap of the water against the underside. She could see stars overhead, millions of them strewn across the sky, scattered to infinity. And she could see Clyde, his face silhouetted against that backdrop of stars. Feel him, too—yes, she could feel him. She wanted to touch him, wanted him to touch her. And her breath came in small gasps, her heart beat in tempo with the lap-lap of the water. Louder and louder in her ears, mingling with his breathless words of tenderness. His touch. His kiss.

"Stop," she said.

"Admit it. You remember."

"How could I ever forget?"

"We could have a nice life, Mildred."

The words were so soft she almost missed them. She looked at him, not trusting her ears.

"I mean," he fumbled, "I know there's not much in the way of excitement . . . life in a small town . . . I suppose it would seem provincial after Manhattan."

"Oh Clyde . . ."

He ran a big hand through graying blond hair. "I'm not very good at this, Mildred." He straightened up, trying for the life of him to remember words that had been so carefully rehearsed in front of his bedroom mirror. "I've been thinking about it. It would be nice to travel. I've always wanted to see the Orient. And ball games, we could go to ball games."

"Ball games?" she repeated in amazement.

"The Yankees. I'm a Yankees fan, remember?"

"Yes," she said.

"And we could go out to dinner"—he waved his arms—"like we're doing now. And rent videos and curl up on the couch and watch them. And read the Sunday paper in bed and plant bulbs in the spring." He stopped. "You know. Do the things married people do."

Married people, thought Mildred. Even after all my years with Connor I'm still not sure what married people do.

"I miss those things, Mildred. I miss them all. And I miss you, too."

She stared into the flame of the flickering candle and listened to his proposal, for that is surely what it was.

"Mildred?" he said at last. "Mildred?"

"Clyde ..." She took a deep breath. "I left my husband only last week."

"But—"

"Just seven—no, six—days ago." Then she said something else. "You could do better than me."

"Oh Mildred," he protested. "Don't ever say that. I couldn't do better in a million years. You're the best."

"I'm still shell-shocked, Clyde. I need time to sort things out. Time to stand on my own two feet." She looked at him and saw the disappointment on his face. "If you were to say these things to me in six months or a year ... if you still felt the same way ... well, I'd be in a better condition to listen."

"I see," he said sadly. "Six months. A year. It seems so far away."

"I hope you do see."

"I hope you don't think I'm foolish."

"No, Clyde. I'm flattered. More than flattered."

"Promise me you'll think about it at least."

"I promise," she said. "But not so soon."

The waiter interrupted, bringing their appetizers and breaking the mood. He opened the wine, poured, and waited for Clyde to sip. Clyde nodded his approval. The waiter poured for both of them, then disappeared.

The wine was delicious—a blush wine from California, not exactly a white and not exactly a rosé, just the barest tinge of pink.

"This is lovely," said Mildred.

"I'm glad you like the wine."

"No. I mean everything. Everything is lovely."

"I'm glad. I wanted tonight to be special."

They ate in silence for some moments. The waiter whisked away appetizer plates and replaced them with entrées. Mildred had ordered boneless breast of duck and Clyde veal piccata. The waiter poured Mildred another glass of wine. She told herself to slow down, to pace herself. She hadn't had much to eat all day, and right now the martinis and the wine had only a few lonely shrimps from her appetizer for company. But she was having such a good time that she ignored herself. The prospect of a hangover in the morning seemed a small price to pay.

"How long are you staying in Raven's Wing?" asked Clyde tentatively.

"It depends," said Mildred mysteriously. She took yet another sip, unaware that her face was starting to match the color of the blush wine. The room seemed very cozy. Clyde seemed so nice. Everything was wonderful.

"Depends on what?" He looked at her keenly. "Remember, you said six months or a year. You owe me that now."

"Oh you!" she laughed. She felt as though her smile were a mile wide. She smiled as she'd never smiled before. He was such a cutie, Clyde was. She felt like leaning over the table and kissing him on the lips, a long, lingering, meaningful kiss. Fortunately she had the presence of mind to realize that the candle would singe her breasts if she acted on this impulse. So she just sat there, smiling.

"I hope it depends on me, because I intend to do my best to keep you here."

Mildred was enjoying herself immensely. "Well," she said gaily, "it depends on you, but I also have some business to attend to." The formal words came out slightly slurred, but Mildred didn't notice.

"Business?"

186

"Can you keep a secret, Clyde?" She looked at him with the most serious expression she could muster.

"Yes," he chuckled. "Anything you tell me is off the record."

"Swear."

"I swear."

"Okay." She leaned forward conspiratorially. Her face was bathed in candlelight. If she could have seen herself, she would have seen a woman who was very happy, very attractive, and very tipsy.

And then she told him, told him everything. Told him about Forrest. About Trevor. About Irene. She told him about Hermine Goldman and the five letters and her visit to Marcel Wintermute. All of it came tumbling out.

"Good God." Clyde was stunned.

"You swore," she said. "You promised you'd keep a secret."

"Yes," he said, "yes. Just let me get this straight. You've got Forrest Haggarty stashed in your house?"

"Well, not stashed exactly. He's just recuperating for a while." She hiccuped on "recuperating," making it "re-coooop!-erating."

"Mildred, his kids are frantic. They've been turning this town upside down looking for him."

"Trevor told them Forrest went fishing."

"Yes, and Scott Haggarty—Forrest's oldest boy—doesn't believe it. He wants his father home now. He even asked me to run a story in the paper, some kind of missing persons report."

"He wants," corrected Mildred, "to put his father in a home. That's what he wants." She stopped drinking then. She stopped eating too. Suddenly she felt cold sober.

"Well, Haggarty has been a little odd these past few years. Senile, some say."

"He is not odd! He's just a man with a mission."

"A mission," repeated Clyde in amazement, shaking his head.

"You're making fun of this whole thing," blurted Mildred. Tears sprang to her eyes.

"No," he protested quickly. "Honestly, Mildred, I'm not making fun. I've always sympathized with Haggarty, felt the town gave him a raw deal. And Dr. Bradford . . ." His face softened. "Well, anyone can tell you that I'm especially fond of Dr. Bradford. He was my mother's doctor, Paula's too, and he saw me through some rough times."

Clyde remembered Trevor Bradford's late night phone calls—calls others never would have made at such ungodly hours. But Trevor knew better. "Staring into the fireplace, Clyde?" he'd say without preamble. "Want some company?" Mostly Clyde said no. "No thanks, Trevor. Go to bed. Don't worry about me, I'm fine." But sometimes, just sometimes, he'd say yes. Then Trevor would come over and the two of them would wait out the night together. They talked about everything in general and nothing in particular and never, never, about death and dying. Trevor called it "waiting for the sunrise."

"I respect his opinion, Mildred, and if Dr. Bradford thinks there's something to this, then maybe there is."

Mildred exhaled a sigh of relief.

Clyde's face clouded as he seemed to consider the possibility that Mildred and her friends might indeed be on to something. "I'm frightened for you, Mildred."

"Oh . . ." she scoffed.

"I mean it." He grabbed her hand, almost spilling his wine in the process. "Jesus, Mildred. You're talking about a murder here. Maybe more than one."

"Well, yes," she admitted.

"And those men you're after—the ones who wrote the letters—they could hurt you. They're powerful people, Mildred. They run this town."

"So do you," she said, and at that very moment an idea came to her.

"Not like them, not by a long shot."

"Oh, but you do," she protested. "Don't you see? You own the newspaper—"

"Yes . . ."

"—and so you could help us—"

"I don't see how—"

"—by keeping copies of everything. The letters. The old files. Our reports—we each write daily reports. Forrest makes us."

"I don't see how that will help."

"Because," she said patiently, "they won't dare do anything if they know the media would become involved."

"Maybe," he said reluctantly. "You might have a point there."

"So you'll help us?"

He looked at her. "Oh, all right. How can I refuse you? I'll help as much as I can. Lord knows, I don't want you in this alone."

Mildred raised her glass in a triumphant toast. Somehow she would explain to the others. She was sure they'd see the logic to her thinking.

"Don't celebrate yet," cautioned Clyde. "I don't want to scare you, Mildred, but there are a couple of other things you should consider."

"Like what?"

"Like maybe you're dealing with a madman. You said so yourself. And if he's crazy, it won't worry him a whit that the media might tell his story. He might *want* it to be told. Did you ever think of that?"

"No," she admitted.

"And another thing. What if it's none of the five who wrote the letters? Maybe it's someone else entirely. Or someone related to one of the five. You yourself said Jimmy Perkins had a motive."

"I know," she said. "But we've got to start somewhere, don't we?"

"Yes," he said grimly. "I guess we do."

24 Forrest, Irene, and Trevor passed the time that evening watching *The African Queen*, followed by the eleven o'clock news.

"And in Raven's Wing, Connecticut," a boyish newscaster was saying, "police report no new leads in the death of Agnes Peabody last weekend."

"No new leads," snorted Forrest. "Ha!"

"In a statement to the press today, Chief Richard Boyle speculated that the murder may have been committed by a vagrant or hitchhiker passing through the small New England town . . ."

"Speculation," sneered Forrest. "That's all Boyle was ever good for."

The program segued from the newscaster to footage of Main Street. "Raven's Wing, Connecticut, is considered one of the most picturesque towns in New England, and many commercials have been filmed on Main Street here . . ."

"I can't believe it," said Trevor. "Even under these macabre circumstances Ripley Crane gets a plug in for the Chamber of Commerce."

"Turning a lemon into lemonade," said Irene. "Ripley always was good at that." She got up from the rocker and flipped off the set. "I can't stand it."

"Where the devil is Mildred anyway?" fumed Forrest.

"She's a grown woman," said Irene, "without a curfew."

"Well, I don't like it."

"Who's her escort?" asked Trevor.

"Clyde Thompson," replied Irene.

"Really?" said Trevor, looking both surprised and pleased. "Clyde Thompson?" He paused, considering the match. "Well, that's wonderful. They used to date back in high school, as I recall. And Paula's been dead for going on two years."

"He took it awful hard, Clyde did," said Forrest.

"Terrible," agreed Trevor. "Held it all inside, but I could see it eating away at him."

"Well, he's a fine fellow," said Irene. "Not bad-looking neither."

"Yep," agreed Forrest with a self-satisfied smile. "Clyde turned out just fine. Course, I take part of the credit for that."

"Listen to him, will you!" exclaimed Irene. "He takes part of the credit! And how, Forrest Haggarty, can you take credit for Clyde Thompson? It's not like he's your boy or nothing."

Trevor fumbled with his pipe and dropped it to the floor, spilling loose tobacco on the braided rug. He knelt down and silently swept threads of tobacco up with his hands.

"Well, well," said Forrest smugly, "you two certainly have short memories."

"I seem to remember something," said Trevor as he stood up. He now proceeded to gather empty soda cans and put them into a paper sack. "Clyde's father ... Macon, wasn't that his name?"

"Yep," said Forrest.

"Yes. Macon Thompson died some years ago, as I recall. Clyde must have been in high school at the time."

"It was a nasty business," said Forrest. "A real nasty business."

"What happened?" said Irene, leaning forward in her chair and planting both elbows on her knees.

"God, Reenie, you musta been spending too much time with the sheep. Everyone in town was talking about it."

"I'm not one for idle gossip," sniffed Irene.

"Oh pardon me," said Forrest in mock apology. "So I guess we better not discuss it now, it being idle gossip and all that."

"Forrest, if you know what's good for you later, you'll tell and you'll tell quick." She arched an eyebrow seductively.

"Okay, okay," said Forrest, smiling. "I'll tell. But it ends here, you understand?"

"Who we gonna tell, Forrest?" said Irene. "Ain't no one we could tell even if we wanted to."

"Okay. Well, you remember Clyde's mother—Endora was her name."

"Yes," said Trevor gravely. "Endora was my patient. Suffered from terrible migraines. I did what I could for her, but I couldn't do much. I always thought they were more psychologically than physically based. She never did fit in this town. Always held folks at arm's length. Hardly had any friends."

It was true. In a town where everyone (even those who could afford otherwise) wore plaid and tweed, Endora Thompson wore velvet and silk. She served lemonade in cut glass goblets even to the handyman and carried a parasol in summer to shield her ash blond hair from the sun's burning rays. People might have snickered at such airs in anyone else, but instinctively they seemed to know that Endora was a lady.

No one knew Endora Thompson well, so no one knew the unplumbed depths of her loneliness, a loneliness Endora herself was unaware of. And that may well be the most dangerous kind of loneliness of all. At least in this case it was.

If you had asked Endora if she was happy in her marriage to Macon, she would have said yes without hesitation. And she wouldn't have been lying because Endora Thompson was a woman who never expected much in the way of happiness or anything else. She married Macon when she was very young. Twenty years her senior—more years older than she had lived on the face of the earth—Macon was her total opposite. Macon was gregarious (some said coarse), he was given to expansive gestures, and he was newly rich. Macon had amassed an unexpected fortune when he invented a special valve that had particular application in the petroleum industry. The more money he made, the more confident (some said obnoxious) he became. Where Endora was quiet, Macon was loud. Where Endora practiced the art of understatement, Macon was prone to exaggeration. Where Endora pursed her lips if she was annoyed (which was hardly ever), Macon displayed explosive fits of temper (on a regular basis).

They might have grown old together, living in the old stone house on Whipstick Road, living lives on separate planes that intersected only at breakfast when Macon chose to look up from his *Wall Street Journal* or at night when they passed each other in the hallway on their separate ways to separate rooms. Yes, they might have settled for such an existence. Many people do.

But one day Endora Thompson took a lover—a person, like herself, of breeding, character, and sensitivity.

This clandestine relationship, too, might have gone on for some time. Endora and her lover were very careful. They met in the carriage house apartment on the Thompson property only when Macon was away on one of his frequent trips to Texas. The carriage house was secluded, virtually hidden behind overgrown hemlocks. Uninhabitable, Macon believed. Macon didn't know that Endora had fixed the place up. She, who never so much as lifted a finger in the main house, scrubbed and cleaned and scoured until her knuckles were raw. She sewed lace curtains and patched the leaky roof herself and beat the braided rug with a tennis racquet. She was a woman possessed, a woman possessed by the joy of intimacy, however fleeting, with another kindred spirit. But if you're thinking that the carriage house was a den of heavy breathing and sweaty sheets, think again. Endora and her lover spent more time reading Elizabeth Barrett Browning aloud than making love, though they indulged in that, too, on occasion.

This almost innocent relationship might indeed have gone undetected had Macon not come home unexpectedly from one of his trips. Had Macon not spied a strange car in the side driveway (a tragically careless error). Had Macon not stumbled in on the couple while they were, well, most certainly not reading poetry.

"I came on the scene," remembered Forrest, "an' there's Macon on the floor lying in a pool of blood, dead as a doornail."

"You don't say!" exclaimed Irene.

"I most certainly do say. Clyde was there, too. All shook up. She waited till the boy came home from school and had him call me."

Trevor shook his head. "It must have been awful for him. What happened exactly?"

"As near as I could tell, Macon came upon the couple, spied them through the window. Then he went to get his gun. It was his shotgun, mind you. He and the lover struggled. Endora tried to intervene. The gun went off, and it was Macon who got the blast, not the boyfriend. The guy panicked and took off. Or maybe Endora told him to take off. Either way, he was gone."

"Who was it?" asked Irene.

"Who was who?"

"The guy! The lover! The one who took off!"

"Dunno," said Forrest shortly. "Endora never told me."

"You don't know?" boomed Irene. "Course you know! You gotta know! You can't tell us a story like that and leave us hanging."

"I sure as hell can," said Forrest firmly. "And I did. I left the whole damned town hanging."

"I remember gossip," said Trevor. "Something about an accident up at the Thompson place. But never anything official."

"Oh, there was an official report," said Forrest. "A report about an accidental shooting. I wrote it up right an' proper. But I saw to it there was no grand jury and no publicity neither."

"And how did you manage that?" asked Irene. "Everything ends up in The Blotter." This was true. The *Raven's Wing Gazette* printed all police business in The Police Blotter column. It was standard practice. Anything and everything that was police business, no matter how sensitive, no matter how embarrassing, no matter how influential the people involved, went into The Blotter. The People Had a Right to Know, the editor said.

Forrest smiled knowingly. "I put a little pressure on the editor. It was Matt Ransom back then. His son got into a minor scrape 'round about that time, and we made a deal, him and me."

"You let Matt's son off?" said Irene.

"I did," said Forrest flatly. "And I'd do it again. It was important. Endora Thompson was a nice lady who married a lout and got caught up in tragedy. Here she was sayin' she wanted to die. She was on the edge, I tell you, the very edge. The last thing she needed was an ugly newspaper story. So I hushed things up. I told her plain and simple that one life might be over and there's no use to adding a second to the list. Told her to take care of her boy. Told her Clyde needed her. Told her to put this behind her and build a new life."

"And did she?" asked Irene. "Build a new life?"

But Irene never got her answer. Trevor interrupted abruptly. "Here's Mildred now," he said.

25 Noah Lockwood knelt before an old moldering trunk in his attic. His eyesight wasn't as good as it had once been, and the feeble 40-watt bulb hanging from the frayed cord overhead didn't provide much illumination. Deftly he inserted a screwdriver in the corroded brass lock and snapped it open with one flick of his wrist.

Sentimental, he muttered to himself. I'm getting sentimental in my old age. He reminded himself that late fifties wasn't old age. He reminded himself, too, that he, above all others, had never been influenced by sentiment.

Scared, an unbidden voice within him hissed, *That's what you are. Scared. Scared shitless, Noah Lockwood, and you know it.*

"Shut up!" he muttered aloud this time, startling himself in the process.

He eased open the trunk, propped the lid against the planked, nail-studded wall, and reached inside. It was filled with women's clothing—soft dresses, lacy blouses, filmy nightgowns. His hands lingered momentarily, caressing the soothing fabrics. Remembering. Then inwardly he seemed to shake himself. Roughly he pushed the delicate garments aside. He reached down deeper, down through folds of women's underthings and ropes of fake pearls. Groping now, he reached all the way into a corner of the trunk and grasped a small bundle.

Noah Lockwood withdrew a packet of papers bound with dried raggedy red rubber bands. They broke easily at his touch. He rearranged himself, sitting Indian-style in that cobwebbed room, hunched over these memories. With another deft flick of the wrist, he fanned the papers out like a deck of cards in one hand. Letters, that's what some of them looked like. These he ignored. From their midst he plucked a photograph. Then another. And another. Soon he had a neat little pile of ten, maybe fifteen, photographs nested in his lap.

Carefully and precisely, Noah Lockwood arranged photos of varying dimension, shape, and hue on the splintery floor before him. Except for his age, the slump of his shoulders, and the obvious grayness of his hair, he might have been a child lost in a game of solitaire. He picked up the flashlight at his side and directed the beam to the faces in the photo. Noah stared bleakly into these faces, faces that mirrored his own. Faces progressing from infancy to boyhood to adolescence and beyond. Faces that looked innocent but weren't. He looked at these reflections of himself and tried to understand. Tried not to panic, too.

My fault, he told himself bitterly. It's all my fault.

26 Quietly, Mildred eased inside the front door, leaving Clyde on the porch for the moment.

"Have a nice time?" said Irene suddenly into Mildred's ear.

"My God," gasped Mildred, "you gave me a start. What are you doing down here? Waiting up? You're worse than my mother."

"We've all been waiting up," said Irene without apology. "So did you have a nice time?"

"Yes," said Mildred. "As a matter of fact I did. We went to dinner at the inn. It was lovely."

"You look a little flushed."

"I'm fine, Irene."

"Did he kiss you or what?"

"Irene!"

"Well, did he?" The woman was relentless.

"Irene," said Mildred evenly through clenched teeth, "I'll thank you to kindly keep your voice down. Clyde is right outside."

"What?" barked Irene.

"I told him, Irene."

"You told him?" Irene's eyes narrowed suspiciously. "Told him what?"

"About us. About the letters. About all of it."

"Jeesum!" cried Irene. "Oh, Jeesum! Now you've really gone and done it, Millie." Irene flew upstairs with Mildred in her wake.

"She told!" Irene cried, careening into Forrest's room.

"Calm down, Irene," said Trevor, "or I'll have two patients on my hands."

"Told what?" asked Forrest.

"About everything," Irene wailed. "Just couldn't keep her

mouth shut. A glass of wine and some sweet talk and it all comes tumbling out. Oh Millie, I'm so mad I could just spit!"

"Hold on, Irene," said Trevor. "Mildred's not the only one who spilled any beans. You admitted that you told Ripley Crane about the other letter writers, remember?"

"Aha!" cried Mildred.

"I didn't see the harm," said Irene defensively.

"Perhaps there isn't any," said Trevor.

"Right," Forrest chimed in. "It's possible that they all might just get together and help us flush out the murderer. Then again they might turn on one another, which wouldn't be so bad, either."

"Yeah," said Irene, as if she'd planned it that way all along.

"Now Mildred," said Forrest, fixing his eye on her, "who did you tell and what did you tell?"

"Clyde," she said miserably. "But I had a reason. A perfectly logical, sensible, rational reason."

"Let's hear it," sighed Trevor.

Mildred explained the value of having someone from the media on their side. She told them to consider Clyde as insurance. Insurance against unexpected accidents.

"She has a point, Forrest," said Trevor.

"You're just saying that 'cause you've always been partial to Clyde Thompson," Forrest shot back.

"Come on, Forrest, you know it's not that. Besides, you've looked out for him, too. You told us so yourself."

"Well, maybe ..." Forrest stared gloomily at the ceiling. "So where is Clyde now?" he asked finally.

"On the porch," said Mildred. "Waiting to join our meeting."

"Think we oughta let him?" Forrest asked no one in particular.

"I don't see why not," said Irene, "*now*."

So it was that Clyde Thompson joined the group in their search for Agnes Peabody's killer. Except for Mildred, he was younger than the rest. He had more stamina, and he had more clout. They knew it, too, and for this reason they accepted him.

They sat, each in his or her own particular place, drinking coffee laced with honey (or, in Forrest's case, bourbon) from steaming mugs. Irene spoke up first, forgetting all about her annoyance with Mildred. She told of her meeting with Ripley Crane. Told how at first she'd been sure he was the one since he'd killed his own wife.

"I beg your pardon?" said Trevor, thinking maybe his hearing was going.

Irene recounted her conversation with Huey Crane. She did so with gusto, first playing the part of Huey, then playing the part of herself. She gestured wildly, moving back and forth beween he-saids and I-saids. When she was finished, she stood there, quiet and regal, as though waiting for applause.

"Jesus," muttered Forrest. "He pulled the plug. Pulled it on his own wife."

"That's what I thought, too," said Irene slyly. "Until I talked to Ripley."

"Huh?" said Forrest.

Irene then recounted her conversation with Ripley. She told how, according to the esteemed first selectman, Sally Crane had begged him to kill her. "*Begged* him," said Irene. "Can you believe it? And he said he couldn't do it. Just plain couldn't. But Huey, well, he said Huey could do it. And did, too."

"Son blames father and father blames son," mused Mildred.

"Well, somebody sure killed her," said Clyde. "What do you think, Forrest? You did the investigation."

"Huey's prints were on the plug," said Forrest simply. "I checked as a matter of course. I questioned the boy—gently mind you, but thoroughly—and was satisfied that it happened the way they said it did. What about you, Trevor? You were Sally's doctor."

"I'm sorry, Forrest," said Trevor, "but the doctor-patient relationship is confidential."

"Oh for pity sake, Trevor," Mildred put in, "the woman is dead. Confidentiality can't help her now."

Trevor looked torn, but forced himself to respond. "Oh all right," he sighed. "Yes, she spoke to me about wanting to die. People in helpless situations often feel that way. But helpless isn't hopeless. They feel that way for a time, and then they come to grips with it. They deal with it. Don't ask me how they do, but it happens. I thought Sally was dealing with it. She was managing, despite her infirmity, to have a loving relationship with her children."

"Do you think Huey could have killed her?" asked Irene. "Intentionally, I mean."

"I don't know," said Trevor. "But I'll tell you one thing. Huey was always a troubled boy. And he hated his father. A child goes through something like that, and invariably he looks for someone to blame. Most children blame themselves, which is tragic. But Huey never did. He always blamed his father."

"What are you getting at?" asked Clyde.

"What I'm getting at is that Huey is unpredictable. Maybe even dangerous. Especially to his father. On more than one occasion I told Ripley to seek help for Huey, but I don't think he ever did. And I told him another thing."

"What's that?" said Mildred.

"I told him it was a potentially explosive situation to live with Huey. When the boy got bigger, I told Ripley that. I thought it was my duty."

"What'd he say?" asked Forrest.

"He laughed at me," said Trevor grimly. "He just plain laughed."

"Ugh," shuddered Mildred. "It gives me chills."

"So what you're saying," Irene put in, "is we got two suspects where we had one before."

"In a way," said Trevor.

"Right," agreed Forrest in frustration. "Because if Huey hates his father so much . . ." He let the words dangle.

". . . he'd do anything to get even," finished Clyde.

"Even set him up for murder," said Mildred.

"Right," confirmed Forrest.

"Well," said Trevor wearily, "I'm afraid I'm not going to make things any easier."

"Oh?" said Mildred. "Why is that?"

"Because I've got another prime candidate. That's why."

"Not Spencer McCloud?" gasped Irene.

"The very same."

"But Spencer was always such a gentleman," protested Mildred.

Trevor emitted a quiet sound of disparagement and then proceeded to describe Spencer McCloud's perverted sexual proclivities to his shocked friends. Mildred looked as though she might faint. Irene clicked her dentures and shook her head. Clyde slumped back in his chair. And Forrest Haggarty simply said, "Good God. What are we getting into here?"

None of them thought it would be like this.

"It's sorta like lifting up a rock and finding creepy crawly things underneath," said Irene.

No one argued with this summation.

Mildred said she was glad about one thing: several suspects seemed decidedly more probable than Marcel Wintermute. She couldn't help it—she felt protective toward Marcel.

"Don't write off Marcel so quickly," said Forrest. "He doesn't have an alibi. And he always was a strange bird. As far as the notion of him getting married, well, that's a joke and a half."

"You wouldn't think so if you'd been there," insisted Mildred. "Not if you'd heard him."

"That sure would upset Jimmy Perkins," said Irene absentmindedly. "Seein' his gravy train derail like that."

Forrest made notes as Mildred, Irene, and Trevor told their stories. He asked several questions. And he was impressed with Clyde's questions. But he remained silent about

Lenny Pulaski's visit. Why bother the women with more gory details? he reasoned. Besides, he was the professional here. He would tie all the threads together. And Forrest T. Haggarty would catch the killer. He had waited too long to let the opportunity slip by.

"I move we press on," said Forrest, giving his friends some semblance of choice in the matter.

"And I second the motion," said Mildred.

"Me too," put in Irene.

"Me three," said Trevor.

"What am I supposed to do?" said Clyde.

"The best thing you can do," instructed Forrest, "is to remain uninvolved for the time being. And for God's sake don't go contacting any suspects. You're our wild card. Our ace. Just take everything in. Keep the files in a safe place. And take these letters, too." He handed the packet to Clyde.

"It's the story of a lifetime," admitted Clyde, not masking his enthusiasm.

"You bet it is," said Trevor.

So it was agreed that Irene would confront Loomis Brewster. Trevor would try to get to Leslie McCloud again, a prospect he did not find wholly disagreeable. And Mildred would see Noah Lockwood.

As they said their good nights, Forrest smiled and told the others to sleep well. He was in fine spirits. The hunt was rejuvenating him, he could feel it. Already a plan had taken shape in his mind. A plan of action for tomorrow. Because one thing he knew for sure: he did not intend to spend the day flat on his back while the others solved this case. No sir. It would be Forrest T. Haggarty who made the next move.

27 Forrest opened one eye and spied his breakfast tray at face level. God, Irene would surely kill him with this food. Her forte was clearly bedroom and not culinary arts. He surveyed dry wheat toast, a small pot of raspberry jam, lukewarm cream of wheat, black coffee, and some blackened mess that looked like dead tadpoles. Stewed prunes.

"Reenie, I told you I can't abide prunes."

"You need them, Forrest. To keep you regular." She tiptoed around in the dimness of early morning light as she gathered her garments. To Forrest she didn't look like a hippo doing the ballet. She looked beautiful.

"No one's more regular than me."

"I'm not gonna argue with you. You've been grousing for days about how bound up you are," she whispered. "An' keep your voice down. It's early yet. Millie's still sleeping." She glanced in the direction of the door. "I hope she doesn't sleep all day."

"You're the one who said she deserved a little fun."

"I know, I know. I just never expected her to have so much fun. She'll probably be conked out most of the morning."

Forrest agreed and tried not to look too happy about it. Things were working out exactly as he'd hoped.

"Me," said Irene, "I'm gonna pay a visit on Mr. Loomis Brewster bright and early. Catch him before he goes to work. You know, now that I'm gettin' the hang of this investigating business, I'm kinda taking to it."

"That's nice, Reenie. You just run along."

She looked at him askance. "If I didn't know better, Forrest Haggarty, I'd swear you were trying to get rid of me."

"Oh no, Reenie." He tried to laugh. To prove his point, he grabbed for her and pulled her down on the bed.

"Well," she said into the crook of his neck, "every other morning I had to pry myself away. You couldn't bear to let me go."

"I was afraid you might not come back," he said, surprising himself with this bit of truth.

"Oh Forrest . . ." She gave him a squeeze. "Now that I got you, I'm not gonna let you go."

Forrest lay back into the pillows and stared at faint spiderweb cracks in the ceiling. If Irene would leave now—while Mildred slept late—he might have a chance to make his way to Noah Lockwood's. At this minute, frustration gnawed at his insides. He felt useless lying here, a prisoner in his own body.

"You gonna be all right?" said Irene, her face etched with concern.

"Oh sure, Reenie." He waved her away with false cheer.

"Right. You want I should turn the TV on?"

"Naw. I don't want to wake Millie."

"I'll bet she's nursing one heck of a hangover." Irene rolled her eyes toward Mildred's door.

"A beaut. She's paying the piper now. So we oughta let her get some sleep," he said with sly consideration, "before she sees Noah Lockwood. So just set the TV clicker within reach. And hand me some of those *Yankee* magazines. I'll catch up on my reading." Irene turned to leave, but Forrest suddenly reached for her hand. "Just be careful with Loomis, you hear? He's got a wicked temper."

"You bet, Forrest."

Thinking of the day ahead, Irene sallied down the sweeping staircase, spilled into the foyer, and trundled smack into the starched white shirt of a stout man she'd never seen before.

"Who're you?" She clutched the banister and recoiled a step.

"I might ask you the same thing," he said, surveying her with ill-concealed distaste.

Irene didn't like the way this man looked at her at all. Oh, he was dressed nice as could be — camel hair topcoat, charcoal gray suit with a vest and a glittering watchchain across his expansive midsection, yellow silk tie with itty bitty polka dots all over. He was fancy, all right. But now his nostrils were flaring as if she had dog mess on the soles of her shoes. His piercing blue eyes were open a mite too wide, revealing whites etched with tiny bloodshot chicken tracks. Her own eyes shot to his finger, poised and pointed in her direction. The finger trembled ever so slightly, and Irene guessed that despite his imposing demeanor this man had been under considerable strain of late.

"I'm Irene Purdy, and I'm a houseguest here."

"A houseguest?"

"Yes. Millie's houseguest."

"Millie?" The word plopped from his mouth like a beetle. "You mean Mildred? Mildred Bennett?"

"The very same."

"Good God." The man suppressed a shudder, then collected himself. In one smooth motion he shucked off his coat and dumped it on a chair. "Well, Miss—"

"Mrs."

"Mrs. Whoever-You-Are—"

"Purdy. Irene Purdy. I told you that before."

"Fine," he snapped. "Mrs. Purdy." The man drew himself up to his full five feet ten inches. He straightened his yellow tie at the gold stickpin. "I am Connor Bennett. Mildred's husband."

He said it as if she should curtsy or something. "You don't say," she replied.

"Indeed I do say. It's painfully obvious to me that Mrs. Bennett has suffered a breakdown of some kind. Gone right off the deep end. But that's all over now." He moved to go upstairs, but Irene remained planted firmly in his path.

"You can't go up there."

Connor Bennett looked at Irene as though she were mad. "I most certainly can, and I will. Now, if you'll kindly allow me to pass."

Irene would have liked to stick around longer just to make things difficult. To stir the pot, as they say. But she had to get to Loomis Brewster's before he left for work. So she settled for one last parting shot.

"Well," she said in a secretive whisper, "you really oughtn't to go up there. I mean it might be embarrassing." She rolled her eyes toward the ceiling.

"Embarrassing?" Connor Bennett didn't want to know about embarrassment. He was a man of order and precision. A man who rotated magazines in the rack weekly and discarded any outdated ones. A man who surreptitiously arranged spices in the cabinet alphabetically. A man who could not abide the merest speck of dust or lint on his bifocals. The last time he'd been embarrassed was in kindergarten when he'd wet his pants during story hour. Since then he'd made it a habit and an obsession never to be embarrassed again. He gave Irene Purdy his best frown. "Embarrassing to whom?"

"Well," she said, leaning forward conspiratorially, "it's just that there's a man up there—"

"Good Christ. It's worse than I thought."

"—and Millie's got one wallop of a hangover."

With that Connor Bennett bolted past and shot up the stairs. Irene had never seen such a portly man move with such grace and speed, except maybe Jackie Gleason years back. She smiled to herself and reluctantly headed for her meeting with Loomis.

28 For both the best and worst of reasons, that day would turn out to be one Trevor never forgot. It was the day he got to know Leslie McCloud, the day he fell a little bit in love with her, too. And it was the day he lost Mary Margaret. Forever.

It was morning, and Trevor congratulated himself for being so clever. He called Silver Glen yet another time and did something he was most unpracticed at doing. He lied. He told the battle-ax on the switchboard that his name was Mark McCloud. Mark was Leslie's son. He never visited and rarely called—only once, maybe twice a year. Usually when he needed money. But his name was on the approved list.

Leslie was surprised, then delighted to hear Trevor's voice—so delighted, in fact, that she agreed to meet him by a brook that ran along the edge of the property. Leslie had grounds privileges and used them frequently to take long solitary walks when the weather was pleasant. So no one raised an eyebrow when she walked out that morning. Later, when she didn't come back for lunch—well, they raised plenty of eyebrows then. They raised a real hullabaloo in fact. But by then it was too late.

They were like two kids playing hooky. Never before had Trevor felt such an exhilarating sense of freedom. Before, there was always Mary Margaret to worry about. Before that there were his patients. And before them there was medical school. Somewhere along the line he had forgotten how to have fun.

Trevor put the pedal of the old Lincoln to the floor and they fairly flew along the Merritt Parkway. They headed for New York City with vague intentions of maybe taking in a museum. As it turned out, they did more than that. Leslie and Trevor toured the Metropolitan, savoring the Impressionists most of all. They ate lunch at Tavern on the Green. They rode through Central Park in a horse-drawn carriage. And they spent a hilarious hour ice skating at Rockefeller Plaza. It was the first time in a long time that Trevor really laughed, and the first time in a long time that he didn't feel old.

He had such a good time that it hardly occurred to him to ask about Spencer. When he did, he held his breath. Despite everything, he didn't want Leslie McCloud's husband to be a murderer. For her sake, he didn't want that.

"I don't know where he was," she said flat out. "He never showed up that night."

"Ah," sighed Trevor, "that is a shame. Well, we won't think about it just now."

It wasn't until three o'clock that he thought to call his answering machine. He called from force of habit more than anything else and almost didn't bother because there were never any messages anyway. But this time there was.

"Hello, Daddy . . ." The voice was Penelope's but it didn't sound like her. It was small and fragile, ready to break. Trevor's hand went clammy on the phone. "Please call, Daddy . . . as soon as you can . . ." The voice cracked and broke then. Trevor listened helplessly to a wrenching series of choked sobs. "Oh Daddy, she's gone. She's dead . . ." There was a long pause. Frantic now, Trevor gripped the phone and waited for Penelope to say more. Waited for her to tell him that it was only a joke. Or maybe that the cocker spaniel died. Yes, that could be it. Penelope was the sort to get hysterical over a dead dog. Just like her mother. But Trevor waited and listened to the silence of the machine. The recorder finally made a squealing beep that signaled the end. To Trevor it sounded just like the heart monitor in surgery. And the line went dead, just like that. Just like Mary Margaret, he thought. At that very moment a heavy, steady, relentless heartache grabbed hold of him and squeezed his breath away.

Numbly he dropped the receiver back on the hook. More than anything else, he would like to turn this day off. He would like to roll it back and make it stop. Just moments before, he had felt young. Now he felt old and brittle. He felt too dry for tears.

"What is it, Trevor?" Leslie put her hand gently on his arm.

"My wife," he said thickly. "Something's happened."

In what seemed to be a dream, Trevor reached into his pocket and fished out a quarter. Blindly he tried to feed the coin into the phone. He couldn't see the slot because tears, real ones now, flooded his unfocused eyes. Finally the quarter tumbled into the chamber. As he heard the internal clang he thought to himself, I'll wake up soon. The alarm will be ringing and I'll wake up. I'll make Mary Margaret's favorite breakfast ... But his finger stabbed at "O" and the operator was talking to him, taking his credit card number, telling him he could have his quarter back, you don't need it for a credit card call. He wanted to tell her to keep the damn quarter but waited silently instead as she punched the combination of digits that would connect him to his daughter.

By the time Trevor's call came through, Penelope had pulled herself together. In fact, she had done more than that. She had transformed herself from a basket case to a drill sergeant. It was her way of coping, Trevor supposed. As he listened numbly, she started in and went on and on, like a chain saw ripping through ironwood.

They didn't know what had happened exactly, but it looked like a heart attack. Mary Margaret had died in her sleep. Last night. Are you sure, Trevor found himself asking inanely. Sure? Yes, Daddy, of course I'm sure. It must have been quick and painless, at least that's what Penelope said. Because this same woman who cried out at the slightest twinge or ache slipped away in sleep without so much as a whisper or whimper.

"We're on our way," said Penelope firmly.

"Who?" said Trevor, suddenly panicking.

"The family," she replied. "Judson and me. Seth and Jeanette."

"Seth and Jeanette," he repeated in a fog.

"Your grandchildren," she said impatiently. "And the relatives. Bob and Doris from Chicago, Louella and Herb from Seattle, and Irene and Joe from Boston. I've called them all." She said it as if he should give her a prize.

The names pounded against Trevor like fists. He hadn't seen these people in years. Now that Mary Margaret was dead they'd swarm like vultures. It was not a comforting thought. He felt he might suffocate. Suddenly the phone booth seemed to shrink around him.

"And Mother too, of course." Penelope said it as if Mary Margaret were still alive. "I've already booked reservations."

"Reservations?" Trevor repeated. Bile rose in his throat. Careful, he told himself. Easy does it.

"Supersavers," she said, sounding like a well-trained travel agent. "Nonrefundable, nonchangeable, noncancelable."

Mary Margaret's already been canceled. The thought popped into his head. The words flew to his mouth, but he choked them back down. Suddenly he felt very angry at Penelope. He tried to remind himself that her heart was in the right place, but nevertheless he saw his private grief being turned into a three-ring circus. Be kind, he told himself. She's had a shock.

And what about me? I've had a shock too.

Still she blabbered on . . . "I never knew this, Daddy, but when someone dies you've got to embalm them before shipping. It's the law. And then you've got to pay full coach fare for the body, even though the airline puts it in freight. What a racket."

"Don't come," he blurted.

"What?"

"Don't anyone come."

"Daddy, I don't understand—"

"I can't stand it, Penelope. Just don't come. Send your mother back, that's all I want. But stay where you are. Tell the others too."

"Daddy," she pleaded, her voice edging up hysterically, "we're a family. We belong together at times like this."

A family scattered to the four winds like so many fallen leaves. A family that exchanges Christmas cards and gifts dutifully sent for birthdays or graduations or weddings. I know the UPS man better than I know my own children, he thought bitterly. No, we're not much of a family anymore.

"I have a family," he muttered to himself.

"What?"

"I have friends," he amended out loud, and he snapped to his customary good posture as a new conviction was born. "Friends who will see me through this."

"Since when do friends mean more than family?"

Since today, he wanted to say. Since right this minute. "I'm not arguing with you on this, Penelope."

"Well!" said Penelope. "I never—"

"Send Mary Margaret back. I'll bury her here ..." He thought about Irene's Earl in the meadow. "Have a memorial service there if you like. But don't come. Not just now."

"But what about these tickets?" she wailed.

"I'll pay for them," he said. He was too sad to be disgusted, just too damn sad. The receiver slipped from his fingers into the cradle.

Once again Trevor Bradford would show his grit. The moment of wanting to run, of being overwhelmed, of wanting to turn his back—that moment had passed. He straightened up, took Leslie by the arm, and led her to the car. They barely spoke during the drive back.

"You know what makes me feel the worst?" he said softly as they reached the outskirts of town.

"What, Trevor?"

"That I knew this was coming. I knew it. And I sent her away anyway."

"Oh Trevor, you couldn't have known. She'd been sick a long time."

"That's true, I suppose. But somehow I think I saw it coming. A sixth sense or something. Sounds funny coming from a doctor, a man of science. But deep down I think I knew it, and I think I couldn't bear it, not anymore."

"Oh," she said, not knowing what else to say.

"Our relationship changed over the years. From husband and wife to parent and child. No—more like doctor and patient. We stopped communicating. I don't know how it happened."

But he did know. His hands gripped the wheel as he admitted this to himself. He had never been completely honest with Mary Margaret. And at the end, before she left, he had been astounded when she confronted him.

"I would have liked to tell her," he said hoarsely, staring ahead at the road through tear-filled eyes.

Leslie touched his sleeve. "Tell her what, Trevor?"

But he never answered. He left Leslie at the gate of Silver Glen. "I'll call," he said. But he couldn't think about such promises now.

"I would have liked," he whispered to himself as he drove away, ". . . would have liked to tell her I'm sorry."

29 Irene Purdy paused at the row of little mailboxes by the entrance to Victoria Ridge, an elegant brick and clapboard condominium complex just a short distance from the center of town. She couldn't for the life of her figure why anyone would pay good money for a house that was attached to someone else's when they could have a free-standing log cabin in the woods for a fraction of the price. She shrugged her shoulders. Irene had long since given up trying to figure folks out.

Loomis Brewster lived with his mother, Hattie, in the last unit on a cul-de-sac that formed the heart of the complex. Loomis had built Victoria Ridge and was proud of it. He took special pains to install every conceivable creature comfort—whirlpool Jacuzzi tubs, central vacuum, central air, track lighting, energy-efficient heat pumps, vaulted ceilings, balconies, built-in bookcases, Jenn-Air ranges, microwave ovens, premium wall-to-wall carpet—the list went on. Loomis found that folks who didn't give a damn about the quality of the concrete or the thickness of the plasterboard went absolutely gaga over creature comforts. Glitz, Loomis called it, and a little bit of glitz repaid itself tenfold. People wanted and wanted and wanted.

So Loomis obligingly upgraded. As he upgraded, he upcharged. And if he skimped a bit on the lumber or substituted PVC pipe for copper, well, no one was the wiser.

Over the years Loomis was increasingly amazed and delighted at the prices people were willing to pay for real estate in Raven's Wing. "Do you know the average price of a house in this town?" he'd ask. "Do you know?" Then he'd laugh and answer his own question. "Three hundred and eighty thousand dollars! Keee-rist!"

Soon Loomis and Hattie would have to vacate the model they were living in—there was a contract on it now. They would move to yet another condo complex or housing development built by Brewster Construction. But Loomis didn't mind. He lived a nomadic existence, never occupying the same house for more than a year, never accumulating any personal effects to speak of, and that suited him just fine.

Irene gave the beveled glass door a couple of sharp raps with her knuckles and waited. Soon a form appeared behind the organdy curtain. The form opened the door, and Irene stared into a face that looked like a bleached raisin. The face of Hattie Brewster.

"Morning, Hattie," said Irene.

"Morning," said Hattie shortly. She looked at Irene over the tops of her half glasses, looked at her as if she didn't recognize her, even though she did. "What do you want?" she said.

"I'm collecting for the March of Dimes," said Irene. It was the first thing that popped into her head. Irene knew that Loomis Brewster might be made of money, but he never gave any of it to Hattie, leastwise not outright. Hattie had manic ways about her, and when she was on one of her upswings, money flew from her fingers quicker than blackbirds from pie. On one such binge, Hattie purchased twenty hats, a dozen pairs of shoes (all black), and sixteen lace brassieres in a variety of colors. People snickered behind her back, and her son impounded the checkbook.

"Humph," grunted Hattie. "You'll have to speak to Loomis about that." She hollered over her shoulder. "Looooooomis! Looooooomis! Visitor!" Then, grudgingly, she opened the door.

Irene stepped into an overdecorated foyer with electric green wallpaper in a jungle floral pattern. Hattie led her past a large family-style eat-in kitchen with island work station, past a half bath with seashell pedestal sink, along a hallway of gleaming Armstrong Solarian No-Wax tile, and into a generously proportioned living/dining room combination. This room was decorated in pink and lavender with black lacquer accent pieces.

"Nice color scheme," remarked Irene.

"Indeed," said Hattie. "He's getting dressed for work. He'll be down shortly."

Hattie waved a dismissive hand, indicating, Irene supposed, that she should sit. She did so. Hattie planted herself in another chair not ten feet away and proceeded to fix gray, unblinking eyes on Irene. At first Irene wondered if maybe she was having some kind of spell.

"Something wrong?" ventured Irene.

Hattie's nostrils seemed to flare slightly, but that was it.

"Think I'm gonna steal something?" Irene tried again.

Still there was no response.

"Cat got yer tongue?"

It was like talking to a dead person.

"Aw, screw it!" muttered Irene under her breath.

"What was that!" snapped Hattie.

"Never mind," sighed Irene. She sat in silence for some moments until she couldn't hold back anymore. "What's wrong with you, Hattie? How come you treat me like dirt?"

Hattie recoiled as though she'd been slapped. Her white raisin face took on the barest blush of color.

"Whatever do you mean?" she gasped.

"You know very well what I mean. I pass you on Main Street, you don't say hello. I nod at you in church, you look the other way. I bump into you in the market, you act like you stepped in a cow pie."

"I'm sorry if I gave you that impression," sniffed Hattie.

"Well, I just don't get it. We were in the Order of the Eastern Star together. Sewing circle, too. We used to be friends, you an' me."

"I know," said Hattie quietly.

"I helped you when the kids were born. I nursed 'em through the measles, mumps, an' chicken pox. If it hadn't been for me, Timmy woulda died of meningitis."

"I know," said Hattie. Her words were choked this time. She coughed into her hand.

"Well, I wanna know why. What'd I ever do to you?"

"Nothing," said Hattie. "It has nothing to do with you."

"Aw, screw it," said Irene, giving up again.

"It has to do with him," blurted Hattie. Her gray eyes rolled to the ceiling.

"Him who?" whispered Irene. "You mean Loomis?"

"Yes."

"I don't get it."

"He said . . ." began Hattie timidly, ". . . he said, uh, we had to cultivate the right people. If he was going to be successful, that's what we had to do."

"The right people," repeated Irene, having no earthly notion of who the right people were.

"People who have *connections*." Hattie spat out the word. "People who have money. People who can give him building contracts and variances. People like that."

"Oh."

"He made me give up the sewing circle and join the garden club. I felt out of place, I've got to admit it. None of those women knew the first thing about growing tomatoes or pole beans. They grew decorative-type flowers like gladiolas and roses. Stuff you can't eat."

"Hattie, he can't make you do anything."

"Oh, can't he?" She arched a penciled eyebrow. "Who do you think puts a roof over my head? Who puts food on my plate? Who buys the nitroglycerine pills for my angina? Him, that's who."

"That doesn't mean he owns you. He can't—"

"Look, Reenie"—Hattie's face flushed with embarrassment —"we all make our choices. We all need a place in this world. Not all of us are strong like you. Not all of us can live alone."

"But he should treat you better," Irene insisted. "Treat you with respect."

"Respect?" Hattie hooted the word.

"He should let you live your life. The way you want to."

"Please," said Hattie, looking alarmed now. "Be quiet. It'll be bad for me if he hears you. Please."

"Okay, okay."

"My life is all right. Not what I expected exactly. Back when I was raising six children. I never expected Vern to take off like he did, never expected to be dependent on one of my children one day—"

"You could move out," said Irene suddenly.

"What? And live on social security? In this town? No. My home is with Loomis. He's a good boy, really."

Before Irene could say more, they heard a toilet flush upstairs. Hattie looked at her with pleading eyes.

"Listen, Hattie," said Irene quickly, "would you like to go to lunch sometime? Just the two of us?"

"Oh, I don't know . . ."

"Come on. We'll talk over old times."

Hattie Brewster stammered with embarrassment, and the words she said cost her dearly. "I don't have any *money*, Irene."

"Oh," scoffed Irene, brushing the concern aside, "my treat, Hattie. I shoulda said that right off."

"That's awfully kind of you, Irene." She clasped the woman's hand in a squeeze and hastily left the room.

"Why, Irene, what a pleasant surprise." Loomis Brewster

216

clunked into the room in heavy steel-toed work boots. Success does different things to different people. In the case of Loomis Brewster, it made him fat. Some might have called it portly or stout or even chunky, but not Irene. Fat was fat and Loomis was it, plain and simple. He had acquired a shape like a watermelon, a shape stuffed with some degree of difficulty into a pair of chino pants, a twill shirt, a cable-knit sweater vest, and a corduroy jacket. Unselfconsciously, he rehitched his belt, which was painfully extended to the last notch. His shirt was unbuttoned at the top, his knit tie loosened, the better to accommodate his expansive neck.

"The pleasure's all mine," said Irene dryly. "I had a nice chat with your mother, Loomis."

"Oh. That's nice, Irene. Real nice."

His face is so fat, thought Irene, his eyes are slits. Reminds me of a pig I once raised. Irene realized she was becoming entirely too engrossed in this fatness, pulled herself up short, and reminded herself of the purpose of this visit.

"Mama said something about you wanting a contribution—"

"That's not why I'm here, Loomis."

"Oh?"

"Let's not play games. I figure Ripley already called you."

"Yeah," said Loomis. His slit eyes turned flat as nickels. "That he did."

"Good," said Irene, not feeling so good at all. She wished he'd sit down. She wished he wouldn't stand over her like that. She wished she'd never gotten involved in this mess, that's what she wished most of all. "At least we know where we stand," she said.

"Look, Irene . . ." Now Loomis did sit, nested himself right alongside Irene, comfy cozy like. "I don't see why you're planning on making trouble."

"I'm not planning on anything," said Irene, edging away ever so slightly.

"Can't we discuss this reasonably?"

"Course, Loomis. I have an open mind." My mind is so open, thought Irene wildly, my brains are gonna fall out.

"I'm a good man, Irene. A decent man. You know that."

I don't know nothing, is what Irene felt like saying. But she didn't. She sat there in silence, wanting to throw up at his closeness.

He spoke with exaggerated patience, as though reasoning with a child, and this was not lost on Irene. "I've always taken care of Mama, haven't I?"

"Yes," she said evenly.

"And lots of folks don't know it, but I put every one of my brothers and sisters through school. Sent Bobby to U Conn. Put Henrietta through beauty culture school. Set Freddie up in the plumbing business."

"You're a saint, Loomis. Everyone says so."

Irene's sarcasm was totally lost on Loomis.

"And when Timmy's boy was born with a hole in his heart, who paid for the operation to fix it? Me, that's who!"

"No one's disputing your devotion to your family, Loomis."

"So why go making trouble, Irene? I'll be honest with you . . ."

One thing Irene knew for sure—whenever someone says "I'll be honest with you" it meant he wasn't about to be.

". . . I don't need this trouble. Not right now. You don't understand the pressure I've been under. No one understands. I've got a bid in on the Yankee Mall project. It's the biggest project in the state, Irene. Maybe the biggest on the East Coast."

He waited for her to be suitably impressed, but Irene could only look bored.

"Do you have any idea how much I want that project, Irene? Well, do you!"

"No," she said.

"I want it so bad I can taste it. And I intend to have it, Irene, oh, indeed I do. Everything is set, see? If you and your cronies sully my good name, well, that will tip the balance. There's a lot of competition for this job, a *lot* of competition. The slightest hint of scandal, and my name's off the approved list."

"That," said Irene sarcastically, "would be a pity."

Loomis lost it then. His reasonable buddy-buddy demeanor vanished. "Well, let me tell you one more thing." He pressed his red face to Irene's pale one. She could smell stale cigar breath. She wanted to gag. "You just forget this whole business, see? Back off. Or—"

"Or what?" she snapped, sitting up straight, staring him down.

"Or I'll call a few friends. About that land you're squatting on—"

"You wouldn't!"

"—and you'll be out on your ass, pardon my French. You'll be in a home right along with Forrest Haggarty."

"Forrest's not going to any home!" cried Irene.

"I wouldn't be too sure about that. And the home you end up in won't be like Craigmore, either. It won't have carpet on the floor and devoted nurses. No. It'll be more like Soundview. An asylum. You can sit there all day, babbling your drivel about murders, drooling out the side of your toothless mouth, and you know what? No one will care. No one."

"Stop!" she cried. The pink and lavender and black of the living room swirled around her. It was a hideous picture, this picture he painted of her future. It was false. A lie.

"Just so's you understand," said Loomis. "Just so's you leave it alone."

"Loomis," said Irene, striving for reason and control, "it doesn't have to be a big deal. All you have to do is tell where you were on Saturday night, and I'll be on my way. We'll cross you off the list."

"Oh," he said with false cheer, "I see. No big deal. Well, I guess I have to spell it out for you, Irene. The big deal is that

I had business to take care of on Saturday night. Business—a business deal, if you will—about the mall. Money changed hands. I needn't be more explicit."

A kickback. Irene might not be wise in the ways of the world, but instantly she grasped what he meant.

She left then. Later she would hardly remember hurrying out of the house, out of Victoria Ridge, past the tidy row of little matched mailboxes. Wearily she made her way back to her rusty VW. And she never looked back, so she never saw Hattie staring bleakly out the second-story window.

Loomis Brewster picked up the portable phone and carried it into the bathroom. He closed the door, lowered the lid on the toilet, and sank down heavily. He waited for the thumping in his chest to subside. Irene's visit had shaken him badly—not just because of her dogged persistence but also because she'd stood up to him. Why, she'd almost dared him to hit her, almost dared him!

Control, thought Loomis. Control. Thank God I didn't lose it.

He leaned back against the tank and surveyed the tiles on the wall. He studied the black streaks in the plastic vanity with the look of marble. He counted the pink and perfect rosebud soaps nested in the rippled lidded jar. Usually these things gave him a feeling of comfort, of rightness in the world. Now he felt no such reassurance.

Loomis punched out numbers into the handset and fervently hoped Noah Lockwood would know what to do.

"Hello?"

Loomis lost control right off the bat. "Noah? Jesus Christ, Noah, have you heard? Do you have any idea what's going on? Of all the stupid things, of all the frigging dumb luck—"

"I'm well aware of the situation, Loomis." Noah Lockwood sounded totally unperturbed. Bored even.

"This thing'll ruin me, Noah. I can't afford any trouble right now. You know my precarious financial situation. The barest hint of scandal, Noah, and the shit will hit the fan." His voice escalated to a piercing whine. "I tell you, the shit—"

"Quit your goddamn sniveling!"

Loomis leaned forward, ripped off a streamer of pink toilet paper and blew his nose noisily. "Easy for you to say," he said hoarsely. "This is nothing to you."

Silently Noah Lockwood wished that were true. But it wasn't.

"I want you to listen to me, Loomis. There's nothing to worry about. Those letters don't mean squat. None of us did this thing."

"Right," said Loomis. He reached for more paper and mopped his sweaty face. "Are you sure, Noah?"

"Christ, Loomis! Of course I'm sure!" He said it with a conviction he didn't feel. "We're solid as rocks. All of us. Not a nuthatch in the batch."

"Well," Loomis reminded him, "there's Marcel. If he doesn't qualify as a nuthatch, I don't know who does."

"True," admitted Noah. "But Marcel is no murderer. He doesn't have the stomach for it."

"I guess you know these things, Noah, being a judge and all."

Noah chose to ignore this questionable compliment. "Marcel would never commit such violence. His friend Jimmy Perkins is another matter, however . . ."

"Right," said Loomis quickly. "Yeah. Jimmy Perkins. Why he coulda done it easy. He always was a sadistic son of a bitch." As relief washed over him, another disturbing thought shot through Loomis. "But Noah, Jesus, there'll be an investigation. Shit, Noah, an investi—"

"There won't be any investigation," broke in Noah firmly. By God, he would prevent that if it took his last breath. "Don't you worry. It won't come to providing alibis or anything as sordid as that."

"It won't?" Loomis's voice was pathetically hopeful.

"No. We're going to nip this thing in the bud."

"How, Noah?"

"We remove the catalyst for this trouble. We get rid of Forrest Haggarty."

"You mean *kill* him, Noah?" His voice edged up hysterically once more. "My God, you don't mean that. Although," he reconsidered, "maybe some kind of accident . . ."

"No, I don't mean that!" thundered Noah, losing patience now. "There are other ways, Loomis."

"I, uh, I'd prefer not to know, Noah. I mean, I'll rely on your judgment." Loomis wasn't an attorney like Noah or Ripley but he knew enough to know that knowing might make him an accessory of some kind.

"Yes," Noah went on, almost oblivious to Loomis Brewster. "I'll find a way to take care of Haggarty. You just go about your normal routine. Get out of the house. Go to work. Play with your dump trucks or whatever the hell you do. And put this mess out of your mind. You hear me?"

"Yes," said Loomis obediently.

"Good."

"There are others, Noah. Other people involved."

"Of course," said Noah, with exaggerated patience. "And once Haggarty is out of the way, I'm sure they'll listen to reason."

"I hope so, Noah." Loomis squeezed his eyes shut tight and rolled them around in the sockets. He decided to try Noah's patience one more time. "I think we gotta have a meeting, Noah."

"Now that's a damn fool idea if I ever heard one."

"The five of us. I think we gotta."

"And why would we want to do that?"

"To get our stories straight. Just in case. And to figure out who did it. Maybe that, too. Wouldn't that be a pisser?"

Noah froze, the phone cold as stone in his clammy hand. "Why?" he said evenly. "What does it matter?"

"I really think we gotta," said Loomis doggedly, for he could be decidedly stubborn when he set his mind to something.

"Okay!" snapped Noah. "Okay. Arrange any damn meeting you want." Loomis Brewster's whining ways were starting to close in on him. "Goodbye, Loomis."

"Noah?" Loomis clutched the phone tightly in his sweaty hand. "Noah?" But Noah Lockwood had already hung up. This gave Loomis a creepy kind of courage, if you could call it that. A creepy kind of courage to ask one last question on his mind. He asked it to the dial tone: "Was it you, Noah? Were you the one who did it?"

30 Mildred held her coffee cup very tightly. They sat in Richie's Luncheonette, not two tables away from the booth she and Clyde had shared. She hoped Clyde wouldn't come in now. She'd die of embarrassment, just die. She started to rearrange the silverware on the plastic Currier and Ives place mat. She moved the fork a millimeter to the right, the spoon a millimeter to the left, the knife—

"Will you quit with that!" snapped Connor.

Startled, she looked up and into the face of the man who had been her husband for thirty-five years. She felt as though she didn't know him anymore. "Quit with what?"

"With that fiddling! Christ."

She folded her hands in her lap and consoled herself with the fact that at least she'd gotten his attention, which was more than she'd accomplished in all those years of marriage.

"I might have guessed Molly would tell you where I was," she said wearily. Of course, she thought. Molly would never take my side.

"Molly told me nothing," he said flatly. "It would have made things easier if she had. As it was, some slug at the post office finally told me where they were forwarding your mail."

"That's an invasion of my privacy," said Mildred, feeling a stab of anger.

"You might like to know that Molly told me I could find you—if I cared enough to try." Connor Bennett winced inside, remembering his daughter's caustic words.

"And did you?" said Mildred sarcastically. "Care, I mean?"

"I'm here, aren't I? What more do you want?"

So much more, she thought. At least once I did. But she said nothing.

"Well." Connor took a deep breath as though preparing to deliver a speech. She supposed he had rehearsed it coming out on the train. "I want you to know that everything will be fine. I intend to stand by you, Mildred. You're my wife, after all."

Yet another flash of anger surged through her. He made it sound as though she were a bitter pill. Or a dose of castor oil. The proverbial ball and chain to drag around for the rest of his life. But she pushed the anger aside. She tried to give him the benefit of the doubt. "And how, may I ask, do you intend to stand by me?" At this late date, no less, she almost said but didn't.

"I broke it off with Heather . . ."

"Broke what off? Your pecker?" The words flew from Mildred's mouth before she could stop them. She said them too loudly. Several heads swiveled. Someone over at the counter snickered.

"Mildred, for God's sake." Flushed with embarrassment, Connor glanced at the door, and she supposed he was considering making a run for it. Cutting his losses. Or perhaps he would simply act as though she were a crazy woman—look up at the plaid-jacketed townies sipping coffee at the counter and shrug his shoulders. But instead he simply said "Jesus" and began to butter his whole wheat toast with a vengeance.

"We will go home." Connor went on as if by rote. "We will take up where we left off. There are so many years invested after all . . ."

Invested. He spoke of their marriage as though it were an interest-bearing account.

". . . First, of course, we'll have to get rid of the riffraff you've ensconced in your mother's house."

"Riffraff!" She spewed a mist of Folger's all over him and didn't even care. Why, he made it sound as though they should call the Terminex people to take care of some kind of noxious infestation. "I'll have you know that the people to whom you refer are *not* riffraff. They are people of character. People of depth. What's more, they are my friends."

"Bah." He waved one hand and reached for a mono-grammed handkerchief to mop his face with the other.

"And furthermore we most certainly will not, as you say, 'take up where we left off.' Our marrige is a husk, Connor. A shell. We stopped communicating, stopped being close a long time ago."

"I tried," he said sullenly, looking around now, nervous to think that someone might know that he'd tried. And failed.

"No, you didn't, not by a long shot." She put down her napkin and tried to be fair. "Oh, Connor, I'm not even saying it was all your fault, not entirely. Neither of us tried. Not nearly enough. But that's all by the board. I have a life now. Things to do. Friends."

"Are you dating?" He sat rigid, face frozen, waiting for the answer.

It was okay for him, but not for her. She could see that plain as day.

"A little," she said, feeling a small pang of pride that she was truthfully able to say so. "But it's much more than that." He looked at her questioningly. She was a woman who dutifully clipped recipes from the *New York Times* and had her hair done on Thursdays. Who did charity work and bought sensible classic clothes at Lord & Taylor. And who never, never really, did anything exciting. Never anything venturesome. He thought she was so predictable. So dowdy. So dull.

"Look at me, Connor. I'm wearing blue jeans. Can you imagine? Me, in dungarees."

He didn't even look up from his runny eggs. "Well, I did think it a bit out of character—"

"And my hair. It's different now. Looser." I'm looser too. She almost said the words but decided they might sound lewd.

"Very nice, Mildred. Very nice." The words were automatic. He was blowing his chance, and he didn't even know it.

"But that's not all," she went on, almost desperate to provoke some kind of human emotion, some kind of reaction. She paused dramatically, then lowered her voice. "I'm working on a murder case."

Connor Bennet inhaled a cloud of whole wheat bread crumbs and doubled over in a coughing fit. He clutched the stainless steel sides of the Formica table. His face took on a purple cast. For one excruciatingly long moment Mildred feared she might have to administer the Heimlich maneuver.

"Excuse me," he said, regaining control and forcing a smile. "I must be losing my mind. I could have sworn you said you were working on a murder case." He chuckled at the very thought.

"I am," she said angrily. The hell with him. She told him all about it.

"Good God," he said when she was finished. "Good God."

"I knew it would knock your socks off, Connor."

He ignored this expression, which he was sure she'd picked up from the bumpkins she'd surrounded herself with

226

of late. "Of all the dumb-ass things, Mildred, this really takes the cake. You listen to some old geezer—"

"Forrest Haggarty," she corrected. "Chief Haggarty."

"Okay." He forced himself to be patient. "Chief Haggarty. You listen to him, then parade around as though you're some kind of—who's that ditz on television?—Angela Loudberry—"

"Angela Lansbury!" she shot back. Angela Lansbury was Mildred's heroine. "You never liked her, I could tell. Never wanted to watch shows I enjoyed. Your word for them was 'drivel,' as I recall. It was always 'Wall Street Week' and 'Meet the Press' until I was blue in the face. I begged you to see *Terms of Endearment* with me—"

"Terms of what?" he said, totally mystified now.

"Endearment! But you wouldn't know about that, would you, Connor?"

"Mildred, don't go off on one of your crazy tangents."

"You were the one who brought up Angela," she snapped.

"Very well, very well." He heaved a deep sigh. "I'm sorry I did, Lord knows. But the larger issue here is that you've allowed yourself to become entangled in something that at the very least is a figment of an old man's senility and at the very most a dreary little sordid affair."

"A fine choice of words, Connor. Especially from you."

"All right, Mildred. Let's forget my transgressions for the moment, if we can. Let's at least try. This mess you're involved in—it's another kettle of fish entirely."

She set her mouth stubbornly and said nothing.

"I don't suppose you've given much thought to the kind of trouble you're exposing yourself to—"

"Oh, I'm being careful. We all are. We know the man we're after is dangerous."

"Bah!" He waved his hand, dismissing her words. "That's not what I mean. The man, indeed—if he exists at all. I mean this business with the letters. Sneaking around and talking to this one and that one. About some important people, I might add. It smacks of a kind of whispering campaign. You're exposing yourself to charges of slander. Exposing yourself to unnecessary court expense and unwanted publicity. And exposing me, too."

"Aha!" she exclaimed. "That's really all you care about, isn't it? The money. And your reputation. Well, the scales have fallen from my eyes, Connor. Just never you mind. Don't lose any sleep over this. I won't tell anyone I'm your wife."

"Stop it! Just stop it!" To her astonishment tears of frustration popped into his eyes. Mildred looked at him with amazement. He was the same old Connor. Pompous. Dictatorial. Stuffed with Styrofoam. And yet he was the same and not the same. He had lost weight, and not for the better. The three-piece suit hung on him limply. It looked as if it hadn't been cleaned in a year. The only creases in evidence were those framing the bags under his eyes.

"Connor, are you all right?"

"You're my wife," he said almost to himself. "Of course you're my wife. Pretend not to be? How can you even say such a thing?"

Clearly his world had turned upside down and inside out. Conflicting emotions swirled within her. She felt a tug to him that surprised her, but she stopped herself. She couldn't make things right, couldn't keep them glued together. Not anymore.

"I almost killed myself, Connor."

He never even heard her. "We can put this marriage back together," he said blindly. "I'll even go to one of those marriage counselors, if you insist. I'll take more time off. We'll take a vacation. We'll—"

"Connor," she interrupted gently. "Connor."

"Huh?"

"It's over. Can't you see that?"

"Just like that?" he said in disbelief.

"No," she said sadly. "Not just like that. It's been over for a long time. We were just going through the motions."

31 To Forrest it was a stroke of good luck that Mildred's husband showed up unexpectedly and dragged her out to breakfast. He knew she'd stand her ground. Knew she wouldn't go back to him, at least not until they had solved the case. And since she wouldn't be seeing Noah Lockwood this morning, he would. Somehow, by God, he would manage it.

Grimly chewing a double dose of Trevor's medicine, Forrest managed to dress himself. It was painful and it took a long time. Finally, though, the medication took hold and movements came easier. Through a dreamy state, he fairly floated downstairs, thinking that he would have to drive very slowly and carefully. But when he reached the front door he was plagued by second thoughts about Mildred, Irene, and Trevor. If one of them came back for any reason, they'd be frantic to find him gone. So he wrote a note, which he left on the kitchen table. He told them not to worry. Told them he was paying Noah Lockwood a visit himself. Told them he had to do just this one thing.

As Noah Lockwood spoke with Loomis Brewster on the phone that morning, he had no way of knowing that Forrest Haggarty would make it so easy for him. When Forrest arrived, the judge was eating his usual breakfast of dry toast and black coffee. Forrest rapped once on the kitchen door and walked in uninvited. He had to hand it to Noah. The man didn't so much as look up from his *Wall Street Journal*.

"Morning, Forrest," said Noah. "I sorta thought you might drop by. You or one of your cronies."

Forrest took a chair opposite Noah and tried to hide his surprise.

"Ripley called me," Noah went on, still not looking up.

229

"Loomis too. Not Marcel, of course. He's too busy wetting his pants. And Spencer? If I know Spencer, he's in front of his video camera rehearsing the fine art of denial."

"So you know," said Forrest. "You know why I'm here."

Noah looked up then. Forrest noticed a sprinkling of crumbs on his dry lips.

"I know you and some of your friends have some letters. Letters written by a bunch of widowers and bachelors seeking companionship."

"I didn't think you were the type, Noah."

"Don't assume so much, Forrest. You think I don't get lonely? You think I'm not human?"

"I didn't say that."

"You're grasping at straws, Forrest." Noah seemed to consider his words. "Listen, I'll give it to you straight. You did me a favor once, so I suppose I owe you. And maybe I even like you, as much as I can like anyone."

"I'm flattered," said Forrest without emotion.

"Don't be. Because I don't like anyone. Not really. Let's just say I dislike you less than I dislike the rest. You've got ideals and you've got character, but like so many with those qualities you're a fool. You're a poor miserable son of a bitch."

"You just hold on!" Forrest moved to jump up, but Noah waved him down.

"This business with the letters, Forrest . . . I don't think any one of us killed Agnes Peabody, and I've been on the bench long enough to have a nose for this kind of thing. But okay, let's for the sake of argument say one of us did it. Let's say you go around asking your questions. Let's say you start raising a stink until by God there has to be an investigation. You think it will accomplish anything?"

"Maybe."

"Maybe, hell! It won't accomplish a damn thing. Because sure as you and I are sitting here every one of us will have an ironclad alibi. Oh, I can hear it now." Noah smiled sardonically. "Spencer's wife will say he was visiting her. Of course, Hattie Brewster will swear up and down Loomis was home. Marcel's boyfriend will back him up. And Ripley? He'll get Huey to say any old damn thing he tells him, if the price is right."

"And what about you, Noah?"

"Me?" Noah shrugged with false nonchalance. "I'll just tell the truth. That I was home reading a copy of *American Jurisprudence*. Home alone. Just like I am every other night of the week."

So my instincts were right, thought Forrest.

"So maybe they'll think it was me," Noah went on. "Maybe, maybe not. But it won't matter because they haven't got a shred of evidence. The point is, even if all of us are innocent, even if we're all cleared, we'll always be tainted. People will always look at us sideways. They'll whisper. They'll wonder. You think Marcel will ever sell another kiddie book? You think Spencer will do another commercial? You think Ripley will get reelected? You think Loomis will get another government building contract?" He rammed each point home like a nail.

"I'll apologize for the inconvenience," said Forrest dryly. "Be sure to remind me."

"Just tell me, Forrest. What did we do to deserve this? Tell me about this vendetta of yours. What did *I* do?"

"Nothing," muttered Forrest. But he was tired of lies. "I always liked Jessica," he said quietly.

"God damn you!" Noah Lockwood jumped up as though electrified. The plate went flying. So did his coffee cup. There was a quick clatter like gunfire, and Noah raised his fist. "You think I killed her! You think it like all the others!"

Forrest looked up wanly. He was tired. The walk and the drive had sapped his strength. He hardly cared if Noah hit him. They were frozen for a moment, and Noah stared numbly at his upraised fist. He let if fall to his side and sank back into his chair.

"Well," he said hotly, "maybe I did kill her in a way. It was what she deserved."

Forrest hardly allowed himself to breathe. "What happened?"

"There's nothing much to tell." Noah got up and stooped to collect broken bits of crockery on the linoleum floor. His royal blue velour robe opened to show a bony white-haired chest. "When I married Jessica, I loved her. I told myself that this was my chance for happiness. I told myself that she loved me, even though she never said so right out. And I believed all those things. She was such a lady. She had ideals. She was decent. Or so I thought."

"I remember her," said Forrest. "She was all of those things."

"Everyone thought so, and so did I." Noah smiled grimly to himself. "Then our child was born."

"Stillborn," said Forrest, remembering.

"Everyone thought so," Noah repeated quietly.

"Huh?" said Forrest. His head swung around. "The child was dead—"

"No, Forrest. Damaged, yes. Mentally deficient. But very much alive. Unfortunately."

Forrest paled.

"It was a difficult pregnancy," said Noah. "Jessica and I went to New York to a specialist when it was time for the baby to come. And when he told me about the child's condition, well, we simply didn't bring it home."

"What'd you do with it?"

Noah ignored the question and went on. "Jessica wanted to, of course. She begged me to let her keep it. But she didn't have much say in the matter, not after what she had done."

"Noah," asked Forrest in disbelief, "what the hell did she do?"

"Why," said Noah in amazement, "she's the one who created this monster."

232

"Jesus, Noah, you can't place the blame for that one on her."

"I can and I do. Yes. I still do." He stared at the wall, and when he spoke the words were harsh and unforgiving. "She had syphilis—the doctor said so. A disease she'd contracted before she met me. A disease almost impossible to cure at that time."

"Good God." Forrest was stunned.

"She had it. She didn't tell me. She married me. And she had my baby. My *damaged* baby!"

"And then she killed herself," Forrest finished, feeling a wave of compassion for that desperate woman.

"Yes. I heard her go out that night. I knew her intention. And I didn't stop her. If she had faltered, I would have tied the blocks on her myself."

Forrest listened and held himself very still. "The child," he said at last, "what happened to the child?"

"He's in custodial care. Has been all these years. With good people, caring people, not far from here." With that, Noah slapped pictures on the table in front of Forrest one after the other. Snap! Snap! Snap!

"He looks just like you," breathed Forrest.

"Looks can be deceiving," said Noah cryptically. "Examine his feet. What do you see?"

Forrest squinted. In some photos the feet were cut off, in others oversized pants hid the boy's shoes. But in one, the boy was wearing short pants. It was out of focus, fuzzy. Forrest saw . . . he thought maybe he saw . . .

"Chains?" he whispered, not trusting his eyes.

"You have a fine eye for detail. Yes. I prefer to call them 'restraints.' Sounds more humane. Yes, the boy looks perfect," said Noah. "And so does the man." He snapped down yet another picture, this one of a man in his forties. "But his mind is gone. Eaten away by the disease he was born with."

"So you put him in chains?" Forrest asked in disbelief.

"He's more than dim," said Noah without emotion. "He's demented. He killed things. They showed me carcasses. Birds. Cats. Another child."

Forrest said nothing, numbed as he was by these words.

"So they shackled him. It seemed that best thing. He managed to get out once that I know of. He brutalized a woman. Almost killed her."

Once, thought Forrest. Once that you know of. "Do you think he could—"

"I *don't*," said Noah, slamming down the word, "think about what might have happened. But since you ask, no, I don't think he killed Agnes Peabody. Unfortunately, I'll never be certain. He's very clever when it comes to escaping. It's become an obsession with him, you see. And good help is hard to find. His caretaker was drunk that night."

"I see," said Forrest.

"No you don't. What you don't see is that I will do anything to protect this son of mine, damaged as he may be. Anything, you understand? And he'll do anything to protect me."

Forrest wondered who needed protection more, the son or the father.

"If pressed to the wall, I'll tell the truth. I'll say I was with him on Saturday night. And he'll back me up. You see, I'd even expose this secret I've taken such pains to conceal. But I'd never forgive you for it."

Noah Lockwood spoke with such force, with such tightly controlled rage, that Forrest felt a ripple of fear pass through him.

"Of course, it won't come to that," Noah went on. "I simply won't allow that to happen."

There was nothing more to say. Forrest struggled to get up.

"Not so fast, Forrest." Noah reached out and clamped a restraining hand on Forrest's shoulder. "Just hold on there."

"Huh?" The barest hint of alarm crept into Forrest's voice.

"Don't you know this has got to stop, Forrest? Can't you see that?"

"What?" Forrest looked around wildly. He heard a car pull up in the driveway, then a door slam, followed by footsteps on the porch.

"Let go of me," he cried. He tried to shrug off Noah's grip, hating his own infirmity.

Scott Haggarty stepped into the kitchen. He looked at his father with relief and pity.

"Scott," said Forrest, badly shaken now, "what are you doing here?"

"Noah was kind enough to call me when your truck pulled into his driveway. Jeez, Pop, you scared us half to death, disappearing like that."

"I didn't—"

"And you look bad, Pop. Your color's all gray. It scares me to see you like this."

"My back—"

"Sure, Pop, sure." Scott helped the old man up. "It'll be okay. You're coming with me. We'll see that you get proper care."

"But I don't want—"

"For your own good, Pop. That's why I'm doing this."

So that was how they put Forrest away. He was old. He was sick. He was weak. And after all, it was for his own good.

Noah Lockwood watched Scott Haggarty drive Forrest away. He wondered if Forrest had believed him, not that it mattered anymore. He would lose little sleep over Forrest T. Haggarty. And Forrest? Forrest would find out that there are worse things in life than incarceration. After all, there are all kinds of prisons in this world. Noah stared down at the pictures of the boy who was the image of himself and could almost feel the bite of metal against his ankles. Soon he would feel it full force. Some things you never forget.

32 Mildred came home to find Irene in tears, and it took some time to extract a coherent account of what had happened—that they'd trapped Forrest and taken him to Craigmore and "there wasn't nothing " they could do about it. That Mary Margaret had died. That Trevor had given himself a sedative and was up on the third floor in an unoccupied maid's room, stretched out on a mattress without a sheet, wrapped in the cocoon of his own grief.

"Everything's going to hell in a handbasket!" Irene wailed.

It was hard to disagree with her summation.

Dinner that night was grim. Mildred picked at her chicken. Trevor sat like a stone, and Irene, who couldn't stop crying, was drinking far too much Chablis. She looked at Mildred with plaintive red-rimmed eyes. Finally Mildred could stand it no longer.

"Don't look at me like that, Irene."

"I'm not looking at you," said Irene, looking at Mildred.

"There's nothing I can do."

"He said you were in charge. Forrest said—"

"Well, he was wrong! I refuse to be in charge. I'm ill equipped to handle a situation of this magnitude."

"Ladies," sighed Trevor, "must we endure this bickering?"

"Yes, we must!" hissed Irene, losing all patience.

"Well," said Trevor, straightening up in righteous indignation.

"Listen, Trevor," Irene pressed on, "I'm sorry as can be about Mary Margaret. Everyone from here to East Jabib knows how fond you were of her. It's a terrible thing, her passing—"

236

Mechanically Trevor began to eat, refusing to absorb Irene's words.

"But there ain't nothing we can do about her, Trevor. She was sick, she died peaceful, and she's gone. Not that it's nothing, mind you. But now we got other troubles. Pressing troubles. Troubles we can do something about. Forrest—"

"Oh, don't start, Irene," said Mildred. "Just don't start. There's nothing we can do about Forrest, and you know it. We're not allowed to see him. They don't allow him access to a phone. He's probably sedated." She rattled off the obstacles.

"We gotta do something," said Irene doggedly.

"What we must do," said Mildred, "is to remain calm." She tried to sound like the voice of reason when, in fact, she felt like screaming.

"Aw Millie, he'll hate that place, Forrest will. They won't feed him right an' they won't let him drink. You mark my words, he'll *die* in there." She shot a glance at Trevor, who winced at the word "die." "Ain't that right, Trevor?"

"Well . . ." he hesitated. "I would be more sanguine if Forrest was not such an adamantine personality."

"More what if he wasn't what?" asked Irene.

"Optimistic," snapped Mildred. "If he wasn't so unyielding. Rigid! Stubborn!"

"There," said Irene. "You see?" She took a big sniff and blew her nose into a raggedy Kleenex.

"Please, Irene, get yourself a fresh tissue. And stop working yourself up like this. You make it sound like he's in prison. When in fact Craigmore is a luxurious facility. He'll get the best of care."

"Bullshit," said Irene.

"Profanity won't help, Irene."

"Bullshit and *balls*."

"Well," said Mildred, standing up, "I can see there's no reasoning with you this evening."

"Don't go," blurted Irene. "I'm sorry."

Mildred sat down. She felt terrible about this herself and her heart ached for both Trevor and Irene. But somehow she knew a display of sympathy would not make it better.

"I know I shouldn't oughta carry on like this, Millie. But I can't help it. I know I shouldn'ta fallen for him like I did. I shoulda taken more time. Played hard to get."

"Now, now," said Mildred.

"But we don't got a whole lotta time, don't you see? Forrest is old and I'm no spring chicken, either. There's no time for bein' coy."

"You did the right thing," said Trevor suddenly.

Irene stopped in her tracks. "I did?"

"Yes. You saw a chance, a chance for some happiness. And you grabbed it."

"Right," said Irene.

"And Forrest grabbed it, too," put in Mildred.

"He sure did!" quipped Irene, smiling for the first time.

"Well," said Mildred, "I didn't mean exactly that."

"But nevertheless," said Trevor with conviction, "you were both adults. You did what you wanted. When you look back you won't have any regrets." Like I do, he thought to himself.

"They even have an expression for it," added Mildred. "Make hay while the sun shines."

"Yeah," said Irene. "Make hay. And we did, too." Her face clouded again. "Oh, I just hate talking about it like it's in the past. Now that I have Forrest, I don't wanna lose him."

"You won't," said Mildred firmly, hoping it was true. "We'll find a way to get him back, you wait and see."

"I hope so." Slowly Irene stood up. "I know it's early, but I'm going to bed." She seemed reluctant to leave, as if something was on her mind. "Millie?"

"Yes?"

"Do I gotta move out?" Irene asked the question to the floor.

"Irene, why on earth would you have to do that?"

" 'Cause Forrest, he ain't here no more. And if he ain't here, I guess there's no reason for me to be, either."

"Nonsense," said Mildred. "You're my friend. You'll stay with me."

"Okay," said Irene, trying hard not to betray the emotions inside her. She turned to leave and got as far as the door. When she spoke, it was with her back to Mildred. "Millie?"

"Yes?"

"Thanks."

"Oh, go on," said Mildred, trying to brush it off.

"For letting me stay, I mean."

"Never you mind, Irene, just never you mind."

"And for cheering me up. That too. Thanks to you both."

With that, Trevor started to cry. But he managed to laugh through his tears. "Now look what you've gone and done," he said. "Get to bed, Irene. Doctor's orders."

Later that night after Trevor had gone home and the dinner dishes were done, Mildred sat in her robe and fuzzy slippers trying to read the same page in a paperback novel for the third time. She just couldn't concentrate. Her mind kept wandering back to the five suspects, back to Forrest, and back to the four of them who in their blundering way were trying—and failing—to solve the series of murders.

Well, she thought sadly, things are in a sad state of affairs now.

We gotta do something. That's what Irene had said.

You're in charge now. Irene had said that too.

"Damn," said Mildred. She snapped the book closed and threw it across the living room, where it hit the phone, knocking the receiver to the floor. Wearily she got up, went to the phone and replaced the receiver. At that very moment, it rang.

"Hello?" she said, wondering who could be calling.

"Mildred? It's Clyde."

"Oh," She tried not to sound so depressed. "Hi."

"I'm calling to see if you might be free for dinner again this Saturday night."

"No," she said. "I mean yes. Oh, I don't know what I mean."

"Mildred, what's wrong?"

"Oh . . ." She groped for words. "Everything. Just everything. They've taken Forrest. They've got him stuck up in Craigmore."

"I know," said Clyde. "Scott Haggarty stopped by the paper this afternoon and told me not to run the missing person story. He said he had his father back. Said he was putting him under full-time custodial care."

"Everything's falling apart," said Mildred. She twisted the telephone cord around her wrist. "Everything."

"Listen," said Clyde, "why don't I come over?"

"Oh," she said gratefully, "would you?"

"Sure. We'll talk. Put on a pot of coffee."

Mildred rushed to get dressed. And by the time Clyde arrived, she had made up her mind.

"I've made up my mind," she said to Clyde as they sat in the kitchen at the old planked pine table with coffee mugs in hand.

"About what?"

"About going public."

"Now, Mildred—"

"We'll go public with the letters," Mildred rushed on. "We'll go public with all of it. It's time the police knew everything. We'll blow the lid right off. We'll tell people what happened, and then they'll have to take Forrest seriously."

"And just how," asked Clyde cautiously, "do you plan to go public?"

"With a story. On the front page. Of your paper."

"Now wait a minute," said Clyde quickly. "I don't think

that's such a good idea. It's too soon, Mildred. We need more evidence. You could be charged with libel, and so could I."

"It's not libel to print the facts. Simply report the existence of the letters. Then publish them."

"And how were they obtained?" he pressed.

"Well, I don't see what that's got to do with—"

"How, Mildred?"

"Well," she stammered, "a lady gave them to me. Hermine Goldman, that was her name. Yes. She gave them to me."

"You obtained them illegally," he reminded her. "They were the property of the deceased. What's worse, Mildred, you withheld them from the police. You withheld *evidence*. That's called obstructing justice."

"You won't help," said Mildred. "That's what you're saying, isn't it."

"Not exactly," said Clyde.

"Well, then, what are you saying? Exactly."

"Just that we shouldn't rush into this without thinking it through."

"God," she snapped, "you sound just like my husband."

It was the worst insult she could have handed him. He started to get angry, then laughed.

"Well, you do."

"Come on, Mildred. You folks have done so much spadework, it won't hurt to wait a little longer. One of those suspects is going to give himself away. I'm sure of it."

"You are?"

"Of course. The heat is really on now."

"Maybe you're right," she said reluctantly.

"Thank you," he said.

"And I suppose it wouldn't do any harm to let Forrest have some quiet time. That's what he calls it. 'Quiet time.' "

"Quiet time for what?"

"For thinking. I never cease to be amazed at his mind. He

may be old, but he's got excellent recall. He's got details stored away you wouldn't believe."

"Stored away where?"

"Here." Mildred tapped her forehead.

"What kind of details?" Clyde was genuinely curious now.

"Details about the previous murders. Details about the victims. Oh, mark my words, that computer of his is clicking away and he'll figure things out."

"That," said Clyde, "will be exciting." He sat back and seemed to dismiss the subject from his mind. "Let's sit in the living room," he said, and without waiting for a reply, he took her hand.

Mildred wondered if he would try to seduce her. If he did, she wondered if she would go along with it. And if she did, she wondered if she would enjoy it. And if—indeed, there were so many ifs, she thought maybe it wasn't worth it.

They sat on the couch. Two statues. Mildred positioned herself off to one side. She sat rigidly upright with her legs primly crossed. She smoothed her skirt. She brushed away an imaginary piece of lint. She uncrossed and recrossed her legs. Suddenly she was aware of all the clothing she had on—brassiere, panties, hose, girdle, slip, blouse, and sweater. As many layers—and as much armor—as Bloomingdale's had to offer.

"Mildred," said Clyde, "relax."

"Relax?" For a split second she forgot the meaning of the word. She certainly forgot what it felt like. But all the same she sank back into the cushions and tried to appear relaxed.

"I'm not going to bite you."

"I know." She relented a wee bit more. She eased the barest bit closer. He put his arms around her shoulders and gently tugged her to him. Somewhat stiffly she settled her head against his shoulder. She hoped she wouldn't get a cramp in her neck or, worse yet, a cramp in her foot. Sometimes she got terrible toe cramps at the worst possible moments. Lack of calcium, that's what Molly said it was. She was a prime candidate for bone degeneration.

"Penny for your thoughts," said Clyde dreamily.

"Osteoporosis," she blurted.

"What?" Clyde looked at her as if she were crazy.

"Never mind," she said. She wished he would just kiss her and get it over with. She didn't know how to make what the young people today called "moves." And she was sure that when he kissed her, her lips would turn to plaster of paris. She'd freeze, that's what. But at that very moment, while her mind was whirling with unromantic thoughts of brittle bones and stony lips, he did kiss her. And it wasn't bad at all. In fact it was quite nice. More than nice, it was delightful.

After an interlude of kissing (which, Mildred discovered, she had not forgotten how to do), Clyde progressed to touching. And after some moments of smoothing her hair, of stroking her face, and reaching around and massaging her back, well, it seemed perfectly natural that he would unbutton her blouse. Perfectly natural, too, that he would reach inside, tenderly cup her breast, and put it to his lips. Yes, it all felt perfectly natural, perfectly right, and perfectly delicious.

There was a fleeting moment when she thought of Connor. When she thought, I am a married woman. But she was so very weary of being lonely, and her body ached for a touch, a caress, and a simple act of closeness.

He undressed her carefully, almost reverently, and held her close. Then, to Mildred's embarrassed chagrin, her hips started moving in spasmodic little upwards jerks, as though they had a will of their own. His hand traveled from the soft round-ness of her breast down to the place of her aching desire. He stroked and soothed and was ever so gentle. How, she wondered through a haze of yearning, how have I lived without this for so long?

Sometime much later she reached up and flicked off the lamp. They slept there on the couch cradled in each other's arms.

33 While Mildred and Clyde lay entwined, Hattie Brewster tossed and turned in her bizarrely furnished bedroom at the Victoria Ridge condominium complex. Since the unit was a model, Hattie's room, like all the others, played a specific role. That role was Teenage Bedroom. The motif was a heavy-handed caricature of femininity so blatantly virginal as to reflect a demeanor Loomis believed most fathers wanted for their daughters. Hattie slept in a white lacquered bed under a pink eyelet canopy. A mirrored vanity with billowing ruffled skirt was set coyly to one side. A menagerie of glassy-eyed stuffed animals peeked from bookless bookshelves. A small magenta television tilted toward the bed from a white French provincial bureau. Posters of rock stars with hair like cotton candy and pouting ruby lips adorned the walls.

Hattie hated rock and roll. As far as she was concerned, the Rolling Stones could roll right out of existence and the world would be better for it. Madonna was a ludicrous contradiction of a name, downright sinful even. And rap music? Crap music, that's what they should call it. Hattie might not be educated, but she preferred classical. Brahms, Mozart, Beethoven. Especially Beethoven. Now, as she slept fitfully, one of her favorite pieces played in her mind. Beethoven's Fifth Symphony in C Minor. Usually it was a comfort. This time it turned into a nightmare.

Hattie's body went rigid as she was forced to sit, chained, in her dream—forced to listen as violins screeched a cacophony and to watch as faces of the musicians rearranged themselves into features she recognized. There was her boy Loomis, decked out in a crimson uniform with dripping gold braid. And Spencer McCloud, his once handsome face now contorted and purple as he puffed into a tuba. Ripley Crane tapped gaily on a xylophone that bore an uncanny resemblance to a rib cage, and Marcel Wintermute played an instrument that looked more like a male member than a clarinet.

The vision was horrible. On and on the musicians played, laughing and writhing with furious abandon to a frantic beat dictated by a baton waved by Noah Lockwood. Noah's visored military cap perched askew on his head. He flailed his arms like a manic marionette. His face, the only part of him that looked real, was flushed and dripping with sweat. The music swelled and screamed, and Hattie watched with horror as clots of blood started to pour from the mouths of the instruments.

"Stop!" she cried in the dream and jolted awake. Her flowered flannel nightgown clung damply to her bony body. Visibly shaken, she threw back the sheets and stepped onto the cold floor. A wave of dizziness washed over her, and Hattie wrapped arthritic fingers around a bedpost for support. She placed her feet in raggedy slippers and took tiny steps, seeking firm ground.

"Mama! You okay?"

At the sound of her son's voice a new wave of panic flooded through her. It's okay, she told herself. Okay. She forced a calm reply, for after all, she'd had years of practice at this. "Fine, Loomis," she said weakly. "Fine. It was just a dream."

"You've been having too many dreams lately," called Loomis back. "I don't like it."

"The medication," she said. "That's probably it. The doctor gave me a new prescription." It was a plausible lie. She knew, of course, that it wasn't any pills that started her dreaming these awful dreams. It was her weakness for eavesdropping. Years before, loneliness and boredom had driven her to do so, and now it was something that came automatically. It was this habit that had led her to listen in when Irene Purdy had visited, and that had led her, in turn, into these nightmares.

"Go back to sleep," Loomis said impatiently. "I got company coming, and I don't want you bothering us."

Company? thought Hattie. She gazed at an illuminated rhinestone-encrusted kittycat clock on the wall. The cat looked back with revolving cueball eyes and an enormous leering grin. It was one A.M. Company?

She knew better than to ask questions. Instead, she reacted according to habit. She moved the skirted stool over from the vanity. She sat herself down in the darkness and nudged the door open the barest crack. She prepared to listen.

It did not take long for the players from Hattie's dream to assemble. And as she listened, she thought she might be dreaming still. She had no trouble putting voices to faces. She had known these men for a long time. They had met under various roofs constructed by her son Loomis on and off for years now.

Glasses were distributed and a bottle passed from hand to hand. Hattie could hear clinks of ice dropped into glasses. There were murmured hellos and hasty inquiries about each other's business, but preliminary niceties were dispensed with quickly.

"Now," said Noah Lockwood, taking charge, "I realize that some of you have been rather concerned about Forrest Haggarty's apparent obsession with some letters he's unfortunately gotten ahold of."

"Damn right," fumed Loomis.

"The fellow's like a terrier with a bone," said Spencer McCloud. "He's not about to give it up. Just a bit of harmless revelry, and he twists it around from here to Sunday."

"You know how this town is, Noah," Loomis whined. "People always think the worst. No one'll understand. The scandal will ruin us—"

"Not just scandal," corrected Spencer. "The merest innuendo would ruin us as well."

246

"Well," said Noah expansively, "I'm happy to report that there's no reason to worry about Haggarty anymore." He tipped his glass in salute.

"Huh?" said Loomis, thinking perhaps, indeed, that Forrest Haggarty was dead and not knowing whether to look sad or glad.

"As of this morning," said Noah, "Forrest Haggarty took up permanent residence at the Craigmore Convalescent Home. I don't think he'll cause us any more trouble."

"Well, well," said Loomis, "that does call for a celebration! Drink up, boys!"

"Not so fast," said Ripley carefully. "Haggarty's confinement is a help, of course, but who's to say he won't keep making trouble from inside? There are telephones. He's got friends."

"You forget, Ripley," said Spencer smoothly, "that I'm on the board at Craigmore. It's one of my many good works, which will finally reap dividends. There are certain patients—those who are infirm, or demented, or highly exictable—who are kept in isolation. For their own good, of course."

"Oh," said Loomis, "I get it."

"But what about his friends?" reminded Ripley. "As I understand it, there are three of them. Trevor Bradford—"

"Mary Margaret just died in California," said Noah, his voice properly regretful. "From what I hear, Trevor is so distraught he's taken to his bed."

"Well, well," said Spencer enthusiastically. "This is coming together rather nicely, I'd say."

"But there are two others," persisted Ripley. "That woman Mildred Bennett and Irene Purdy."

"Irene Purdy," said Noah with disdain, "is a simple woman from the back woods. And it just so happens she's in love with Haggarty."

Loomis almost spit out his drink. "Love? How do you know that?"

"The woman must have called Craigmore twenty times

yesterday afternoon," said Noah. "Don't worry, we didn't allow her calls to go through. She is, I think, rather frantic by now. I believe we can bargain with her. Her cooperation in return for visiting privileges. Or, if necessary, for his safety."

"I do hope," said Spencer in his best actor's voice, "that it won't come to an overt show of strength."

"Oh indeed not," agreed Noah. "I would never presume to threaten the poor woman. A thinly veiled hint would, I think, suffice quite nicely."

"You mean we might kill Haggarty?" blurted Loomis with characteristic lack of finesse.

"I wouldn't put it that way," said Noah sharply.

"Craigmore is a home for the aged," said Spencer easily. "The near-deads, if you will. People pass on there every day of the week. It happens."

"The place," Noah went on, "is quite understaffed. Regrettably so. Prescriptions can be forgotten or mixed up . . ."

At the mention of medication, Hattie Brewster clutched at her own chest. She waited, hoping Loomis would speak up. Would object. But he didn't.

"What about the Bennett woman?" asked Ripley.

"Yeah, Noah," said Loomis. "She won't be so easy. She's got money, I hear. It won't be easy to intimidate her."

"I remember Mildred Bennett," said Noah crisply, "and she's never had an independent thought in her life. Once her friends give up on this nonsense, she'll cave in and go back to New York."

"What about Haggarty's family?" asked Loomis.

"They're pathetically grateful," said Noah, "that a group of distinguished citizens such as ourselves has offered to repay in some measure Haggarty's devoted service to the town of Raven's Wing by underwriting the cost of his care."

"Now wait a goddamn minute!" cried Loomis. "You mean we're gonna pay? Bull*shit!* That place costs an arm and a leg."

"Look, Loomis," said Noah coaxingly, "it won't be for long.

Take my word for it. Haggarty is an old man. He could go any day."

"The sooner the better as far as I'm concerned," said Loomis, gulping down his drink.

It was then that Marcel Wintermute spoke for the first time. "I cannot believe what I am hearing here tonight. I simply cannot believe it."

"Believe it, Marcel," said Loomis. "Take off the rose-colored glasses."

"These measures are inordinately extreme," protested Marcel. "It's not worth destroying an old man's life for the sake of some stupid letters that don't amount to anything."

"Is that all you think's involved?" snapped Spencer McCloud. "Some letters?"

"If those letters come out," said Noah reasonably, "we will all suffer the indignity of looking like fools."

"More than that," murmured Spencer, "we will have to verify our whereabouts on the night Agnes Peabody was murdered. Publicly. I, for one, am not prepared to do so."

"Oh?" said Marcel. "So where were you? What are you so afraid of?"

"Yeah," Loomis chimed in. "What about it, Spencer?" He turned and faced the group. "Maybe one of us did do in the old lady. Yeah. Maybe it was one of us. Ever think of that?"

"Now, Loomis," said Ripley Crane hastily, "let's not make a bad situation worse with a lot of half-baked accusations."

"I don't have a lot of half-baked accusations," said Loomis doggedly. "I've only got one. For one person."

"Somebody killed Agnes Peabody," said Marcel, almost chanting the words. "Maybe somebody right here in this room."

"Will somebody shut him up?" snapped Spencer.

"I do not think," broke in Noah, "it's going to do us one iota of good turning on each other at this juncture. Perhaps Loomis is right—perhaps it would be a good idea to clear the air right now." He turned pale unblinking eyes on Spencer

McCloud. "So where were you on Saturday night, Spencer? And don't give us any cock and bull about visiting Leslie."

"Very well," said Spencer, struggling for composure. "But I expect the same courtesy from the rest of you. I expect you to tell me—"

"Fine," said Noah.

"There was," began Spencer, "I mean, is, a young lady who resides in South Salem. I was with her for the evening."

"So she can verify your whereabouts," said Noah. "If need be."

"I would prefer," said Spencer, "that it not come to that. For one thing, it would, ah, prove difficult for her to speak right now."

"Why's that?" asked Loomis.

"Her jaw is broken."

"Oh God," said Marcel into his hands. "Oh God . . ."

"There was," said Spencer quickly, "no malice intended. Believe me. It was just a bit of sex play that got out of hand. Her parents were quite understanding, actually. They, too, are concerned about adverse publicity. I have paid generously for the girl's plastic surgery. Paid for that, and then some."

"How old was she, Spencer?" said Noah.

"What?"

"You heard me. How old?"

"About eighteen, I'd say."

"You'd say?'

"All right. Sixteen. Sixteen goddamn years old. How was I to know? She was all gussied up. Makeup and tits out to here. How was I to know? I met her at Touchstone's. She was hanging around the bar. A trollop. Trash. She got what she deserved."

"Enough!" boomed Noah in disgust. "As you said, Spencer, we'll hope it won't come to unearthing this girl. But I think you can see, Marcel, why Spencer here is reluctant to have such dirty linen aired in public." He then turned to Loomis. "Okay, Loomis. It's your turn."

"Well," said Loomis self-righteously, "I didn't beat anybody up. I had a dinner engagement that evening. Strictly business."

"A dinner engagement with whom?" said Noah.

"A gentleman by the name of Louis Pontella."

"Gentleman?" echoed Marcel. "Are you kidding?"

"You mean *the* Lou Pontella?" asked Spencer in disbelief.

"Ah, yes," said Noah. "Louis Alberto Pontella. A man who has graced my courtroom on more than one occasion. And one, I regret to say, who always gets away."

"My goodness, Loomis," said Spencer in a clucking voice, "we know you have to deal with all kinds of riffraff in the construction business, but organized crime? Isn't that a little bit out of your league? You could end up wearing concrete anklets."

"I can take care of myself," said Loomis sullenly. "Besides, I don't have a whole lotta choice. This mall project is a whole new ball game. If I don't make the right connections, I don't stand a chance of getting a contract."

"You mean," corrected Marcel primly, "if you don't grease the right palms."

"Yeah?" challenged Loomis. "Yeah? Well, maybe so, rich boy. But some of us hafta earn our money, see? Some of us didn't step in hot shit so early on in life."

"Take it easy, Loomis," cautioned Noah.

"Easy?" Loomis shot back. "Easy! Keeee-rist! How the fuck do you expect me to take it easy? You think Lou Pontella's gonna be thrilled if he has to testify on my behalf? You think he's gonna like having his method of operation exposed for all the world to see? No, he's not gonna like it, he's not gonna like it one fucking bit. And Lou Pontella's one enemy I don't need."

"Calm down, Loomis," said Noah. "As I said, it certainly won't come to our having to offer evidence regarding our whereabouts that Saturday night. But even if it does, I assume all of you are adroit enough to arrange for, let us say, more acceptable alibis."

"You mean get someone to lie?" said Loomis, seizing on the word.

"If you must put it so crudely," sighed Noah, "yes. Lie."

Now here was a word Loomis Brewster could understand.

"Okay, Ripley," said Noah. "Your turn."

"I know this might sound slightly farfetched," said Ripley, "but I was at the dump Saturday night."

"The dump?" said Noah.

"Yes."

"And what, may I ask, were you doing? At the dump."

"Inspecting a shipment of refuse."

Loomis Brewster let out a guffaw.

"Cut the crap, Ripley," said Noah. "Since when do you inspect incoming garbage?"

"Since it comes to Woods Hole, that's since when," shot back Ripley.

"Woods Hole?" said Marcel. "But that's all swampland. Way in back of the dump. No one puts garbage there."

"Wait a minute," said Noah, suddenly understanding. "You're telling us someone's dumping in Woods Hole, not a mile from the town reservoir, under cover of darkness? What were they dumping, Ripley?"

"Just refuse," said Ripley. "That's all."

"Bullshit," said Noah. "Come clean here, Ripley. Just like the rest of us. Don't dick around with us, or we'll be pointing the finger at you."

"If you must know," said Ripley, "it was refuse from Matrix Chemical over in Danbury. Danbury has unreasonable environmental regulations. I told them Raven's Wing could accommodate their needs."

"Toxic waste!" laughed Loomis. "Well, I'll be damned. Our lily-white first selectman on the take. God, that's beautiful, it really is."

"Shut up, Loomis," said Ripley through clenched teeth. "I'm warning you."

But Loomis was not about to be put off. "Jeez, I used to watch you, Ripley. Watch you standing up there at those town meetings wearing your three-piece suit and stuffed shirt. And I'd think to myself, Christ, I bet that guy shits Ivory soap bars, he's so fucking clean. Ninety-nine percent pure. Good old Ripley Crane, Raven's Wing's little darling. Whatta laugh."

"I said shut up!" screamed Ripley.

"Ripley," said Spencer placatingly, "I don't understand. Your involvement with the more sordid details of the transaction, I mean. Couldn't you have delegated the dirty work to that boy of yours? Huey?"

"No," said Ripley hotly. "I could not. For some reason—don't ask me why—Huey detests me. And he can be perversely honest when it suits him. Of course," he looked around the room, "that's something none of you would understand."

"I understand it," said Marcel. "I'm honest."

"Oh sure," said Ripley. "You forget, Marcel, we remember when you were giving blow jobs to caddies out at the club."

"That's enough, Ripley," commanded Noah.

"Yeah?" Marcel shot back. "Well, that was a long time ago. And if memory serves, I didn't limit my clientele to caddies. Other people begged for it. Respectable people. I seem to remember you and Spencer—"

"Why, you miserable little faggot!" roared Spencer. "You, with your trashy behavior. Always playing to a man's baser instincts, you were—"

"At least I never broke anyone's jaw," countered Marcel. "At least I never drove my wife to an asylum. At least I never mooched off my wife's money."

"I'm gonna break his ass!" screamed Spencer. "I swear to God, I'm gonna break his ass!"

A scuffle ensued. Bodies came together. A table overturned. Hattie heard Marcel scream.

"Hold on!" cried Noah Lockwood. "Hold on a damn minute! You think this is going to solve anything? Well, do you?"

For some moments there was silence.

"Very well, then," huffed Noah. "Let's finish what we started. Marcel, where were you?"

"I went to the movies," said Marcel defiantly. "Over in Danbury. *Rain Man*."

"How convenient," snorted Ripley. "You take your pretty boyfriend with you?"

"I went alone."

"Hey, I get it," said Loomis. "Marcel was out catting around. Hunting fresh meat."

"That's a lie!" cried Marcel.

"Oh no," said Loomis. "I bet it's true. And I bet old Jimmy Boy's gonna be jealous. Ha, ha. You don't wanna make Jimmy jealous now, do you, Marcel? He might get nasty."

"As a matter of fact," said Marcel, "I don't. But that's not the point. The reason I'm scared is that no one can verify where I was. The theater was mobbed that night. I already went back and talked to the ticket taker. He can't remember me."

"Maybe if you offered the man some measure of remuneration," said Noah, "his memory would be refreshed."

"Maybe," conceded Marcel. "But that could backfire. He could refuse. Tell the police, too."

"Indeed," said Spencer nastily. "Your best hope, Marcel, is that your fat-assed boyfriend feels inclined to back you up."

"We haven't been getting along too well," said Marcel wretchedly.

"Well, kiss and make up," hooted Loomis.

"Noah," said Ripley, "I guess that leaves you. What were you doing on Saturday evening?"

"The same thing I do every Saturday evening," said Noah. "Reading *American Jurisprudence* in my study."

"Alone?" said Spencer.

"Quite," said Noah.

"Well, well," chuckled Loomis gleefully. "I guess you don't have a very good alibi either, Noah, old pal. No sirree."

"An alibi can be arranged," said Noah. "I'm not concerned about that."

The meeting wound down soon afterward. As goodbyes were said and guests headed toward the door, Hattie heard Ripley Crane ask one last question; "What do we do if Purdy, the Bennett woman, and Doc Bradford won't listen to reason? What then?"

"Accidents," said Loomis, "can be arranged. Just like alibis."

34 Early the next morning Mildred fussed happily around the kitchen. She was in a world of her own. She wiped already clean counters. She rearranged spices in the rack in alphabetical order. She cleaned the refrigerator shelves. And as she wiped, arranged, and cleaned, she sang to herself.

Last night had been wonderful. Clyde had been tender and gentle and caring. When he nudged her awake before daybreak, he gave her a lingering goodbye kiss and promised to call again. Mildred believed him, because she was in love. I'm in love, she wanted to shout. I'm in love! But because she was also fifty-eight and a proper New England lady down to the tips of her toes, she restrained herself. Instead she sang. "What the world needs now is love, sweet love. It's the only thing that there's just too little of . . ."

"My my," said Irene, shuffling into the kitchen in a pair of red woolen pajamas with feet, "aren't we cheerful this morning."

Mildred looked at Irene. In the red outfit, she looked like a little fireplug. But she also looked well rested, less sad, and ready to meet the day head on. There was a new sparkle in her eyes. A determined sparkle, but Mildred didn't know that yet.

"Cheerful?" said Mildred, pausing in midwipe. "Yes, I suppose I am." She went back to humming the song and set the table for breakfast.

"Why you holding your head funny?" asked Irene.

"My head?" Mildred tried to straighten her neck and winced.

"Yeah. It's kinda tilted to one side. Twisted. Like you got a crick in your neck."

"Oh," said Mildred. "That." She turned away from Irene and perused cereals in the cupboard. "I fell asleep on the couch last night. I must have slept on it funny."

"Come to think of it," said Irene, "I didn't hear you come up last night."

"Right," said Mildred primly. She extracted boxes of Nutri-Grain Wheat, Grape-Nuts Flakes, and Captain Crunch. Then she rememberd that Captain Crunch was Forrest's favorite. Hastily she shoved it back. She didn't want to spoil the mood.

"Come to think of it," Irene pressed on, "I also heard someone come in last night. Saw a car in the driveway, too. Looked like one o' them Cadillacs or some such."

"I had a visitor," said Mildred airily, determined not to let Irene's nosiness get the best of her.

"Come to think of it—"

"Come to think of what, Irene?" Mildred was getting exasperated now.

"—the car was still there when I got up to go to the bathroom. Musta been round about three A.M."

"I had a gentleman caller, Irene. He stayed overnight."

"Oh." Irene seemed to chew on that thought. "Was it your husband?"

"Irene!"

"Sorry. I spose it ain't none of my business."

"No," said Mildred. "It ain't. Isn't."

"Well, don't go getting your feathers ruffled, Millie. Just set yourself down here." Irene stood up and indicated her chair. "Let me give that neck of yours a good massage. I know just the trick for getting rid of a crick."

Mildred sat down. She supposed Irene was trying to make amends in her own way. She tilted her head back, resting it on Irene's ample stomach. She closed her eyes. Irene massaged her shoulders and lower neck with practiced fingers. Mildred found herself relaxing. Floating. Almost drifting away.

"Millie?" said Irene tentatively.

"Yes?"

"You remember how I said I get my best ideas when I sleep on something?"

"Um-hmmmm." Mildred was so relaxed, she was totally unprepared for the magnitude of Irene's idea.

"Well, I know what we gotta do. I got it all thunk out."

"That's nice, Irene."

"We're gonna steal him back."

"What?" Mildred's head snapped up and away from Irene's flexing fingers.

"We're gonna steal Forrest back. It'll be easy," said Irene quickly.

"Don't tell me. I don't want to hear."

"I got a friend by the name of Josephine Dunlop," said Irene. "She's head nurse over at Craigmore—"

"Forget it, Irene."

"Josephine owes me a favor or two and I'm gonna call in my markers. She don't have to do nothing bad or illegal or nothing like that. She's just gotta look the other way."

"Look the other way when?" Damn, thought Mildred. Damn me and my stupid curiosity.

"When we put Forrest in the laundry cart. When we wheel him out. That's when."

"That's insane."

"No, it ain't neither. Monday's laundry day. That leaves me enough time to get hold of some uniforms. We'll get there before the regular laundry company and pick up some dirty sheets. Only we'll pick up Forrest, too. Under the sheets, see?"

257

"No," said Mildred. "I don't see. The only thing I see here is that you've gone completely off your rocker."

Irene ignored the insult. "No one's gonna know, not till it's too late. I seen those carts, Millie. They got wheels an' they're real big. They got plenty of room for Forrest."

"Irene, what you're contemplating here is illegal. Illegal entry. Theft of a cart—"

"Borrow," corrected Irene. "That's all we're gonna do."

"Kidnapping," Mildred continued.

"It ain't kidnapping if he wants to go."

"Not to mention impersonation of a laundry employee." Mildred stopped and realized how ludicrous her words sounded. She gazed heavenward, praying for strength. "Look, Irene, I'm in enough trouble already, what with those letters and all. We could go to prison, Irene. Prison. Think of that." A picture of Irene Purdy flashed through Mildred's mind. Irene Purdy in a similar pair of pajamas, only with black and white stripes. Irene Purdy behind bars. In her hand was a tin cup, which she raked across steel bars to the tune of "Nobody Knows the Trouble I've Seen."

"If you won't help me, Millie, I'll do it alone. I'll go ahead without you. It'll be harder, but I'll manage. Somehow." Irene studied her sideways.

"Irene, I really think this merits further thought," said Mildred almost desperately.

"Think about it till Monday," said Irene stubbornly. "If you want to come along then, you're welcome."

"Oh Irene, for pity's sake," said Mildred. And right at that very moment the front doorbell rang, and Winston erupted with a throaty bark.

"I'll get it," said Irene.

"More bad news I'm sure," said Mildred. "And to think I was in such good spirits when the morning started."

Irene returned momentarily with her arm wrapped protectively around a tiny birdlike woman. The woman's gray hair was twisted tightly into a neat bun, and her blue eyes darted around the kitchen nervously.

"I'm afraid I haven't had the pleasure," began Mildred.

"This here's Hattie," said Irene. "Hattie Brewster."

"Oh," said Mildred. "You mean Loomis Brewster's—"

"Yes," said Hattie. "Loomis is my boy."

"Oh, boy," sighed Mildred. Suddenly she realized that Hattie Brewster looked very frail indeed. She swayed on tiny feet. She looked, in fact, as though she might topple over right on the kitchen floor. "Please," said Mildred quickly, "sit down. I'll get some coffee."

"There's a taxi waiting outside," said Hattie quietly. "I'm afraid I didn't have any money. Loomis never gives me any money . . ."

"Irene," said Mildred quickly, "my purse. It's on the table in the foyer. Please pay the cab."

"You bet," said Irene.

"Now," said Mildred, once they were all seated at the kitchen table, "what's this all about, Mrs. Brewster?"

"I've come to warn you," she said. She was so nervous her coffee almost spilled as she tried to raise the cup to her lips. She set it back down, untasted. "I felt I had to. Loomis isn't a bad boy, you understand. He's just so anxious to prove himself. We were poor, Mrs. Bennett. I don't know if you can appreciate what it's like to be poor in this town, but we were."

"I'm sure it was difficult," said Mildred. She tried to remember Loomis Brewster back when he'd been poor. Back in grade school and junior high. She couldn't remember him. Couldn't remember any poor people in Raven's Wing. She remembered Girl Scouts and dancing lessons and sailing at Great Pond but not poor people. Was I so protected? wondered Mildred to herself. So insensitive too?

"Loomis didn't have a father," Hattie rattled on, "not really. The one he had, well, Vern—my husband—used to drink, and he used his fists more than I like to remember. That's where

Loomis learned his ways, I'm afraid. Vern wasn't around much and when he was he didn't work. So I took in laundry and the children did odd jobs. Loomis especially. I was happy for him when he got his lucky break with Herb Palmer. You know, the chance to go to college and the fancy clothes and all that."

"Yes," nodded Mildred. That she remembered. Loomis Brewster not taking his good fortune in stride, not at all, but taking it in an arrogant way instead.

"Loomis was like a sponge, though," said Hattie. "Nothing was ever enough. Not money, not possessions, either. He always had to have more. What he wanted most, of course, was admiration. And love, too, I suppose."

"I'm afraid I'm not following you, Mrs. Brewster."

"Those others are swaying him now," she said adamantly. "My Loomis never was a good judge of character. I've never said this aloud, of course, but, well, he's just not as bright as folks think. So now he's going along with them."

"Along with whom?" asked Mildred, trying to swallow her impatience.

"Well," began Hattie, "I've been having these god-awful nightmares, and last night one woke me up . . ."

Hattie Brewster proceeded to recount the events of the previous evening as Mildred and Irene sat there in stunned silence.

"Oh, Jeesum," said Irene. "The cat's really outta the bag now. And they're gonna hurt poor Forrest. Oh Jeesum . . ."

"Not if you do as they say," said Hattie urgently. "That's why I came, you see. To alert you. You should know what they're planning. Be prepared. And you mustn't fight them, no indeed."

"So lemme get this straight," said Irene angrily. "We're s'posed to leave Forrest to rot in that nursing home? So's he can stay alive? That's what we're s'posed to do?"

"Not to rot," said Hattie quickly. "They'll let you visit him, don't you see?"

"Let me visit him?" shouted Irene, jumping to her feet. "Listen to that! Let me *visit*!"

"Irene," said Mildred, "get hold of yourself."

"Get hold of myself? I've got a shotgun up in my cabin and I'll get hold of that. Yes sir. I'll blow 'em all to kingdom come, that's what I'll do!"

"Irene!" said Mildred. "I hardly think you should vent your anger on poor Mrs. Brewster here. She's only trying to help."

"Oh," said Irene. She sat down. "Sorry. I didn't mean to shout at you, Hattie. Honest. I'm not mad at you. I'm grateful you took the chance coming here."

"I've been too meek for too long," said Hattie quietly. "And, well, you were nice when you came to visit, Irene. You spoke up on my behalf."

"Oh, that's okay," said Irene, trying to brush off the compliment. "What are friends for?"

"Friends," repeated Hattie, almost to herself. "Why, yes. I guess we are."

"Darn tootin'."

They let Hattie rest a bit. Fed her breakfast. Then Irene drove her home. As soon as she returned, she stormed up to Mildred. "Well," she demanded, "what're we gonna do now?"

"I think," said Mildred, thinking aloud, "you'd better get hold of those laundry uniforms. And tell Trevor, too. Somehow we must convince him to let us use the Lincoln. It's got more room in the back in case Forrest can't sit up. Yes. We'll get him out on Monday."

"Great," said Irene. "Then we'll go to the police?"

"No. Then we'll go to Clyde. He'll put it in his paper then. I'm sure of it. Because now it's gone too far. We're going to need help—no matter what Forrest says."

* * *

As expected, Noah Lockwood paid a visit to Mildred and Irene the very next day. Plainly, bluntly, without couching any phrases, he laid out the deal. Visits with Forrest in return for their co-operation. When they didn't reply, he looked at them and spread his hands, as though appealing to their sense of reason. "I really don't see what choice you have, ladies."

"And what if we don't cooperate?" snarled Irene.

"Irene, Irene," chuckled Noah, "why make this more unpleasant than necessary? I'm sure you want what's best for Forrest during his golden years. The last moments are the most precious, after all."

"Last moments!" repeated Irene. "Did you hear that, Millie? Last moments, he says!"

"I think you'd better leave, Judge Lockwood," said Mildred evenly. Winston growled menacingly.

"Fine," said Noah, drawing back a step. "Am I to take it that that's your answer?"

"Tell the others we'll think about it," said Mildred.

"I hope so," he replied.

"Just tell them," she repeated. And she closed the door.

Irene pounced on her as soon as he was gone. "Millie, you didn't mean that, did you? That we'd think about it?"

"Most certainly not," sniffed Mildred. Never an independent thought, indeed. Well, she'd show them.

35 Days passed. Trevor buried Mary Margaret following a small service attended by a few friends. And somehow—Mildred didn't ask how—Irene managed to snag two uniforms from Consolidated Laundry. She then set up logistics for Monday with Josephine Dunlop at Craigmore.

Meanwhile, the five suspects went about the business of arranging for agreeable alibis ...

* * *

"Lila?"

"Yes suh, Judge Lockwood."

"You've been working here a long time, haven't you?"

"Mor'an twenty years, I'd say, suh."

"Well, I want you to know I appreciate it. You've taken good care of me."

Lila Franklin looked at Judge Lockwood as though he was crazy. Never before had a compliment crossed his lips. Then she thought on his words some more and decided maybe he was about to fire her and she frowned.

"Thank you, Judge Lockwood," she said sullenly.

"Well, I'm going to do something about it, Lila. Yes indeed. Thanksgiving's coming up. You got all those grandkids and they'll be needing winter coats soon ..."

In fact, Lila Franklin had four grandchildren living under her roof plus three foster children. Her home was a snug haven for the unwanted, the forgotten, or the malformed. She took each child, be it blood relation or frightened wanderer, to her big bosom, and she loved each child with an even bigger heart.

"Then, of course, there'll be Christmas. Those kids'll be wanting presents ..."

Lila Franklin couldn't figure out if Judge Lockwood was stupid or just plain cruel. No way were her kids getting any presents, unless you counted the toys from the dump that her son Lionel retrieved and repaired. No way. Socks, maybe. Yes, they might get socks. Or woolen hats. You had to have a hat in Connecticut in the wintertime.

"So, Lila, here's a little something to help out. Consider it a bonus of sorts."

Lila stared at the envelope he offered as though it were on fire.

"Go on. Take it."

She took it. She looked inside. Suddenly she felt unsteady. "There's a mistake here, Judge Lockwood, suh."

"It's no mistake, Lila."

"But inside here looks like a bunch of fifty-dollar bills."

Judge Lockwood smiled kindly. "Twenty of them, to be exact. One for each year of employment. Not an exorbitant gift, I think, considering years of devoted service."

"But—"

"But nothing, Lila. You've worked very hard here, at considerable sacrifice to your family, I'm sure. Take last Saturday night, for instance. I know you like to be home with those youngsters on the weekend, but here you were helping me clean out my study. What a job! I appreciate that kind of sacrifice, Lila, I surely do."

"But Judge Lockwood, suh, I weren't here last Saturday night. You be mixed up. That was the Saturday before we was workin'—"

"Last Saturday," Judge Lockwood repeated, still smiling but his eyes as flat as slate. "Think hard. I'm sure you'll remember it that way."

"But—"

"You like working here, don't you, Lila?"

"Yes suh," she said quickly, sensing a threat.

"Then I suggest you take that gift. I further suggest that you think hard about last Saturday night."

Silently, Lila stuffed the envelope in the breast pocket of her white uniform dress. She didn't know whether to be mad or glad and thought maybe she was both at the same time. A thousand dollars would buy a lot of things. Fuel oil for the winter. Winter jackets. New shoes instead of used.

"I would like," said Judge Lockwood, "to make things easier for you and that family of yours."

"You would?" Yes, decided Lila, Judge Lockwood is surely crazy, crazy as a loon. Well, if he was gonna start throwing his money around, Lila was gonna position herself to catch some of it.

"Indeed," he went on. "I'll be inclined to repeat this gift around Christmastime."

"Lordy," breathed Lila.

"So that business about Saturday night, Lila . . . If anybody asks . . ."

"I was right here, Judge Lockwood. Helpin' you clean out the study."

It was a small thing, after all. Why should it matter? And those kids needed shoes, the way their soles were flappin' to beat the band when they walked . . .

Spencer McCloud sat across a mahogany desk from Dr. Harlan Warren, chief administrator of Silver Glen, withdrew a Dunhill cigarette from a gold case, tamped it down on the monogram, and lit it with a slim onyx lighter.

"So," said Dr. Warren, smiling expansively, "to what do I owe the pleasure of this visit?"

Spencer exhaled a ribbon of blue smoke, totally ignoring the THANK YOU FOR NOT SMOKING sign just in back of Dr. Warren's left shoulder. "Oh," said Spencer, "it's a small matter, really. Hardly worth bothering about. But I need a minor favor." He stressed the word "minor."

"Anything," said Dr. Warren quickly. "Just name it."

Spencer looked at Dr. Warren, carefully masking his disdain. You bet your ass, snotnose. You bet your ass you'll do anything. For your biggest benefactor you'll do anything and then some.

"When I visited Mrs. McCloud on Saturday night—as, of course, I always do on Saturday nights—I neglected to sign the register." Both men knew the register was a ritual of entry that was meticulously maintained. Residents of Silver Glen were delicate in nature. Only approved visitors were allowed access. "Hell," Spencer went on, "I've been visiting this place for so many years, I guess I just forgot. Breezed on by, you know."

An expression of puzzlement crossed Harlan Warren's face. "Nurse Chapman would have been on duty Saturday night—"

"Right," said Spencer quickly. "She was at the desk."

"She's a stickler for detail," said Dr. Warren. "I can't imagine anyone getting by, Mr. McCloud. Even you."

"Maybe," smiled Spencer, "she was in the can."

"Oh, she'd have gotten coverage. She's very reliable, Nurse Chapman is."

"And I'm not?" said Spencer, putting the barest edge in his voice.

"Oh, I didn't say that, Mr. McCloud. Certainly not." Dr. Warren looked decidedly uncomfortable now. "I'm afraid I don't understand. What seems to be the trouble?"

"Questions may be asked, Dr. Warren. Potentially embarrassing questions. About me. About my whereabouts on Saturday night."

"I see," said Dr. Warren, not seeing at all.

"I would prefer to avoid any repercussions, any, ah, fallout from such questions . . ."

"I beg your pardon?" said Dr. Warren.

"I was here," snapped Spencer, losing patience now. "On Saturday night. I was on your premises. There is a possibility— a remote one, of course—that I may have to verify that."

"Oh."

"Yes. And it will be easier all around if you allow me to sign the register now."

"Oh," said Dr. Warren. "My goodness. Well, surely Mrs. McCloud would be in a position to verify your presence that night."

"I would prefer not to subject her to an interrogation of

that nature," said Spencer smoothly. "I think you'll agree that it might disturb her."

"It might," said Dr. Warren, sounding unconvinced.

"And besides," said Spencer, "her memory is highly unreliable."

"Oh my," said Dr. Warren. "Well, it would be highly irregular for us to alter the register after the fact. Dear, dear, we are in a dilemma here, aren't we?"

"There's no dilemma here, Dr. Warren," said Spencer icily. "There are other considerations. Other irregularities, if you will. For one, there is the fact that it would be highly irregular for me to cancel my pledge for the new south wing—"

"But," blurted Dr. Warren, "the ground-breaking is tomorrow. A deposit has been paid." Dr. Warren looked very distressed now.

"For another, there is the irregularity of your private form of entertainment."

"I beg your pardon," said Dr. Warren, blanching visibly.

"I am talking, Dr. Warren, about that nasty compulsion you have to indulge in narcotics."

"I don't—"

"Cocaine, Dr. Warren. Nose candy. Or have you graduated to freebasing?"

"I'm off that stuff now," said Dr. Warren pleadingly. "Mostly. I'm in therapy. I'm off—"

"Maybe," said Spencer skeptically. "Maybe so."

"And you were the one who supplied me," said Dr. Warren. "You said you had access to good stuff in the city."

"Your mind is playing tricks," said Spencer. "With cocaine it often does, I understand. Paranoia sets in. But in any event, who would believe you? And who would care?"

"What do you want from me?" said Dr. Warren. The man looked ready to crumble in his chair.

"The register, Dr. Warren. And your cooperation, of course."

"Of course," said Dr. Harlan Warren hollowly. And he got up to get the book from the front desk . . .

"Huey, my boy, glad I found you here. Care to bend an elbow with your old man?"

Huey Crane looked at his father warily as he set two Budweisers on the coffee table and popped each one open. Something was up.

"Sure, Pop," said Huey carefully, his curiosity overriding his disgust for the moment.

"So, Huey," said Ripley, leaning back in the recliner, "how's the job going?"

"Fine," said Huey.

"Sal Monti giving you any trouble?" Sal Monti owned the septic cleaning service Huey worked for.

"Nope."

"That's good," said Ripley. "Real good. How's your social life?"

"Dad, why don't you cut the crap?"

"Huh?" Ripley almost snapped forward in the extended recliner. His face turned the barest shade of pink.

"What is it you want?"

"Can't a man even talk to his own son?" said Ripley in a wounded voice. "Can't a man try at least?"

"Dad, we haven't been father and son for a long time."

"Well," Ripley nodded his head sagely, "I'll admit we haven't been as close as we might have been."

"We've been enemies, Dad."

"Enemies?" Ripley's pink face turned slightly pale. "I wouldn't say that, Huey. Oh no, I wouldn't say that."

"I would. You want me to say why?"

"Uh, no," said Ripley quickly. "That won't be necessary."

"I kinda thought not," said Huey, moving to get up.

"Wait!" Ripley shot up and grabbed his son's arm. Huey looked at his father's hand as though it were a claw. "I need your help, Huey."

"Take your hand off of me," said Huey quietly. "I don't want you to touch me, never wanted you to touch me, not after—"

"Okay, okay," said Ripley contritely. "Sorry."

"So spit it out, Dad. How do you need my help?"

"I was, ah, attending to some business on Saturday night. It was nothing. Just, you know—"

"I don't want to know, Dad." Huey held up his hand. "Don't tell me. I can imagine what kind of business. If you were involved, that's enough."

"Okay," said Ripley, "okay. Suffice it to say that there seems to be an ugly set of circumstances that might make things difficult for me and that it would alleviate the problem considerably if I can place myself at home on Saturday night."

"But you weren't at home," said Huey, being deliberately dense.

"I know that!" exploded Ripley. God, how he hated conversations like this. Unpleasant conversations. Conversations in which he had to squirm.

"Don't shout," said Huey, "or I'll leave. We'll forget the whole thing."

"Okay," said Ripley. "The long and the short of it, Huey, is that I want you to say, if it proves necessary, which I'm sure it won't, I want you to say—"

"Say what?" said Huey blankly.

"Say that I was here on Saturday night."

"Which you weren't," said Huey doggedly. If Huey Crane had his way, no one would ever get their facts mixed up again.

"Right," said Ripley, striving for control. "Right."

"Wait a minute," said Huey. "Saturday's the night that woman was killed. That Peabody lady." His eyes widened.

"I didn't do it, Huey. I swear. I swear to God I didn't

do it. Surely you don't think I'm capable of cold-blooded murder."

Huey looked at his father and realized that the man had no idea how ridiculous his words sounded. "I think you're capable of almost anything," he said back.

"Well, I didn't. Please God, believe me. I didn't do that. I *was* doing something else. Illegal, if you must know. Something that, if it comes out, will ruin me. All this that we have here" —he waved his beer can, spilling some in the process—"all this that we have *together* will be gone."

"Big deal," said Huey. "I can live a simple life."

"Yes," said Ripley. "Maybe that's true. I think you can. And me? No, I don't pretend that you care about me at all. But what about your pregnant girlfriend?"

"What?" Huey's head snapped around. "How'd you know about Bessie?"

"I know about most of what goes on in this town, Huey. I know about Bessie. Know she's had something in the oven for three months without proper prenatal care—"

"We don't have a whole lotta money," said Huey. "I didn't want to go to you. We're gonna try to make it on our own. There's a clinic over in Norwalk—"

"A clinic!" Ripley spoke emotionally, sliding with ease into this new role. "A clinic for my grandchild? Oh no, I won't have it. No indeed. Bessie deserves the best of care."

"You never liked Bessie," Huey broke in. "You said she was white trash, said her teeth looked bad. If she was a horse, you said, you'd never buy her."

"Well," Ripley tried to smile, "a man can mellow in his old age. And a grandchild changes a lot of things. I want you to have a nice wedding. Soon, so she won't show that much."

"Bessie's folks can't afford any nice wedding."

"I'll pay."

"You'll what?" Huey was sure he'd heard wrong.

"I'll pay. For the wedding. For the honeymoon. For the

medical expenses. I want my grandchild to have the best. You can both move into this house."

"Oh no," laughed Huey. He knew there had to be a catch somewhere. It all sounded too good to be true. The catch was Ripley. Bessie and Huey and a little baby living under the same roof with Ripley Crane.

"I won't crowd you, Huey. A young family, I can understand. I plan to move into the apartment over the garage."

"Holy shit, Dad, you must be sweating Saturday night pretty bad."

Ripley Crane looked at his son and almost said, It's not that. Almost said, I really do want to help my granchild. But for once he decided to tell the truth. "I don't want to go to prison," he said.

"Okay," said Huey. He set the wet can down on the table, then picked it up again, remembering that it would leave a ring and that the table would be his. "Okay. But I'm doing it for my child, just remember that. Not for you . . ."

"Jimmy?"

"Yes, Marcel?" Jimmy Perkins looked up over the edge of his *Wall Street Journal* only briefly. "We're taking a beating on that Kodak stock. I guess I should dump it. Duke Power doesn't look too hot either. But Loew's is holding steady, always does."

"Jimmy?"

"Yeah?" Still he didn't look up.

"Jimmy," said Marcel, his voice getting slightly shrill, "we've got to talk."

"Talk?" repeated Jimmy. He put down the paper. "Sure. Okay. Let's talk." He grabbed a delicate porcelain teapot and poured pink tea into a translucent cup. He added a generous amount of milk, preferring to drink his tea the English way. He lifted the cup to perfect lips.

271

"We used to do that," sighed Marcel. "Talk."

"Oh," snorted Jimmy, "you're starting on that jag again. The we're-growing-apart crap. Look, get off it, Marcel. As soon as your book's done, we'll take that cruise we were talking about. You know, the one to the Mediterranean."

"I don't know if I can finish the book," said Marcel miserably.

"What?" Jimmy set the cup down in its saucer.

"I can't concentrate."

"And why not?" Jimmy sounded like a petulant child. The threat of Marcel not working hit him where it hurt the most—in the pocketbook. "Something wrong?"

"I guess you could say that." At that point Marcel fled from the table and threw up his Rice Chex into the sink.

"Jesus," said Jimmy. He rushed over to Marcel and put his hand on the small man's back as he retched up the last of his breakfast. AIDS, he thought in a panic. Jesus Christ, he's got AIDS. "Stop this, Marcel. You're scaring me, you hear?"

"Sorry," said Marcel, straightening up. He ran a fistful of paper towels under the faucet and dabbed his face. He tucked in his shirt. He went back to the table and sat down.

"So tell me, Marcel. What's this all about?"

"You remember the night we had that fight?"

"Which night?" said Jimmy. "We've had a lot of fights lately."

"I know. But the last time. Saturday night."

"Oh," said Jimmy easily. "Yeah. I remember. You stormed out of here, jumped in the Bentley, and spun gravel all over the lawn. I had to redistribute it the next day. You also, I might add, completely demolished a nice azalea I planted only last spring. Drove right over the thing."

"Jimmy," said Marcel all at once, "a woman named Agnes Peabody was murdered that night. Perhaps you've heard about it."

"Oh that," said Jimmy, lighting a cigarette. "Yeah. I heard."

"Well, it seems I could be charged with this crime."

272

"You?" Jimmy Perkins choked on his own smoke. "That's the most ridiculous thing I ever heard of."

"Not so ridiculous," Marcel shot back, his pride stung now. "I went out with the woman. On a date."

Jimmy's expression scared Marcel more than anything he could remember in a long time. It was cold. Bloodless. He looked Marcel in the eyes and he smiled. "I know," he said.

"You know?" Marcel felt the bottom of his stomach drop out.

"I knew all along. I knew about your little soiree at the dinner theatre and I knew about your pathetic plans. Marriage," he hooted. "That's a laugh."

"How," whispered Marcel, "did you know?"

"You're a writer, Marcel, and like most writers you keep a diary."

"That's mine! You had no right—"

"It's pretty boring reading usually. But the part about Agnes Peabody was a kick."

Marcel looked at Jimmy Perkins and felt revulsion. How, he wondered, could I have lived with him all these years. "You make me sick," he said.

"Yeah? Well that's tough. Just think about this. I make you sick, but I also make you safe. I mean, who knows? Maybe you went out with her again. That night. See, without me, you don't have an alibi for Saturday night, do you?"

Marcel considered lying but knew it wouldn't do any good. "No," he said miserably. "But what about you, Jimmy? You knew about Agnes. You could have hurt her. You could have—"

"Shut up!" snapped Jimmy.

"Well, what about you? Don't you think the police will want to know where you were on Saturday night."

Jimmy looked at Marcel with guileless eyes. "Why, I was here on Saturday night. With you." He paused, letting the words sink in. "Let's face it, ol' buddy. We both need each other. And we're going to need each other for a long, long time ..."

Of all the suspects, Loomis Brewster was the most direct.

"Mama" he said one night as Hattie sat knitting, "anybody asks you, you tell 'em I was home last Saturday night."

In her nervousness, Hattie dropped a stitch. She had known this confrontation would be coming, but that didn't make it any less difficult. She let the knitting fall to her lap and twisted the needles in her hands.

"What's this all about?" she asked softly.

"What's what about?" snapped Loomis, who was unaccustomed to having his directives questioned.

"Saturday night," she pressed on, hardly able to speak through the dryness of her mouth. "You weren't here Saturday night, Loomis."

"Doesn't matter," said Loomis. "You'll say I was."

He sounded so sure.

"I will not," she said in an almost whisper, "say that lie for you." She said it so softly he almost missed it. Almost.

"What?" he said, not believing his own ears. His face took on a mean, dangerous look. "What's that you say?"

"You heard me, boy. I don't know what kind of trouble you're in with that Lou Pontella. I don't think you killed Agnes Peabody, either, but when you look at me that way, I think maybe you did."

"Why you, you—"

"But I will not lie for you."

"—miserable old cunt!"

She couldn't believe it. Her own boy calling her such a name. He sprang from his chair, the flat of his hand raised to strike her the way he'd done before. But this time she rose to meet him. In a blind panic, Hattie Brewster raised a knitting needle to protect herself. The hand came down expecting to hit flesh and hit needle instead, causing the sharp stationary object to ram right through the soft center meat of his open palm.

"Arrrrrrrrughhhhh!" screamed Loomis in pain. Like a wounded animal he careened around the living room, shaking the bleeding hand in the air spasmodically. Blood spattered on Hattie, on the knitting, on the color-coordinated furniture and the hot pink carpet. In spite of her terror, Hattie took a small measure of satisfaction in the fact that the model would be unsuitable for showing.

Loomis bolted to the kitchen, held his throbbing hand over the stainless steel sink, and yanked out the needle. Breathing hard, he wrapped a dish towel around the wounded hand. "Now you're gonna get it," he said under his breath. "You've pushed me too far this time."

He stepped from the kitchen into the garage and grabbed hold of a length of snow chain with his good hand. In one swift motion, he swung it around his fist, allowing eighteen inches to dangle to the floor.

"You're really gonna get it this time," he said hoarsely as he came back into the living room jangling the chain up and down. "Gonna get it now."

"Loomis," said Hattie as she backed away from her son. "It was an accident. Don't, Loomis. Please." But he kept coming. "Someone will hear," she said in desperation. It was the worst threat she could think of.

He swung once and caught her across the stomach, knocking the wind out of her. When she doubled over, he swung the chain across her back.

"All right," she cried. "I'll lie. I'll lie for you."

Maybe Loomis didn't hear Hattie. Or maybe he was so angry he just didn't care. Because Loomis hit her once more before he managed to stop himself. And when he looked down at his mother crumpled on the floor, Loomis felt his anger turn to revulsion. Revulsion at what he had done. And sadness at the futility of it all. And fear, too. He reached down to touch her and hoped nothing was broken. After all, his mother might have to stand up for him. And when she did, she would have to look good.

36 He sensed her before he saw her.
"Mother? Is that you?"

Noiselessly he closed the door behind him. He listened. She could be so quiet sometimes, purposely walking on her toes so her high heels wouldn't go click-click-click. She liked to creep up on him. Scare him. It was a game.

Well, today it was a game he wouldn't play. He was tired. He was irritable, irritable when he had every reason in the world to be happy. Things were going well, not just some things, either. Everything. His work. His stature in the community. His social life. Even his health. The headaches had stopped, the dizziness, too. He was sleeping better. There were no bad dreams, at least none he could remember.

Deliberately he ignored her. He moved to take off his topcoat, but stopped first to search the pockets, checking for car keys. Yes, they were there. And something else too. He withdrew a cylindrical object and held it in the palm of his gloved hand. A roll of cherry Life Savers.

Now what on earth had possessed him to buy those? Then he remembered. It had been a man. A man brushed against him in the news store, distracted him, just as he'd been reaching for a pack of peppermints. He'd been startled. Afraid? Of course not, that was stupid. But even now a tingle of anxiety traveled down his spine. No. He'd simply been distracted and grabbed cherry Life Savers instead of peppermint. It was no big deal. He let them drop into the umbrella stand that doubled as a wastebasket in the foyer. Even Mother wouldn't eat cherry Life Savers.

"Sweets rot your teeth."

The words popped into his head. Her words. Her voice.

"You hear me, boy?"

"I knew you were here, Mother."

"Brush, boy. Brush. Up and down, up and down. Not across. Listen to me, boy. I *said* up and down. You never listen, do you? Never learn. Here. I'll show you."

"You're hurting me, Mother." He could taste Pepsodent in his mouth. "Please." Menthol clogged his throat. The brush went up and down, up and down, up and down, stiff white bristles tearing at tender pink gums. Harder and harder. "Please!" She rammed it in the back, all the way, better to brush the back molars, rammed it with such force that he gagged. "Ach! Stop! Please!"

"You listen to me, boy. You hear?"

Sticky warm liquid flooded his mouth. Blood. But still she brushed. "Stob," he glugged. Tears streamed down his face. She held his chin fast between bony thumb and forefinger. She looked into his swimming eyes with her own—eyes bright as icepicks. He was drowning in foam and blood and the lavender odor of her own sweet breath.

"Listen to me, boy! Or the next time it will be lye soap! Hear?"

"Yes! Yes! I swear!"

"I swear," he whispered to himself now. He looked up from the umbrella stand wastebasket and into the living room. It was then that he saw her.

She was sitting in the bow-back Windsor, an old chair, an uncomfortable chair, but the one she seemed to favor nonetheless. She sat erect and regal, her back arched away from the spindles, her ankles crossed demurely. Her hair, silver gray, was perfectly styled. Her clothes, a Pendleton skirt and white silk blouse, were obviously expensive, fashionable yet understated. Yes, she always did have style. Her skin was the skin of a much younger woman. She barely bothered with makeup, just a hint of pink lipstick, just the barest blush of color on her high cheekbones. He looked at her now, sitting in that chair, her body framed in firelight, and once again he was amazed. She never seemed to grow old. Everyone else did, himself included, but not her. She was ageless. Timeless.

"You made a fire," he said, hoping he sounded properly appreciative.

"Somebody had to see to it. A body could freeze in this house the way you keep the thermostat down."

"I told you, Mother—if you get cold, turn up the thermostat." He tried to speak politely. Patiently. It would be unwise to anger her, most unwise.

"Far be it from me to meddle in a house that's not my own."

"It is your house. What's mine is yours. You know that."

"Far be it from me to raise the heat when no one's here anyway. It would be a waste. Just for me."

"I want you to be comfortable. Really." Please, Mother. I want you to be comfortable. And happy, too. Yes, please God, she must be happy.

"You're never home," she accused, going back to her favorite subject.

"I told you," he hastened to explain. "My work. It keeps me so busy. We're short on staff. I have a lot of responsibility—"

"Don't talk to me of responsibility!"

"I didn't mean—"

"Me, who raised you by myself! That's responsibility, let me tell you. A woman alone with a boy, an ungrateful boy. A sick boy."

"I wasn't ungrateful," he blurted. "Never, I promise. I was never ungrateful." He was whimpering, and he hated it when he did that, hated it. But he couldn't help it. And I wasn't sick! Not then I wasn't! This he wanted to shout. He wanted to shout it and throttle her as well. But of course he did neither.

"You've found another girl, haven't you."

"No, Mother, I swear." He felt the prickle of perspiration under the armpits of his starched white shirt.

"Don't lie to me, boy." She fixed unblinking gray eyes on him, allowing no room for escape.

"I'm not lying."

"You've found another girl. Yes, I can see it plain as day. You feel something for her, don't you? You think it's love."

"No, no . . ."

"You're such a fool. Just like your father—a skirt chaser. You want to fuck her, that's what you want to do."

"Mother!"

"If you haven't already, that is. You're just like your father."

He forgot himself then and lost his temper. "He wasn't like that! He wasn't! He was a simple man, a loud man maybe. An unrefined man. But it was you! You who chased . . ." He choked on his own words, shocked.

"What did you say, boy?"

Such a simple question. But the sharp tongue, the icy look, the set of her jaw, he'd seen it all before. What he felt now was raw terror.

"Nothing," he breathed. "Nothing."

"Nothing?" She smiled. "I don't think so. Well, just remember, boy—you were the one who called your father. Made him come home. Made him see what he shouldn't have seen, was never meant to see. You were the one who—"

"Stop!"

"—got him killed. You!"

He couldn't fight her. He was crying now, crying openly in front of her. It was what she wanted, after all. His humiliation.

"There, there," she said soothingly. She indicated a spot on the floor next to her, pointed to it with the toe of her patent leather shoe. Sit, that's what she was saying. Sit down next to me. Beneath me, boy. Sit.

Meekly he sat by the chair. He rested his cheek against her

279

knee. She patted his head, just as she'd done so many times in the past.

"Now tell me," she said. "Tell me about this new girl."

"She's not like the others," he whispered. Oh, he hoped she would believe him. This time he hoped she would. She had to believe. Otherwise . . . but no, he wouldn't think of that now.

"I'm sure she's not," said his mother, not sounding sure at all. "But tell me about her anyway."

And haltingly he did. He told her about the new lady in his life. He told her about this rekindling of an old flame. He talked in the firelight, his body framed by the glow from the hearth. And as the fire died, he talked well into the night, talked to an empty chair.

37 "You got a new roommate, Pops."

Forrest cast a jaundiced eye at the orderly who was pushing a gurney into his semiprivate room. He bit his tongue and turned his face to the wall. Pops. Who the hell did this snot-nosed kid think he was?

"Not that he'll be much company," the orderly went on. "This fella's *really* crackerjacks."

Worse than me, thought Forrest angrily. That's how he's saying it. Worse than me. Out of curiosity he turned to look at the neighboring bed at the precise moment the orderly unceremoniously dumped the body of a middle-aged man onto it.

"Easy there!" snapped Forrest.

"Right," said the orderly indifferently. He tucked the covers around the man very tightly, too tightly, it seemed to Forrest. "Like I'm gonna rot in hell. Sure." He glanced at Forrest. "This guy's a priest, would you believe it?"

Forrest looked hard at the man. Balding. Hands folded on his stomach. Staring straight up, unblinking, at the ceiling. A body's eyes could dry up the way that guy was staring. It gave Forrest the willies.

"Well, just don't get too attached, okay?" said the orderly. "He's not staying long. A few hours is all. He's, like we say, in transit. We're only keeping him until the diocese can transport him to the home they got up near Hartford. Yep, this guy is headed for the Starlight Express. Be able to say his beads all he wants."

"Why don't you just get the hell out of here?" said Forrest, losing patience. "Go play with yourself. Grow yourself some fresh zits."

"My, my. Aren't we testy today."

Forrest turned again to the wall. It was all so futile. He closed his eyes, trying to blot out the orderly, the crazy priest, the antiseptic room, and the whole damn convalescent home.

"Look, Pops," said the orderly, determined to get in his parting shot, "you may as well make the best of things. You're gonna be here till the day you die."

"Fuck you."

"Thomas!" The shrill voice belonged to Nurse Dunlop. "Are you upsetting Chief Haggarty?" She was the only halfway human being in the whole place. She barreled into the room with the determination of a drill sergeant on the way to inspection. She grabbed the orderly by the front of his starched white uniform and hoisted him up on tiptoe. "I won't have it, you hear? Doctor Munson said Chief Haggarty is not to be upset. For any reason. You just haul your ass down to the second floor before I have you out of this place on your ear."

Nurse Dunlop was a woman after Forrest's own heart. In better times—in times before Irene, too—Forrest might have surveyed Nurse Dunlop with interest. But now even the reaming out of Thomas couldn't bring a smile to his lips. He was too depressed.

Nurse Dunlop looked over her shoulder to be sure Thomas was gone. "A man called," she said in a whisper.

"What's that?" said Forrest loudly.

"A man," she repeated. "He didn't leave his name. He left a message for you, though."

"Oh?"

"It doesn't make any sense to me, but I promised I'd deliver it. He just said, 'Tell him the flavor was peppermint.'"

"Huh?" said Forrest. Then he remembered. Lenny. The Life Saver in Agnes Peabody's hand. Well, fat lot of good such knowledge would do him here. "Oh," he said, slumping back into the pillows. "Right. Peppermint."

"Does it make any sense to you?" she asked.

"No," he lied. "No sense at all."

"Don't be so down in the mouth," she said as she smoothed the covers over him. "Things will be all right soon. Your friends haven't forgotten you." Then she winked and hurried out. Forrest wondered what she meant. It seemed like some kind of code. Today certainly seemed to be the day for messages.

For a long time Forrest lay there in silence, not talking to the man in the other bed, not looking at him, either. Finally he could stand it no more. "Hey you," he called. "What's yer name?" When no reply was forthcoming, he climbed out of bed to take a look at the name card taped to the steel frame of the man's bed.

Flynn, Clement t. That's what it said.

"Pleased to meet you, Clement." He walked up and looked into the man's unblinking eyes. "I'm not Catholic, so I hope you don't mind if we skip saying Father and all that." He extended a hand, waited, then let it drop. "Christ," he muttered and climbed back into bed.

"Dominus vobiscum," came a voice from the bed.

"Don't start with that," snapped Forrest, leaning up on his elbows. "Just don't start, you hear? I'm not Catholic and I'm not religious and if you're gonna talk papist gibberish I won't know what the hell you're sayin'. So talk straight or don't talk at all."

Clement Flynn blinked once and snapped his mouth closed. Forrest was certain he'd been understood.

"I didn't mean to be rude," Forrest said after a while, trying to make amends. "It's just that this place is getting to me. I don't remember you from these parts. Where you from?"

Clement Flynn didn't answer. He didn't change position. He didn't blink, either. He just lay there like a dead man.

"Clement, ever play cards? Hearts? Acey-deucey? How 'bout it, Clem?"

But Clement Flynn still didn't respond. He remained a mystery. Silent. Ashen-faced. His mouth set tight. And because he was so mysterious, because he never said anything stupid like so many other people, Forrest chose to view him as a wise man. He vested in Clement Flynn powers and perceptions far beyond those of mortal men. It was, after all, more comforting than thinking he shared his room with a man who was cracker-jacks.

"Do you believe in God, Clement?" This question came to Forrest only after he had exhausted his life history, the solution to the national debt, an opinion (pro) on aid to the Contras, and pessimistic predictions about the impact of sexually trans-mitted diseases on the American family. "I guess it's a stupid question, you being a priest an' all."

Clement Flynn lay there listening. The string of a prayer pulled through his head. *I believe in God the Father almighty, creator of heaven and earth and in Jesus Christ, His only son, Our Lord, who was conceived of the Holy Ghost, born of the Virgin Mary, suffered under Pontius Pilate, was crucified, died, and was buried ...*

"When a man gets to be my age, he thinks about such things. I s'pose I seen a lotta things in police work should make me not believe in God. Raven's Wing's a quiet town, but still I seen some god-awful things. Forty years o' keeping' track of people's trespasses, well, a body's bound to get a snootful."

If Forrest had been looking, he might have noticed that

Clement Flynn's face was flushed, that his head was turned, that he was looking right at Forrest with a kind of desperate intensity. But Forrest was rambling and he wasn't looking.

Awful things, thought Clement. Awful things and trespasses. Oh, we could trade war stories, this policeman and I.

Forrest tried to decide whether or not to tell Clement about the time Carl Perlmutter shot both his parents. Or the time Billy Kramer at the age of twenty put his neighbor's German shepherd through the town wood chipper. (A pilot in Bethel subsequently murdered his wife in the exact same fashion. A copycat killing, the newspapers called it.) Or the time Forrest had to unstring Axel Sherman from the ash tree in his folks' yard and Axel was only ten but just as dead as if he'd been thirty. An accident, said the coroner charitably. Children don't commit suicide. Forrest saw that for what it was: a lie. But he didn't say anything to Axel's parents. He couldn't, seeing their faces.

No. Forrest decided not to tell Clement those stories, even though they were true.

"I'm not what you'd call religious, but I must believe in God. You know why? 'Cause I never experienced what people call despair. You know what I mean, Clement? Even at the worst times I never had that."

Oh, thought Clement, I know despair. I know it well. The despair of my impotence in the confessional. The despair of my impotence right here and now. He turned his gaze back to the cracks in the ceiling.

Forrest pointed his chin in Clement's direction and studied the man respectfully, as though expecting his companion to ask a question. Or concur. Or argue. Clement didn't, though.

"Somewhere along the line," continued Forrest, "a fella told me—or maybe I read it—that despair reflects a disbelief in the Almighty. It reflects a belief that everything is really nothing. Now that sure don't make sense, something being nothing.

"Sides," Forrest went on, "I'm working on a case now. A big case. It gives a body a sense of purpose, I can tell you that."

What case? Clement Flynn wanted to scream the words.

And, indeed, Forrest did tell. He told everything. He told about Agnes. Told about Betty and Marilyn and Emmylou and Muriel and Harmony, too. He told about the letters and the suspects, described them in detail, even.

"Oh my God," said Clement.

"Don't start that again."

"No," whispered Clement. "No. You don't understand."

"What?" said Forrest, startled now. The man was talking English, not gibberish. "What're you saying, man?"

"Nothing," said Clement quickly. "Never mind." The sanctity of the confessional must be preserved. The thought bounded through his brain, and he clung to it. If he broke, if he violated that trust, his beliefs—his very life itself—would be a mockery. Meaningless.

Forrest swung his legs over the side of the bed. He leaned forward. "Look, Clement, don't go getting yourself excited. It's gonna be okay, see?" He walked over to Clement's bed and leaned over Clement Flynn's face. Nervously, he looked toward the door. Then he took a deep breath and dropped his voice to the barest whisper.

"I know who did it, Clement."

"No," breathed Clement softly.

"Yes!" He grabbed the priest's shoulders in glee. "Don't you see? I figured it out! And when I get out of here—and I will, Clement, yes I will—we'll nail the bastard."

Father Clement Flynn sighed hopelessly. Sick at heart, he turned his face to the wall.

"What's wrong, Clement?" Forrest shook him.

Slowly Clement Flynn turned his face back to his tormentor. "I am sworn to a vow of secrecy. Surely you can accept that."

"I accept nothing," Forrest hissed fiercely. "Nothing! For the love of God, Clement, if you know something about this, tell me now."

For the love of God, thought Clement hopelessly. For the love of God I can't. I can't tell. But he looked into Forrest's desperate blue eyes, eyes from which there was no escape, and he wavered.

"Tell me," pressed Forrest through clenched teeth.

"I have not met him," sighed Clement.

"But you know him?"

"In a way." The words came slowly, haltingly. "I met him twice. Once in the confessional, when he . . . ah . . . he spoke of these things . . . these crimes."

"Yes?" pushed Forrest.

"I didn't see him then. There's a screen. You could look through it, but we don't. We press our fingers to our temples and cast our eyes down . . ."

"But you saw him later?"

". . . That's what they teach us, you know. Don't look up. A safeguard for us, really. If we don't know who it is, we're not tempted to break the vow of silence. The sanctity . . ." Clement babbled on, relieved to have shared a measure of his burden. "But a voice is as bad as a face. I couldn't forget. I just couldn't! I would hear that voice. In my dreams. As I said Mass. Everywhere, over and over again. There was no escape, no peace. I thought of this man constantly. It made me crazy, you understand? Crazy! And I thought of his victims, thought about them, too."

"You said you met him twice," demanded Forrest. He shook the man in his hands, shook him like a rag doll.

"What's going on here!" Nurse Dunlop stood in the doorway, flanked by Thomas and a second orderly. "This is a fine kettle of fish. Chief Haggarty, you get back in bed this instant."

Thomas stepped forward and put a hand on Forrest's elbow, but the old man wrenched free. "Tell me I'm right!" he shouted into Clement Flynn's face. Desperately he leaned forward and whispered a name into Clement Flynn's ear before both orderlies grabbed his shoulders and forced him back to bed.

"Please!" he yelled.

"And you..." Nurse Dunlop regained her composure and turned her attention to Clement Flynn. "Well, it seems you've regained your power of speech, Father Flynn, and I congratulate you for it. But you've got Chief Haggarty here all stirred up, and we can't have that now, can we? It's just as well you're on your way out of here." She nodded to Thomas and his companion. "Well, don't just stand there gaping. The ambulance is waiting outside. Kindly prepare Father Flynn for transport."

"Clement," pleaded Forrest, "just tell me I'm right. I'm not asking you to break any vows."

Clement's mind whirled. The orderlies stripped back the covers. They lifted him onto a gurney. There was no time. Wildly he plunged into speech, saying whatever popped into his head as it came to him: "In the news store! That's where I saw him!" Clement had reached for a pack of gum and brushed against someone. "Excuse me." That's all the man said, but it was enough. Clement would never forget that voice. Stricken, he looked up and into the face of a deceptively ordinary man. "He was none of those you described. None of them!"

"No," said Forrest, shaking his head. "You're wrong."

"Blond hair!" cried Clement. "Fair, he was." His voice trailed off to a gasp.

Forrest lay frozen in bed, trying to make sense of Clement's words.

"Tall, he was. With dirty hands."

"Dirty hands?"

They were wheeling Clement Flynn away.

"Yes," Clement called back. "Blackened fingers. Smudged. Like ink." And he was gone.

Ink, thought Forrest blankly. Ink? He lay there for a long time, thinking. Finally he fell asleep.

38 Forrest sensed him before he saw him, a form moving through the darkness of the room. Groggily he opened his eyes. The door was open, and light from the nurses' station far down the hall cast an eerie glow. Groaning inside, Forrest looked at the man by the foot of his bed, thinking it was probably Thomas come back to torment him once again. Then he recognized the shadowy figure.

"Hey!" he exclaimed in relief. "You come to get me out?" The moment the words passed through his lips his relief turned to fear. All at once he understood. The center of town . . . the news store . . . a man with dirty hands. Of course. Lord, he'd been so blind. His heart started beating rapidly, but his face froze and he showed not the slightest trace of emotion.

"I'm just here for a visit," said the man softly. Nervously he glanced toward the door.

Where, wondered Forrest desperately, was the nurse call button? The right or the left? Think, he told himself. Think! Any sudden move would be risky. He wouldn't get a second chance.

"That's nice," said Forrest through dry lips.

"Do you have any more ideas on this murder thing?" asked the man suddenly.

"Hell, no." Forrest tried to sound convincing. "It's like the Hydra in one of them mythology stories. Eliminate one suspect and two more pop up." He twisted his head as much as he dared, searching for the call button cable, but could see nothing in the dim light. "Say," he said gruffly, "don't you have anything better to do than waste time in a midnight chat with an old man?"

"Actually," said the man, "I came here because of my mother."

"Oh?" Forrest felt prickles of sweat under his arms. His skin went clammy.

"She's been having a hard time of it lately," explained the man, oblivious to the expression on Forrest's face. "She was never a well woman, you know. Always so fragile. Out of touch."

"Sure," said Forrest.

"It's become painfully obvious that I can't keep her at home any longer. I worry about her, you see, when I'm not there. And when I am, well, it just seems to upset her. So I'm looking for a place . . ." He let the word drift off. "I feel guilty about it, but then I've been good to her all these years. Considering."

Forrest knew he should make his move. Knew he should grab for that call button. But his curiosity got the best of him. It was as though now he could see the Devil and he had to step closer for a better look. "Considering what?" he breathed.

"Considering that she killed my father."

"No," said Forrest weakly. "It was an accident."

"You never guessed, did you? Thought such a cold-blooded crime beyond a lady." He read distress on Forrest's face and hastened to add reassurance. "Don't take it too hard. She fooled everyone. My father especially. He came home unexpectedly. After I called him, I admit it." He sneered, remembering. "I knew something was going on. I called him from school, and waited for him to kill her."

"I see," said Forrest, buying time.

"Only it didn't happen that way. Somehow the bitch got the gun. Somehow she twisted it around and shot him."

"It was a long time ago," said Forrest.

"She thought it would make her happy, his being dead." He looked at the ceiling and shut his eyes. "Of course, nothing makes her happy. Nothing ever."

So that, thought Forrest, was the start of it. No. It probably began long before, with seeds planted in infancy. And here he lay after so many years of trying to understand. After so many years of wondering. Helpless. Crazily. Trevor's words came back to him. *Helpless isn't hopeless.*

"Anyway," said the man, "I thought maybe they'd have a space for her here. It's frightfully expensive, but I want the best. And I have to be sure, of course, that it is the best. That's why I decided to come here. In the middle of the night." He dropped his voice to a whisper. "It's the best time, you know. For checking."

"Yes," said Forrest. His mouth was dry. It was difficult to speak. But he forced himself to act nonchalant. Slowly he snaked his hand down the left side of the bed in search of the cable. Please, he thought. Please.

"I just hope they have a place for her," said the man again.

Forrest tried to joke. "She can have my place."

"Maybe," said the man suddenly, "that can be arranged."

No. The cable was not on the left. It had to be on the right, where the man stood. It would be risky to grab for it. A sudden move would be a tip-off. With effort, Forrest rolled onto his side. He could not see the wire draped from the headrail.

"How're they treating you here?" pressed the man.

"I've been treated worse," said Forrest. It was hard to form words. His tongue stuck to the roof of his mouth. "Listen," he said all at once. "My mouth is dry. Would you get me a glass of water?"

"Here," offered the man. "Maybe one of these will help."

Forrest stared, transfixed. There on the man's outstretched palm was an offering. A silver and blue roll of Life Savers. Peppermint. Of course. I am frightened, he thought suddenly. Yes, I am frightened to the bone. And he gave in to his fear. His tongue turned to cardboard in his mouth. He lost control of his bladder.

"What's wrong?" said the man at once, his voice taking on an edge of alarm.

"Nothing," lied Forrest. But the game was up. They looked

into each other's eyes, the hunter and the hunted now flip-flopped by condition and circumstance, and each recognized the other for what he was.

"I was wondering," said the man softly, "how long it would take you to figure things out."

"Figure what out?" said Forrest hoarsely. His heart was racing much too fast. And there was pressure, too, so much pressure he could barely breathe. No, he thought, no. Not now, not yet.

The man went on, oblivious of Forrest's condition. "The letters, of course. I knew they'd lead you to me. Sooner or later. Who knows, maybe I wanted them to."

"It wasn't the—" In a foaming sea of pain, Forrest lunged for the call button.

"Don't," said the man, grabbing his hand. "Just don't." He squeezed very hard and held on to Forrest in a kind of desperate handshake. "I wanted someone to know," he said through clenched teeth. "Can you understand that?"

"Yes," gasped Forrest. There was yet another explosion in his chest, larger than the first, a terrible explosion of pressure and pain and blinding light. "I'm having . . ." he gasped, "having . . ." He thought of Irene. Then he thought of Mildred. "Oh no," he cried.

He never got to say more. Because he drowned then, drowned in a sea of pain and blackness, blackness as dark as ink on the oldest linotype press.

39 Promptly at six the next morning, Irene, Mildred, and Trevor cruised along silent dark streets and headed toward Craigmore Convalescent Home. Trevor, still bleary-eyed from too little sleep, was at the wheel. He had refused to let

Mildred or Irene drive his prized Lincoln, and in the face of their determined pleadings had finally allowed himself to become a participant in the plan. As he drove he muttered to himself, "In for a penny, in for a pound . . ."

"What was that?" Irene piped up nervously. She wore an unpressed silt-colored uniform with *Consolidated Laundry* stitched across the breast pocket in red. The garment was much too tight.

"Nothing," said Trevor.

"I'll be happy when this is over," whispered Mildred as she looked out the window.

"Won't we all," agreed Irene.

At first, everything went according to plan. Trevor parked the car between two massive hemlocks near the back service entrance. Mildred and Irene slipped inside without any trouble. A rubberized canvas hamper on wheels was exactly where Josephine Dunlop had said it would be. They wheeled it into the elevator, closed the gate, and silently ascended to the third floor.

"Room C-eleven," whispered Irene as they stepped into a carpeted hallway. "That's what Josephine said."

Mildred was too nervous to respond but relieved to see that the hallway was deserted. According to Irene, this section of the home was reserved for the most feeble patients. In addition, it was Thanksgiving week. Patients who were able had already gone to relatives for the holiday, and several staff members had taken vacation. The timing, as Irene had been quick to point out, was perfect.

Irene counted rooms on the left as they went by. "C-five. C-seven. C-nine. C-eleven."

"This is it." she said, hardly able to contain her excitement. She pushed open the door and rushed inside. Josephine Dunlop straightened up from her task. She had been tucking in hopital corners on a bed. An empty bed.

"Where is he?" asked Irene anxiously. "Did you move him?"

Josephine wiped her hands on the sides of her white uniform. She seemed at a loss for words.

"Come on, Josie. We don't have much time here."

"I'm sorry, Irene. Really I am."

"Huh?"

"Forrest had a heart attack last night."

"No!" cried Irene. Immediately Mildred stepped forward and put a protective arm around Irene's shoulders.

"We don't know how bad it is yet. They're running tests. It doesn't look good."

"He can't have had a heart attack," Irene insisted. "He just can't. We're gonna take him home."

"Irene," said Mildred gently.

"No! No! We're gonna take him home."

"Home," said Josephine firmly, "is a place he simply cannot go. Not now. Maybe not ever."

"Shut up!" shouted Irene, losing all control now. She wrenched free of Mildred's arm. "Come on, Millie. We're goin' to that hospital."

"Don't bother, Irene," said Josephine not unkindly.

"And why not?"

"He's on machines right now. Until they've done more tests, they've got to assume it's an extremely fragile situation. The next twenty-four hours are critical. No visitors are allowed except for immediate family."

"Well, we'll just see about that!"

"But even if you were allowed, he wouldn't know you. He's heavily sedated. Totally unconscious. Irene, look . . .I've seen a lot of this. You should prepare yourself for the worst."

"The hell I will!" cried Irene. "He's gonna be okay!"

Later, on the way home, she would repeat those words. "He's gonna be okay. He's gonna be okay." She looked bleakly out the window of the Lincoln and seemed to deflate. "It's all my fault."

"Nonsense," said Trevor, his eyes on the rain-slicked road ahead.

"I shoulda moved quicker. Shoulda gotten him outta there sooner. Shoulda taken better care of him, too. I shoulda—"

"Listen to me, Irene," said Mildred. "You took excellent care of him."

"That's right," agreed Trevor. "This never would have happened if he'd behaved himself. He's just so damned contrary."

Irene wiped tears from her face. "Well, don't go picking on him now."

"No," said Trevor, "I won't do that. But when he recovers . . . when he's up and about . . ." He grabbed the wheel tightly as though by sheer force of will he could make his friend strong. "Well, then I'll give him a piece of my mind."

"See, Irene?" said Mildred. "He'll be fine."

"I wish I could be like you, Millie." Irene looked out the window at children heading for Veterans Park School, burdened with colorful knapsacks filled with books.

"And how," asked Mildred, "am I?"

"I wish I could be like you. Strong. Sensible. I wish I could not cry."

Oh, thought Mildred sadly, that's no way to be. No way at all.

40 Later Mildred, Irene, and Trevor sat in the living room. Just as Josephine Dunlop had predicted, attempts to see Forrest that afternoon had proven futile. They were politely but firmly turned away at Norwalk Hospital, where they were told that the patient was under evaluation—with no visitors allowed except immediate family.

As the sun went down, they didn't bother to turn on the lights but sat, instead, in semidarkness. They spoke little, only when a random thought or memory occurred to one or the other. Irene would say, "I think I'll sleep in the sewing room tonight. I can't bear to look at his union suit hanging in the closet." And Mildred would respond, "He sure did like that bourbon." Silently she remembered the rest of the case and wondered if Forrest would ever get to drink it.

"Well," said Trevor reluctantly, "I guess I better be going." Although he never said anything, it had become painfully obvious to Mildred since Mary Margaret's death that Trevor hated going home to an empty house.

"I would be ever so grateful," she said carefully, "if you would consider staying here for tonight."

"Oh no," he said too quickly, "I couldn't—"

"There are a half dozen empty bedrooms up there. Although maybe they're not up to your standards. There are tumbleweeds under the beds. They haven't been cleaned—"

"It's not that," he said.

"People will talk," said Irene. "That's what he's afraid of."

"You can't be serious," said Mildred in disbelief.

The distinguished doctor flushed slightly. "Well, after all, Mildred, you are a woman alone. A woman separated from her husband. An attractive woman—"

Mildred almost choked on the olive in her martini.

"—and I'm only recently a widower." Clearly the words were agonizing for Trevor. Mildred didn't know whether to be flattered or angry.

"Oh for heaven's sake!" she blurted . "Let them talk, then."

"Well," he said, "if you're sure. What with you two here alone and all, maybe I could stay up on the third floor. Just to keep an eye on things, you understand. Until Forrest comes back."

"That would make me feel ever so much better," said Mildred without batting an eye.

"Me too," said Irene.

They were interrupted by soft chimes announcing a visitor

at the front door. Winston hoisted himself up and went to investigate. Mildred and Irene looked at each other. They weren't expecting company and didn't want any either. Reluctantly Mildred got up to answer. She had long since given up the notion of Irene as servant, and besides, it was her house and her responsibility.

"Clyde," she said in surprise as she opened the door. "I didn't expect you."

"Well," he smiled, "that's a fine welcome. We had a date, remember?"

"Oh Lord," sighed Mildred. She pressed her fingers to her temples and closed her eyes wearily. "I forgot all about it."

"I'm that forgettable?" he joked.

"No, of course not. It's just that there's so much trouble right now."

"What's wrong?" he said, his face full of concern.

They stood in the foyer and she told him about Forrest.

"He's alive?" Clyde asked anxiously.

"Yes. But we don't know the prognosis. They're running tests. So you see I can't go out with you tonight. Not under these circumstances. I wouldn't be very good company. And besides"—she lowered her voice—"Irene's very upset. Someone should be here with her."

"I'll speak for myself, Millie, if you don't mind." Irene had come up behind her, creeping as was her fashion.

"And I'll be here to keep her company," Trevor put in, a little too gruffly, Mildred thought.

"But what if there's a call . . ." From the hospital, she meant. Bad news. But she didn't say it.

"If there's a call, we'll find you," said Trevor. "Where are you going to be?"

Irene looked at Clyde.

"At my house," he said quickly. "I'm cooking dinner myself. Roast beef."

"There," said Irene. "It's all settled. We'll be fine, Millie."

"Well, if you're sure . . ."

"We're sure," said Trevor.

Why, it almost seems as though Trevor is pushing me out the door, Mildred thought as she put on her coat. But then why on earth does he seem so grumpy about it?

41 Trevor tried various methods to keep Irene's mind off Forrest. They walked Winston, played double solitaire, worked on a jigsaw puzzle, and even watched "A Current Affair," a program Trevor detested but tonight endured because Irene enjoyed it immensely under most circumstances. This evening, though, her eyes kept welling up; Maury Povich must have looked like a fragmented jigsaw man to her. At eight o'clock the phone rang shrilly, causing Irene to scream and Trevor to drop a log he was carrying to the fireplace.

Both lunged for the phone, but Irene was more determined and wrested it from Trevor's grip.

"Hello," she said hollowly.

"Mildred Bennett?" came the voice on the phone. Irene could barely hear, what with the phone tilted askew in Trevor's hand between her ear and his.

"No, she's not here. I'm her friend, Irene Purdy. Who's this?" Just get it over with, she thought miserably.

"This is Scott Haggarty. Forrest's son."

"He's dead, isn't he, Mr. Haggarty. That's what you're calling to tell me." A fresh cascade of tears spilled silently down her cheeks and onto her checked flannel shirt.

"No," he reassured her. "He's a tough old bird. Tougher than I gave him credit for."

"Tough," she repeated, hanging on to the word. "Yes."

"They think he's going to be all right. It was a heart attack, yes, and there was some damage. But if all goes well, he should recover."

"Recover?" she echoed, hardly daring to hope.

"Yes!" Scott, laughed. "Can you believe it? They say he's probably got years left. Years."

In her excitement Irene dropped the phone into Trevor's hand. So great was her happiness and gratitude that she did a little dance around the room.

"This is Dr. Bradford," said Trevor. "I'm afraid Miss Purdy has been overcome by emotion. It is most kind of you, Mr. Haggarty, to inform us about this blessed turn of events. Most kind."

"Actually," admitted Scott sheepishly, "that isn't why I called."

"Oh?"

"I need a favor, Dr. Bradford."

"What kind of favor?"

"Well, they say Dad's going to be all right. *If* he follows doctor's orders. Most important, he has to get complete rest. No excitement of any kind. But he's not cooperating at all."

Trevor laughed. "Oh, tell me about it. Is he pinching the nurses? Drinking bootleg bourbon?"

"I wish it were something like that," said Scott. "It's much worse. He's extremely agitated. Very upset. Causing one helluva hullabaloo. Even the sedatives don't seem to work."

"What's he upset about?" asked Trevor, suddenly listening very intently. He waved his hand behind him, motioning Irene to be quiet.

"Just nonsense. Says he's got to talk to you folks. Keeps babbling something about Mildred being in danger. Something about a man named Clyde—"

"Clyde?" repeated Trevor. His heart lurched. No, he thought, please God, no. Frightened now and sick at heart, too, he asked, "Are you sure?"

"Of course I'm sure."

"Oh, my God," said Trevor softly.

"Does this make any sense to you?"

"Mr. Haggarty, listen very carefully. This is very important."

"Huh?"

"I want you to do two things. First, call the Raven's Wing police, and tell them to send help immediately to Clyde Thompson's house on Main Street." He said a silent prayer that Lenny Pulaski would be on duty. With Lenny, no questions would be asked. He'd go.

"Help for what?" Scott said.

"Just do it!" yelled Trevor. Alarmed at the tone of his voice, Irene now clung to his elbow.

"Okay, okay. I call the police. Tell 'em to go to Clyde Thompson's."

"Then go to your father. Tell him we got the message. Tell him everything will be okay."

"I don't get it," said Scott.

"Just tell him that. It should calm him down."

"If you say so." Scott sounded skeptical, but Trevor never heard. He slammed down the phone, grabbed Irene's hand, and rushed to the car.

He thought reason and logic would prevail as they always had in his life. Thought maybe, even at this late date, he could make a difference. It never occurred to him to take a gun.

42 Mildred took a tiny sip of Bailey's Irish Cream and leaned back in the chair contentedly. "Dinner was superb, Clyde. Really exceptional. And the company, too. I didn't think I could enjoy myself this evening, but thanks to you I did." She reached for her purse and moved to get up.

"You're not going so soon?" he protested.

"Oh, I've really got to get back."

"But I thought . . . I hoped . . . well, I thought you might stay here. For the night."

She let him take her in his arms. "You really are a dear," she said into his shoulder. "And I'd love to stay. But I can't. Not tonight."

He talked with his chin on her shoulder, his eyes wide open, staring off into space. "It's just that . . . well, being here alone . . . ah . . . Oh, I know it's foolish. But Mother has been impossible lately."

"Clyde." Mildred pulled away and looked at him with concern, then tried to laugh it off. "Goodness, I'd better not stay! You do need some rest. You've been alone a long time now. Your mother indeed." But in spite of her light chatter she felt a chill pass through her.

"Oh," said Clyde quickly, "I mean the memories. That's all. Her ghost, I guess."

"Well, just stop this talk of ghosts and get yourself some sleep. You're running yourself ragged at that paper, I can tell."

"Ragged," he said, almost to himself. "Yes. I suppose."

He helped her on with her mink, put on a grease-stained ski parka, one he used for work around the yard. He led her to the garage, an enormous four-car wing attached to the house. She remembered him saying that he liked to tinker with old automobiles.

"Watch your step," he cautioned her. "There's a leak in the roof I've been meaning to get fixed, and with this cold there's ice on the floor." He flipped on the light.

She saw it then. The vintage Cadillac. The burgundy fender gleamed like a mirror, so shiny it almost looked wet.

"Clyde!" she exclaimed. "I don't believe it!" She ran over to the car. "You kept it all these years!"

"In perfect condition,'" he said proudly.

"You took me to the prom in this," she said softly. "Do you remember?"

"I'll never forget," he said.

"Oh you!" she laughed. "Always with the flattery. I'd think you'd want to forget. We had a fight that night. Do you remember that?"

"No," he said carefully.

"Well, we did. I'm certain of it. You took me home early. Said you had to get home to your mother or some such excuse. On prom night, no less. We had a terrible row. We broke up that night, Clyde."

"Funny," he said, looking perplexed. "I have no recollection of that. I must have been crazy."

"Crazy, no. Sly as a fox is more like it. I was sure you had another date."

Even as she was saying the words, she saw it. Something almost lost in a clutter of paraphernalia on the walls. Almost but not quite. A red STOP sign with a handle on the bottom. Bolted to the wall. A souvenir of sorts. She saw it in an instant and masked her horror a split second later. But that was all it took. Clyde Thompson didn't miss a trick.

"I did," he said.

"Did what?" she asked lightly, her heart pounding all the while.

"I had another date."

"Oh," she said carefully. "Well."

"With Betty Murphy."

"I don't think I remember—"

"Oh, you remember her, Mildred." His voice took on a badgering, angry tone, one she'd never heard from him before. "You know very well you remember her."

I've got on high heels, she thought wildly. Just like Agnes Peabody. How can I run? Frantic, she looked around the garage for escape. Or a weapon. Anything.

"I don't understand," she said weakly, playing for time.

"Stupid bitch," he snapped. "You understand very well."

Horrified, she realized he was working himself into some

kind of frenzy. Before her very eyes he was changing into some-one she didn't even know. She backed away a step.

"I tried to warn you, but you're just like the others. Mother was right. I thought you were different. Decent. I thought you would stand by me, but no. Instead you hunt me down. You dare to presume I've done something *wrong*." The word came out a screech. "Don't you know I'm better than that? Smarter than that, too?"

With mounting terror, Mildred realized that this was a man who fully intended to kill her. Just like all the others. She backed away slowly, then bolted. Panic washed over her, and she ran blindly. Into the snow thrower. Between the lawn mowers. Around to the other side of the car.

He followed her almost leisurely. Smiling. "It will be easier," he said, "if you don't struggle."

"Please," she gasped. "I'll do what you want. Anything."

He laughed. "God, you're so true to form. That's what they all said. All of them. Oh, anything. I'll do anything! As if they could do anything to please me." He lunged, and she dodged to the right. His fingers clawed at the fur of her coat and she wrenched free. She bounced off a wall and threw herself head-long toward the workbench. There was a window. If she could just hurl herself through it . . .

A chance, she thought. I only want a chance.

"Not so fast!" He grabbed again at her coat, clutching a fistful this time. Helplessly she sprawled on the workbench. Her hands flew out randomly, grasping for anything. A mason jar full of nuts and bolts fell and shattered on the floor.

"Bitch!" he cried. "Look what you've done!"

She raked manicured fingers along the tool-studded wall. Oh please, dear God, she thought. Please. It was then that she connected with something. A long screwdriver. Des-perately she grabbed hold of it, whirled around and fled once again.

"Get back," she said, brandishing the screwdriver in front of her.

He was breathing heavily now. Enjoying every minute of it, too, she could see that.

"Don't," she said shakily as he came toward her. "Please."

He came slowly. Very sure of himself. "Now, now," he said almost soothingly. "The game's up." He lunged at her once again and she braced herself tightly for his assault.

Clyde Thompson forgot his own words of caution. He forgot about the ice. He lunged—and he slipped—falling face forward onto the rigidly held screwdriver in Mildred's hand. Horrified, Mildred watched the shaft connect with Clyde's left eyeball, pass through it ever so easily, and continue on through what she realized must be brain tissue. She felt resistance—and finally thought to let go—at the precise moment the metal shaft connected with the back of his skull.

"Aaaaaaaaauuuuuuggggggg," he screamed. It was a garbled, inhuman sound. To Mildred's horror and amazement, as he howled in incoherent pain, Clyde reached up and with one swift agonizing wrench pulled the screwdriver from his skull. Blood streamed down his face, dripped from his chin and oozed onto his parka where it formed a sodden and expanding blot. His remaining good eye seemed to roll up in its socket. Blindly he staggered toward her.

Dear God in heaven, Mildred prayed. Make him stop. Please make him stop. He took another jerky step, flailing about wildly with the bloody screwdriver, and she screamed.

"Stop," she cried in terror. "Clyde!"

Then miraculously, almost as if responding to her plea, as if wanting to lie down and take a rest and be done with the whole horrible nightmare, Clyde Thompson collapsed to his knees. He reached out to Mildred with both arms, as though imploring. Transfixed in terror, Mildred stared numbly as Clyde wavered, then toppled onto his back. He lay there in an agonized clutch, shuddered once, and turned his mutilated face toward her. He mouthed something, but the word was lost in a gargle of blood. And in spite of her fright, Mildred leaned forward ever so slightly, straining to hear.

"Help," he croaked wretchedly.

"Oh Clyde," she whispered, torn between revulsion and reflexive compassion for a creature in agony. "Clyde . . ."

His hands twitched spasmodically. His remaining good eye flickered and seemed to fix on her. The other eye became lost in a walnut-sized cavity that quickly overflowed with blood. And he was gone.

Mildred staggered backward. She thought she would be sick. Hardly knowing where she was or what she was doing, she backed into the running board of the Cadillac and collapsed in a heap. She supposed she should do something—call the police or cover the body or cry—but she couldn't move.

"Mother of God."

The words sounded faint, and Mildred hardly heard them. Then she felt someone shaking her shoulder. Weakly she looked up and into the eyes of Officer Pulaski. Next to him, pale and trembling, her eyes registering shock and disbelief, stood Irene. But Mildred barely glanced at them. It was Trevor who drew her attention. Trevor who drew her compassion, too, as he knelt next to the body, knelt in a pool of blood.

"My boy," he said through his tears. Gently he smoothed back Clyde's sodden hair. "Oh, my God. My son . . ."

43 "Do you want to tell us about it, Trevor?" Mildred sipped cold coffee from a Styrofoam cup as they sat in Forrest's hospital room the next day.

He sighed bleakly. "I don't know. Maybe." He crushed his own empty cup in his hand, got up wearily, and tossed it in a waste can. "It was so long ago ... Sometimes I remember it like yesterday ... The panic. The shame."

"Yes?" said Mildred gently.

"We were children, Endora and I. Only fourteen years old. Children having a child.

"My," said Irene, at a loss for words. "My my."

"Marriage was out of the question. And here she was pregnant. People think you can't be in love at fourteen, but I could argue that point ..." He paused, losing himself in the memory. When he spoke at last, he filtered emotion from his voice, laying it out as best he could, unadorned and without sentiment.

"Endora's father was a practical man. Angry to be sure, but by God he was practical." Trevor smiled grimly. "Macon was much older than Endora, but he was convenient. Bright, with lots of ideas and no money to finance them. Macon was in the market for a bride, and Endora's father had money. It was that simple. An arrangement of sorts was made. A deal, I guess you could call it."

"How sad," said Mildred sympathetically.

"Yes," agreed Trevor. "How very sad. My fair-haired, fragile flower with Macon Thompson, a bruising sort of man. A crude man. They married. I was helpless to stop it. The baby was born."

"Clyde," said Irene.

"Yes. Clyde. I finished high school, went through college and medical school. But I never got over Endora."

"So you came back," concluded Irene.

"Yes. It was foolish, I suppose, but I couldn't stay away. I thought I would live apart from them, you know ... Just see them from a distance, know that they were alive and well. I thought it would be enough. And for a time it was. I married Mary Margaret and tried to build my own life." He shook his head. "I loved Mary Margaret, you know. Whether you believe it or not, I loved her in spite of all this."

"We know," said Mildred.

"So what happened?" said Irene.

"I was caught so unawares. Endora came to my office one day. Just like that. As a patient." He spoke haltingly. "And we started seeing each other again. We saw each other for years. I was the one who was there when Macon came. I was the one who struggled with him. I was the one who shot him, too."

"Don't you think I knew that?" said Forrest quietly.

Trevor looked at him in amazement. "You knew?"

"Yes. I knew it was you. Knew what happened, too. It was an accident, Trevor. Don't torture yourself about it."

"But I do," said Trevor. "Don't you see? I left her to take the blame. It was her idea and she insisted, but I went along with it."

"It was," said Forrest flatly, "the best thing to do, under the circumstances. Endora was no dummy. She knew it. She knew if you were involved, the affair would come out. People would think it was premeditated. That the two of you plotted to kill him."

"That's not the half of it," said Trevor miserably. "I kept seeing her, don't you see? All those years. Even after Macon's death. We were ever so careful. We only met away from Raven's Wing. I thought I was protecting Mary Margaret. Thought she never suspected. But she did. She confronted me about those disappearances before she died. She knew, don't you see? She knew!"

"Mary Margaret," said Irene, "was sick a long time. A long, long time, Trevor. And she was a god-awful hypochondriac before she took sick for real. No one blames you for seeking a little happiness."

"I blame me," he said softly.

"Did Clyde ever know?" asked Mildred.

"No," said Trevor quickly. "I'm sure he didn't. He knew there was someone involved with his mother before Macon died. But not afterward. And he never knew it was me."

306

"Well," said Mildred shakily, taking his hand in hers, "there's nothing to be gained by looking back in regret."

They were interrupted by a sharp knock on the door. It was Richard Boyle, chief of the Raven's Wing police department, along with some of his subordinates.

"I'm here to verify your statements of last night," he said formally.

"Chief Boyle," said Trevor, standing up, "Mr. Haggarty is in no condition—"

"I'm in fine condition, Trevor," cut in Forrest. "I'm feeling better by the minute." He smiled cryptically at Boyle. "I'd have thought an unfortunate accident wouldn't merit your presence, Chief."

"It seems," said Boyle reluctantly, "that more may be involved here."

"Oh?" said Forrest, playing this for all it was worth.

"Yes," said Boyle uncomfortably. "We found things in the house. Things of a questionable nature."

"Things like what?" blurted Irene.

"Things like women's clothing," said Lenny Pulaski, smiling behind the chief. "All different sizes. Jewelry, too. And some letters."

"Dr. Bradford," said Chief Boyle with respect in his voice, "You've got your head on straight—"

"Well, thank you," said Trevor dryly.

"First I had one murder on my hands. Agnes Peabody. Now I've got another. Clyde Thompson."

"That wasn't murder," put in Forrest quickly.

"It was self-defense," said Irene.

"It was an accident," said Mildred.

"Whatever it was," said Boyle impatiently, "maybe you'd be kind enought to fill us in. From the beginning."

Wearily and with great patience, Trevor related the story from start to finish. A painstaking and thorough man, he started by explaining that it had all begun more than forty years ago with the murder of Betty Murphy.

"Good Christ," said Boyle in frustration. "You mean there are more murders? More than two?"

"Six including Agnes Peabody. Probably more, depending on what clothing and jewelry you've found."

"Jesus!" groaned Chief Boyle.

"Of course," Trevor went on, "Forrest Haggarty was onto this case right from the start."

"Oh, no," said the chief. Right then Boyle developed a nervous tic that would plague him through early retirement.

"I think," said Officer Lenny Pulaski discreetly into the chief's ear, "we should continue this interrogation behind closed doors. Before the media gets ahold of it."

But indeed the media did get hold of it, thanks to Officer Lenny Pulaski. Over the next week the whole story came out. Forrest, his recovery fanned by the blitz of attention and overdue recognition, recounted every gruesome detail with unbridled relish. The twisted route to Clyde Thompson was exposed, layer by layer. The letters were examined in detail.

A stringer from the *New York Post* phoned the story in to his paper. From there, the wire services picked it up. And Channel 7 Eyewitness News.

Connor Bennett was not a man to watch local New York area news, which he deemed "trash." But later that evening as he sat in his living room nursing his third martini, he flipped through the channels with his clicker and caught the end of "20/20." Connor inhaled his olive and sprayed a mouthful of Tanqueray all over the picture tube as a jolt of recognition hit. There she was. Mildred. Being interviewed by Barbara Walters.

*   *   *

A week later, a story appeared in *People* magazine:

> When Forrest Haggarty, former chief of police in
> Raven's Wing, Connecticut, tried to find out why
> women were disappearing from his picturesque
> New England village years ago, people said he was
> crazy. Now Haggarty and three friends are heroes,
> having solved what many consider the most brutal
> case of serial murder in the region. In their unflag-
> ging effort to see justice prevail, these senior citi-
> zens also uncovered sordid criminal activities of
> the town's most prominent citizens.

"Senior citizens indeed," sniffed Mildred as the four friends
sat around the fireplace, toasting their own success several
weeks later.

"Oh, I don't know, Millie," said Forrest contentedly. "I can't
say it bothers me. I've been called worse."

"Well," Mildred went on, "I was more than a little bothered
that Chief Boyle didn't believe it was self-defense. Can you
imagine? He wanted to charge me with murder."

"Until they traced Betty Murphy's sweater," said Trevor.

"And Muriel Guthrie's sign," added Forrest.

"And a whole lot more besides," Irene put in. "Gosh, it
makes me shiver just to think of it. All that stuff in his attic. Stuff
from women we don't even know about."

"Well, remember," said Forrest, "Clyde was well liked. And
he left all his money to the town. They would have liked to
make him a hometown hero."

Trevor was strangely silent.

"What's wrong, Trevor?" asked Mildred gently.

"He was my son. This murderer we speak of. My son."

"And he was my lover," said Mildred, her eyes stinging

with unshed tears. "But the man in that garage wasn't the Clyde I knew. He was a stranger."

"There's no explaining some things," said Irene simply. "He was a freak of nature, like a two-headed calf. Only we didn't know it."

"Irene's right," said Forrest. "Sometimes things are born. Things we can't explain. Things that look human but aren't. I call them God's mistakes."

"God doesn't make mistakes," said Irene flatly.

"Do you have a better explanation?" asked Trevor.

"No."

"Well, I for one can deal with it better if I know the good Lord screws up once in a while."

"Maybe," said Trevor. But he was not going to be able to deal with it, not like that at least.

"What gets me," fumed Irene, "is that those letter writers get off scot-free."

"Well, they didn't do it, Irene," said Mildred. "We know that now."

"Yeah," responded Irene grudgingly. "I guess. But some of them still did some pretty gruesome things."

"Don't despair," said Trevor. "They didn't really get off scot-free. Think about it. The letters caused everyone to take a closer look at those men."

"Right," said Forrest, slapping his knee. "I'd lay odds Ripley Crane will be convicted of taking bribes for allowing the dumping of toxic waste. Funny how Huey turned on him, isn't it?"

"Oh," said Irene, "Huey always was a good boy. I coulda told you that. And Hattie, she's got gumption, too, the way she finally filed a complaint against Loomis for the abuse."

"Because of your friendship and support," said Trevor.

Forrest hooted gleefully. "Why, they've got Loomis doing volunteer work at the senior citizens' home over in Bridgeport. Emptying bedpans and brushing dentures. Hah!"

Even Trevor had to smile at this picture.

"I hope Marcel does all right," said Mildred with concern.

"Oh, Marcel will be fine," said Forrest, "once he unloads Jimmy Perkins. Of course, it won't be easy. See, there's no legal recourse for homosexuals. There's no cut-and-dried divorce. No legal way to divvy up property and such. But he's awful riled up, and he'll manage somehow. He might lose part of his fortune, but he won't lose all."

"It's a shame about Noah, though," said Trevor.

"Crazy as a loon," sighed Forrest. "He sure had me fooled. When he showed me all those pictures of himself and starts talking about a son—a son that never existed, mind you—well, I knew he was crackers."

"Sometimes I think everyone in this town's crackers," put in Irene.

"Yeah," said Forrest. "Sure seems that way sometimes. Anyway, I thought for sure he was the one."

"The abuse in his childhood, combined with the loss of his son and wife, took a sad toll," said Trevor glumly. "At his age the prognosis isn't so good. He's lived so long with his guilt, lived so long with his delusion, too."

"Never really hurt nobody, though," said Irene. "Maybe they'll let him out of the state hospital someday."

"Maybe," said Trevor.

"The one that sticks in my craw," said Mildred, "is Spencer McCloud. He's doing more commercials than ever. Every time I turn on the set I see his grinning face—selling Preparation H, Dentu-Creme, or Dr. Scholl's."

"Yes," agreed Trevor. "Spencer finally hit his golden years in more ways than one."

"At least Leslie is divorcing him," said Mildred. She kept her voice light and turned to Trevor. "Now that Leslie's free, I suppose you'll be spending more time with her."

"Oh no," said Trevor earnestly. "All I wanted was for her

to be all right. And she is. Remember, I had one wife who turned into my patient. I'm not looking to have that happen again."

"Right," said Forrest, winking conspiratorially at Irene. "What you need, Trevor, is a strong, independent-minded woman." Both of them shot meaningful glances at Mildred, who was oblivious to this heavy-handed hint even if Trevor wasn't.

"What you two should do," said Trevor gruffly, "is start answering some of those letters that have been piling up."

"Fan mail!" exclaimed Irene. "And people all over the country who want us to solve unsolved mysteries. Don't that beat all?"

"Yes," said Trevor. "Indeed it does. So sift through those offers, Forrest, and forget about giving me advice. There's no romance in my future. An old goat like me."

"Well, don't give up so quickly," said Mildred, not yet seeing the possibilities that stretched before them. She remembered lying on the floor of her living room on Twelfth Street . . . She remembered considering suicide, then choosing Connecticut instead . . . She remembered an old man crashing through her woods . . . And she remembered Trevor's words: *God knows, we all could use a little adventure*.

Well, she thought, we certainly got some of that.